SUFFER THE CHILDREN

For my school friends, the characters in all my best stories.

Alfred DePierre Beeken IV
Daniel Harrington Benckart
James Scott Clancy
David Wayne Davis
Richard Courtney Eakins
William Henry Guterl Jr
Donald Howard Humbertson
Scott Lendon Hutchinson
Thomas William Ladley
Randolph Ward Linhart Jr.
James Bailey Ludwig Jr.
In memoriam David William Maiorana
Edward Joseph McCague III
Gary Edward Midock
Marc Anthony Puntereri
Michael Sanford Ratway
Michael Wallace Rigatti
James John Ruggeri
In memoriam Thomas Reid Shook
In memoriam John Michael Speer
Lloyd Franklin Stamy Jr.
John Allan Strange
Robert James Whitacre III
Paul Frank Ziemkiewicz

And the friends of thy boyhood—that boyhood of wonder and hope,
Present promise and wealth of the future beyond the eye's scope.

—Robert Browning, "Saul"

CONTENTS

SUFFER THE CHILDREN

It was not a path, but there was no reason it shouldn't have been one.

"It doesn't go anywhere," Duke said.

"It starts out," Wheaty said.

They were walking along something less than a road but more than a trail. They referred to it as the track. It ran parallel to and below the streets their houses were on, and they found themselves on it every so often. It was dirt, but studded with gravel and stones. You couldn't tell if the dirt had worn away to expose the rocks or if the rocks had been sprinkled on the dirt. And there were traces of grass down the middle. The easiest way to get there was to follow the gully from the low point of Rockingham Road. Today, though, they had cut straight through the woods across from Hondo's house. They had emerged onto the track staggering down the steep slope, holding onto a branch till the last minute to slow their descent.

Their destination was a creek still farther down the hill, through the woods that resumed on the other side. Probably technically the same woods. But they were on no schedule. School had been out for long enough that these endless days seemed routine, and the next school year was not even a blur on the horizon. Being between fourth and fifth grade was a little like being on this track halfway down the hill. The woods to either side seemed impenetrable. They took it on faith that their neighborhood, a grid of ranch houses, was still there, up above. The creek they were less sure about, since they explored that way only once in a while. The development was surrounded by forest, and each direction exerted its unique claims. Every time they found the creek it seemed miraculous, especially the bend where it deepened under the plank bridge. The water in the pool there was anything but blue, more amber, almost sap-colored. The big minnows in its depths behaved as though they were faintly aware of their presence as the three boys knelt on the bank and peered at them. It didn't matter, though, if they didn't get there that day. There was plenty to occupy them in the woods. They had all stopped at Wheaty's observation.

"See," he said. "It's shaped a little like a shovel. It starts out a wide and gets a little narrower. I mean, like someone took a scoop with a shovel."

"That was one shovel," Duke said. His snort was not completely dismissive.

"Maybe on some kind of machine."

"But then it stops," Duke said.

"Our driveway is like that," Hondo said. "But the opposite. At the top there's a wider part."

"Every driveway is like that," Duke said. "They're all the same, if you haven't noticed."

"Don't forget the Politos," Wheaty said. "They have a sidewalk out front. It connects to the driveway."

Their parents' expression was that the Politos had gone a little overboard. First the sidewalk, the only one on the street, like a slip of city block transplanted into the suburban neighborhood. Admittedly, it was fun to tightrope along it on your way home until you fell off back into the street. Then two big patios and, the finishing touch, a front yard filled with rocks instead of grass. "That's one way to get out of mowing the lawn," Duke's father said. Mr. Polito was a mason. When his crew was working on his yard, the boys moved whatever game they were playing up the street so they could watch and listen. The men wore slacks but took their shirts off, revealing skin not exactly tan but more like the color of Hondo's father's army jacket. Their chests were oily with sweat and occasionally tattooed. Whatever they were speaking, it wasn't English. It not only sounded funny but, to judge from their chatter, was funny. The boys laughed along with them. They pretended it was at something they were doing.

"Say it was a path," Duke said. "Where would it end up?"

They stood shoulder to shoulder and sighted along what was really no more than an indentation in the fringe of trees. Still, its features were both ordinary and distinctive, certainly worthy of study. Its mat of grass and fern, the rocks that projected from the ground not quite at random.

"Not my house," Duke said. "It would be over that way."

"I don't know about that," Wheaty said. It wouldn't pay to press an issue he had raised.

"Maybe it wouldn't hit the streets," Hondo said. "Just hit more woods."

"It would at least have to cross the main road," Wheaty said.

"That's true," Hondo said.

"Did somebody make it?" Duke said. "Or was it just there?"

"Maybe they started a road there and changed their minds," Hondo said. "Like what Wheaty was saying. About the shovel."

Wheaty himself found that unlikely, but he had to be gratified that the subject was receiving such consideration from his friends. He would have conceded that there were comparable spots all along the track where sparse cover gave the illusion of a portal.

"Maybe they started and got rained out," Hondo said. He could have wished that his father coached little league or at least came to some games. His mother did, dutifully, usually sitting at the end of the bench with a couple other moms. They managed to look pleased, even delighted, at the action, buy they didn't really understand how to cheer. If his father wasn't working late at the office, he had a meeting at church after dinner. At least for those he didn't have to wear a tie, as he did on Sundays. As Hondo had to. "I'm going up it," he said.

"You can't," Wheaty said. "I didn't really mean it was a trail."

He and Duke watched Hondo, already nearly on all fours, scrambling up the bank, fingertips grazing the ground. His father wasn't seeing that, either. Duke and Wheaty looked blankly at one another and then followed. It was a fact that once they got past the first row of saplings, clawing through the curtain of leaves and branches, other spaces appeared. The slope grew more gentle, and it was possible to make their way upward from one clearing to another.

"See," Hondo said.

"Okay," Duke said. "But I wouldn't say it's a trail."

Wheaty felt a little swell in his chest that he associated with spring, whatever the season. His friends had not only entertained his idea; they had embraced it as their own.

"This way," Hondo said, turning to his right, if you could call it turning when you plunged back into foliage.

After a few minutes, Duke said, "Congratulations. Now we're lost."

His remark was sarcastic, yes. But there was no sting to it. You couldn't get too lost in these woods. They routinely got lost on purpose.

"Now watch," Hondo said. He motioned for them to follow him along a faint but verifiable path. It seemed not quite diagonal to the direction they had come, in fact in a different dimension. They emerged into a space they recognized.

"Okay," Duke said.

The trees were sparser here, creating the effect of an arena. They had reached the vines. Coming on them unintentionally, from an unusual direction, felt as though they had discovered them.

"Want to swing?" The minute he made the suggestion, Duke knew that, though well-intentioned, it was misplaced. Vine-swinging wasn't something you did as an afterthought. A day could be devoted to it.

"Maybe," Wheaty said, but sat down. The clearing also contained stumps. You could stand on different ones to begin a swing.

After a while, Duke said, "Want to go down to the creek?"

Of course it was now in the other direction, across the track. The lack of response was a response in itself.

"We're basically home," Wheaty said.

They all knew that from there they could take a few steps one way or another or climb only partway up a tree and see roofs. If they followed the path where it continued on the other side of the clearing, they would break not into another clearing but into someone's back yard.

"We could go tomorrow," Duke said, comfortable at least for that day in his role of advancing doomed ideas. He knew full well that tomorrow the sentiment of the group might be entirely different. At the same time, they could all be pretty sure each of them had an image in his mind of the creek unspooling along the edge of the field far below and felt the chill coming off the water.

"Let's not rule it out," Hondo said. It was another of his father's favorite phrases. "The creek will still be there."

* * *

David laughed under his breath.

"What?" Brian said.

"The smell. It never fades."

"Are you making an argument for immortality?"

David smirked. "The immortality of the smell?"

"Should we know him?" Brian said.

The usher who led them halfway down the right aisle looked familiar. He smiled as they edged into their seats and handed each of them a bulletin.

"We could share," Brian said.

"I've got a million of them." The usher's nod was comradely, almost conspiratorial—some mixture of fellow feeling and solemnity. But it was clear they didn't know him. It was the type they recognized: hair thin but neatly combed, an athletic frame blurred by his suit coat and by middle age. He had the authority of a father with kids in high school. He was them maybe fifteen years ago, just barely of their generation.

"I take it back," David said. "It's that the smell has always been fading." He looked around at the filling pews. "Still hanging on. It's all the same. They're still at it."

Brian looked at him. "When's the last time you saw the inside of a church?"

"It was probably this church," David said. "And not the sanctuary. And look at us. Sitting here like a couple. It didn't help that you offered to share a bulletin. We must stick out."

"I don't know," Brian said. "These days."

"But in this church."

It was about as suburban a sanctuary as could be. They could remember when the church was built, in the sixties, when developments were eating into the forests and farmland like lichens. The sanctuary was scandalously modern at the time and now seemed furnished like a living room. The pews were covered in fabric rather than velvet; the wood of their arms and backs, as well as of the pulpit and choir loft, was light. The windows were not quite stained glass; some panes were pastel colored, but in a design rather than a picture. A trapezoid of sunlight fell across the room; it could be taken for summery, since the room was slightly, they would have said typically, overheated. They looked in unison at their bulletins.

"I'm not sure I knew his middle name," Brian said. "I must have at one time. Is it his mother's maiden name?"

"We could ask her," David said.

When someone came through the left door of the sanctuary they could see the family gathered in the hallway outside. His mother was flanked by two elderly men. They would be his two older brothers. Even during their childhood they seemed vaguely parental. You were never sure where their sympathies lay; they would as likely lecture you as run interference for you if you broke a household rule. They knew whom to expect from the death notice. *Michael Hogan Burr (April 20, 1951-October 15, 2019). Longtime educator. Pre-deceased by his wife. Survived by his mother and two brothers, Peter J. and John L., both of Pittsburgh.*

"There's a reception afterward," David said, turning over the bulletin. "Downstairs."

"No dance?" Brian said.

Something caught David's attention. He turned and then turned farther, with a half-wave. "There's Skip Proctor."

Brian looked over and smiled. "Let the reunion begin," he said.

The choir entered. When the singers had their places, they sat down as one. With a grimace, one of the men opened his folder, rearranged two sheets of paper, and closed it, then gazed grimly into the distance. They noticed the pastor sitting off to one side of the pulpit.

"How long has he been there?" David said.

"You mean today?" Brian said.

"I meant today, but you're right," David said. "He's not Reverend Moore."

This pastor was young and pleasant looking. Approving, maybe, as the sanctuary swelled with arrivals. A couple edged past them into the pew. They exchanged apologetic smiles, unsure who should welcome whom. On the arm of one of her sons—Peter, it must have been—Mike's mother led her family to the pews up front.

* * *

"Right on schedule." Duke's mother laughed softly. She was standing in their living room at the picture window, gazing out onto the still Sunday morning. It was both bright and gray outside. The air was gelatinous with unfallen snow. A lone sedan glided along the street lined with ranch houses. She yanked her skirt straight at her waist. "And he didn't forget his scarf."

"Bless his heart," Duke's father said.

"Isn't he about the most unlikely person for the job you can imagine?"

Mr. Amick left for church an hour early, week in and week out. They would see him later setting his hat, coat, and scarf on the clothes rack in the lobby. He was undoubtedly the most formally dressed man in the congregation, which didn't seem to bother his daughter, Susan, Duke's classmate both in sixth grade and in Sunday school. They didn't talk to each other much either place.

"You never know what's in someone else's heart," Duke's father said. "Dr. Moore would say we each have our ministry. That's his baby."

Duke's mother wheeled from the window. "Mine is to get those girls ready."

"That counts," Duke's father said.

His mother smirked.

"Seriously," his father said.

She stepped into the hallway as Duke and his father got ready. Duke was in his suit pants, which he had trouble convincing his parents were scratchy. It was cold enough that day that he could resort to the device his mother had suggested: he wore long underwear underneath. He would pay for it later in the overheated church. His father had moved around behind him and draped a tie across his shoulders like a yoke.

"Regimental stripe, Duke. Can't go wrong with that. Never goes out of style. Give it a try. Remember the Half Windsor?"

"Wheaty's clip on."

"You're too old for that," his father said. "You're a young man." He rubbed his head, a gesture of affection that Duke could have lived without. "I'm also going to introduce you to a new invention called the 'comb.'" He managed to mispronounce the word. He made many jokes about the object. "Remember what my father told me: a man is never well dressed unless he has a shoeshine and a haircut. I am half well dressed all the time." Sometimes he was the object of the joke: he was bald.

They left early, too, since his father was in the choir, just not as early as Mr. Amick. Duke's younger siblings would go to the nursery. Duke would meet his friends. One or the other of their parents had to arrive early also.

The boys could agree that turning twelve was a mixed blessing. They would soon be exempt from the children's sermon. No longer would they be the oldest kids trooping with infants up front, where it became more and more incumbent on them to answer one of Dr. Moore's rather open-ended questions. "What is love?" And they were more likely to attempt an intelligent answer. The youngest kids got the laughs. They would get to take communion, not all that appetizing a prospect. The grape juice would be okay, and the little glasses would be fun to lift from their sockets. But the other tray contained what looked like pasty pills.

These developments were all contingent on their passing confirmation class.

"Everyone passes," Hondo said. "They want you to pass."

They had gathered before Sunday school in what seemed to be a forgotten room in a passage from the sanctuary to what was known as the "new wing" or the "education building" completed just a few years before, not that long after the old wing. It contained classrooms, the music rooms, the gym—almost everything besides the sanctuary and the main office. Neither here nor there, this plain, dingy space could have belonged to either wing. It was now obviously used for storage. Either that or it was furnished with a vengeance. Chairs and lecterns seemed to have been bulldozed against one wall like felled timber. Boxes of old books were stacked against another. Apparently there were such things as used Bibles. A relief map of the Holy Land took up a whole table. They sat at student desks that they salvaged from the debris. This space would be their resort after church as well, if their parents had a meeting, which they usually did. The custodian, a colored man, enjoyed acting surprised to find them there when their parents finally tried to round them up.

They each had the notebook they had been given for confirmation class. Each had his Bible open to the first few pages.

"If I can just get past Obadiah," Hondo said.

"If you get to Amos, you're there," Wheaty said.

"If I can just get to Amos," Hondo said.

"Reverend Moore always helps you out," Duke said. "I don't think he really expects anyone to get them all. When Susan Amick did it last week, he looked confused. Like he didn't know what to do."

"He likes giving clues," Wheaty said. "Real obvious ones. 'Well, I don't think it's Andy.' That's what he said when I got stuck on Amos."

"Have they read these?" Duke said, opening a hymnal. "'I believe in the holy Catholic Church.' Then why don't we go to the Catholic church?"

"He explained that," Hondo said.

"I was never too sure about this one," Wheaty said. "'He descended into hell?' Would they let Jesus in?"

Hondo got up and looked at the map. "Look," he said, reading the label at the bottom. "Another class made this."

"We made one like that at school once," Wheaty said, joining him. "Remember, you use salt and flour."

"You can't tell if it's a big country or a small one," Hondo said.

"Small," Wheaty said. "It's hard to find on a globe." There was one of them in a corner, too.

"I hope it doesn't rain there," Hondo said. "The country would dissolve."

The ridges of the map had started to crumble, like stale cake.

"Not much, I don't think," Wheaty said.

Duke had stayed at his desk. "What about this one? 'Very God of Very God.' You're already God. How could you be very God?"

"We don't have to memorize that one," Hondo said.

"It's in there, too."

"It's time for class," Wheaty said.

They walked down a flight of stairs that would have been spiral if it weren't square.

"They descended into hell," Hondo said.

"You shouldn't joke about that," Wheaty said.

Their classroom was in the basement, one of several along the hall for elementary school grades. The upper grades, junior and senior high, graduated to a whole different atmosphere, not classrooms but lounges a couple of stories up, above the gym. Teachers were always somebody's parents, not teachers in real life, and it usually showed. They would be more uncomfortable than the kids, who would pretend not to notice. They were usually very formal. "You're not addressing the Board of Directors, Steven," Duke's mother told him one morning when it was his turn, as he collected some charts. Duke was just as glad he wasn't in the class his father was teaching.

This class was different. It was taught by a real teacher, but not at a real school. They passed it sometimes on the way in to town. The students were preachers. Once in a while they made a special trip to pick up a person from a different country to bring to church. There were buildings but no football field. But it was a college. This teacher lived in the next town over from theirs, though he was more often than not in Egypt. His children had their own children. Their parents said they should address him as Professor. So far they liked him. He was old but didn't seem to mind.

They had been the first kids into the building, but they were last to enter the classroom. That was normal. The other children seemed neither surprised nor disappointed when they walked in. But that day they got there before the teacher. They shrugged and found seats.

A minute later they heard scraping in the hall. Then, at about doorknob level, Professor Davies's head appeared. He looked at them pleadingly. When he entered the room, he was stooping, struggling to walk. He had a rope around his neck, and from it swayed what looked like a big wheel. Every few steps it dragged on the linoleum floor. He staggered to the desk up front and sat down. Bending over, he heaved the object into his desk with a clunk. The he sat back and gasped, catching his breath. All at once, he sat up and smiled. "I wouldn't wish that on anyone," he said.

The class, which had been stunned into silence, broke out in laughter and chatter.

"Come up and see what I've been lugging around."

The children gathered around the desk, looking for an opening to reach through and touch the object. "Try to lift it," he said to a student. One of the huskier boys stepped forward. When he pulled, it almost flew off the desk. He and everyone else laughed.

"It's Styrofoam," Professor Davies said. "Paint it gray, and it looks like rock, doesn't it? This is from an exhibit that I borrowed from our museum. Let's look in our Bibles and see what it is and what it has to do with anything. Today we are going to look at two passages in Matthew that are almost next to each other but not quite. I will need some people to read for me."

Not surprisingly, Susan Amick volunteered for the first. "Matthew 18.1-6: At the same time came the disciples unto Jesus, saying, Who is the greatest in the kingdom of heaven? And Jesus called a little child unto him, and set him in the midst of them, And said, Verily I say unto you, Except ye be converted, and become as little children, ye shall not enter into the kingdom of heaven. Whosoever therefore shall humble himself as this little child, the same is greatest in the kingdom of heaven. And whoso shall receive one such little child in my name receiveth me. But whoso shall offend one of these little ones which believe in me, it were better for him that a millstone were hanged about his neck, and that he were drowned in the depth of the sea."

More surprisingly, Hondo stepped up for the second. "Matthew 19:13-15. Then were there brought unto him little children, that he should put his hands on them, and pray: and the disciples rebuked them. But Jesus said, Suffer little children, and forbid them not, to come unto me: for of such is the kingdom of heaven. And he laid his hands on them, and departed thence."

"Thank you both," Professor Davies said. "Can we say that one thing is very clear from what you both read? That is that children were very important to Jesus. And teachers and parents have a great responsibility. We don't want one of these things hanging around our neck, especially if they are real. This is supposed to be a millstone. Real ones are very heavy. They are supposed to be heavy: Israelites used them to crush grain. We adults hope you like church. We don't want to stand between you and Jesus. Duke, I think you have a question?"

"Then why do the children suffer?" Duke said. "It seems to hurt. Either the children or the disciples. Maybe both?"

"Thank you, thank you, Duke," Professor Davies said. "You have led me to the next thing I wanted to share with you. Grown-ups have their toys, too."

He also knew their nicknames.

First he passed around a book that contained what seemed to be words but in different, curvy letters.

"That is what you just read, if you can believe it. That is Greek, the first language the book was written in. It has been translated into many, many languages. But sometimes those languages get old, too, and it has to be translated again—even into the same language."

Another nice thing about him was that he didn't ask them questions all the time, like other teachers. To which whatever they answered was correct.

"Susan and Hondo both read from what we call the King James Version of the Bible. It is a wonderful translation, but it is now almost 400 years old. This may not look like it, but it is also a Bible."

He held up a white book.

"We have that in our house," Duke said.

They did. The exact same one. They didn't have many books, but the ones they had were prominent, in a bookcase in the living room. His parents made them seem like events; they had "just come out." There was one called *Dr. Zhivago*, another *The Tin Drum*. They were both foreign, too. His mother said they helped his father think about the war he was in. And there was this one, the New English Bible, New Testament. It was a paperback.

"It is in language that we actually speak, the way the other Bibles are written in what they spoke at the time. Will you read from this for me, Duke? You might like it better. Just read Matthew 19:14 for me."

Duke read: "But Jesus said, 'Let the little children come to me and do not try to stop them, for the kingdom of heaven belongs to such as these.'"

"Yes, that's all that 'suffer' means. It was a way of saying 'let' or 'allow' at that time. Jesus did not want the children to hurt. And I don't think he meant the grown-ups to hurt, either, even though he rebuked or scolded them—the way they rebuked the children. I imagine their feelings were hurt. That happens when you're grown up, too. He wanted them to remember how important children are. That's you. So teachers have to be very careful not to hurt them, even if they think they are helping them." He winced. "They have to try not to be boring."

He passed around another book, a big one, open to glossy black-and-white pictures of disks that looked even bigger and heavier. "These are real millstones. You can tell from the story that you don't want one hanging around your neck, especially if you are also being thrown into the ocean. May I take this one back to the museum, where it belongs? Take it off while I preach?"

They left for a bigger room and sang a song with the other classes, with Miss Cowsley at the piano.

There was a fifty-fifty chance that on the way to meet their parents in the sanctuary for the worship service they would see the other students.

There was no time to stop off in the storage room before church. The hallway was thronged, and they were swept along with the surge of their fellow students headed into the main lobby to mingle with the adults, who could be coming from their own classes or just arriving. Then from another hallway Mr. Amick appeared, back in his uniform. Behind him, single file, came the students from the Home. Although they were dressed up, too, you could tell they were all a little different. Their features might droop, or they might walk at an angle. One boy's head was much too large for his body. He had a very short crew cut, which made his head seem more normal, or less. It reminded Duke of a light bulb, or of pictures in comic books of what human beings would look like in the twenty-third century, as their brains continued to evolve but they relied more and more on labor-saving inventions. He was always nodding cheerfully, though that may have been from the effort of supporting his head. He and the other children followed Mr. Amick out a side door, where he helped them into a van. Mr. Amick was allowed to be late for the worship service.

That day they left right after church. Duke sat in the middle of the back seat. On either side of him, his sisters slumped into the car doors. They were not twins, but since Debbie was big for her age they seemed to be.

"So there are no miracles after all?" his father said. "They can all be explained. That helps, I suppose."

"I've read about that," his mother said. "There's some special wind in Egypt, for example, that blows along the coast of the Red Sea and could push water back. So the Israelites could pass over land that was under water a minute before."

"Yes. Or some kind of tide."

"So the waters didn't exactly part."

The day had cleared. Cold enameled the bright blue of the sky and the white of the snow. The streets glistened with melting ice.

"Well," his father said. "Did you know that the biggest fault line in the United States is not in California but Missouri? In the nineteenth century there was an earthquake so violent that the Mississippi River flowed upstream. Something like that could look miraculous."

"Or what he said today. When Jesus walked out to the boat, did he actually know where there was a sandbar? To the people on the boat he seemed to be walking on water."

"And then we miss the miraculous things that happen every day. Like where did those little guys in the back seat come from?"

"That didn't happen overnight, as I remember it," his mother said.

"Or he said that maybe at the feeding of the five thousand the bread and fish didn't magically multiply, but when Jesus pointed out a need the people responded and produced food they had kept hidden for themselves out of their clothes and shared it with their neighbors."

"But we should believe in the miracles even if we think we can explain them. Did I get that right?" his mother said. "I sometimes feel I get everything in a sermon but the point."

"That was his point, I think," his father said. "That it was more important how people interpreted an event. In faith. Could you follow his sermon, son? Professor Davies can be a little over our heads, too. What did he talk about in your class?"

"We did the story about Jesus and the children. He said that they didn't suffer. That word means something else."

"Interesting," his father said.

"But the children from the Home were here today."

His mother spun in her seat. "We hope those children aren't suffering. We want them to come to church, but we worry about how it would make you feel to be in the same classroom with them, and also how it would make them feel. We don't want them to feel conspicuous. We think it's best for them to have their own room. We worry."

"We talked about it in session," his father said.

Duke was remembering Professor Davies stooped over. He stooped a little anyway, without the stone. He remembered the boy supporting his head. His parents were worrying in the front seat. He was the only person he could think of who was not suffering. Or probably Mr. Amick.

* * *

As hillsides went, it had much to recommend it. From where they stood, on the track, it was a green disk, tilted a little. Its border with the woods above was so sharp that the grass looked wedged under the fringe of trees at the top the way you would tuck a carpet under living room furniture. Furthermore, toward the middle there was the suggestion of a notch, as though two separate woods had been folded onto each other, with a slightly visible overlap. Any one of them would have acknowledged that they should have observed it sooner. But it was Hondo who discerned its crucial quality.

"You could roll down it sideways," he said.

The notch might turn into a valley. Who could tell how far back it went? Maybe indefinitely, if the angle missed the county workhouse. Though the leaves had thinned, they still couldn't see a roof. Conversely, once they got up there, they might not have been able to be seen from where they now stood.

"Well, not sideways," Duke said. He disagreed in a way that showed he saw Hondo's point, maybe before Hondo had.

"You know what I mean," Hondo said. He swept his arm from right to left. "From that corner there to down here."

Though the border of the woods was semicircular, you could think of it as having a corner.

"Diagonally," Wheaty said.

"Right," Hondo said.

This particular geographical feature hadn't existed until a couple of years before, not until they built the bypass that took out the lower third of their development, down the hill and closer to the river. A new road had to be built up to the grid of streets on top of the hill, so that they had to enter the woods from a different point, not to mention that there were fewer woods. Some parts, luckily, were untouched, such as the vines. A set of cliffs, however, had vanished. The creek was underground now for part of its course, issuing from a huge corrugated pipe back into its bed. That made it more mysterious, in a way.

So the cleared area was new and it wasn't. It was a hill and it wasn't. Immediately after it was bulldozed it was undeniably fun to climb. You scrambled over the crumbly footing from what looked like one boulder to the next. They were actually just big chunks of dirt. You could slalom between them sitting on cardboard sleds made by flattening out boxes that lay around the construction site. You could slide a fair distance just on your pants. Either they had come back and smoothed out the surface or it had just settled, and it was now covered with thick, crisp grass.

"We can't do that now anyway," Duke said.

"Why not?" Hondo said.

"Because we're supposed to be doing an assignment. Supposed to, like, last week."

"Like you're suddenly on the honor roll," Hondo said.

"We're still in our school clothes," Duke said, appealing to Wheaty.

"My mother doesn't mind if I come home with grass stains," he said. "She'll frown, but I think she likes it. It's a sign of a normal childhood."

Apparently that was endorsement enough for Hondo. He set down his shoebox and jar and took one oversized stride onto the bank. Then he pivoted sideways and took shorter, quicker steps upward, tacking toward the corner. The other two watched his progress.

"You could roll straight down it, too," Duke conceded to Wheaty. Having dismissed the project, he spoke confidentially.

"Not to here," Wheaty said, eyeing the bank that Hondo had vaulted over. Farther to their left it tapered to merge with the track. "That last roll would be a long one."

"Thank you, Wheaty, Sr."

It was something any one of their fathers would have said. They set down their own equipment and followed Hondo. Duke took a more vertical route. By unspoken consensus, they waited until they reached the stand of trees at the top of the slope before they turned around to look back down at the track. From there it seemed to go off at an angle.

"It's the same place, but in a different place," Hondo said.

After a pause, David said, "I hate to be the one to tell you, but what you just said doesn't make too much sense. Or maybe it makes too much sense, if you know what I mean."

"I know what you mean," Hondo said. "I don't think it came out right."

"I know what you both mean," Wheaty said.

A minute later they were taking turns rolling down the hill crosswise. Hondo had already perfected a technique. After a couple of crouching steps, you tucked and tumbled. The trick was to find the right angle. Too shallow and you'd stop dead; too sharp and you were out of control. No one made it to the bottom. Duke, the sceptic, had some of the better runs.

Half an hour after that they were at work. It was appreciably later in the day, but the air was still saturated with sunlight.

"That's two down," Wheaty said. "Only eight more to go. Hondo, you want to hand me the jar?"

"Let me see," Duke said. He walked over to Wheaty's station. "That's the same."

"What are you talking about?" Wheaty said. "This one is smaller and a different color. That one's brown; this one is green."

"It's still the same species," Duke said. "You can let it go."

"I knew it couldn't be that easy," Wheaty said.

It was a hot day, as hot as summer, though school had been in for what seemed like months. And in junior high the days were longer. They still weren't used to that. In the afternoons the teachers threw the high windows open. You could imagine the radiators were on full blast, but they were cool to the touch. After school the boys often repaired to their old haunts in the woods, but the track had a different character now. It was broader, since construction vehicles had plied it. Also, by this time of the year, though only scattered leaves had started to turn, the foliage had frizzled. The hillsides in the distance were still green, but the trees looked feathery. The track had horizons now; the sky had a curvature. The sun was ablaze somewhere out of sight. Crickets were everywhere, as though in that conflagration life on earth was down to two species: humans and grasshoppers. They flew up at your legs out of the straw-like weeds as if sparks.

"Look for a beetle, a slug," Duke said. "Something."

He stepped off into higher grass. Wheaty resisted the urge to follow him. He obviously knew what he was doing. When they had caught a few specimens, they gathered for the part that was grisly but also satisfying. It helped to remember that they were told to do it. It worked the way their science teacher, Mr. Harvey, said it would. Wheaty laid a pad of cotton wool over the mouth of a bottle of nail polish remover, requisitioned from his mother, then tipped the bottle so the pad would get soaked without getting his hand wet. He transferred the pad to the mouth of the jar that contained the insect, which by that time was poised, as though privy to the operation. Once the pad was in place, the insect would stiffen and grow still, completing its part in the assignment. From there it could be pinned in a shoebox.

"What do you think you got, Duke?" Duke said.

Wheaty looked up sharply, first at Hondo and then at Duke. "You're Duke."

"What if I wasn't? What if I was Hondo? Hondo could be you, Wheaty."

"If you liked that name better you could have told me at the time," Hondo said.

"I mean just for today. What do you say, Duke?" Duke said to Wheaty.

"Sure," Wheaty said. He handed the bottle to Hondo. "Your turn, Wheaty."

With a couple of slips, with mostly straight faces, they kept it up until they dispersed again into the woods for one last sweep. When they reconvened they could feel the cool seeping along the track from the woods above like a parallel creek.

"They look different to me," Wheaty said. "I might have discovered a new species. You know that? Did I hear someone say 'extra credit?'"

"They're all grasshoppers, sorry to tell you" Duke said. "In the Bible they're locusts."

"Speaking of which, did anyone do their homework for tomorrow?" Wheaty said.

Hondo dropped his hands. "What do you think we're doing?"

"I mean for Bible study."

"Is that tomorrow?" Hondo said.

"It's not homework if they don't get mad at you if you don't do it," Duke said.

"Sue Curry does it," Wheaty said.

"Her mother's the teacher, for crying out loud," Hondo said. "Still, I should at least know the verse for the week. What is it again?"

"Second Corinthians five seventeen," Wheaty said. "'So if anyone is in Christ, there is a new creation: everything old has passed away; see, everything has become new.'"

"That shouldn't be too hard to memorize."

"You do the assignments, too, Wheaty," Duke said. "You get your share of stars."

"I take it back," Hondo said. "I don't have to memorize it. Wheaty can be me tomorrow."

"It's at Ralstons' house," Wheaty said.

"That's something," Duke said.

Every other Wednesday afternoon they met with some other neighborhood kids at either the Currys' or the Ralstons'. Although they were identical, the Ralstons' house seemed bigger. The living room was all angles; the furniture had more metal and skinnier cushions. There were no pillows to speak of. The glass ashtrays were always clean, but you could smell smoke.

"I like it when Mrs. Ralston leads."

Mrs. Ralston was mostly angles, too, but also some padding.

"So do I. But she makes me a little nervous."

"That makes a lot of sense."

"I know what you mean. But I wouldn't call it nervous."

"She can be kind of, I don't know, tricky. Remember last time at her house we had this sort of game. She made that list of Bible verses we had to see who could look up the fastest. Some were in those short books we never read, like Obadiah, I think. Titus. But there were some easy ones, from Genesis and Psalms, but she split them up and put them at different places on the list. Sue Curry saw that and looked up the ones from the same book at the same time, so she finished first. Mrs. Ralston said she did that on purpose. She said, 'I wanted to see if anyone would notice.'"

"She talked to me alone one day."

"If you haven't figured it out, they do that every time. One of them talks to you by yourself."

"This was the day they talked about boy-girl stuff. Dating."

"No, thanks."

"She said if I felt a little uncomfortable talking about it that was natural. She said she knew what I was thinking. I hope she didn't know what I was thinking."

"Our mothers are pretty, but not like that."

"She looks like she could snap shut in the middle, like a jackknife."

"Like a centerfold."

"They bend in two places."

"Don't forget she's younger than our parents. Having children is hard on your figure."

"She was supposed to have a baby, but it was cancelled. I heard my parents talking about it. I remember, because it was the only time I saw my mother cry."

"Why was it cancelled? Who cancelled it?"

"That's what my parents said."

"My parents said 'miscarriage.' They were probably talking about the same thing."

"You never see Mr. Curry."

"My sister went to the Ralstons' house once and Mr. Ralston answered the door in his bathrobe. It was in the day."

"I like him. Remember when he picked us up after the rally, he asked if we wanted to see him lay some rubber?"

"He's saved, too."

"He don't act too saved, if you know what I mean."

"Mrs. Ralston found a verse in the Bible. She was all excited. I heard her tell Mrs. Curry about it. It says if one person in a family is saved, the whole family is saved."

"One time Mrs. Ralston said she could pray for me anytime. She was smiling. She said she could pray for me while she was talking to me."

They sat in a rising pool of shadow. By now the sun's rays skimmed the ground farther down the track. Behind them, the glow turned the fringe of trees on the hill into embers against the sky. They gathered their apparatus.

"Are we ourselves again?" Wheaty said.

"Absolutely, Duke," Duke said. "I mean Hondo. I mean . . . "

Wheaty half laughed, half groaned.

"We'll get our names straight tomorrow," Hondo said.

* * *

Mr. Huizinga was at the door. That was quite possibly by design: he was both an elder of the church and a civics teacher at the high school. Beyond him, their fellow students milled around, in some cases probably dancing. They had entered at the school-like wing of the church, down a sidewalk edged with evergreens and through fire doors into a linoleum vestibule. The air was faintly antiseptic. They must have used a brand of floor wax akin to the high school's, Pepsi to their Coke. Neither Duke nor Wheaty had had the hairless but still bearish Mr. Huizinga in class, so they couldn't be sure he recognized them. His expression wore just a hint of humor as he took their dollar and stamped the backs of their hands. He couldn't have known they all felt he had married above himself. He and his wife, an undeniably attractive Spanish teacher, lived in one of the two towns in the school district, and they might see one or both of them at the shopping center. They didn't seem to have children, which was somewhat reassuring to Mrs. Huizinga's admirers.

For Wheaty these monthly events were more patrols than dances. Opportunities for conversation with the opposite sex were thankfully few, given the din of the music, but he would skirt the dance floor as though in search of them. He was chronically without a girlfriend; Duke was in the midst of some sort of concordat with his. They drew their vocabulary of dating from past history classes. Until Hondo and Duke broke ranks in tenth grade, they defended their bachelorhood as a policy of "no entangling alliances." Wheaty was finding it more and more difficult to follow this line unilaterally. Already Duke and his quasi- or crypto-girlfriend had breached their neutrality, approaching each other gradually from opposite sides of

the floor. It was like a slow-motion square dance in the midst of the frug-
ging and jerking going on around them; each of them spun off one group
of friends after another until they found themselves exchanging pleasantries, the most courteous couple in the joint. Their moves could have been
chalked out; they stood on a free throw line.

Wheaty continued on his rounds. He gravitated to groups of other single guys. That tactic was viable for a while. There was even a sort of bravado
in it, as though they had abjured or needed a respite from female attention.
At some point he would have to talk to a girl. The trick was to catch one
right after she had danced or when the band took a break. Alternatively, he
could accost a girl with a known boyfriend. In none of these cases would
he be expected to request a dance. None of them, however, prevailed at the
moment. The music had only gotten louder; the margin of spectators was
now virtually pressed to the walls as the dance floor expanded.

On stage, eyes closed, Hondo leaned into his mike, all but osculating it
as he sang. Whether that was acoustically effective or not, Wheaty couldn't
say, but it didn't seem terribly sanitary. Paradoxically, his voice seemed muffled, though you could clearly hear the twang of his trademark twelve-string
electric guitar. Predictably, Duke and his girlfriend were dancing. Wheaty
found himself edged near the entrance.

Another adult winced at Mr. Huizinga. "They're having fun," he said.

"Gives the phrase 'Suffer the children' a whole new meaning," Mr.
Huizinga said.

When the song ended, Wheaty met the eye of Cindy Morgan as she
parted from the beefy Buzz Strickland, with whom she had danced ami-
cably. He was one of the older guys there, the ones you weren't sure had
graduated or not. He was old enough to be gainfully employed; the story
was that his father had bought a service station so he could pump gas. It
was the most craven of all ploys to talk with your friend's girlfriend, but
Wheaty took it. Cindy's role at these dances was anomalous. How was she
to conduct herself when her boyfriend was in the band? By definition, they
didn't dance together. Their conversations, snatched over a dixie cup of juice
during breaks, had an aura of the tragic. Even as she and Wheaty talked,
they glanced toward the stage with a shared sense of Hondo's responsibility.
As it happened, that was the last song before a break. After a last couple of
pleasantries, Wheaty left Hondo and Cindy alone.

Since their hands were stamped, patrons could come and go as they
pleased. The urge to get a breath of fresh air, especially as the gym-class
scent of rubber on hardwood singed your nostrils, was one more valid
reason to withdraw from the dancing, though it could be overused. At the
same time, as the evening grew later, the vigilance of the chaperones was

palpable. A couple of adults lounged conspicuously on the sidewalk. Fights had broken out in the past; six-packs had been secreted under bushes. The fall night was one step from frigid, with a spanking clear sky and the cidery smell of fallen leaves in the air. They were on an isthmus, the chill coming off school on one side of the weekend night and church on the other. In thirty-six hours they would be back, this time at the business end of the building, for Sunday school and the worship service. Farther out on the parking lot, past the huddle of parked cars, the asphalt landscape was deserted, lunar. When Wheaty reached its verge, the big back yards of houses on the street behind the church, he turned around. A shadowy figure approached him. It was Duke. His slouch rendered any explanation unnecessary, but he said, "We couldn't come to terms."

Wheaty commiserated appropriately. "I trust though that your talks were candid and productive."

Duke shrugged but smiled. Wheaty was reasonably sure that negotiations would be reopened Monday at school.

Then they realized that a third person was there. They couldn't place him at first. He was dressed for the dance, in slacks and a crew-neck sweater. But he was too big or too old, or both. Too substantial.

"You were expecting someone else?" he said. It was Rev. Moore, their pastor. "Where's your better third? You don't want to break up the three catechumens."

Hondo and Wheaty recognized this as a joke and laughed.

"I'm glad you came to the dance," Rev. Moore said. "I tend to keep my distance. I'm not sure my presence would add much to the general mood. When I leave, the room lights up, right?"

A laugh seemed called for there, too.

"Hey, what's so funny?" Rev. Moore said. "Think fast."

Duke ducked and put his hands up in front of his face. But Rev. Moore had only pretended to toss something at him. "Name the books of the Bible. In order. Both barrels. Just kidding. We're all off duty tonight." He gazed across the parking lot. "What do you think? Are these dances a good idea?"

The boys thought so.

"Are our motives ulterior? You betcha. If we can get young people to put their foot in the door . . . .Literally, right? Their feet on the dance floor. I'm not speaking in parables here. If we can get them in the door Friday night, maybe we can get them in the pews on Sunday morning."

They could see that.

"On the other side. We get ridiculed for objecting to the music, but have you ever actually listened to the words of these songs? A lot of the time you can't make them out, but that's probably on purpose. Some of them will rot your socks right off. Do the kids listen to them? Even if they did, would they be influenced by them? What about the beat and the volume, all the gyrating? That can't be wholesome, can it? Whereas basketball breeds well-mannered young Christian gentlemen. Yeah, right."

Basketball was Tuesday nights. They both played.

"There's always the other side. What do you boys think?"

They were undecided.

"Welcome to the session," Rev. Moore said.

They had known that Rev. Moore lived by the church. His home was referred to as the manse, but it looked like any other house in the street, two-storied, with dormer windows. The yard had flowers and bushes and other indications of normal life. The Moores had three grown daughters who sometimes visited on the same occasion with their families, taking up two solid pews up front. Their pastor was a strapping guy even in his sixties. He had been a celebrated athlete at a New England college—though Wheaty's father said that people used the term "All-American" loosely. At church picnics, cajoled by the kids, he would uncork a few long passes with a perfect spiral. He had a crest of gray, crinkly hair and wore glasses.

A few electronic screeches and blasts came from the gym. "That's not the music. You can't always be sure." Rev. Moore paused. "You want kids to be happy. They might not believe it. I have kids. I started out as a kid." He struck a linebacker's pose, crouching, his hands spread out in front of him. "I want you to have fun tonight. But I'll see you on Sunday. That's where the real fun starts, yes?"

They watched him pick his way across the lawn back to his house in his loafers. The grass had grown after the last mowing of the fall, and it was wet with dew.

"No wonder his socks rot," Wheaty said.

Duke was shaking his head. "You want to like the guy," he said. "If he would only let you. It's nice that he speaks to us as adults, but whose side does he think we're on? If only they did listen to the words of our songs. Is there something the matter with peace and love? They only hear what they don't like. Stamp out sex anytime you see it sprouting. Meanwhile, napalm villages. They don't listen to the words of their own songs. That's because they sing them week in and week out without thinking about what they're saying. 'Praise him above, ye heavenly host.' Ye? Host? What are they picturing? I'll bet they see a guy in a tuxedo holding the door for them. I do. Repeating the words just makes them feel better. It doesn't make them better people. It stops them from being better people. They could be out feeding the poor." Duke strummed an invisible guitar. 'Hate your next-door neighbor, but don't forget to say grace.' They don't hear that."

As they neared the gym, they passed a few people on their way out, among them Cindy. Her father waited for her in an idling station wagon. She turned to them as she got in and made a face. "Curfew," she said. "I was allowed to come and hear Hondo's band. Only because they played first." They had forgotten: tonight was a battle of the bands. Hondo's arch rivals would play the second half of the dance. On the way down the steps Duke and Wheaty mingled with some people just arriving. They reported to the table to pay their dollar as the boys showed their stamped hands and entered the gym. Up on the stage, the players stepped around amps, picking up power cords and dropping them in a different place. Abruptly dateless, leaning against the far wall in professional detachment, Hondo observed. The group's centerpiece was an electric organ. "Just hardware," Hondo's father would say. Skip Proctor adjusted dials and jabbed at the keyboard, producing random riffs that still sent jolts through the crowd of which he seemed oblivious. No doubt, the band meant business. In lieu of madras shirts and khaki slacks, they wore army surplus and sunglasses. Their hair was as long as the school's dress code allowed. When Bill Guterl, the bass player, combed his hair straight forward in the boys' room, it touched the tip of his nose.

It seemed the crowd had ebbed and flowed over the break. It was about as big as before, but the demography was subtly different. More single guys and more surly single guys. They were likely the band's supporters, some of them Buzz's friends or coworkers. His father had reputedly bankrolled the organ as well as the microphones as well as the gas station. They had amperage in abundance. With good effect, Duke and Wheaty would have to concede, as, without transition, their tuning up turned into their first number, a note-for-note rendition of the Stones' "This Will Be the Last Time." Like a frog leg galvanized by electric current, the crowd twitched into motion. Dancing started even before couples had formed. That could be sorted out. To all appearances, though, Duke's girlfriend was dancing with both Ted McCague and Scott Clancy.

"Wrong band, wrong guys," Wheaty said.

The next song began with five familiar notes on the guitar, repeated several times.

"Hey, I just heard that," Wheaty said. "Do they pay you royalties on that?"

The opening words followed in due course: "The eastern world, it is exploding."

"Let's get out of here," Duke said.

"But it's your song."

"I only like it if I'm singing it. Or Barry McGuire."

Duke headed not toward the front door but the kitchen.

"All right," Wheaty said. "But where?"

Unobserved, they slipped into the kitchen. Barely lit, it looked more like a lab, all gleaming stainless steel counters and vault-like freezers. On the far side was a passage into the old wing of the church that most of the adults would not have known about. They walked up a flight of wide, rubbery steps into a back hallway lined on one side with closed steel doors. Some sort of security light was on that bleached the cement block of the wall of whatever color it would have had during the day.

"What's the smell?" Wheaty said. "Mothballs?"

"Moths don't eat brick," Duke said.

True, there wasn't a trace of fabric in the hallway. Its other side was the outer wall of the original church.

"It's something like that," Wheaty said.

Each door hade a small vertical window. They looked through the first one at the miniature chairs and tables inside.

"We fit into those?" Duke said.

"Miss Grundy," Wheaty said. "She was a battle-axe, but she kept us from damnation for a year."

"Look at this," Duke said. "You were a handsome devil in your prime."

Between doors, the bulletin boards along the wall held a lot of kids' drawings, but also pictures of past Sunday school classes. There were two kindergarten classed from 1956, each brimming with crew-cut boys and pigtailed girls. Wheaty sat on the far right of one of them wearing a grin that struck him as fatuous even for a five-year-old. Duke was standing behind him, in the second row, glaring.

"What was your problem?" Wheaty said. "Did the photographer remind you of the man who murdered your parents?"

"I guess I just wasn't overflowing with Christian charity that day."

The hallway led to the church's main office. A turn onto the stairway to the left would have led them to the music rooms. But they crossed the lozenge-shaped lobby to the back doors of the sanctuary.

"The doors have to be locked," Wheaty said.

"They can't lock," Duke said. "They're swing doors."

He was right. They stepped noiselessly inside onto deep carpet. The sanctuary lay in front of them a little like a clearing in an autumn forest, the pews and pulpit like fallen tree trunks, stripped of leaves and branches. The walls held panels with Biblical scenes carved into them barely visible during the day, almost line drawings. In the gloom they looked and felt like bark; Wheaty ran his hand over one as they edged along the back wall. They took no more than a couple of steps down the right aisle before Duke laid a hand on his shoulder and nudged him into a pew.

"Listen," he said. "Someone else is here."

They saw the form at the same time, all the way across the sanctuary and a couple of rows ahead.

"I think that's Hondo," Wheaty said, starting to rise. But Duke stopped him. "Okay. Maybe he's praying.

"Maybe he should be," Duke said. "Buzz's band wasn't half bad."

It wasn't one form but two. The first stood up and took the other by the hand, leading it down the aisle and out the front door of the sanctuary. It swung closed behind them.

"It was Hondo," Wheaty said.

"But it wasn't Cindy," Duke said. "We'd better get back, too. We don't want to get locked in the building till Sunday."

They retraced their path, less cautiously, until they were through the kitchen. They inched the door to the gym open and slid inside. Just in time: the crowd was already separating into two groups heading to opposite walls according to which group they judged the better.

"Which side is ours?" Wheaty said.

* * *

"Hondo . . . " That was as far as Mack got before he doubled over again in a spasm. It was not his first attempt that evening at forming a sentence. He was too amused not only to speak but to laugh. "Oh, shit," he gasped, and leaned back against the wall. He was sitting on a couch cushion on the floor. Putting his fingertips to his forehead, closing his eyes, he began again. "Dig it. Hondo . . . " But he had no more success. He leaned forward, shaking his head.

The four or five other young men in the room—there was some coming and going—watched him indulgently. They could afford to be patient. It was Friday night, and nothing was going on or was going to go on. It wasn't Homecoming, it wasn't Parents' Weekend, it wasn't quite midterm. The football team was away that Saturday. The campus would be inert and sodden all weekend long, the quad tiled with wet, fallen leaves. The boys could have gone home, only about an hour away, but they hadn't. It wasn't Homecoming there, either, and now that they were juniors in college they would no longer be recognized at the high school football games, let alone adulated. So they sat in Mack and Hondo's room and passed around a joint.

Mack's fit had passed for the moment. He was a lanky guy with an incongruous combination of shoulder-length hair and heavy black glasses. "What time is it?" he asked.

It was around 7:30. A long night stretched ahead of them. Another frat was having a party where they would be welcome, in fact expected. They would probably drift over at some point with no prospects beyond beer and loud music. They apparently weren't expected to study; the library had closed at 5:00 and wouldn't reopen until noon the next day. Maybe they were obliged to carouse. Somehow though their college experience had been less orgiastic than they had envisioned. Theirs was more a mill town than a college town. The school's buildings were only slightly more stately than the blocks of shops and delis that surrounded them. A few were a sooty white brick that made them stand out a little. A walk around downtown wouldn't fill a Saturday morning. There was a decent music store where Hondo and Mack whiled away some afternoons shooting the breeze with the proprietor, Max Callian. Duke and Wheaty sometimes tagged along just to overhear the shop talk and wander among the amps and drum sets. They referred to Max as the Wild Armenian, which was a joke, since he was fat and bald and rarely stirred from his stool behind the counter. He was a great pianist, however, and led a jazz trio he let Hondo and Mack sit in with. They had their own band, too, which meant they were out playing more nights than not.

"It's acky pro time," Duke said. "Right, Hondo?"

At the phrase, Mack let his head fall back with a rictus, a silent howl of amusement. Or maybe he was preparing to sing. "Acky pro, time to go," he chanted. He reached languidly for his Stratocaster, which he grabbed by the neck and dragged toward him over the cushion. Laying it across his lap, he played a riff. Even unplugged and twangy it sounded great. "It's always time for acky pro."

"Not to worry," Duke announced to the room. "They're both going to ace their midterms."

Everyone knew that wouldn't happen. But they also knew to a certainty that Mack would wriggle off academic probation once again. Routinely sleeping through his morning classes after jamming half the night, he maintained the most precarious possible standing in the school. He was not known as Macky Pro for nothing. While Hondo kept the same schedule as his roommate, he lacked his brinkmanship. The previous spring he had been suspended and was now a semester behind Duke and Wheaty.

"I meant, like, what time of day is it," Mack said. "Like a. m. or p. m.-type time."

"Quarter to eight," Wheaty said.

"Okay, no problem," Mack said. "Our gig is late tonight." His relief was short-lived, because he convulsed again. This time he managed to produce a few squeaks recognizable as laughter. "Hondo. Duke. Wheaty. It just hit me tonight. What kind of names are those for grown men?" He shook his head. "And that's not the best part about it."

If it wasn't a fraternity house, with Greek letters over the front door, the building where they lived would probably be deemed a tenement. The brothers described its architecture to fellow students as Urban Decay Style. Their housekeeping didn't help. Mack and Hondo's was only slightly below the norm. Their room contained two beds, two desks and the disassembled couch. The hardwood floor was littered with laundry. If a shirt was unworn for three days, it was pronounced clean. As though a piece of furniture, a column of men's magazines occupied one corner of the room. There were about as many guitar cases as books. Mack and Hondo's band would be playing that night at a bar on the outskirts of town among the motels and fast-food restaurants near the interstate. The clientele was blue-collar; they suspected that their hippie-looking group offered as much novelty as musical value. But it was a paying gig.

"We drawing you guys to the club tonight?" Mack said.

Only the seniors among them would be legal, but they would cause a stir of their own if they trooped into the bar wearing their letter jackets. Mack and Hondo were just about the only non-jocks in the house. Having a couple of freaks in their ranks gave the Fijis a little heft on campus. And Mack and Hondo were fundamentally normal. Hondo had swum in high school.

"No can do," Duke said. "We have practice tomorrow morning. In the pool at 7:00 a. m."

"On Saturday?"

"Saturday morning workouts just started. We've been training informally till now. Formal practice opened this week."

"Informal? Formal?" Mack said. "What's next? Speedo and white tie? See what you're missing, Hondo? In the meantime, shotgun me."

He put a joint to his lips while Hondo crouched in front of him, cupped his hands between his face and Mack's and blew. Mack swiveled on the cushion and lay back, arched in the middle, since he was longer than the cushion. First he reached behind him and grazed the floor with his hands; then he raised them and fluttered his fingers at the ceiling.

"This guy is going to play a musical instrument tonight?" A linebacker, this brother had grown up a few blocks away, but he lived in the frat house. His campus persona combined athleticism and chauvinism: *Serb* was stitched into his letter jacket.

"Oh, yeah," Hondo said. "He'll be ready to rock and roll. Except that . . ." He picked his guitar out of its open case and strummed a few chords. ". . . we do not play no rock and roll. If Mississippi Fred McDowell does not, we do not."

Mack sat up, hands first, clutching at air. "Gimme," he said. Hondo handed him the guitar. "Like this. Remember that chord. It's a substitution. Use this shape."

Mack gave the chords some kind of edge. He handed the guitar back, leaving his fingers on the frets until the last possible moment.

"Right," Hondo said. "I keep forgetting."

"Your fingers keep forgetting," Mack said. "That's what practice is for."

"That makes it a ninth or a thirteenth, right?"

"Just think of it as a diminished chord," Mack said. "The best part about it is they come from John Wayne movies, right?"

"What?" Norm Cable walked into the room as though answering a summons. He was the fraternity's eccentric; he wore shorts to class through the winter. He was hefting something in his right hand. "Never mind. Anyone got a cartridge on him? Or just a needle? This one is, like, incredibly dull."

"Here you go," Mack said, shifting his position on the cushion so as to reach into his pocket.

"Thanks," Norm said.

"You always keep a cartridge on you?" Serb said.

"You never know when you'll need one."

"What do you need it for, Norm?" Duke said. "You having a party in your room? Beer? Babes?"

"Share the wealth, Norm," Wheaty said.

"I'm listening to records for music appreciation."

"You're studying on a Friday night?"

"I find that if I do an hour on a weekend night it will save me more than that during the week. But I've got to have the tools." New cartridge in hand, he found an unclaimed cushion and sat down. "So. What?"

"We were discussing the etymology of these guys' nicknames," Mack said. "I had deduced that they come from John Wayne movies." The humor had evaporated from his observation; he had either sobered up or attained some state beyond stoned. "*Hondo* was, what, a Western? So John Wayne single-handedly wiped out a couple of nations of indigenous Americans, like a good patriot? Warmed his audience up for the Vietnamese?"

"I know," Hondo said. "I was hoping most people would have forgotten about that movie by now. It came out when we were kids. One of our dads took us to see it somewhere. It was probably quite formative."

"It's an intelligent movie," Wheaty said. "I was surprised. I saw it on TV recently. John Wayne's character is half Indian, don't forget. He was a marginal figure, not quite at home with either whites or the Apaches. Not exactly the hero you'd expect. *The Searchers* was even more ambiguous."

Mack hooted. "You deserve some kind of prize. You just used 'ambiguous' and 'John Wayne' in the same sentence. Talk about black and white. That's where he started, and that's where he belongs, with his politics. And then he won the Academy Award."

"That was for *True Grit*," Wheaty said. "He was parodying his earlier characters. There was *The Man Who Shot Liberty Valance*. That was in black and white, and that was 1962. I remember being disappointed when I saw it. But now I see the point. It was about right and wrong, which turned out not to be that different. John Wayne didn't get the girl, by the way."

"'Duke,'" Mack said. "That was his nickname, right?"

Duke shrugged. "Guilty as charged."

"What about 'Wheaty?'" Mack said. "What John Wayne movie did that come from?"

"It didn't," Wheaty said.

"What were we going to call you?" Duke said. "Rocky? That was his name in the *Three Mesquiteer* series. Get it, Mack? Like in three musketeers, except they were cowboys? What were you watching? *Sky King*?"

"Stony," Wheaty said. "John Wayne's name was Stony Brook."

"As clever as I would have expected," Mack said.

"'Wheaty' had already stuck," Hondo said. "We couldn't dislodge it."

"So where did it come from?" Mack said, intrigued now.

"My own family doesn't know. There are different theories. My father's name is Thomas. His family called him T. Since I took after him, a smaller version, I was wee T. Or I couldn't pronounce TV, which I obviously watched all the time. Saturday morning Westerns. Or I liked Wheaties. I went through a phase where that was all I would eat. Take your pick."

"At least it saved you from the John Wayne brand," Mack said. "What a bummer that guy is. Did you see that picture of him in Vietnam with the troops? Signing autographs while the shells were exploding around him? In fatigues? Except no helmet. He supposedly declined one. I guess that goes to show he has no fear. He can take on the gooks with his bare hands. He's bald as a coot, by the way. He's probably the reason we're there. That mentality. Meanwhile, he's the biggest draft dodger going. When other actors were off fighting World War II, he was back in Hollywood making movies about it."

For someone as loosely affiliated with the college's academic program as Mack was, he was quite well informed. He had attended a prestigious private school in the eastern part of the state and seemed to have read or at least heard about many of the books that they were studying. You often caught him in the lounge watching the news on the house TV before dinner. For his rare classroom appearances he favored a glen plaid sport coat over a sweat shirt and jeans, and he liked to take issue with his teachers as early as possible in a lecture. "I would dispute that" was his favorite opening. He kept his professors on edge with phrases like "power elite" and "objective correlative."

"John Wayne was kind of old for military service when World War II started, wasn't he?" Serb said.

"Mid-thirties, maybe," Mack said. "Older people than him served."

"And he had children," Wheaty said.

"Ditto," Mack said. "I know: let's civilize and Christianize the third world. Let's do it with napalm. That sounds like a job for eighteen-year-olds. Civilized Christians make good consumers, by the way. Too bad for you John Wayne fans the draft ended. I can't spare you, though, Hondo. I'm going to get you RG status. The rhythm guitarist deferment. People need music even or especially during wartime, and I need you to back me up. You others can always enlist."

The one class Mack would never miss was music theory. If he had to, he would drag Hondo out of bed for it.

"Why did you come back to school, Hondo?" Serb said. "Hey—don't get me wrong. I'm glad you did. But Mack's right. You don't have to worry about the draft."

"I've got another kind of gun to my head," Hondo said. "The guilt gun. I've told my father innumerable times that I'm getting nothing out of college and that he's wasting his money. He doesn't care. That's a direct quotation: 'I don't care.' At least he's honest about it. He says that finishing college is all he asks of me as a son. He'll pay the bills and keep me in Stratocasters. Which is a little counterproductive. He says, wherever I want to get to in life, I can't get there from here. I have to have a college degree to get other places. What if I like where I am? I just want to explore my music for a while. I don't have any illusions I'll be rich and famous. That takes talent. Well, talent is one way to be successful. I just want to find out what I can do. I know he still wants me to be a doctor. Talk about an illusion. He'll say, just get through college, then see. Do you know what they call the lowest-ranking graduate of the worst medical school in the world?"

"Doctor," Norm said. "I've heard that one. Good luck. If you want that title, you'll have to go through me."

"I try to explain to him that that only works if you're not also the lowest-ranking graduate of a no-name college. I don't know how I got in here. Then I flunked out. 'No, you were suspended. Use that to your advantage.

You learned from the experience. That could sound good in an application letter.' Right. I learned some Grateful Dead songs."

"I'm convinced," Mack said. "One way or the other, Hondo's out. If you can handle the civilizing, Duke"—he shook his head and repeated, "Duke"—"Wheaty here will take care of the Christianizing. He's already going to church, sneaky-like. I think he secretly wants to be a missionary."

Two Sundays before, Mack had caught Wheaty *in flagrante* entering the Presbyterian church a few blocks away. Mack was just getting back from a post-gig jam.

"It's for a research paper for Hooper's class. I'm doing the different worship styles topic."

"You're working on that already?" Mack said. "That assignment's not due until the end of the semester. I'll wait till Thanksgiving break. There's plenty of synagogues and temples back home. I can't start a paper early. I work better with a deadline."

They were all four of them religion majors. It had the fewest requirements and prerequisites. It was true that the churches in town were all pretty much the same flavor. There was a big one with onion domes, but Wheaty could never figure out when it was open. Serb attended functions there with his family sometimes. Apart from the services at the Presbyterian church, which weren't especially inspiring, Wheaty rather enjoyed getting up early on Sunday morning. There was a cloister-like silence in the frat house; the brothers claimed to be devout followers of the Z-god. There would be some stirring in the streets as Wheaty walked down to enter the sanctuary on the stroke of 10:00. It struck him as a sheepish group, as shy of him as he was of them. He would seat himself apologetically in the street end of the pews, which formed a semicircle around the pulpit. There were a few young children, but he was the only one remotely his age. He enjoyed that status. Men in general were in short supply on the floor and in the choir loft, where there were just two, a tenor and a bass, Wheaty assumed, though he couldn't always make them out over the female warbling. The pastor was closer in age to him than to most of the congregation. His baby-faced smile verged on the rapturous. He always worked a Greek term into his sermon. Judging from the smiles of his parishioners, that was almost a running joke. Toward the end of the service, the smell of baking seeped into the sanctuary. But Wheaty departed as punctually as he arrived, pleading his pressing studies when invited to fellowship time. What he wanted was to get back to the house unnoticed, just as the brothers were rising.

Mack leaped off his cushion, flailing his arms, not for balance but in alarm. "Jesus Christ, it's 9:30, We've got to get to the bar to set up. Hondo, what are you doing? Pack up the guitars. Hey, guys, a little help?"

At Hondo's direction, a couple of the brothers gathered some cords and gizmos and walked them down to the front entrance. By the time they came back, a consensus had formed to join the Sig Eps' party.

"What about your homework, Norm?" Duke said. "You're equipped."

Norm looked down at the cartridge in his hand, then set it on a desk. "It's the wrong kind," he said. "Let's go."

* * *

"Michael. Good of you to come. I know you're just home for a few days."

"But of course," he said.

Brian had lost weight. That was immediately apparent because of the way he was dressed: bare-chested, wearing only a pair of cut-off jeans. His frame was still athletic and well-proportioned, just somehow a size or two smaller. He had no body fat but also not much muscle tone. Then he hugged Michael. They must have wrestled around as kids. They were both on the swimming team in high school and used to being in close proximity to each other wet and in bathing suits. But he wasn't prepared for the feel of Brian's skin. At least he had all his clothes on.

"This is Jenna."

"Hi," Michael said.

A slight young woman in scrubs appeared in the door behind Brian.

"Come in and meet our guest," he said.

It was hard to find their development but not their house. The suburb was diametrically across the city from the one where they grew up, identical but alien. Michael couldn't swear he had ever been in that district before, though he had heard it referred to all his life. He wondered what fate could have translated his friend into this anti-neighborhood, as though into a photographic negative. He found a street of near-identical two-story brick houses, but theirs stuck out. Form the road, its front yard seemed overgrown, obscured by a jumble of foliage like a fogbank. But as he followed the curve of the sidewalk he noticed a wheelbarrow and bags of potting soil in among the scrubby trees and low shrubs. A shovel and a rake leaned against the front wall of the house under a picture window. Very little of the yard was grass. He had a glimpse of the back yard, which was more conventionally a lawn. A clothesline held colorful laundry.

Michael followed them into the dining room, identifiable by the long table and six chairs. That was all it contained. Through an archway they came to what must have been the living room, which was just as sparely furnished. What objects it contained were standard. With one exception. It had a throne. Or perhaps altar. In the center of the couch, in lotus position, sat a man with a shaved head in an orange robe. The sight of a Buddhist monk in a suburban living room was so incongruous that Michael thought for a minute the figure might be levitating. When Brian introduced them, the monk's expression was not unfriendly, just quizzical. For him this ceremony obviously required explanation. A handshake was not in order; the monk's arms were disposed somewhere deep inside his drapery. The flowing robe left no room on the couch for anyone else. There were also two chairs—though the two speakers in the room looked substantial enough to sit on—but the three of them stood. If felt natural enough.

"Where are you from?" Michael said. In that monastic atmosphere, the remark seemed as gauche as turning on the TV, had there been one in the room. In his dress shirt, slacks and sport coat, he wasn't sure if he felt overdressed or naked.

"I grew up in Cherry Hill, New Jersey," their guest said, with the same reserve.

"The bonze is itinerating," Brian said, with a smile at the word. His demeanor was new. More formal, in contrast to the surroundings. He was as pleased with the line of conversation as the monk was nonplussed. "He's based in Colorado. He's on a teaching tour. He's stopped here for our retreat. Michael will be with us for the rest of the day."

The monk seemed partially enlightened, or at least not mystified.

Brian had reached into the next room for a scrub top and put it on. "Shall we?" he said.

To Michael, the monk looked if anything more out of place in the passenger seat of a Buick Special station wagon than he had in the living room. They wound their way through the labyrinthine neighborhood until one of the streets turned into a ramp onto the freeway. They followed signs to the airport. The gray sky was so low that they could have been traveling through one of the tunnels that led into the city in the other direction, behind them, that Michael had come through on the way there that morning. The buildings on either hand were monoliths of sheet metal or concrete— nameless, windowless office buildings, warehouses, air freight depots. But surprisingly soon they were in farmland. The exit they took was flanked by a truck stop and a gas station; once beyond them they followed a meandering two-lane country road. The sporadic traffic was more trucks than cars. At intervals they passed a clump of mailboxes.

"I've never understood that," Brian said. "If you own a hundred acres of land, why do you build your house right on the road? Or right across the street from another house?"

"Why a brick ranch house?" Jenna said. "They could be transplanted from a development."

The atmosphere in the car grew solemn for a moment at those observations. Then Brian explained that he was painting houses while Jenna worked as a nurse in an emergency room. "It's not what I thought I would be doing when I was twenty-eight years old. But, whatever I'm doing, I'm not doing it so I can do something else in the future. That's what college was like. That's why I quit, though I might not have understood that at the time." The monk's glances at Brian were stern but approving. Nods might have been too emphatic. "Jenna's job is good for that, too."

"That's what I like about it," she explained to Michael, who sat beside her in the back seat. She spoke with her hands turned upward in her lap, as though pleading. "You're so absorbed. A case comes in, and next thing you know your shift is over."

"If you're wondering how a house painter and an e. r. nurse can afford to be homeowners, my grandmother left me some money. Like a down payment-type amount of money."

Michael knew that Brian's father was a lawyer and still living.

They slowed and turned into a drive with an open metal gate. A squat man in overalls waved from his porch.

"We rent land for the center from him," Brian said.

Jenna turned to Michael with a smile. "Think Woodstock without the music."

"Or the nude mud-sliding," Brian said. "We have other sorts of activities, but we're going to start you off easy, with lunch."

They pulled off the drive and parked on grass beside other cars, then stepped out into a gray, humid western Pennsylvania day, clouds like drying plaster, the air steamy with the scent of fertilized soil. After a short uphill walk they crested the drive and saw several outbuildings. Brian led them to the largest one and held the door for them into a screened-in room. Maybe twenty folding chairs were arranged in a semicircle around two other chairs. One of them was empty. In the other a woman in a robe sat smiling. Her robe seemed less complete than the monk's; she might have had street clothes on underneath. She wore glasses, and her hair seemed dressed.

"We're all here, I think," she said. "And welcome. We're glad you found us. Please take a seat. And Bonze Bruce, our special guest, won't you join me up front?" She spread her hands. "We are the Buddhist Meditation Center. Which one? Of course: the one just past the Wal-Mart off Route 119. With the Angus Steer sign out front." She smiled and leaned slightly forward on the punch line, arms folded in her lap. After each pleasantry, the smile settled into something between a frown and a pout. That was a sign to Michael that the levity would not go on forever. "We will begin our time together with a meal. For those new among us, we eat communally and intentionally, refraining from conversation, appreciating our plain fare gratefully and consciously. Consciously grateful, yes, but also gratefully conscious. Call it communion, if you will." She rocked back upright with a smile. "Please. We would like our guests to go first."

The monk stood. With a glance at Brian, Michael got up. One other person rose as well, a young lady across the semicircle from him. He followed the monk and her to the far end of the room and a counter. On its other side, from a simple kitchen, two women set out bowls of soup and pieces of brown bread. Michael thought at first they were food service workers in hair nets. They were Mennonite. Back in their chairs, they all sat straight-backed, eyes ahead, and ate meditatively. That was the only word for it. Michael's gaze might have been the only one that strayed. He would not have been able to identify the other novice. There was a variety of dress, and everyone seemed at ease. A couple of men were dressed as semiformally as he was. He had left his sport coat in the car and rolled his sleeves up. His fellow lay guest wore jeans and a loose, flowered blouse. She was attractive, he decided. He would have taken her for a regular.

Sitting with a bowl in his lap, as opposed to a plate of hors d'oeuvres or a full meal, was comfortable, especially when everyone else was doing the same thing, especially when he didn't have to, in fact was not supposed to, talk. Without any announcement, people began to get up to return their bowls to the counter. He thought better of asking Jenna if he could take hers. She followed him. He brought a cup of water back with him.

"Meditation is at the center of our gatherings," the leader said. "We will have silent time soon. We will try to let all the mental chatter that we hear all the time dissipate. We know that's what our minds get up to when we leave them to their own devices. Like children when we turn the light out and close the bedroom door behind them, right?"

Though her feet were planted on the ground, her swaying gave the impression she was in the lotus position. The monk, beside her, was. Somehow he had drawn his legs up underneath him in his chair. It was only as they walked up the drive that Michael had realized how large a man he was, half a head taller than Brian and him. Broad, too—rangy. He could have been a power forward on a basketball team. There was a lot of leverage locked in place under that robe. Before today he would not have thought of Buddhists as either athletic or jolly.

"Before we still ourselves, let's open that door again. Let's turn on the light and ask those uninvited thoughts to account for themselves. We'll ask which of them are genuine and which are disguising themselves as thoughts.

Who's crashing the slumber party?" She nodded sideways. "Bonze Bruce, would you start us off with your reflections?"

"I am glad to be here," he began. His public speech was rather clipped. Not South Jersey. "But in order to be with you I had to get here. I have been in motion more than I like. That is not the same as moving. How can we be in motion without moving? That is the world's problem, and that is our challenge. Our world is in motion. I see that when I travel through airports. People are in motion, but are they going anywhere? Sometimes in an airport I get the feeling that no one ever leaves. People are trapped, moving both directions, dragging luggage with their lives packed away inside. Do they think that they have a destination, really, and that they will find satisfaction there? Or will they need to keep moving? Those airports make me think of our minds, with impressions and sensations and ideas bustling back and forth, back and forth. Do they think they will find truth and contentment, or do they just crowd out reality and comfort us with noise and trample on the ground of being? Even on those pedestrian conveyor belts the people walk; they can't relax. Sometimes when I see someone just standing still, alongside or above the commotion, I think maybe I'm seeing a demonstration of how our consciousness can rest in the midst of life."

The leader uncocked her head from its position of attention and said, "Thank you. Reactions, anyone? Thoughts? Say what's on your mind. Don't ask whether it belongs there or not. Maybe it's at the surface of your consciousness on its way out."

A middle-aged but girlish woman to Michael's left began. Her thick, springy hair looked as though it had just been released from a pony tail. "I can't express the relief I felt when I let go of the idea of a personal god." A murmur ran through the arc of chairs. The leader rocked backward this time. "It may seem strange to say, but I no longer have to worry how I behave." She grew flustered all of a sudden. "I don't mean that," she laughed, waving her hands. "I'll try to be a nice person! I just mean, the way people talk about God as a father or a teacher or a friend, I think they were just telling me to have good manners. 'Behave yourself; we have company.' Surely there is a more profound way to relate to the divine?"

"I used to try to pray." It was a man's voice, closer to him. He had to lean forward to see him. Aged ten years and in wire-framed glasses, either Brian or Michael might look like him. They were probably that far below the average age of the group. "I would say, 'In Jesus' name.' I grew to hate that phrase. It was like a stamp. Without it, the prayer wasn't official. Does God have a name? And what does it mean to pray 'in' it?"

"Or does God have only one name?" another man took him up. "And is there a special time for worship? Exactly one hour? I love our meals. They're not 'fellowship hour.'"

Brian glanced at Michael. "We know whereof you speak. The meals after services at our church were downright raucous. Back-slapping. People seemed to need to dispel the mood of worship as soon as possible. I think maybe they needed to convince themselves that they were normal. 'See. Christians know how to have fun.'"

"Yes, yes," a woman said, nodding and grinning in agreement. "Even during the service congregations don't seem comfortable with just being with the divine. Children's time is a nice idea, I suppose, but its real purpose is to entertain the adults. They need comic relief. The pastor doesn't dare stop talking until one of the kids says something funny."

"And passing the peace," the first man said. "That was just a preview of fellowship hour. Take a break for small talk. That's peace?" He threw his hands up. "Sorry. That wasn't opening the door to let the light shine in. That was releasing the emergency exit on a school bus full of a childhood's worth of frustration at being ferried back and forth to church every Sunday. Look at us. We were probably all raised in a church. I never sensed the sacred until I came here. I was hoping it would cause me to be a little more mature."

"Whatever brought you to the place you are now has value," the leader said. Her expression was wavering toward its frown again, while the monk maintained his vigilance. "We need to respect other faiths."

"I don't know about that," someone said. Everyone looked toward the far end of the semicircle. "I wouldn't say that you have to respect other religions." It was the woman in the flowered blouse. "I don't know that you can. I don't know enough about most other religions in the world to say I respect them. I would say I have to respect the people who practice them. Maybe not even that. I have to respect their right to practice them. That's one thing. The other is that I'm not sure it makes sense to respect a religion. Without being disingenuous or hypocritical. The only way to respect a religion is to follow it. See, I'm not being theological; I'm trying to be logical. What do you mean when you say you respect a religion? Either you follow it or you don't. Jesus wasn't very respectable, for example. I don't think he particularly wanted anyone's respect. I don't know about Buddha."

"So many words, so many ideas." This woman was white-haired and bird-like, hunched in her chair as though in prayer. She may have been the oldest of the group. "I was raised in an observant Jewish household. When I heard a teacher of the Torah speak in the synagogue, even as a teenager I would want to scream, What about other religions? Get out of your box!"

"Well, first of all, it was probably a pretty big box." It turned out to be Michael speaking. "If he was a Biblical scholar, he probably knows several languages. He's probably done comparative religions. Second, everyone is in a box. It's called your identity. Everyone has his or her perspective. That's all they can have."

"But to say there is only one manifestation of the divine," a man said.

The monk broke his silence. "Duality is the problem," he said. "If we could step back and see that what look like opposites to us are part of a larger whole. We trap ourselves into saying that one religion is right and another is wrong."

"It's true," the young woman said. "It's probably harder for people of different faiths to debate than it is for a theist and an atheist. In that case, one person is right and the other is wrong. There are just the two choices. God can't both exist and not exist. I guess I should say, not even God. You can't get more dualistic than that."

"Take a step back," the woman said. "That's what I meant by getting out of your box."

"Can't you always take a step back?" Michael said. "Don't you just step into another box? If it's just inside or outside it still sounds dualistic to me."

Michael was no better at meditation than he was at prayer. When the leader struck her gong, a couple of people sat on the floor. Everyone else settled in their chairs. Michael could resolve to pray in the meantime, but the problems were the same. Was he thinking or was he praying? Was he talking to God or talking to himself in such a way that God could overhear? Would he have to decide that before he could begin to pray? Could he ask to be told what he should pray for? Was the conversation he was trying to strike up with God the mental chatter everyone had been talking about? Would he have to dispel it, or could prayer go on independently, in the background. Was prayer for him just a way to fill an awkward silence? He had not arrived at answers before the gong sounded again.

Had he meditated? Had he prayed?

Outside, the sky was neither brighter nor darker than when they entered the building a few hours before. The same muffled daylight. Brian and Jenna had stayed behind with a few others to speak with the farmer, leaving Michael and the young woman of the flowers, as he now thought of her, alone on the porch.

"What did you think?" Michael said.

"Well," she said. "Ironically. It made me feel I was in a Bible study. Mostly it was the demeanor. The same posture, half-serious, half-jokey. It's hard to be serious about the most serious things. It just is. 'I told myself, I could never be a Christian. This couldn't be happening to me.' Or, 'I was

trying to meditate this morning, and all I could picture was an English muf-
fin.' And everyone knows what everyone else is talking about."

At first glance, the sky seemed a uniform gray. But there were patches
and streaks of near-white, like a wall that needed another coat of paint.

"Will you come back?" Michael said.

"Honestly, I think probably not. I came because my friends invited me.
I meant what I said. They had experiences that brought them here, different
experiences from mine. What if I had had theirs? Met their mentors instead
of mine? I need to listen. Or maybe I was going to say all that."

"You said it. At least, it came through. I got it, anyway."

"Good."

Aware of some fluttering, Michael glanced up at the eaves of the porch.
"I didn't notice those on the way in. They had them at Brian's house."

"They're prayer flags."

"Oh," Michael said. "So, then, what house of worship would I have to
attend to see you again?"

"You could try Fourth Presbyterian Church."

"Is that the one by the park on Fifth Avenue?"

"You know it?"

"I think I went to a meeting there once. It has a big food kitchen around
to one side? And tapestries in the foyer?"

"That would be us. We feed the homeless in style."

"Okay," Michael said.

"If you want to sit beside me, you have to join the choir."

Brian stepped out onto the porch and stood, smiling self-evidently
from one to the other of them. After a moment's silence, Michael said, "Anyone got a gong on them?" Brian shrugged another smile. The couple who
brought the young woman emerged also. They were the man in glasses and
the woman with the wiry hair; when they stood together they seemed the
same age. "Michael, this is Pat and Owen," David said. They all shook hands,
a little belatedly, it seemed to Michael.

"And Marie," Owen said, gesturing toward the new woman. "But you
knew that by now."

"I was working my way around to it," Michael said.

Those three left. Then the leader and the monk joined them, and they
walked to the cars. Only two were left, the Buick station wagon and a BMW.
As they stood outside the car, Michael said to Brian, "Did you settle with
your landlord?"

"Even Buddhists have to do business."

"I think I made a date in the temple. That probably ranks right up there
with money-changing."

"Dating," Brian said. "Good luck. I'm glad to be out of that."

They climbed into the car and rode back to Brian's house in silence. By the time Michael was on the freeway on the way back to the far side of the city it was rush hour.

* * *

Growing up in the sixties in an Eastern suburb about equidistant from steel mills and farmland, it was only natural that Brian passed a certain number of fallow summer adolescent afternoons sitting in his friends' houses listening to surfing music. After a morning of mowing lawns to earn some spending money and to satisfy their parents of their work ethic, they would repair to someone's paneled basement or side porch and put on Beach Boys or Jan and Dean records. One year the songs were about drag racing, the next about surfboards. It may have been in the other order. Conversation was minimal; the vision of a realer life somewhere was self-evident and called for no comment beyond wistful stares. Such discussion as there was, when someone got up and flipped a record over, was heavy on jargon—hanging ten and shooting the tube in the latter case, dual carbs and 389s in the former. Brian was as fluent as the next guy. Meanwhile his father was taking him to the high school parking lot before dinner and teaching him to drive a Plymouth Valiant with a three-speed on the column, and they vacationed at Tionesta, in the Allegheny National Forest, where a few of their neighbors water-skied on the straight stretches of the olive-green river. So flying into California for the first time was like watching a mirage materialize.

"Is that the Golden Gate Bridge?" Jenna asked, looking out the window of the plane as a jigsaw of brown and blue, interlocked land and ocean, tilted toward them.

The African-American man on the aisle looked up from his newspaper to say, "Bay Bridge."

It didn't sound as romantic, but they got a better price flying into Oakland, which was also a little closer to their destination than San Francisco was. Once they had picked up their rental car and left the lot, they felt as if they had been fed like a can onto the conveyor belt of the freeway. Or maybe it was more like an abacus, since the vehicles slid bumper-to-bumper like beads up and down the lanes. There were no apparent exits from the freeway except onto other freeways. Eventually though they saw signs to the district where they were spending the night and pulled off onto streets so regular, with yards so neat, it seemed like a game board. Even the shops looked manicured, with low hedges between the parking lots and the street. An auto parts store could have been a boutique. The summery vista through the windshield was misleading; they stepped out of the car into a cool, abrasive breeze that seemed to have scrubbed the sky to a fine-grained blue. Jenna asked for her jacket.

They were staying for just the one night in the motel. David had arranged a good rate for them. They could have stayed with him and his wife except for the baby, whose arrival had pretty well trashed their apartment. Somehow though they were hosting a party the next day, a "closing party," perfectly timed for Brian and Jenna's visit.

When they located the apartment complex, its parking lot was full of cars. Any empty slots were assigned; they had to drive around to find the visitors' section. The building on the other hand looked deserted. They entered by the nearest door but then followed what seemed miles of blank, beige-carpeted hallways, chunking though fire doors only to look down another, identical corridor. Furthermore a sequence was not readily apparent in the units' numbers. Finally they arrived at what could have been the right door and knocked. It was opened by a pretty young woman who smiled and struck a pose of hospitality, spreading her arms. One hand held a plastic cup. She said, "Could this be Brian and Jenna?"

Her guests looked at each other. "Yes in the aggregate," Brian said. "Let us synchronize our watches before we tell you who's who."

"Welcome to Pacific Standard Time," she said. "Come in and join the closing party."

"Yes, come in." David had appeared behind her. "As always, my wife Meg and I are of one mind. Meg," he said, speaking distinctly, as though to a slow student, "this one would be Jenna. Let's see. How are we going to do this?" He looked himself over: beer can in one hand, baby dangling from his neck.

"Here," Meg said, plucking the baby from its pouch.

"That's better," he said, stepping forward to embrace Jenna. "I trust we're on hugging terms even if we've just met. For this guy, a firm handshake will suffice. We might be bicoastal, but that's as far as it goes. How are you, buddy?"

"Been worse," Brian said. "Hey, I was just explaining to Jenna here what a closing party is, except I don't know. Is the furniture for sale?"

"No," Jenna laughed. "But make us an offer."

"My firm closed a deal last week," David said. "We took a company public. After much deprivation of sleep."

"For everyone involved," Meg said, hefting the baby.

"Your fellow guests are mostly my partners in crime," David said.

"Only that crime," Meg said. "I'll give you a good price on the item in there." She gestured toward a doorway, through which they could see a skeletal contraption in front of the television.

"Right this way," David said with a theatrical flourish, turning to block the doorway and nudge them into the living room.

The next hour or so was devoted to introductions. Everyone looked about their age, one side or the other of thirty. The chief topics of discussion were business, babies and triathlons. Brian and Jenna jumped in when they could, but they were clearly not expected to carry the conversation. Jenna was soon drawn off into a group of women that had separated off onto the patio. David had told him dress would be casual. That was true to a point. However, Brian thought he detected a dress code. Almost to a man, David's friends wore shorts, tee shirts and running shoes. Brand new running shoes, with one of a few different logos. The tee shirts might have been pressed, and they announced various events: *Redwood Shores Triathlon, Back Bay 10K*. Even the couple of older men there, with razor-sharp businessmen's haircuts and steel-framed glasses, had adopted this attire. Brian could believe they had come by it honestly. Everyone looked fit and tan, even in February. Through the back door he could see the corner of a lap pool; he and Jenna had counted three public pools on the way from the motel to the apartment complex.

A particularly conspicuous guest made his way over to Brian and David. He was tall and angular enough that you didn't realize at first he was also muscular. His tee shirt was like a canvas stretched on a frame; his calves looked as though they had been molded and then snapped in place on his legs. "Blitz today," he said when he arrived.

"I'm pleading my hosting duties," David said. "And, if I need them for my defense, my parenting duties. I ran eight this morning."

"Eight?" The guy turned to Brian. "What do you say? I guess everyone is entitled to a day off now and then." He extended his hand. "Don Plantinga."

"This is my childhood friend Brian. Visiting from the East. He's in computers."

"You came to the right place," Don said.

"Programming, not designing," Brian said. "Well, learning to program. I'm back in school."

"He's from Steeler country. Blitzburgh. Don's talking a different kind of blitz. You swim, bike, and run all on the same day. You're simulating a triathlon."

"Fifteen hundred in the pool—long course—twenty-five miles on the bike, six on the road. International distances," Don said. "And go, Lions."

"Oh, God," Meg said as she passed by. "These guys feed off each other. Now David's going to have to outdo that tomorrow. So our family Sunday's shot. Thanks, Don."

"Don't worry, dear," David said to her retreating back. "My policy is, in the off-season you concentrate on one of three events. You don't try to keep them all going at a reduced level. That way you get out of shape in all three. For me it's running; I think that's the best exercise for base endurance. I'll get back to fifty miles a week. Once in a while I'll get in the water or on the bike, just so I don't lose my feel." He nodded toward Don. "This guy has no off-season. He's training for the Iron Man."

"Now if I can just get in," Don said.

"Get in?" Brian said.

"There are so many maniac baby-boomer triathletes out there they have a cut-off for our age group," David said.

"It's like applying to college all over again," Don said. "I'm asking President Reagan to write me a letter of recommendation."

"Training gets to be like a sickness," David said. "I'm like an alcoholic: now I'm hiding it. Meg will ask me how many miles I put in in a week, and I'll say, 'I don't know. Thirty?' And she's like, 'Yeah, right.' Then when I get home from work it's on the Starship Enterprise to watch the nightly news." He jerked his thumb toward the den.

"What is that gizmo?" Brian said.

"That's a turbo-trainer," Don said. "They come standard in every California residence. Hook your bike onto it and spin to your heart's content in the comfort of your own home." Given his height, he had a way of crooking one knee and leaning over you with an overhead grin as he spoke. "Actually, I'm a roller man myself. I don't want a machine keeping my balance for me."

Another guy had joined their group in the course of the last few remarks. He was as noticeably wide as Don was tall. But not short. Brian learned he was from Long Island and had been lacrosse player of the year in his conference. "That translates as 'land animal,'" he said. "I have exhibited great potential as a triathlete, if you spot me the swim and the run. You swimmers have such an advantage."

"I don't know," Don said. "The Iron Man bike leg is 110 miles. They say it's not weighted to the cyclists? Give me a break." He nudged David's shoulder. "Qualcast is up ten points."

David nodded and frowned. "If it sells at twice book value, I made a mistake. I'm going to check on the food."

Conversations did laps around Brian like a relay; he was passed from one group to the next. Every so often though there was an individual event; someone seemed singled out for attention as though on a starting block. A tanned, boyish, short-haired blonde woman in a sort of burnoose was holding Brian and Meg's baby. He had a gleeful, vise-like grip on the neckline of the robe, which he seemed intent on pulling down to her waist. Bent at the knees, the woman laughed as she tried to stay decent without dropping the baby.

"You've got competition, Scott."

"Someone's making a move on your date."

"She's just practicing. She wants one of those items of her own."

"Better deliver, stud."

Recoiling, the young man at whom these remarks were directed, as athletic-looking as everyone else, became a study of amused, self-deprecating celibacy.

Another male guest, dateless, was ostentatiously preoccupied in the midst of the festivity.

"What's the problem, Derek?" Don said. "We just closed. You didn't get the memo?"

Derek shook his head. "The whole industry is getting ahead of its skis. I've taken that position publicly. You don't feel a headwind?" He raised a finger. "I'm convinced that the market is overvalued a minimum of five percent."

His doomsaying didn't spoil the mood; it seemed to heighten it. The joking went on; bets were made on basketball games to be played that week on snowy campuses between eastern alma maters. It became clear that there were few if any native Californians at the party. It was particularly clear that there were several Ivy Leaguers. A pastime of theirs was to get the name of David and Brian's college wrong, assigning it any presidential names but the right ones.

"So, how's the basketball program faring this year at Garfield and Eisenhower?"

"No, they went to Buchanan and Hayes."

And other such hospitable abuse. Brian felt included.

They were summoned to dinner. From somewhere an impressive spread had been produced.

"Under normal circumstances, the host would not serve himself first," David said. "However, I want to demonstrate to any visitors present, of which we know there are two, and perhaps also to some of our guests not so assimilated to West Coast culture as I am the proper way to assemble a taco."

Beyond him, in the kitchen, three young Hispanic women were at work. At Brian's side again, Jenna leaned into him and said, "Even the caterers are good-looking."

Since the dining room table was serving as the buffet, people dispersed around the premises to eat. Brian and Jenna ended up sitting around a low table in the living room with David and Meg. Most of the other guests dragged lawn chairs into loose clusters in the small back yard separated from its neighbors by latticework fences. Some sat on the living room carpet with their plates in their lap. Jibes were still lobbed into the cooling evening air like volleyballs as people walked back and forth to get more food or another can of Miller Lite. But the atmosphere had settled. Jackets were put on.

"You could have been hosting me," David said. "Back in college we probably would have voted you most likely to end up in California."

"Had guitar, would have toured," Brian said. "Had. I should not have sold that Stratocaster. I hope no one brings that subject up."

"I won't," David said.

"David said you were going on a retreat?" Meg said.

"It's pretty well known in our circles," Brian said. "Sort of a Mecca of meditation centers, if that makes sense. We've been planning the trip for a long time."

"It seems funny, though," Jenna said. "We were looking forward to a time of tranquility, and to do that we have to fight our way through airports and freeways."

"I just think spirituality is so important," Meg said. "Something to ground you."

"It can be crazy here," David said, hunching over his plate. His forehead was higher, and he was wearing his hair short, so that it gave the impression of a skull cap. "That's why I want my son raised in the church." He looked up at Meg. "I'm very serious about this."

"You have no idea how rare this is," Meg said. "This is the second night this weekend we've been home. If David isn't at work, we're at some business meeting disguised as a social event. If you think you've heard shop talk tonight? This is mild."

"My release is working out," David said. "That's the one place I can get away from everything. In the water, on a bike in the middle of nowhere. This is a nice time of year to bike. Anyone who says California doesn't have seasons is blind. If you want to see daffodils, this is the time. Sunday mornings is the only time I can do that."

"So when is your son going to church?" Meg said.

"He can make his mind up about things when he's older," David said. "Be anything he wants. I want him to have a moral base when he's young."

"I'm not taking him by myself," Meg said. "That's the kind of hypocrisy that drove me from the church. And where would we go? Which church would we pick? They're different from the ones back East. Denominations you never heard of. Most of them don't look like churches. No steeples."

"Find one with a 9:00 service," David said. "That would help. You'd think they would realize that people have things they want to do on a Sunday. You get out at noon, the day's shot."

"Oh, oh," Meg said. "I think I'm being summoned. Got to put the baby down. This was a nice break."

"You don't need a meditation center," David said. "Come out with me tomorrow on a four-hour bike ride."

Brian laughed. "I don't think I would equate oxygen debt with enlightenment. Or carbo depleting with emptying the mind. You triathletes and marathoners strike me as pleasure-pain types. Work hard at the office so you can get to the pool to work out hard. Then relax hard."

"Nolo contendere," David said. "That's the culture."

"'Culture' seems like an odd word for it to me. I associate culture with leisure and appreciation. There's a pertinent Zen parable. Short version, a guy is hanging from a cliff by a vine with one tiger peering over the edge at him and another tiger waiting for him below. Two mice are gnawing away at the vine. What does he do? He plucks a strawberry and eats it. Best-tasting strawberry he ever had."

"Nice non sequitur," David said. "Sounds like a 'fractured fairy tale' out of *MAD Magazine*."

"It does," Brian said. "But with a point. First, that pleasure doesn't exist without pain. It has no free-standing reality. Second, you are threatened by duality on every side. Maybe it would make more sense if I said on both sides. Or less. Two tigers, two mice, two emotional states. All illusions: so is the duality itself. People seek illusions. You don't have to; they present themselves to your mind. But if you step back, you see them as part of a larger whole. Give your consciousness space to breathe, expand, like your lungs, along with your lungs. Let the illusions fall back into the nothingness they came from. If other people are anything like me, they're a jumble of feelings and expectations and memories, short-term and long-term, none of them actual. I'm trying to find work that won't feed my fantasy life. The friends of yours that I've met all seem talented, accomplished people. And poised. There's a collective wit here. But they also seem to me to be pre-stressed. You know, like fabric. Are they relaxed or are they tensed? Like they can't wait to get back to work. Who's that guy over there, for instance? I had a nice talk with him."

In fact, Brian had mostly listened to a story he told about driving a sports car non-stop with a friend from San Francisco to Dallas by a certain deadline. It was a great story. It was pretty clear from his gestures that he was telling it again to a fresh sitting—literally: several people sat around him on the carpet. He was currently in the lotus position, but he kept unbending his legs and lifting himself with his hands, shifting his weight, like a gymnast doing his floor routine. You expected him to pop into a handstand.

"I might diagnose him as driven," Brian said. "Especially when you've heard his story, which I'm guessing you have."

"Oh, yeah," David said. "He's the world's most fidgety man, for sure. I met him in b-school. He's with a start-up. He is the start-up. That will do a number on your nerves. Half the guys here are with start-ups; half of them won't make it. I know how it seems. We're the stereotypical capitalists. What's worse, we're venture capitalists. I think people react to that term today the way they did to 'politician' in the Watergate years. Guilty until proven guilty. The older I get, the more I see life as a selection of stereotypes. The choices are many, but not infinite. Pick one, go with it. If I had to explain the appeal of this place to outsiders, I would use the word 'possibility.' Unbelievable things are happening. There's so much ingenuity and innovation collected in one place. You want to be in, but you have to be all in. That guy is 24/7, you're right. Worse than me. That's what I mean by culture. The rewards are great, but the risks are great.

"Then I hear people say we don't do any social good. Hey. Our firm employs secretaries, custodians. We pay rent. We create jobs; we generate wealth for other people, too. You know the parable I remember from Sunday school? The guy who was rewarded for investing his money. I know it has a moral, but I think people ignore the literal. And I always felt our teachers secretly sided with the guy who buried his talent. I might be the only one who got the point."

"I can hear it now." Meg had returned, holding their baby. "'The Parable of the East Coast and the West Coast Friends.' Well, I gave you the title. You can fill in the details."

* * *

With every meeting after that day at the retreat, Michael had another first impression of Marie. He still could not decide whether she was pretty or plain. Eventually he decided that was because he was making a false distinction. She was neither. She was pleasant looking. And maybe the 'looking' was irrelevant. She was pleasant. That satisfied him for a while. But in the half-light, in profile, she was angelic.

That light came from the street outside her apartment in one of the older districts in town, a mile or so up the boulevard from the university campuses and cathedrals, the synagogues and hospitals strewn like boulders at odd angles from each other up side streets and along the hillside. Marie had the front half of the second story of one of the old houses with which the streets of the neighborhood were lined. They had been built for single families, but almost all of them had been converted to apartments. "Who could afford to heat them?" one of your elders could be counted on to ask as you drove by. Marie's block was a small business district. The dimmed windows of the deli and dry cleaner added to the glow of street lights that suffused her three rooms as you entered, before you turned the lights on or after you turned them off. The apartment retained many of the fixtures of the original residence. The appliances were new, but it still had radiators and scrolled woodwork. The bathroom floor was tiled in black and white octagons, and there was still a claw-footed bathtub.

That first meeting set the tone for their dating. That was probably a fair term for the time they started to spend together. Taking her invitation at face value, he attended a service in her church. It was right on the boulevard, at a big corner with a traffic light at which he had stopped hundreds of times without particularly noticing the building, typically massive and sooty brown, with the standard placard outside announcing services. They were standard, too: 9:45 AM Sunday School; 11:00 AM Worship. All were welcome. He couldn't remember ever seeing anyone going in or out; the big metallic doors looked welded shut. But then he had never driven past on a Sunday morning until he walked up the front steps to find those doors flung open, an usher on either hand. The male was just this side of ancient. His tie was knotted tight, but his collar was loose around a ropy neck. Michael declined his offer to show him to a seat. An empty pew was not hard to find in the cavernous sanctuary. Apart from a few people sitting in the very back, twenty or thirty people clustered in the first few pews. He took a seat on an aisle about two-thirds of the way down. He could maybe do his part by filling in the void. Hidden somewhere in the loft, the organist had begun a prelude. A cross hung up front, and, just in Michael's field of vision, an enormous mirror was suspended on a side wall.

Before too long the choir filed in from either wing. About as numerous as the congregation, they were mingled in sex and age. From the grey-haired and bald to what looked like college students, whose sandals and running shoes were visible under the robes. It took him a minute to pick Marie out; there were a couple of other women about the same size and coloring. She was not the youngest or even the prettiest, but she had the openness and alertness he remembered from the retreat. After they sat in unison, as the organist continued to play, she exchanged a remark or two with her neighbors. But when they stood to sing the introit she was all business, balancing her folder like a tray on one hand, the other poised to turn the page. She looked away from the congregation as she sang. Michael thought that was strange until he realized she was following the organist's direction in the mirror. During the service she scanned the sanctuary. Michael had the impression that at one point she stared at him. He was certainly conspicuous, the only human being in an expanse of vacant pews. But there was no sign of recognition.

He had come on stewardship Sunday. The pastor apologized, especially to visitors, of whom Michaels assumed he must be the only one, for the nuts-and-bolts, business plan of a sermon they were about to hear. But it was not as dry as advertised. He brought a certain wit to the topic. He reminded them that they were not sitting in Solomon's temple, the subject of that day's Old Testament reading. Carpets frayed, circuit boards blew out, sometimes in the middle of a service. That seemed to be an inside joke. They were blessed with a big physical plant, and they were cursed. Unlike Solomon, they had utility bills. "Our building is magnificent in its way, but does it have a portal?" He encouraged people to look around for one. "I'm not sure," he said. "To be honest, I was never a student of church architecture. I couldn't tell you which is the apse and which is the narthex. But I'm not really talking blueprints here. What is the portal of our church? Where do we open out to the community? Do people know how to get into our church? Maybe not on Sunday morning at 11:00 AM." He smiled around sheepishly at the congregation, which smiled sheepishly back. "The sermons don't seem to be packing them in. Do you know that on any given weekday our soup kitchen serves maybe four times as many people as attend an average worship service?" Maybe they were the congregation. Maybe, down and out as a lot of them were, they were the church. "We just have to keep the shelves stocked." He encouraged everyone to put their pledge cards in the offering plates. "We also accept cash," he said. Michael responded with a ten when the usher who had greeted him at the door held out the plate for him. He half-stood, half crouched to take it to an older woman who had come in late and sat at the far end of the pew, then sidled back to his seat. Marie wouldn't have noticed. The choir was singing again, and her eyes were fixed on the mirror.

After the benediction, Michael observed his policy of declining invitations to post-service coffees, but with a purpose of his own. You could think of it as fellowship. He stationed himself by a side door, backstage, so to speak, where he guessed the choir would come out. He guessed right. He recognized the first few people to rush out the door as the youngest singers. They looked even younger in street clothes. There was a hiatus until Michael heard some rustling. Head down, her arms full of bouquets, Marie almost collided with him. When she looked up, her expression passed from startled to blank to astounded.

"That was you!" she said. "You remembered! You came to Fourth Presbyterian Church. Not Third or Fifth."

"I did," Michael said. "On the first try, too."

She lit up. "We should go to lunch!" she said. Then, equally pleased at the thought, wide-eyed, "But we can't! I have to make some hospital visits, and I have to do it before these wilt, and then I have to do something else."

"A good deed?"

"Always," she said.

"How about I help you to your car?" Michael reached for the flowers.

"I've got these. You could get the door."

So they walked down the steps of the church to the street together as she clutched her flowers. She opened the back door of her uncluttered car and laid them along the seat.

"You can park on the boulevard?" Michael said.

"Just on Sunday mornings," Marie said. "We're special."

"Oh," Michael said. "Then I wonder if there's even a remote chance I could see you again sometime."

"I know!" Marie said brightly. "You could join the church. Then you could see me every Sunday."

"Maybe once in a while in between?"

"Here." She opened her purse and handed him a card that announced her as a home care nurse. "Call me. But don't wait until you need me."

Their second date took place not at her church but at another church, on a Saturday rather than a Sunday morning, and they drove separately. Michael found her car and pulled in behind her. It was a stuffy early autumn day under a low sky. They could have been indoors, maybe in a huge hangar or a mill. The buildings around them might as well have been machinery for any sign of life they showed. The only way in or out of them seemed to be loading docks or fire escapes. They were in the inner city, but not the residential part.

"Should we put money in the meters?" Michael said.

"I doubt these have been operational for a few decades," Marie said. "Look, they take pennies."

"Mine has a nickel wedged in the slot," Michael said. "Somebody has a conscience."

"It's Saturday morning anyway," Marie said.

"I guess you can park anywhere in the city you want," Michael said.

"I guess I can," Marie said. "You should follow me around more often."

She was wearing jeans and a gray sweatshirt. Though the sweatshirt was shapeless, the jeans were not.

"I've never been down this street," Michael said. "I've passed it a zillion times. It's all warehouses."

"This building's a church," Marie said. "We're around back."

Once they rounded two corners, they came upon activity. The curb was lined with cars; doors were opening and shutting almost in a cadence. From the front, the structure looked more like a church, and in fact there was another one across and up the street. This one was more horizontal than Marie's church. It felt like entering a high school, especially when they walked into the gym.

"Grab a box," Marie said. "One for me, one for you. This is an A. M. E. church. We have mission partnerships with them and a bunch of other churches in the East End."

Folding tables had been set up to form a big rectangle. On the inside, mostly African-American helpers stood by heaps of food—cartons of eggs, bags of potatoes, packs of cheese. On the outside, people shoved their boxes along the tables from station to station.

"Mmm-hmm," a heavyset black man said, holding up a canned ham to put in Michael's box. "I'm going to get me one of these."

Marie wagged a finger at him. "No sampling the product."

"You're no fun," he said.

"That's what everyone keeps telling me."

When they had worked their way around the circuit, Marie said to the man at the money box, "Ah, Bill, I forgot my coupons again today."

"Don't you try that on me, Miss Marie." He was a grizzled guy with a frayed gray crew-cut. He grinned at Michael. "It's cash on the barrelhead here."

"Geez oh man, what does a girl have to do to get a discount?" She dug into her jeans' front pocket for some bills. "Here's your twenty-six dollars. That's still not a bad deal for two boxes full of food, huh, Michael?"

As they carried their boxes of food down the front steps, Marie said, "That was pick-up. Now delivery."

Michael stopped short on the sidewalk.

"What?" Marie said.

"Maybe we shouldn't look."

But the people across the street didn't seem to mind. A young African-American woman, formally dressed in a lavender coat and matching hat, was bent double, hopping and shrieking, while an older man held her around the waist from behind, heels dug in, hanging on for dear life, shuffling along as she pulled. The coupling looked unseemly, if not obscene.

Another older man, also in coat and tie, walked alongside. He held Michael's eye in a near-glare. Glancing up the street, Michael saw people leaving the church opposite. Its main entrance was on the corner.

"Don't you wish we knew how to mourn?" Marie said. "Believe me, that's how I felt like acting at my mother's funeral."

Marie's box was destined for a shut-in only a few blocks away. Michael waited in his car while Marie walked it up the porch steps and handed it through the front door to a woman and took an envelope from her. Marie got back in her car, and Michael followed her again. This time they drove for a little while. They were still in the city, but, subtly, the neighborhood altered. It contracted. Both the houses and the streets were narrower; when they weren't one-way, they had to take turns yielding to cars coming the other way, since people parked on both sides of the street. At the same time, everything from the curbs up looked scrubbed or spiffed up somehow. On the main street shops seemed to lean into each other, shoulder-to-shoulder; restaurants had names like Veltri's and Montemurro's. So the name alone of the nursing home they drove into, Wellington Place, was incongruous, and it looked like a Tudor manor in the middle of Little Italy. They parked side-by-side in visitors' spaces out front by the porte-cochere and entered a vast, elegant lobby, plush with green-and-gold patterned carpet and polished woodwork. They were alone. The reception counter was unattended.

"I feel like we should have luggage," Michael said. "This is like a hotel, except no one ever checks in or out."

"Oh, they check out," Marie said. "Come this way." She led him up steps to a fire door. On the other side they stepped from carpet onto matting that ran the length of a long concrete hallway. "We're on the other side of the tracks. The other side of the lobby, that is. The nice apartments are on the other wing."

They stopped at one of the many steel doors along the hall and knocked. "Come in," a voice answered. "I left the door unlocked for you."

"It's, Marie, Mrs. Liscak. I brought a box of food and a friend. You can keep the food."

Mrs. Liscak sat ready to receive them in a chair against the far wall. Her wave was a greeting, an acknowledgment of Marie's joke, and a surrender all in one. She was dressed for her levée in a hair net and a robe, but she wasn't about to get up, even though she gripped her cane. Her swollen calves were swathed in tape under the smock, which parted slightly at the knee over pasty thighs. To approach her they had to wind their way through stacked-up boxes and newspapers.

"Have a seat," Mrs. Liscak said. "You can move any of that stuff. Just set it on the floor."

Under the clothes and magazines piled on them, the outlines of a couch and chairs were visible, like objects under a snowdrift. Michael cleared the front of a kitchen chair. For the next fifteen minutes or so he balanced on its edge and tried to comprehend what unfolded before him. It was a little like the moment on the sidewalk outside the funeral. He wasn't sure he could believe what he was witnessing.

"Let me show you your food before I sit down," Marie said. "I can put it away for you. Some things need refrigerated."

"I'll do that," Mrs. Liscak said. "You can just set the box here."

"Pretty much the usual."

Mrs. Liscak pulled a couple of items from the box and turned them over. "Hand me my reading glasses, hon."

"It's all okay, Mrs. Liscak," Marie said. "It may all be overstock, but it's not expired. We won't let them poison you."

"You just don't know," Mrs. Liscak. "And then you can't get them open." She gestured to the kitchen counter. "That one's from last time."

"Look, see," Marie said. "You have to break this tab first."

Mrs. Liscak nodded in guarded assent.

"It's good you're eating healthy," Marie said. "Remember the magic words: balance and moderation."

That was one example. Everything Marie did, she exaggerated. She talked a little too loud. She mimicked Mrs. Liscak's facial expressions. No, she amplified them. She repeated Mrs. Liscak's platitudes and produced her own. Another one:

Out of the blue, Mrs. Liscak said, "My best friend had to go into the hospital last week."

"Did she?" Marie said.

"I take it back. It was the week before that. She was my one friend here. I don't know if she's coming back. They won't tell me."

"Oh, now, it's hard to lose someone close like that. Close both ways. Nearby, and a good friend."

Mrs. Liscak absorbed that thought. Marie's consolations seemed unbelievably transparent to Michael. What was more amazing was that they worked. They seemed to be exactly what Mrs. Liscak needed to hear.

"You know what?" Marie said. "We could sit here and gab all day, but we have to be on our way."

"Here," Mrs. Liscak said, handing her an envelope. "Is it still thirteen dollars?"

"Still thirteen bucks," Marie said. "And still the best deal in town. Now, do you want us to take anything with us? We do recycling, too. You know that? You remember what we said about hoarding?"

"Maybe next time," Mrs. Liscak said. "I need to go through these things here."

"All right. But someday I'm coming over and we're going to do some serious cleaning. I'm talking about scrub buckets and brushes. Right?"

They stood to go. Marie walked over and took both of Mrs. Liscak's hands in hers. "Who wants to pray?"

Mrs. Liscak's head neither shook nor nodded. It oscillated slightly.

"Does that mean me?" Marie said. "All right. Lord, we just ask that you be with your creature Mrs. Liscak until we meet next time. Nourish her with this food and with your love through Christ our Lord. Amen." She kept hold of Mrs. Liscak's hands. "That about says it all, doesn't it? You stay well. I'll be back in a month. Maybe I'll even bring Michael back with me. He sort of dresses the place up, doesn't he?"

Mrs. Liscak looked up at Marie with a smile that somehow mingled desperation and bewilderment. "Why are you so good to me?"

"It's a privilege, Mrs. Liscak," Marie said. "You might be the one helping me. Did you ever think of that?"

As though dialed, Mrs. Liscak's expression registered another complicated smile. You couldn't tell if it was amused or appalled.

In the hallway, Marie said, "Now we go to lunch."

By 12:15 the serving line had already begun to dissolve; this was a punctual lunch crowd. Michael and Marie stood with a few other young people behind the table, while a crew in the kitchen was at work on pots and pans.

"We're a clean-as-you-go operation," Marie said. "I didn't say we were going to *eat* lunch."

"However," a young man named John to Marie's right said, "I don't think we are needed anymore. And I see four very desirable places, all together. The others can hold the fort."

Each with a paper plate of spaghetti, salad and bread in one hand and a cup of iced tea in the other, the three of them along with a girl named Donna slid into the end of one of the tables that ran the length of the room. It was long and low but, with its stone walls and pipe-like metal pillars, rather Gothic.

"My compliments to the chef," John said. "Who did the cooking this time?"

"Jimmy and them," Donna said. "Italian cuisine is their specialty."

"You want me on the sloppy joes," John said.

"You're all a church group?" Michael said.

"We're the SWAT team," Marie said. "We try to help people out. You're unemployed, overwhelmed, a single parent. Maybe your apartment needs painted or your porch needs repaired. Call us."

"It sounds better than Young Adults," Donna said.

"Or Not So Young Anymore Unmarrieds," John said. "Try to get your mouth around that acronym."

"What did we say it stood for?" Donna said. "'Single Without a . . . ' I forget the rest."

"So we do the soup kitchen every so often," Marie said. "We also meet for Bible study."

"Did you all grow up in the church?" Michael said.

They looked at one another as though startled.

"No," Donna said. "But we all joined about the same time. There was a real dynamic young pastor. He kind of organized us. What, maybe twenty-some of us?"

John shrugged. "I'm not from around here. I grew up in the sticks." He was deceptively tall, with a round face and shallow features. He wore his thin, blond hair short and parted it in the middle. The effect was puppet-like, but he wasn't bad-looking. Neither was Donna. But sitting side-by-side on the bench as they were, as though on a double-date, there was palpably no chemistry between them. "I came to the big city to have fun. Specifically, that turned out to be to engage in recreational activities of a pharmaceutical nature. The church hosts a twelve-step program, too. Pastor Paul was involved in it."

"I was raised Roman Catholic," Marie said.

"I wondered about your last name," Michael said. "What is Gorski? Polish?"

"Careful," Marie said. "Croatian."

"Hey, Donna," John said, as though on cue. "You see that light bulb by Marie flicker? I think it needs changed."

"All right," Marie said. "How's about let's lay off the Croatian jokes today?"

"There are Croatian jokes?" Michael said.

"Yes, but around here only bad ones," Marie said.

John and Donna were still laughing.

"How about all these folks?" Michael said. "Will you see them in church on Sunday?"

"We have no illusions," John said. "We'll see them next time there's a free meal. We feed them week in, week out. We'll be back, too."

"And that's okay," Marie said. "There's no preaching here. We don't preach; we don't pass out pamphlets. We decided not even to say grace."

"It would be hard anyway," John said. "When we open, the line's half-way out the door onto the sidewalk, and once people sit down with their food it's pandemonium."

"Sometimes I want to witness so bad," Donna said.

"I know," Marie said. "But you are. Maybe when people are full of food and back out on the street they'll have the feeling they still need something else in their lives. Like maybe Jesus?"

Marie was not kidding Mrs. Liscak when she said that they did recy-cling. Two Saturdays later her crew assembled on a bank of the Allegheny River. It was not far upstream from Michael's old neighborhood, two mill towns north, but it was still another territory Marie was introducing him to.

"I've crossed this bridge before," Michael said. "This is the first time it's crossed me."

That's what it felt like, seeing the massive, stone-block stanchions and the rooted steel girders at eye-level. It looked like a fort.

"Who brought the pigskin?" someone said.

It was true: it was football weather. The gleam of river's surface and sky, the same blue-gray, was metallic, and they stood on a field of coarse, curly grass. They were dressed for a pick-up game; not just Marie but everyone there wore jeans and a sweatshirt. The logos read either 4P SWAT Team or Steelers.

Someone else put his finger in the air. "Let's check the wind."

"He doesn't mean for kickoff," John said. "There's a waste treatment plant over that way." And, sure enough, they caught a whiff of it.

Business was not as brisk as the breeze. A trailer with slots for different kinds of refuse stood off to one side. When the odd car pulled onto the field it was swarmed by team members ready to take boxes and stack and sort. In between deliveries the team members drifted into groups and strayed around the field. Someone actually had brought a football. A handful of people stationed themselves by the trailer; Michael and Marie walked over toward the river's edge.

"Don't you get discouraged?" Michael said. "You're overstaffed here. On the other hand, your church is underattended. You're prepared to do more good than there is good to be done."

"I don't get discouraged," Marie said. "I get busy."

"But seriously. You try so hard. Most people look forward to their Saturday mornings off. You start these programs. Some take off like gang-busters, like the soup kitchen. Some are duds. Meanwhile, no one comes to church on Sunday. Families go shopping. Or they take their kids to play soccer. The stores are full; the churches are empty. The die-hards who do go to church don't seem to notice. They act like everything's okay."

"I notice," Marie said. "Things change. They stop working. The plants are empty, too; they're shut down. My father worked in a mill just around that bend in the river. But, you know, I don't think that's the problem. I think it's that Christians have a hard time talking about Jesus. We just want to help. See, we know what needs done. We'll recycle, we'll do meals on wheels. We're down to earth; we'll pitch in. That's all well and good, but that's not what we have to offer. I know it's awkward. No one wants to sound like a street-corner evangelist. So even though we're doing all this for Jesus's sake we can give the impression we're just being good citizens. We can mix in. Don't be scared of us. Then, hallelujah, we're just another NGO."

The football skidded to a stop at Marie's feet. She picked it up. Feet planted, she lofted it back to the other group.

"Nice toss," Michael said. "You put some air under it."

"I'm a tomboy," Marie said. "What can I say?"

"And then I wonder," Michael said. "What if it happened? What if the kingdom came? What if every knee did bow and every tongue confess that Jesus Christ is Lord? Would people stop going to the store? Stop taking their garbage out? Would they walk down the street singing hymns? No more Catholic or Protestant? The world already looks to me like God's creation. Basically, I like it."

Marie stood and looked at him. Suddenly she put her hands on his shoulders and shoved him.

Michael staggered back a couple of steps.

She did it again. "Get out!"

"What?" Michael said. If it was a blocking drill, she was holding.

"You're saved," she said, her hands still full of his sweatshirt. "Listen to you. Yes, you are. You belong to him. And here you were acting all skeptical."

"I was saved, maybe."

"Now, does that make sense? You're saved or you're not. There's no 'was.' There's no 'maybe.' Jesus called you. He's not going to recall you, like a defective car. Paul says so: 'for the gifts and the calling of God are irrevocable.'" She pushed him lightly and let her hands fall. "I can't wait to tell everyone. I know. We're all getting together for dinner. You come. You tell them."

Michael wasn't quite sure how it happened, but he didn't think it was an accident, that he was alone in the living room with Pastor Andy. They sat opposite one another in long, sway-backed, mismatched couches. There was a lot of furniture in the room, but it was miscellaneous. Three female members of the church shared the second floor of a house one district over and a step or two less fashionable than Marie's. After dinner everyone else had adjourned to another room behind double glass doors to watch a video. Maybe that was the living room. Theirs was an old-style layout; it wasn't clear what the function of all the rooms was. There was what Michael thought was probably a foyer. Someone had heard the movie was good—a strong R, however. They agreed that collectively they could handle it.

"It looks to me as though you're a member of the Swat Team," Pastor Andy said. "At the very least an auxiliary. Or maybe honorary?"

"And I gather I'm talking with the founder."

"I suppose that puts me in the annals of Fourth Presbyterian Church."

"They talk about you a lot. They make your time there sound like a golden age."

"I was sad to leave. It was time I had my own church."

"It's a nice group."

"I hear they're hiring."

"I don't know."

"Can I tell you my theory about your generation? Which by the way is my generation. I'm not all that much older than you all. I'm almost a boomer." In his powder blue sweater and slacks he certainly could have been one of the group. He was maybe a little jowly above the crew neck; his youth was fuzzy at the edges. "So let me say our generation. People say we're not believers. Come on; that's not fair. Everyone believes in something. What we're not is subscribers. We want to be sure what we're signing on for. We belonged to enough things when we were growing up. Boy Scouts. Little League. Key Club. I don't know what all. Some people call us Nones. Have you heard that one? 'What party, group, or denomination are you affiliated with?' None of the above. We don't want to be identified with a larger body. We want to keep our options open. Does that ring true?"

"The people here tonight," Michael said. "What do they have in common?"

They had all sat at a massive table in still another room. In the middle of the furniture's random furnishings sat a dining room set out of a Victorian mansion. It belonged to Mary, one of their hostesses. Her roommates referred to it as her trousseau. "You should see her hope chest," one of the guys said. "Don't laugh," Mary said. Dinner was gourmet. The girls had prepared a lamb roast and every conceivable fixing. Despite the holiday fare, Michael would have called the mood at the table subdued, even somber.

"No one fit," Michael said. "So many are unemployed, or drop-outs."

"And single," Pastor Andy said. "Or maybe divorced. You can be pretty sure some have passed up offers and opportunities. They want a Christian marriage."

"Well?" Michael said.

"I know." Pastor Andy shook his head and smiled. "Here they all are. Created male and female. About half and half. I think maybe the problem is that they all also want the perfect match, the one person on earth God intended for them. Whereas I think maybe God just roughed it out. You know. Two sexes, take it from there. I might not go as far as Ralph Vaughn Williams. Are you familiar with him, Michael? He is one of my favorite composers. That's his arrangement of 'For All the Saints' in the hymnbook. You've sung that, I guarantee you. He wrote this gorgeous church music; I figured he must be getting it straight from the source. Then I read a biography of him. Turns out he wasn't a believer. He described himself as 'a cheerful agnostic.' How is that possible? He also held some eccentric social views. He favored compulsory marriage over the age of twenty-five on the grounds that any two reasonable adults could learn to live together under one roof. If he were here tonight he'd have me perform a mass wedding on the spot. I can't say I'm hearing any bells."

Two of the guys at the table had described their ordeals at the same local school at roughly the same time before they left halfway through their first year. *It's a community college, for crying out loud*, Michael was thinking. *How rigorous could it be? You're making it sound like West Point.* There were allusions to former marriages. One of the women reported that her husband "had control issues." Disgustedly, John said, "Was he one of those? How long were you married?" "Three years," she said. "Give me three minutes alone with him," another guy said. He was the one veteran in the group. "Now, Bill," Pastor Andy said. "Don't worry," Bill said. "I'd beat him up in all Christian charity." After many comments there was a pause, almost a moment of silent reflection. The cast needed work on its cues.

"Think of it as a senior high group with some mileage on it," Pastor Andy said. "And carrying some baggage."

"And their names," Michael said. There was Lanny Albano, a Grimek, and of course Marie Gorski. "In Sunday school I was surrounded by Rosses and Watkinses and McClures."

"This is not your grandfather's Presbyterian Church," Pastor Andy said. "We started to have some African-American members when I was there. The church is finally reflecting the neighborhood, praise God."

Even during dinner, in the rhythm of handing around serving dishes and doling out pleasantries, Michael had felt detached and disembodied, like a human movie camera panning around the table, recording one close-up confession after another. It didn't occur to him at first that the camera would work its way around to him. It would be his turn to explain to the other knowing faces that he was lucky to have a good job at the high school he graduated from but that he had always wanted to teach at the college level but that the job market was tight. "Closed shop," a guy said. And that now to pursue that career he would have to gear up his dissertation basically from scratch, and that meant catching up on the literature in the field, and his job search would be limited because he couldn't live too far from home because of his parents' age and in fact it made sense for him to live at home.

"They're all such losers," Michael said. "So why did I feel that I belonged?"

"Even these folks, watching a video is about their only group activity. They have their projects. No more bowling leagues. They're not going out to the bars."

"I noticed there was no alcohol served tonight."

"That's not because they're so puritanical," Pastor Andy said. "That's the stumbling block rule kicking in. Some of them could handle it, but some couldn't. They don't want to make anyone's recovery more difficult than it already is. Tonight you joined a unique club. You know what they say about the church. There is only one qualification for membership: you must demonstrate your unworthiness to belong. And it is strictly observed. When I officiate at the Eucharist, I stand in front of the table with the loaf and say, 'Broken bread for broken people.' If I didn't know that we weren't in a church and that there is no wine on the premises, I would say you took communion tonight."

The double doors burst open and the diners emerged.

"The featured attraction over already?" Pastor Andy said.

"Indefinite intermission," John said.

"Too raunchy?" Pastor Andy said.

"No, just bad," John said. "And raunchy."

"And some of us have to work tomorrow," a woman said. Marie was not the only choir member there.

Afterward, Michael walked Marie to her car. "You had some time with Pastor Andy," she said.

"The bad news is that I'm broken. The good news is that I belong. I think I got that right, though it could be vice versa."

"You know, people think that when you're saved, you're saved."

"In fact," Michael said, "I think you said something to that effect earlier today."

"Saved from everything, they think. What I meant, what I mean is that even though you're saved, you're still a sinner. You make mistakes. You're not saved from being human."

They were standing on the buckled sidewalk between street lamps. Michael realized they were holding hands.

"It doesn't mean that everything in your life from that point on is going to go just the way you want it to. It's a little like falling in love."

Marie was wearing a light scent. It was maybe a little stronger when she blushed. Michael moved his hands up and held her elbows.

"So, just to be clear," he said. "You can be saved and still fall in love?"

A little later in the evening, Marie cupped his cheek and kissed him. "And?" she said.

"I'm not prepared," Michael said. "Equipped."

Marie held his face and looked at him. "Maybe you should have thought of that before you got in my bed. I could be prepared. I'm ready in every other way."

"I am, too," Michael said. "I love you."

"Is there something?"

"I had a scare once. I was young. I was young and in love and un-prepared. I didn't know what I was doing, so I did what I thought I was supposed to do. We thought she was pregnant. She wasn't, but that was the end of the relationship. I did not react well in the circumstances. I thought maybe that was the end of all relationships, period."

"What was God's first commandment? Be fruitful and multiply."

"Yes, but eventually?" Michael said.

Marie laughed but pulled him tighter, her mouth by his ear. "Give me your hand."

* * *

David liked the idea of word processing when it came along and e-mail even better. And none too soon. At long last—writing was obsolete. He could remember the first time that, with a few key strokes, he made a sentence disappear and then surface in another paragraph. He was glad now he had not gone long on erasable typewriter paper. Talk about one of the truly bad ideas of the late twentieth century—right up there with laser disks. He used to hand in essays for his college classes so smudged they looked as if they had survived a house fire. All through his undergraduate career he had avoided courses that called for papers, especially term papers. That was pos-sible even as a religion major; some teachers took a surprisingly statistical approach to the subject. Or they allowed you to make a presentation in lieu of a paper. The irony was that when he got to law school he did nothing but research and write. By then he was using an electric typewriter with a little side spool of eraser tape. You could backspace over mistakes and, by repeating them, make them vanish. He wondered now if you could find one of those machines outside a museum. It was true that even with computers you had to get some words up on the screen before you could cut and paste them. Now he was in a position where he could dictate most of his correspondence or work from a template. The actual work of corporate law was not particularly interesting, a lot of plugging numbers into blanks on contracts that were all pretty much the same, one deal to the next. It was the people he met, the innovators, that made the work rewarding. And the money. They processed that, too.

E-mail was great. No names, no leaving space for the date. That was all built in. Always in the past when he called someone "dear" he felt he was starting a letter right off with a lie. Now you just let it rip.

> I thought about you when I got home from church today with the kids. Church . . . baptism . . . wedding: a logical progression. To the best of my recollection, which is not legendary for its accuracy, I e-mailed you an apology for missing your nuptials and promised to write more. Or was that before e-mail? Ouch. I'm sure I also congratulated you, though whether it was for getting married or for the fact that your bachelorhood outlasted all of ours I'm not sure. We all thought you would be the first casualty. I don't know if you were aware we all referred to you as "Married Man" that last semester in college, after the art major got hold of you. Who was posing for whom? we wondered. You wouldn't have been around to overhear. One minute you were a frat rat like the rest of us. The closest we got to sexual activity was mooning each other in semi-public settings. We graduated just in time; we were regressing from collegiate to adolescent to infantile. Sometimes I didn't know if it was a fraternity or a nursery. Marijuana didn't help our comportment particularly. Then you vaporized. You vanished into nubility. We never saw you. If we did, you would be wearing her like a wet suit. She was all over you. I remember seeing you once on a weekday evening in the library lounge, out by the periodicals. The two of you were sitting in the same easy chair, and you had somehow both draped your arm and hooked a knee over one of her thighs. I remember thinking that you probably needed to be using contraceptives even when you were fully clothed.
>
> I have no room to talk except that I only became a sex tool after I got married. We weren't ready to have children the first few years. Then we were ready. More like relentless, in her case. Every time I turned around I was expected to produce. That was good for my self-esteem until I realized my services were being requisitioned. She was following some kind of ovulation zodiac.

That was half her research. The other half was into exotic sexual techniques to keep me performing. I shouldn't complain. These days sex has to be scheduled three months out.

She had a plan, though. I basically like that about her. She wanted to have all her kids at once—bang, bang, bang, so to speak. That way they would grow up as friends, she could concentrate on child-rearing, etc. And she wanted three children. That was against her parents' advice. With a third child, they said, your challenges grow geometrically, not arithmetically. It's easier to be fair with two than three, keep things even. They convinced me, just not their daughter. I think it's become a little moot in our case. Meg didn't necessarily want all boys.

She takes the lion's share of the child-raising, no doubt; the division of labor is clear. Sunday is her one day to sleep in. I've missed the first four years with the kids; the question is whether I'm going to miss the next four, too. Partnership is coming up. Or not. I guess the firm will answer the question for me. Either way, I'll be busting a hump for the foreseeable future. And then, assuming I make partner—do you know there was a study that said the period anyone worked hardest in a profession is the few years after rather than before they get vested, tenure, whatever it may be. Out of some kind of perverse gratitude, I guess. You took my prime years; here are a few more. So I can kiss my kids' high school years goodbye. The weekend of your wedding I was at a firm "retreat." Last time we saw Brian he and his wife were out on the West Coast for a retreat at a Buddhist meditation center. I imagine the atmosphere at theirs was somewhat different. Fewer charts, I would bet. Probably also fewer inspirational speakers. So it was work that kept me from getting back for your wedding, not sexual exhaustion.

I always said I wanted my children raised in a church. No argument with her parents there. I didn't stop to think, though, that that meant they had to be baptized. I wince when I see a baby doused. Our first two cried to bust a gut; that can't be a good sign. The third just looked annoyed. When the pastor counselled us beforehand in his office, he made a point of saying it shouldn't be just a trickle; you want to pour water over them. He said however that the point is not to wash away sin. I was glad to hear that someone besides me thought that. How many sins can a newborn have committed? What I worry is that it foreshadows years of brainwashing to come. That's why I go to church with them.

Someone has to be vigilant. I want my sons to come of age with totally open minds, free to be whoever they want to be.

And I want them to be grounded, have a moral baseline. That's the plan. Whether it makes sense or not I don't know. Does it matter which church I take them to? Some of the main drags around here remind me of the cereal aisle in the supermarket. Houses of worship up one side of the boulevard and down the other. Different labels, same contents; probably same manufacturer. Would a synagogue or temple do as well? As far as I can tell the Bible is a book some guys wrote. Is it any better or different than the Koran? How am I supposed to know? Am I supposed to study every known scripture, then practice the prescribed religion for a few years before I decide? Then follow that protocol for the world's other major faiths? Meanwhile, I have to present at a board meeting next week.

The pastor said that baptism looks back. When you see the water, you should visualize all the perils God has brought God's people through. (He says "God's" rather than "his." It can sound a little awkward.) The Flood, the Red Sea. Think of Jesus getting his call waist-deep in the Jordan River. But it also looks ahead. It's a sign and a seal, a promise that God and God's people will rescue the child from the world's dangers and keep it safe. So don't skimp on the water. Like at communion. Why pass out those little yeasty pellets? Hold out a loaf. Have people take a big fistful of bread. I don't know that I completely follow all that, but it's the best explanation I've gotten to date. It's the first and only explanation I've ever gotten. So hose them down. Let them bawl. That's a trauma they'll get over. They'll live.

But that just makes me wonder if the whole shebang is more for our sake than theirs. I happen to have a recent example. Naturally Meg's parents were there for the occasion, and they brought that whole side of the family down with them from across the Bay. We packed the first three pews right under the pulpit, like our own little congregation. Meg's brother Brooks and his wife were there. They looked especially well dressed and wide-eyed, which indicated to me that they got to church seldom enough that it was a novelty. They weren't quite sure how to behave, but they were polite as hell. You can't be that attentive week in and week out. Brooks runs a hedge fund; his work ethic makes John Calvin look like Tom Sawyer. Once you put your name on the door it's total commitment. But it was an uncle of Meg's who caught my eye. He didn't have that exaggerated alertness. Rather, he sat perfectly still with a perfectly pleasant and agreeable expression on his face. It said, "Don't mind me, go about your business. I can see it's important to you." He was also completely impervious to the proceedings. He looked like he had put his brain on energy saver, like the camcorder in his lap. Then, after the sermon, as the preacher stepped down to the baptismal font, he came to life. It was his turn to be all business. He sat up straight, snapped the camera open and held it up to capture it all for posterity.

Once again, I shouldn't complain. He's the guy who taped our service and reception and gave it to us as a wedding present. We pulled it out so often at dinner parties that it started to seem like a video rental. Something tells me you didn't record your nuptials? Brian told me a little about them. No alcohol at the reception, he said. No band. That's kind of brutal after a church service an hour and three quarters long, wouldn't you say? There was a DJ, Brian said, but he couldn't make out any of the songs. Then he realized they were all contemporary Christian. "Good beat, easy to dance to," right? Your fiancée maybe did the planning? I expect you retain the musical tastes we cultivated under the guidance of the Wild Armenian. A little gospel blues wouldn't spoil the mood; Rev. Gary Davis meant no man no harm. Brian said some people tried to dance. So I'm assuming no masseuses at the bachelor party? You can hear me and Brian joking, I hope. Just because he's a Buddhist doesn't mean he's lost his sense of humor. I may make it sound like they were offended by the wedding, but they liked it. "Authentic" was the word Brian used. Still, I wonder what their wedding was like, assuming they had one. As far as I know no one was invited to one. Unlike yours, I doubt it had an altar call.

In this church it's Patsy I'm going to keep an eye on. She has a title, Director of Christian Education, I think it is, and she handles the children's sermon. Earlier in the service we watched our first two go up and sit on the steps so she could explain baptism to them. After the account the pastor gave us in his office, hers was a little bit of a throwback. "Did your parents ever give you a bath? Do they make you take a bath now sometimes?" She's in that camp: start with a question, the more metaphysical, the better. Such as, "What is love?" What do they expect kids to say? Something outlandish. I wince then, too, not just for the kids' sake but because I honestly think that's when the congregation is most engaged. They zone out for the sermon. Sitting through it is their penance. They should be Catholic.

So. Patsy. I didn't think they made that model anymore. She is Miss Guthrie resurrected. You remember her? She supervised Sunday school when we were kids. I think Supervisor was her title. She probably wasn't as old as she seemed to us. She managed to have this dynamite figure and yet remain utterly asexual. The problem may have been that her figure was too well-proportioned, like almost geometrical, at least in those flowery dresses she wore. Two triangles intersecting at that tiny circle of a waist, two cones for breasts. If you're having trouble calling her to mind, think Mrs. Ralston, our neighborhood evangelist-housewife-Jezebel, only more so. She was the opposite of the ample Miss Williams, the one African-American member of the church. How did she infiltrate the ranks? In those Dr. Spock days reprimanding children was out of fashion, but no one told Miss Williams. She was one of the greatest of the old-school scolders. She would chastise any-body's children for anything. "This is God's house, young man. You be respectful. Stop running around like you're outside on a playground." But there was something bracing about her re-bukes; you felt cleansed afterward. Miss Guthrie, on the other hand. She got hold of me in the hallway one day when I guess I should have been in my Sunday school class and just turned me into a pillar of salt. I still feel the ground getting warm un-der my feet. Neither one of them had children of their own. They were the last of the spinster schoolteachers from the days when female teachers couldn't be married. Patsy has children, two grown daughters. They bring their children on Sundays, though you don't see much of their husbands. Those kids seem well-adjusted. But I don't want my children scarred, even if it keeps them out of hell by the skin of their teeth.

Judgment seems a long way off in any direction or dimen-sion. I don't have to worry about my parents'. You know my fa-ther died not long after we got out of college. The timing seemed reasonable. I'm an adult now, right? A college graduate? I can keep the family on track. I can grieve in due course. "Here's your diploma. By the way, your father has six months." My mother lives out here, since my sister is in the Bay Area also. She was always a little sweet on you, by the way. I suppose it's safe to tell you that now. She is one of your many unclaimed conquests over the years, especially during the unaccountable celibacy of your late twenties that we could only impute to the sculptress, who must have burned you right down to the ground and then sowed the soil around the rubble with the sexual version of salt and cinders. We're glad your bride has brought you back to the land of the living.

When Brian visited out here he explained his doctrine of living in the present. Let the past go. Don't worry about the fu-ture. Neither exists, pretty much by definition. They are equally illusions. We project our desires behind and ahead of us to create a fictional life that perverts the present into a mirage so that we never actually experience it. Your mind is always somewhere else. I know you can find that view in other faith traditions. I was a religion major, don't forget. They all have a mystical strain. To me that makes it less rather than more valid. Generic. I realize Christianity has it, too. In college we got assigned some sections in a book called *The Eternal Now*. Same deal. With a scriptural perspective, you can live in a permanent present.

No, thanks. That's where my mother lives. She's in a home for the elderly. I take it back. Excuse me: it's a "memory care residence." It's for people who suffer from Alzheimer's disease, and not only that but "early-onset" Alzheimer's disease. "Old age" won't work, or "senility?" We'll call it a disease. Feel better? Where did all these conditions come from? Autism. No, "the autism spectrum." There's a place on it for everyone. The way it works it looks to me is that first they invent the disease, then they diagnose as many people as possible with it. It's like private prisons. You build them; we'll fill them. We'll get you your in-mates. Mandatory sentences should do the trick. Or air freight. When did it become so urgent that everything be delivered overnight? Suddenly there are all these little, brightly-colored trucks tearing around suburban streets to pick up packages and then haul out to the nearest landing strip and screech to a halt in front of airplanes just as their cargo doors are closing. Everybody's got some syndrome. It's not that kids can't sit still. It's that they have ADD or ADHD or some acronym. I don't blame God. I blame the TV talk-show psychologists and the celebrities who give their career a boost by becoming crusaders for the latest cause. Right after they get out of drug rehab. And the church buys into it. We feel your pain! We're compassion-ate! Our thank offering this week will go to . . . The church is just sucking up to the world. Big screen TVs hanging beside the cross. Praise bands, drum sets. A good family activity, right? Are you aware that the divorce rate among evangelicals exceeds that of the general population? By the way, did I congratulate you on your Christian marriage?

Did you take Knox's psychology of religion course? You would remember: we had to read long sections of that famous book by William James that we all dreaded. There was a unit on conversion. The point was that it takes many different forms than just the trademark one-eighty, sinner-to-saint type. You know: drug dealer becomes social worker. Or like Paul, per-secuting Christians one day and recruiting them the next. For instance, there was one version Knox called "deepening": you hold the same beliefs as before your "conversion," but after whatever experience you've had you feel them more intensely and are more committed to them. A similar one would be something like "clarification," when you realize you had beliefs you weren't aware of. I think that's where my experience falls. Not that I became an atheist but that I realized I had been an atheist all along. Conversely, you couldn't say I lost my faith; I never believed what I assumed I did, or what I allowed others on my behalf to assume I believed. Rather ironic that I should have that epiphany while sitting in a pew in church. It didn't fill me with joy. I didn't feel the urge to testify. I didn't burst into song: "I once was saved but now am lost." It gave me no pleasure to be the only non-believer there. Except I don't think I was. There was the guy with the camcorder. I almost pitied him; I could be more-infidel-than-thou. I doubt it occurred to him that he didn't believe in anything going on around him. I at least was willing to try to see what everyone else did. I just couldn't. I sometimes feel I'm like some kind of specialty receiver that can only pick up certain frequencies. If God is sending some signal through the church, I am not picking it up. I lack that wavelength. I've spun the dial looking for it; all I get is static. Would God design me that way? That theory doesn't compute.

What would that cloudburst mean to any child? Will they remember being baptized? I don't. What could it mean to my child? He doesn't seem to notice; he only seems anxious to get back to his own thoughts. What sense is my mother making of it all, who probably realizes she is in a church but not why. When I said I didn't have to worry about my parents' judgment, I meant both by and on them. My father's gone, and my mother has lost judgment in every possible form. But, by the same token, who could judge her in her current state? How could she be held accountable any more than that dripping-wet baby? Compute that for me. This pastor likes to hold a child up after he baptizes him and carry him around the sanctuary. "This is your child," he says, "the newest member of God's family. You have pledged today to love and nurture him." And he'll repeat those words, or variations, as he walks up one aisle and down another, even into the amen section. That's also a good way to render a father helpless, seeing your child held aloft. You just hope the pastor has good hands. Your son is out of yours. Up front, after the service, the people thronged us, jockeying for position to poke and coo at the baby, who pretty clearly wanted to be left alone. Eyes shut, he glowered, insofar as an infant can. "He's tired," people said.

We didn't take Ross downstairs to fellowship hour. People understood. Meg took him home, and my sister and her family took Mom back to her residence. She gets anxious at the prospect of missing a meal there; that's one thing she remembers. I stayed behind with the other two children to receive congratulations. When the crowd had thinned, the pastor asked me to come up to his office so he could give me some "paperwork"—a diploma and a bag of gifts.

"Among the many emotions I feel after a baptism is gratitude," he said. "You have enlarged our numbers. Never underestimate the value to faith of reinforcements."

I like him. He can be vulnerable in that way.

"Your family has grown, and so has ours. We mean it when we say that we will be here for you if you need us. Literally: right here. It's hard for me to say that children are not always a blessing, especially right after I've blessed one. But some pain and disappointment along the way are virtually guaranteed. At the end of a confirmation class, I would never say to any one of the confirmands that he or she will fail to feel fulfilled in the church or fail to follow Jesus. But, if I were honest, I would say pretty confidently that not *all* of the students will remain students; that's what 'disciple' means. My own children aren't exactly all in the bosom of the church."

He's so youthful that I forget he has grown children.

"There's an old joke about that," he said. "So old I'd be embarrassed to tell you. The only thing less funny than a preacher's joke is an old preacher's joke."

I offered to tell one. I hear a lot in the locker room. There's a good one about a penguin who wanted to join a nudist colony.

He's also a regular guy. He did a very creditable double-take. "Maybe I'd better tell you mine after all," he said.

"Go ahead," I said. "Hit me."

"A church was plagued by bats in its belfry. No one could figure out how to get rid of them. Exterminators had no luck. The pastor was at a loss until one Sunday one of his predecessors in the pulpit, a really ancient-looking guy, came back to worship with him. When the young pastor confided his problem, the old man said, 'It's simple enough. Sneak up on them all some night and baptize them. You'll never see them again.' But that won't work with you. You've kept bringing your kids back. It's true we always remind the congregation of their role. But how much can they really do? I think the hymn-writer got it right, though I take his words slightly out of context. I count on the faith of our fathers. In my experience, that makes all the difference."

And I came home and wrote this letter. Well, not at one sitting—don't flatter yourself. You can thank the "save" function. I'm a little compulsive with it; losing an e-mail—that's the worst. Call me OCD if you want and sign me up in a support group.

The two A's. Alzheimer's and autism. Where the hell did they come from? There were no such things when we were growing up. Five years ago someone comes up with a couple of good names and, voilà, two new conditions to research. Is it a coincidence they start with the same letter?

You probably won't get another letter, at least like this, until we have our next kid. I hesitate to scroll back through it. I don't have to; this computer even counts my words for me. In that spirit I should maybe upgrade my analogy. I'm not a radio missing a wavelength but a computer without a "save" function. Good thing I have friends.

* * *

"What did you get up to?" David said.

"I just had a ten-minute conversation with Denny Vilsack," Michael said.

"Wasn't he a wrestler?" Brian said.

"I can report that he is now a home inspector," Michael said. "And that this summer he and his family vacationed in Canada for the first time. They liked it. Everyone up there drives with their lights on all the time. Now you are up to date."

"Denny Vilsack," David said. "I haven't heard that name in about thirty years. I guess in exactly thirty years."

"That's the way is with reunions," Michael said. "You spend more time talking to people you barely know than you do to with your closest friends."

"We can catch up later," Brian said. "Like at the brunch tomorrow?"

"I won't be there," David said. "I have an early morning flight to New York. I tied the reunion in to a business trip. That way I got it paid for. If you guys claim you were consulting you can write off your registration fees."

"Watch out," Michael said.

He had spotted a woman making a beeline for them. She wore a bright red sheath dress and a blonde bouffant. The effect was confectionary. On closer inspection, she was listing slightly to her left. On still closer inspection, she was making for Brian. She pulled up in front of him. "Do you remember me? No peeking." She clapped her hand over her nametag, incidentally drawing attention to and deepening her creamy cleavage. Whoever she was, her breasts could not have been that ample in high school. She pulled her hand away and pouted. "You don't remember."

"Darlene Dunkle," Brian said. "Of course."

Unnoticed and unlamented by Darlene, David and Michael peeled away from that rendezvous.

"That's one way to get through a series of highly charged emotional encounters," David said. "Plowed. I'm going to get another drink myself."

"I think I see Ed Sheerer over there," Michael said.

It was like that all night. The three of them would reconnoiter after individual forays into the crowd. Their thirtieth high school reunion was taking place at a country club overlooking the Allegheny River, just far enough outside their school district to seem foreign soil. The people around them seemed alien as well. Before they started to identify some of their classmates, they couldn't be sure that they and the middle-aged people mounting the stone stairs to the entrance with them were there for the same purpose. They paused on the mezzanine and looked out over the main floor. Some of their male counterparts had graduated from the husky to the portly. "Is this a high school reunion or a biermeisters' convention?" Michael said. At one end of the bar, a few burly men were jostling for drinks like hippos at a watering hole. The women had held up better.

"Is that Becky Zimmerman?" David said. "Holy cow. From wallflower to belle of the ball. I should have ordered a put on her in twelfth grade."

They walked around a little before they plunged into the crush of classmates. A bunch of smaller rooms radiated out from the ballroom, each one more plushly upholstered than the last. Most were empty, the armchairs and divans open-armed and snubbed. In one though a group of octogenarians in evening dress dined; they seemed as at ease as though they were sitting around the kitchen table. An underscent of food was everywhere, though they got a whiff of blended chlorine and liniment as they passed the hallway to the locker room and pool.

"I think I swam here once as a kid," Michael said. "A meet. One of our mothers would have driven us. I wouldn't have had any idea where I was."

They got drinks and separated. They had reunited again when they saw that Darlene had released Brian.

"Get used to it, pal," David said. "Have you forgotten that in high school you were adulated, revered?"

"He doesn't remember," Michael said. "I'm not sure he noticed at the time. Girls swarmed him. He had to be let out of classes early so he could get to his next one while the halls were empty to avoid riots."

"Under escort," David said.

"I'll settle for the compliment I just got from Darlene," Brian said. "It's the highest compliment you can receive at a reunion: I'm recognizable. Is that because I haven't put on that much weight or because I still gaze into the future with my hair blown by unseen winds?"

Brian held up his name tag, which framed his black-and-white senior yearbook portrait. In fact his hair wasn't blowing anywhere. The regulation bang plastered across his forehead, he looked off to his left with faint foreboding.

"They wanted me to turn my back to the camera and look over my shoulder," Michael said. "I don't think so. Who am I, Errol Flynn?"

"There's our class president," David said. "Your tax dollars at work."

The ever more statesmanlike Floyd Remy was breasting the swelling tide of classmates on the ballroom floor. Now a lawyer with an office downtown, Floyd was ex officio chair of the reunion committee. It was his club.

"Still working the crowd," Michael said. "What's he running for now?"

With dinner not far off, they scattered once more, but this time with purpose, and when they got together again they were briefly sobered. Brian and David had spoken to their former girlfriends.

Floyd strode by at just that moment. The invitations had stipulated informal dress, barring shorts, jeans, or army surplus. But Floyd had set his usual high standard, right down to the tie pin.

"Stand still for a second, F. R. F.," Michael said. "Where is it tonight?"

"What?" Floyd said, reined in.

"Check his cuffs, Brian," Michael said.

The three friends stood around Floyd as though fitting him for his sport coat.

"Got it," Michael said. "Right on his breast pocket. Disappointingly obvious, I'd have to say. Still, I'm just as glad we didn't have to pull his shirt out of his pants to check for it."

No shirt of Floyd's went un-monogrammed. The emblem might appear on the cuff, the collar, the shirttail, but it was always configured FRF, the middle letter, his last initial, enlarged.

Floyd shrugged his jacket back into place but kept fidgeting.

"What's the matter?" David said. "We don't like to see you flustered. We look to you for leadership."

"I'm trying to find someone to say a grace. I'm going to gather and greet everyone, but that's it."

"You do it," Michael said. "Who more qualified?"

"I'm a singer, not a prayer," Floyd said. "I'll sing in the choir, I'll make announcements from the lectern, but I stay out of the pulpit."

"Didn't the committee think of that?" David said.

Floyd winced. "What a menagerie that was. It was democratic, I'll say that. All social strata represented. I didn't know if the menu was going to end up being chicken cordon bleu or ham barbeque. The hunkies had to have their DJ. Most of our effort went into trying to track people down. It turns out that some people don't get all choked up at the thought of a reunion. Some people want to put as much distance as possible between themselves and high school. I felt like the FBI."

"Who was your most wanted?" Brian said.

"That would be Denise Rigatti," Floyd said. "Last seen in Denver, headed west."

"Do you mean to say that our class didn't produce a minister?" Michael said. "What a surprise."

"Do you need a grace?" Brian said. "I mean, it's a party."

"It's a meal," Floyd said.

"Then what kind of grace?" Brian said. "You figure. By now there must be all kinds of beliefs out there. Not just the three or four basic flavors in the sixties. And don't forget the spouses come from all over."

"Right, it would have to be ecumenical," Floyd said.

"Interfaith," Brian said.

"You need something," David said.

"Maybe just to remember deceased classmates," Michael said.

"Are there some?" David said.

"You don't want to know," Floyd said. "More than you'd think. That's the downside of googling someone on the roster of the non-responders. The sleuthing is kind of fun until you find the obituary."

"There could be a moment of silence," Brian said. "Or meditation."

"Good luck with that," Floyd said with a glance at the bar, where drinks were being passed back into the crowd like buckets in a fire brigade. "You don't want to spoil the mood. I'm thinking a simple blessing. Maybe mention the departed. Collectively, not individually."

"Is Norman Hess here?" Michael said. "Didn't he meet some kind of Bible group after school?"

"We want a grace, not a sermon," Floyd said.

"'Please bow your heads for a moment of silent reflection,'" Michael said. "I still remember my line. I should. I recited it every day of eighth grade right before I read the announcements."

"I still can't believe anyone would put you at the console of a PA system," David said. "'The following students won medals in yesterday's track meet: Jim Kee, John Ludwig, Bud Weiser, John Logan.' Bud Weiser? You didn't get busted for that?"

"The principal was amused," Michael said. "I knew how far I could go."

"'A moment of silent reflection,'" Floyd said. "I forgot that phrase. It doesn't sound too hypocritical, does it? When did they stop saying the Lord's Prayer? When we were in sixth grade?"

"And the next day students started dealing drugs in the halls, right?" Brian said.

"At least we kept saying the Pledge of Allegiance," David said.

"That's better?" Michael said. "That's not still a prayer?"

"I'll keep looking," Floyd said. "See what else has come off the rails." He glanced at his watch and waded back into the crush of his constituents.

"Hubba, hubba," Brian said.

Floyd's place in their circle had been taken by a curvy brunette. Her figure was fuller in perfect proportion to its high school incarnation. "'Hubba, hubba?'" Sue Oliver said. "Is this the reunion of the class of '69 or '39? Are you going to ask me to do the jitterbug later on?"

"Hey, babe," Brian said. "Whatever they're playing, we're dancing to it." Sue collapsed into him and kissed him on the cheek.

"And I'm cutting in as soon as I decently can," David said.

"You're sweet," she said. "You always were. Here's a kiss for you, too, Michael."

"I saw you sneak a look at my nametag," Michael said.

She held out puckered lips for him to pluck with his as though from a tree. "I'd know you anywhere."

"That's already more than I got off her in four years of high school," Michael said.

"And the night is young," Brian said.

"Stop it," she said, a hand on Brian's chest. "My jealous husband is over there." They located him standing against a wall with a couple of equally taciturn companions. You could always tell the husbands of classmates; they were the ones you could mistake for bouncers. "I see you boys omitted to bring your wives." She jabbed a finger at Michael. "Do your impersonation of Mr. Lockhart. I loved that."

Jutting his jaw, Michael launched into a civics lecture.

"Stop!" Sue's shriek dropped to a whisper. "I'm going to pee my pants." And she excused herself.

David straightened, suddenly alert. "Hey, Brian."

"What?" Brian said.

"Hey, Michael."

"What?" Michael said, exchanging glances with Brian.

"If you would, cast your minds back to the late sixties and a Friday night dance at our church," David said. "Is the scene materializing in front of you? Two shadowy figures in a dim sanctuary? One of them in our present company and one of them just now departed?"

"In fairness, I can neither confirm nor deny that suggestion," Brian said.

"And what were we interrupting?" David said.

"Nothing much," Brian said. "Come on. It was a church. It was our church."

A ripple in the crowd reached them. Guests turned in all directions to announce dinner. The three friends joined some other unattached class-mates at a table. Floyd stood at the podium as the diners settled.

"Could I have everyone's attention for about the next thirty seconds?" he said. "I know that's asking a lot of this group, but I'm gambling that your attention span has doubled since high school. We'll have a little presenta-tion after dinner, with a few special guests. But now. I'm sure you can tell from the seamless flow of the evening so far that your reunion committee has functioned like a well-oiled machine. No detail has been overlooked. Except one. Not for lack of well-qualified candidates, we neglected to desig-nate someone to offer a blessing for dinner. And, unless this class has been repenting non-stop for the past thirty years, it needs one. So. Any volun-teers?" If Floyd wanted a moment of silence, he got one. A pall fell over the ballroom. Then he said, "I hear the scrape of a chair. Come up front."

"Thanks," someone at their table said.

"All right," Brian said, as David stood up.

"I've heard enough of these at church that I ought to be able to pull one off."

"Just a tip, David," Michael said. "You say 'amen' at the end."

* * *

As people were settling into their pews after the hymn, Brian looked at his bulletin and turned to David. "Do funeral services have sermons?"

"Oh, yeah," David said. "They're standard. He pointed to the bulletin. "'Winter Wheat.'"

"It says 'homily,'" Brian said.

"That's a euphemism," David said. "It's a sermon. Calling it a homily gives you hope it will be shorter. Don't count on it."

The pastor stepped up into the pulpit. He seemed in no hurry to preach. With the same half-smile, he arranged some papers in front of him and paged through the Bible before he spoke. "Our text today is Matthew 13.24-30. Listen for God's word.

He put before them another parable: "The kingdom of heaven may be compared to someone who sowed good seed in his field; but while everybody was asleep, an enemy came and sowed weeds among the wheat, and then went away. So when the plants came up and bore grain, then the weeds appeared as well. And the slaves of the householder came and said to him, 'Master, did you not sow good seed in your field? Where, then, did these weeds come from?' He answered, 'An enemy has done this.' The slaves said to him, 'Then do you want us to go and gather them?' But he replied, 'No; for in gathering the weeds you would uproot the wheat along with them. Let both of them grow together until the harvest; and at harvest time I will tell the reapers, Collect the weeds first and bind them in bundles to be burned, but gather the wheat into my barn.'

"The word of the Lord."

"Thanks be to God," David said.

"I am going to think of this service as a homecoming. Those verses from the first gospel may seem a trifle ominous for the occasion. I will try to justify my choice.

"Many of you know that for most of his adult life Michael was a member of another Presbyterian church, Fourth. That is one of our venerable churches, attended back in the day by the bankers and captains of industry of Presbyterian Pittsburgh. Its bricks still wear the soot of their plants and mills. With time, they left the city limits for newer churches, like ours. Michael made the opposite journey, an exodus in reverse. He left the promised land of the suburbs, where his parents brought him under cover of the night of the Depression and World War II, to rejoin the remnant in the inner city. That church houses some cooperative ministries, at least one of them interfaith. Rooms that held Sunday school classes and women's circles are now offices or food pantries. Our fathers' house has many mansions, even as they left their mansions to be turned into apartment buildings and bought estates in the countryside. Michael was devoted to all those efforts. Of course, he was devoted to his wife as well; she belonged there when they met. When she died a few years ago, tragically young, Michael moved into a nearby retirement community and returned to the church where he was baptized nearly seventy years ago. You might have thought that, returned from exile, led into green pastures, Michael would retire from the vineyard. No. He threw himself into missions here as well.

"Some few of you remember him from his first membership here. From you I learned what I did not know all the years I pastored him, both here and at Fourth, where as you know I served briefly as associate pastor.

He had a nickname. Wheaty. What a great, great nickname. I don't think I've ever heard it before. Maybe it's common in Iowa, I don't know. As his pastor and his junior, I probably wouldn't have been on 'Wheaty' terms with him anyway. But we know that God sets great store by names. So great that he names us in the womb, as Jeremiah tells us. Any good Hebrew name will incorporate God's name, whether at the beginning or the end: Samuel, name of God; Nathaniel, God gives; Jesus, God saves. Michael: who is like God? Suddenly our friend's given name sounds like a burden, doesn't it? I can't imagine anyone like God. Neither could Michael. You might remember one of his bedrock convictions: 'God is God; I'm not.' I can hear him say that now. At critical times, when God chooses someone for a task, he may assign a new name—Abraham, Israel. What about nicknames? When Michael became Wheaty, did God set him on a new course?

"Now, about that text.

"'Pastor Tom. As we gather to celebrate Michael's life, do we really want to dwell on incineration? We crave good news. We want to hear the gospel of salvation. Do we seriously have to worry about Michael's fate? Do we think there is the ghost of a chance he will end up in the fire and not in the barn?'

"I hear you. I suppose more to the point, did Michael have any doubt? Some of you may have seen the recent documentary about our beloved Mr. Rogers, a Pittsburgher and a Presbyterian to the core. If so, you were probably as surprised as I was to learn that, as he approached death, he asked his wife if she thought he was a sheep. Or would he be sent packing with the goats? Mr. Rogers, about as close to a saint as we Protestants are likely to produce, asked that? Was Michael a sheaf of wheat or a weed? Wheat or weed? Would Jesus—the man, not the judge on his throne of glory—have been able to tell him?

"One of the many things I love about this parable is that it sort of illustrates itself: it's almost hiding in the weeds, choked out by the other parables. You could almost miss it. This chapter is chock-a-block with parables, all of which try to describe the kingdom of God. Matthew probably gathered them all in one place—culled them, harvested them, if you like—for our convenience. But the effect is that it seems like Jesus can't quite get it right and keeps trying, one comparison after the other. 'Maybe if you think of it this way . . .' The analogies repeat each other, they overlap, and sometimes I think they conflict. It's hard to keep this story straight from the one right before, the sower and the seed. Jesus explains this one, too, but not right away, only after he throws another one into the mix, the parable of the mustard seed. To me there is a note of comedy in the chapter. After all the attempts to explain the kingdom, Jesus asks the disciples if they understand now, and they say, 'Yes.' Right. Jesus already as much as told them the point is not to understand.

"Maybe what we need is an extension—some more time to figure it all out. And that seems to me the blessing the wheat offers, especially if you feel you might be among the weeds. It buys us some time. 'Should we pull up the weeds?' the servants ask their master. 'No—you'll pull the wheat up along with them.' That means we'll all make it to the harvest, a word that connotes fertility and hope to me, as do other words in the story, like 'fruit.' (That's in the Greek.) What could happen between now and the harvest? Maybe the master will sow more good seed. Maybe some weeds will fertilize the wheat. You can see I'm no agronomist. But I have always loved the phrase 'winter wheat.' They grow that somewhere. It gives me hope of life in death. I know it says the weeds will be pulled up first and burned, I know. But maybe instead of the weeds pulling up the wheat, the wheat will pull up the weeds along with it, gathering the weeds in its arms.

"Joanne Rogers told her husband that, if ever there was a sheep, he was one. If ever there was a sheaf of wheat planted smack in the middle of the ills of the world and the schemes of the evil one, it was Michael. I saw him radiate love in this life, inside and outside our church, and I can see him dragging some weeds kicking and screaming into the barn with him. In our father's house are many mansions. In our father's granary are many silos. I may have mentioned that I'm not an agronomist. But I think that works. How can a mansion fit in a house? Or, I think, a silo in a barn? It sounds to me as though they are full to bursting and have room for more. And that Michael will welcome us. I set great store by his nickname.

"Amen."

Brian and David all but tiptoed down the stairs to the reception. Their trepidation had two sources. It was hard not to imagine the standard fare of church dinners of their youth, ham loaf and pineapple juice, awaiting them. And they assumed that, apart from one or two familiar faces, they would spend their time in small talk with total strangers. They couldn't move quickly anyway through the bottleneck of the staircase but inched along with their fellow mourners. By the time they reached the bottom, the solemnity of the service was beginning to thaw into conversation, and they found a lavish and festive potluck lunch spread before them in the low-ceilinged dining room. On the one hand, the high school reunion they anticipated did not materialize; only a few of their classmates were present. It had been a half-century. On the other hand, they turned out to know many people they hadn't recognized in the pews. Once they were identified as Michael's childhood friends, they were besieged. A number of people their age they felt they must or would have known, but didn't, were members of Michael's other church. Brian and David obliged with many anecdotes of Michael's youth, some of them set in their present location.

By the time they got their food and ate, a good hour had passed, and the crowd had thinned. Eventually they were left pretty much to themselves, as people began to clear the tables. "Did we let you boys eat anything?" a grandmotherly woman maybe ten years their elder said. "Act fast if you want seconds; folks are claiming their dishes." They assured her they had had enough and surrendered their plates. They sat for a minute. "Shall we?" Brian said, and they got to their feet. The people they passed nodded at them as though they were long-time members, and even in the kitchen, even as they headed past the sinks and freezer, they didn't attract attention. Men in late middle age probably did not need to be as surreptitious as their teenage avatars.

In a couple of minutes they were in the hallway they had followed the night of the dance past the church office on their extra-Sabbath visit to the sanctuary. The walls were still lined with Sunday school pictures, but now they stretched all the way down the hall and started back up the other side. Through the window of the kindergarten classroom door the furniture still looked miniature, but plastic and in bright primary colors rather than wooden.

"There we are," David said. "We still have our place in history."

"Yes," Brian said. "In the black-and-white era."

A decade or so later, the group portraits were in watery color. The most recent ones were downright glossy.

"They look like ads in a magazine," David said.

They turned in unison to see a figure approaching them from the other end of the hallway. Blurry at first, it stepped out of the window-lined lobby as though from a pool of light.

"I was on my way to the office and heard voices."

"We know a back way," Brian said.

The pastor laughed. "You probably know the layout of the church better than I do. Kids find every nook and cranny."

"Our former selves are immortalized in a Sunday school picture," David said. "Way down at the end. We're baby boomers."

"I've heard of them," the pastor said.

"We're the genuine article," Brian said. "In living black and white."

"And you are legion," the pastor said. "I have paced this hallway many times. Often with envy in my heart. That's one of the seven deadlies, don't forget. I can't get over those pictures from the fifties. Filled to the brim with kids. You needed risers. And today . . . " He gestured toward the most recent pictures, where a half-dozen children frolicked on the lawn. "Some of those are combined classes. Where are the children? Well, where are the parents? 'The sea of Faith was once, too, full.' That's a line of a poem I can't get out of my head. I usually misquote it as, 'The sea of Faith has ebbed.' Just among us, I consider that an improvement. As it withdraws it leaves naked shingles—something like that—like empty pews. Meanwhile, the tides of other faiths are rising. People explore other religions, sign up for self-help classes. A chapter of AA meets here Tuesday nights. I sometimes wish we had their clarity of purpose. They have something. So is the literal sea rising; that rouses some people into action. What is God's plan? Is God working through other faiths? What about Weight Watchers? Dyanetics? What is motivating their followers?

"Where are the children? Jeremiah shows us Rachel weeping for her children. 'She refuses to be comforted for her children, because they are no more.' We feel her pain. Jesus raised a child at the last minute, on the brink of the grave, at the cemetery in Nain. I ask you, Is or is not today's society a graveyard for today's youth? Do we send them out with no spiritual guidance to weave their way through the open graves of sex and drugs and maybe not rock-n-roll but gangsta rap? Be your own, authentic persons. Save yourselves. And that same prophet insists that God is watching out for us: 'For surely I know the plans I have for you, says the Lord, plans for your welfare and not for harm, to give you a future with hope.' That's God talking. Maybe Jesus is waiting for the last minute to raise our youth.

"That's your bonus homily. You're welcome."

They laughed.

"While we're at it, thank you for the regularly scheduled sermon," Brian said. "You captured Michael's character. He was 'life-enhancing,' as we used to put it so warmly in college. We should probably clarify the nickname for you, however. It dated from his infancy, and no one was quite sure what it signified, if anything. It doesn't seem to have anything to do with grain, however."

"I had a feeling I was claiming what we in the business call homiletic license," the pastor said.

"We all had nicknames," David said. "We dropped them sort of by consensus once we got out of school."

"Were yours more Biblical?"

They both laughed. "That's debatable," Brian said. "In the fifties John Wayne was right up there with the patriarchs. I went by Hondo. That's a character John Wayne played in a movie. Duke"—he gestured at David—"was John Wayne's own nickname. That may be before your time."

"Wasn't John Wayne there in the beginning?" the pastor said.

Brian looked down the hallway. "Michael and Marie might have brought their children to this church. But they didn't have any."

"I've wondered about that." The pastor seemed visibly to relax, almost off duty. He was obviously younger than them, but not by enough to be their son. He was between generations somehow. "I wasn't their pastor, here or at Fourth, until later in their lives. They were already elders of the church of long standing, movers and shakers, respected, the kind of folks that you as a pastor want on your side. Not that they would ever have leaned on me in any way. I don't think their careers got in the way of having a family. They were both professional caregivers, a nurse and a teacher, but they would have had plenty of empathy left over for their own kids. And Michael was good with kids. He was great at children's time. It's so hard to strike the right tone: not to be too serious, but not to play it for laughs."

He was leaning against a wall. It was a nice moment, as though they were killing time, hanging out on a street corner after school. That would put them back in their parents' past, before their parents moved them out to the suburbs, where there were no blocks or corners.

"And what about you two alumni? Are you still in the church?"

"Yes and no," David said.

The pastor smiled and waited. "I give up. Who's yes and who's no?"

"That was just me," David said.

"I'm a no," Brian said. "I came to realize that worship services didn't seem very worshipful to me. Children's time is an example. Not that I don't think children have a spiritual life. I admire Mr. Rogers, too, though he was actually after our time. I have two children, from my first marriage. Church services sometimes feel to me like club meetings. I feel much more in touch with the divine, the transcendent, when I meditate. I have been a practicing Buddhist for a long time. In fact I think I practiced before I was a Buddhist. Though I don't necessarily identify myself that way. I think labels diminish people. For me, unity is the goal."

"I know many Christians who would agree with you," the pastor said. "Look at all the flavors we come in. Jesus could be cryptic, but he made it crystal clear that he wanted all his followers to be as one. What about you, Duke? Am I right to pick up a certain ambivalence? Although it could be scripturally endorsed. Jesus said your word should be yes or no. Yours is both."

"He was a big no in college," Brian said. "He was our house atheist."

David threw up his hands. "I would say I have upgraded to agnostic. I go to church just so my kids will go. Call me hypocritical."

The pastor came to attention. "I'm not going to call you hypocritical. I can't afford to cast that particular stone. You take your children to church out of faithfulness."

"I don't have much faith to spare or share, I'm afraid," David said.

"I didn't say faith," the pastor said. "I said faithfulness."

A silence fell. The pastor extended his hand. "Thanks for coming," he said.

"Thank you," they said.

"We're open for business again tomorrow at 11:00 AM."

"Thanks for the invitation, but we'll be heading to our respective homes," David said.

"Safe travels," the pastor said.

"We have one more stop to make on our tour of the church, though," Brian said.

"I'd say make yourselves at home," the pastor said. "If you weren't home already."

He turned with a wave back toward the office, and they walked back down the hall the way they had come.

"Should we go through the kitchen?" Brian said.

"No, let's be legal," David said. "Through the front door." He held up the back of his hand. "I think I can still make out the stamp."

With a descent and a couple of turns they were in the vestibule.

"What are you hearing?" David said. "Dribbling?"

"I hear a bass. Vox amp, would be my guess."

They pushed open the double doors and stood on the threshold as though on the shore of a lake.

"That's far enough," David said, looking down at their feet.

"I almost forgot," Brian said. "No street shoes."

The lights were off, though the daylight was bright enough that you weren't sure at first. They took one last look at the empty stage and the silent, sterile hardwood floor.

SIMPLE GIFTS

"Not your Martin, Bill."

Mike was either protesting or conceding. With him it was hard to tell which. Punctuating a good many of his sentences would call for something between a period and a question mark.

"It's not a great Martin," Bill said. "It's not vintage or anything. It's not even my best guitar."

"Well, all right." Mike relaxed after having recoiled in mock outrage at the donation Bill was proposing. His reservation on record, he seemed to recognize a fait accompli. He was even amused, as though at a scam Bill could trust him to keep a secret. "But, come on. A Martin is a Martin."

"Sort of," Bill said. "This is one of the few Martins made outside America. They pride themselves on their home-grown product. You know. Made in the USA."

Over the years Mike's features had grown expressive almost to the point of pantomime. You never missed one of his jokes, since he was subsiding in laughter himself as he delivered the punch line, his face creased with mirth. He braced his feet to grin. Bill couldn't pinpoint when Mike had assumed his adult personality. Well, he could, roughly. Mike belonged to that class of people who adopt the ethos of the college they go off to, and furthermore to those alumni who even after they come back home are devoted to the state university of a neighboring state. He had joined a fraternity—or, rather, club, as they were called at that particular school—and had returned with a visibly raised consciousness and broader horizons. He also wore boating shoes back to the landlocked suburb where he and Bill had known each other since grade school and before. Now, more acquaintances than friends, they were elders in the church they had been baptized into within a few months of each other. At the moment, head cocked and eyes narrowed, Mike looked intensely interested in, almost alarmed at, the manufacture of musical instruments.

"The one I'm taking was made in Mexico," Bill was saying. "Not even of wood. It's a composite material."

And now they were in their early fifties, if you began the mid-fifties at fifty-five, as they had decided was strictly accurate. *I'm in my late forties. How late? Quite late: fifty-two.* They had acknowledged that that line would have to be retired for a decade or so when they hit fifty-four, which called for the current euphemism. Pressed again against the back of his chair, Mike gave the impression that the information Bill was sharing with him might revolutionize not just his view of stringed instruments but his subsequent life. They sat in the Calvin Room of Knox Presbyterian Church waiting for a meeting of the mission committee. They were early, having come straight from their respective offices, and resigned, given the membership of the group, to staying late. Even though Mike commiserated with Bill about the dilations of their fellow-members, he contributed to them. At the meeting, Bill could visualize it in advance, Mike would declare some issue simple and settled and then raise a consideration that would extend discussion by half an hour. He loved to revive ideas that had just been discarded by consensus. "What if we did do what Curt suggested?" Then, as they concluded their agenda with a vote over whether or not to fund the purchase of a water heater for a homeless shelter, one of several retirees at the table would ask what they could do as a body to solve the crisis in the Middle East.

Though Mike had settled in his chair, his demeanor was circumspect, implying unexplored depths in the present topic. He spoke. "Your gift isn't more valuable because it's expensive, Bill. You know that? They won't have any idea. They'll just be grateful for a source of music. Or maybe I should say source of noise. Are you sure anyone over there knows how to play a guitar?"

You couldn't be too annoyed at Mike when he so wholly identified with your concerns. He took them more seriously than you did. What was annoying was that underneath all his elaborations and reversals of scenarios he always had a point.

* * *

"Bwana asifiwe!"

Bill was going to have to ask someone what that phrase meant. He was only hearing it for the six-hundredth time since his arrival in Kenya the day before. It was probably safe to repeat.

From the moment they touched down in Nairobi, he was struck by the perpetual motion of the people. The airport was more like a market day or a fair as they milled with other passengers around the lobby, immigration control and then the baggage carousels. They weren't the only whites, but there was something different about many of the others. Some wore African garb or sleeveless bush jackets, like carnival costumes, and in line they pulled out green or red passports. Some could have passed for fellow Americans until they spoke a European language among themselves.

It was 11:00 PM when they arrived, but a team from their host church was waiting for them outside in the crowd on the sidewalk. After their groups identified each other, and after some nodding and shaking of hands, the Kenyans grabbed the visitors' suitcases out of their grasp as though confiscating them and hauled them off toward the parking lot. Some pulled out the handles so they could wheel them; others just hoisted the bags onto their shoulders. They piled into minivans and tunneled three hours into the African night. At around 3:00 AM they swung through a gate, and their headlights raked a low stone building. It was the church's fellowship hall. Inside, the session awaited them with tea and fruit and cakes. "Karibuni," they said. "Bwana asifiwe." They had also prepared formal greetings and speeches, one after the other. Also prayers. Throughout, the women bustled to bring their guests tea. This seemed the most urgent item of business. The visitors were invited to speak also.

Bill turned to Mike. "Where are we, in the Calvin Room?"

"Next time, let's remember not to travel on a Saturday," Mike said, setting his watch. "Church in four hours."

* * *

"Send a check," Mike said. "They know what they need."

"You started without me." Rev. Kerr walked into the room through the far door, the one closer to the front of the church and his office. He had a lot of carpet to cover before he reached them. "Who needs the pastor anyway? You guys are taking this priesthood of all believers stuff to heart."

"Mike here is making it very difficult for me to practice Christian charity," Bill said.

"Bill," Mike said. "Your Martin?"

Rev. Kerr looked back and forth between them agreeably and quizzically as he took a seat at the massive oval wooden table.

Mike re-crossed his legs. It was clear he considered the conversation to have been re-booted with the arrival of a new party. "On the next trip Bill wants to take his Martin guitar to give to a church. That's the Cadillac of guitars."

"You're assuming our pastor has heard of Cadillacs," Bill said.

"Good point," Rev. Kerr said. "And is my salary on the agenda tonight?"

* * *

Bill didn't like to stereotype or profile or anything, but he was coming to the conclusion that speech therapists were maybe a little on the literal-minded side. He was sitting in an office in a rehab center with two of them and his father, who was recovering from a mild stroke.

"Is it A, B or C?"

His father turned to them with a knowing smile.

"Peter. Is it A, the man is chased by the bus; B, the bus is chased by the man; or C, the bus is dogged by the chase? Which caption goes with the picture?"

The therapists sat patiently with his father, one at his elbow, the other behind him at her desk. Bill thought their smiles were crusting slightly.

Finally his father said, "It would depend if you had a bent for personification. That bus could be pretty tired of being run down by latecomers. This one is probably not the first of the day. The bus could feel dogged."

"Would that be C?"

His father shrugged.

"But C doesn't really make sense, does it?"

"You could say B," his father said. "Though that could sound pedestrian." He pointed to the stick figure man in the picture. "Pedestrian."

"Good," the therapist said. "See?" She held the picture up again. "The bus is being chased by the man."

"And if you weren't particularly bothered by the passive voice."

"Dad missed his calling as an English teacher," Bill said.

"Did you?" the therapist by his father said. The other one had started some paperwork at her desk. "Now I want you to practice making some new sounds."

They were also maybe a tad humorless as a species.

"We're working on making *k* sounds today. Repeat after me. *Smoke.*"

"*Smoke.*"

"That's it. We want you to feel that *k* sound in the back of your mouth. Now, *stack.*"

"Stack."

"And *croak*. That's two *k* sounds for you. Two for the price of one. Today only."

"Cloak."

"*Croak.*"

"Cloak."

"Listen. *Croak.*"

"Croak."

"That's that funny sound," Bill said. "I've read that some languages don't distinguish between *l* and *r*. They just don't hear the difference. All those Chinese jokes. It's not just them, I found out. In Kenya you can tell that someone belongs to the Kikuyu tribe in the same way."

"Good job, Mr. Owens," the therapist said.

* * *

Sometimes, when the two friendship committees convened in a vestry or a fellowship hall for one of their many formal meetings, Bill just sat and listened to the speeches of the Kenyan church officials as though it were music. In their clerical collars, seated along one side of a long table, they looked a little like an octet anyway. It didn't matter which language they were speaking. With most of the Kenyans he met, it could be one of at least three: English or Kiswahili, their two national languages, or Kikuyu, their tribal language. They might know a couple other tribal languages as well. One of the younger pastors told Bill about his interview for admission into an American seminary. "They wanted to know how much remediation I would need," he explained. "So they asked me if English was my second language. 'No,' I answered them. 'It is my fourth language.'"

And, whether or not he followed the conversation, Bill maintained his air of aloof interest, which also acknowledged that he was out of his element. For an instant at one meeting he recognized on his face the expression he had seen husbands wear while accompanying their wives in a department store, a show of open-mindedness before a shelf of goods. He would back up in front of his wife, sort of clearing a path for her. He might have stumbled onto the section it was by luck. He would let her operate. He would let her find the items in question. They might even buy something. His hosts mixed up their *l*'s and *r*'s all the time in English and presumably in the other languages also. They had another quirk: they rolled their rs. Every time their lead host, Rev. Nimrod, introduced the Americans, he said, "We have William Owens. We have Michael McGrew, which he pronounced *MacGrrrew*. Bill remarked on the burr to him on a visit to a hospital one day.

"Yes," Rev. Nimrod said. "This area was missionized by the Church of Scotland. We learned English from them. Come, I will show you the original mission."

They walked down a path to a low building. A plaque stood out front.

"Tumutumu," Bill said. "Doesn't sound terribly Scottish."

Nimrod laughed and shook his hand, which he had been holding by the wrist since they had started talking. That was another Kenyan custom

Bill was getting used to. He looked around, hoping none of his team was filming the moment. He would just as soon not have the video circulating in the locker room of his health club back home.

By Monday, their second full day in country, they were back in the vans driving around to the various projects sponsored by Nyeri Presbytery of the Presbyterian Church of East Africa. The approximately three-lane roads held plenty of vehicles, none of them new; in fact, they all looked identically dusty and dated. At regular intervals they had to inch their way up grades behind a heavy truck billowing black exhaust you'd expect from a torpedoed ship. But foot traffic was everywhere; there was something eternal and tidal about it. Women in bright wraps, men in mismatched suit pants and jackets over open shirts trod dusty red channels on either side of the road, past goats and cows tethered in the sparse grass along the shoulders and produce in makeshift stands or just laid out on a bank. The bicyclists walked, too, balancing bales on seats or handlebars or both along toward their destination. Beyond them all lay the landscape of the Central Highlands, quilted in all shades of green.

At the end of that day, Rev. Mathias took Bill and Mike to one of his parishioners' homes for a Bible study. A dozen-odd Kenyan adults were waiting for them on couches arranged around the perimeter of a cinder-block living room. Once tea had been served, Rev. Mathias introduced them. "We have from Pennsylvania (he pronounced it with five syllables) William Owens. We have Michael McGrew (with the brogue). Then each Kenyan got up to speak in turn. They had their own formula: "I am Joseph Munyi, and I am saved. We want just to welcome you. Be at home . . ." "I am Jayne Nguyo, and I love the Lord Jesus as my savior. You are welcome . . ." "I am George Gitai, and I am saved. We wish to greet and welcome you here . . ."

* * *

After a stroke of market luck and a spell of success in his thirties, Mike had announced his intention to retire at fifty. Bill found himself questioning Mike's chronology anew with each passing year. "You know, you're going to have to hustle to retire at fifty now that you're approaching your mid-fifties," he had told him at the last July Fourth cookout. His birthday was July 4, specifically, his fifty-fourth.

"I put my name on the door, Billy," Mike said. "That means total commitment."

"Well, at least you get your birthday off." Bill hoisted his can of beer. "In fact the whole country celebrates with you. But I guess you can't give your life to good works now."

"They're good for my clients. I'm lucky I got to Africa when I did."

The rest of the committee had arrived. They were marooned in the Calvin Room in more ways than one. The eight or ten of them sat around the heavy wooden table in one corner of a room that could hold a congregation and, every Sunday after worship for fellowship, did. And the carpet and curtains were wine-red. Along with the clumps of plush furniture scattered around the room they created deeps of atmosphere around the shallows of the one lit table.

"I know it seems impersonal," Mike was saying. "But send a check. Even if they need it, you can't be sure anything you send will make it through customs."

"We shouldn't have that problem with ties," Ralph Booth said.

"Well, I don't know," Mike said.

"Bill will be taking them with him anyway," George Willis said.

"That's true," several people, including Bill, acknowledged.

"If it seems impersonal, Mike, you take it," Rev. Kerr said. "You can deliver it. We can probably get a third member from our church on this team."

Mike turned his palms out. "Don't you recognize an armchair missionary when you see one?"

That produced lusty laughter in the group. It seemed counterintuitive to Bill, but laughter was not that difficult to elicit from a church committee. It sometimes seemed the reason they gathered.

"I see the armchair," Rev. Kerr said, to more laughter.

Bill had pulled an even more massive chair as close as he could get it to the table. It left him slightly out of the group's orbit. Bill found that a good posture for deliberation. It was appropriate on this occasion, though, because only he and Mike had been on the first trip, and only he and Rev. Kerr would go on this next one. Only he would be making both trips.

* * *

"Let me guess," Mike said, setting his hand on the lid. "A fin says rice." He had turned their midday and evening meals into a shell game. Kenyans served their food in what looked to Bill like crockpots without the cords. Mike lifted the lid. "Greens. I'm down five."

"I like the food," Bill said.

"Oh, I like it," Mike said. "Let's just the say the novelty has expired."

It was true that the same basic dishes were served every lunch and dinner: a beef stew, a chicken cut into small pieces, chopped greens and chickpeas, rice—all in the cylindrical containers. There was usually flat bread, chapati, or as a special treat, *ugali*, a kind of cornmeal that you could mold into a scoop for the other food on your plate. Breakfast was recognizable as such—fruit, bread and maybe a hard-boiled egg. And off to one side always the array of thermoses for tea, milk and coffee.

"How are you, *mzee*?"

Moses and Daniel, an elder and the treasurer of the church, respectively, had approached them from Mike's side. Teams of their fellow Americans were still gathering in Tumaini Hall from their morning excursions. They had been paired up and assigned different host families, who showed them around their parishes. On their way in, one church member poured water from a basin over their hands, and another offered them a paper towel. Bill and Mike had accepted this ablution with smiles and nods and, once though the door, simultaneously and surreptitiously reached for the hand sanitizer they carried at all times.

"Who are you calling *mzee*?" Mike said, then pointed to Bill. "Him, I hope." In a kind of maneuver, he took a step back while his face contorted into its widest, toothiest smile. Feet planted, he writhed with laughter that was silent at first, then booming, lagging behind the grin, like thunder after a flash of lightning. He hadn't gone native, that was for sure. He wore khakis and a blue Oxford-cloth shirt, as at home. Bill dressed as tropically as he could; he had brought a couple of plaid sports shirts. Mike had gone a little soft but was still strapping, with graying hair that you could tell had been blond and not dark. You could figure he was one of those big guys who could play on the offensive line but also be center on the high school basketball team. Now that he thought about it, when he had laughed just then he looked as though he were dropping back to protect a passer. Bill might have worried that Mike's hail-fellow Yankee heartiness would cause offense in Africa. Amazingly, it worked. Moses and Daniel also shook with laughter. Someone taught them a new word in Kiswahili every day; yesterday's was *mzee*, a term of respect for an elder. When Mike said, "*Mimi kijana*," their laughter redoubled. So did Mike's.

"Yes," they said. "You are young. But you are both young. Then what do you say?"

"Vijana," Mike said, and Moses and Daniel pulled faces to show they were impressed. "Ninyi vijana," Mike added.

Moses shook his head. "That is 'you are young.' You want to say, 'Sisi vijana.' We are young. Yes."

They all repeated the phrase, laughing.

"And if we say it often enough, will it be true?" Mike said. "It worked on you."

As they joked, Bill reflected that in fact all his hosts looked ageless to him. Apart from the very old, with their white, wooly hair, he had a hard time distinguishing ages. Young males, they had been told, were absent from the church. They congregated at what they called shopping centers, nothing like malls but rather lines of low buildings with curtained doors along the roads, at corners. There was a stirring. Moses and Daniel drifted to another group and another language, likely Kikikuyu. Rev. Mathias raised his hands to get everyone's attention. "Let's pray for food," he said.

After another encyclopedic Kenyan grace, Mike turned to Bill. "I want to ask you something."

"All right," Bill said.

Just then a couple of their hosts came to usher them into line to get their food.

"After lunch," Mike said.

Bill took a seat by himself at a table and waited for company. His new African friends were not shy. A church elder named Isaac took the seat to his left and explained how he ran his *shamba*, the small farm that many Kenyan households maintained to supplement their own food and also gain a little income. If conversation ever lagged, some of his hosts would simply lecture, and Isaac was one of the more professorial among them. One crop of coffee had just been harvested; local women could be seen along the roads hauling the beans in burlap sacks flung over their shoulder to collection centers. They would visit one that afternoon. When he turned to his food he found that another conversation was in progress to his right. It was so energetic that he was surprised to see, first, that it came from one speaker and, second, that that was not strictly the case: the other speaker was him. The empty chair to his right had been occupied by a Kenyan woman.

" . . . because I am *mwalimu*, too, a teacher, though today I am *mwana-funzi wako*, your student." She went on breathlessly. "So tell me, please, Mr. William, tell me about the life of a teacher in America. See, I am preparing to take notes."

Bill could tell these were pleasantries, partly because of the new words, which he could kind of figure out, partly because she punctuated her speech by doubling up with laughter between clauses. And she had stopped her torrent of words short, positioning her purse in front of her like a notepad, though she had no pencil, before she dissolved in laughter again. He wondered if he should introduce her to Mike. But her laughter was different, apologetic, as though she worried that Bill would embarrass himself by taking her literally. Mike's laughter by contrast was preemptive and triumphal.

Mike dared you not to find his jokes amusing. Bill explained once again that teaching was just one of his duties at the company where he worked, though over the years he had spent more and more of his time training new employees and even more bringing veteran employees up to date with new software. He would admit that for the first time in his life he had a sense of pedagogy and that he took some pride in his classroom technique. Still, he was vigilant not to turn into one of those retirees who discover they are teachers. Their adult Sunday School faculty was overstaffed with them. But despite his disclaimers he could not shake the title *Mwalimu*, with which everyone addressed him, including Mike on public occasions.

Bill observed her. She spoke so briskly that he didn't think she noticed. Her reddish hair was not a wig, he decided, but permed or something so that is seemed like a cap or a shell, with waves or curls that could have been carved in wood. Her skin was dark and slightly pitted in spots, like burnt cork, and her near-purple gums showed when she flashed a smile. At intervals her expression went blank, as though penitent, and she straightened in her chair, her hands in her lap. Her figure was trim and taut. She was likely a little but not much younger than Bill. In the pink of middle age, he would have said. A word to describe her came to Bill: pretty.

* * *

As he stood in the darkened hallway outside the room, Bill had a sensation he wasn't even sure was possible: he was conscious that he should be remembering something that had never happened.

He was listening to his father sleep, waiting for his next breath. All their married lives his parents had each accused the other of snoring. Both from his childhood and from later visits he could attest that they both snored, sometimes in unison. His father was not exactly snoring lately. The doctors weren't sure whether his stroke had caused his fall or the other way around, but in the hospital and in the rehab center he spent much of his time in a chair nodding off and then snorting himself almost awake. In bed at home now he sputtered and gasped and occasionally moaned, even though during the day he was mostly alert and seemed to be recovering. He just couldn't quite get a snore going, like an engine that wouldn't turn over. They were leaving the light on in his bathroom so that he could get to it in the middle of the night. The mirror across the room caught a glimmer of it, like a pool in a forest glade. Bill waded into the room. From years of pre- and post-pubescent forays, he knew it almost as well as his own, knew where to find the jackknives and the army insignia, the occasional men's magazine, so laughably tame by current internet standards, in a drawer or under some sheets on a shelf in the closet. He breathed the scent of soured Old Spice.

One thing his parents weren't was vain: this was the only full-length mirror in the house. It wasn't even mounted but just leaned beside the bathroom door; it could be moved or turned around to face the wall. Bill had stood in front of it in various stages of undress and in various poses as his physique developed. In his middle age he was still in good shape, just more judicious about baring his torso for appraisal. When he walked over to it, he found that his reflection was accompanied. Without interrupting his shallow breathing, without so much as turning over in his bed, his father appeared behind him, lifted his hand and dropped the noose of a tie over Bill's head. *Just slide the knot up and down. Then we'll make one from scratch. Not a full Windsor. Not with the ties they're making these days. You're liable to end up with a knot the size of a basketball. Here.* He took the tie back and a minute later snaked it through Bill's collar. *Oh, yes. The classic button-down. I'm glad it's back. You might prefer to undo the buttons when you put a tie on. Even it up—but not even. Allow for the knot. You don't want the back end to be longer than the front end. Cardinal, sin, Billy. Cardinal sin.* He reached around him to tie the knot that Bill still favored, in fact the only one he knew how to make. *Like this.* He tightened the tie up to Bill's throat.

Bill returned to his vigil by the door, listening to his father's fitful breathing. It was something else he was supposed to be remembering. That memory had happened.

* * *

"You've made a conquest," Mike said.

He had taken the seat Isaac vacated to join his fellow Kenyans in deliberations over the afternoon's itinerary, which they all thought was already set. It seemed that the smallest decisions called for a conclave. *I went to a tea party and a session meeting broke out*, would be a good Kenyan joke. It was as difficult for them to adjourn a meeting as it was to conclude a prayer. Paying a bill at a restaurant after one of their group meals was more like arbitration. It reminded Bill of the way dinner parties at home took forever to disperse, the interval between the first couple's announcement that they should be getting home and the actual departure, the way one spouse stood with his coat on in the doorway striking up one last conversation while the other thought of something else to say to her girlfriend. *Leave already*, Bill felt like saying. *It's not that I care. It's not that I want you to leave. It's just that you said you were going to leave.* And it wasn't even his house. Mike had dubbed the African system of advise and consent "complification." While agreeing, Bill would counter that what they set out to do they eventually got done.

"She likes you."

"She's nice," Bill said. "We were talking."

"She's smitten."

"I don't think our present circumstances encourage passion to smolder. We're in a church. We're on a mission trip."

"Isn't that redundant?" Mike said. "A mission is a trip. You decide. You're the *mwalimu*."

"Not an English *mwalimu*. I'll consult my father."

"How's he doing?"

"Just okay. His sister is with him."

Bill watched the woman he had been talking to. She may have given her name in the rush of her remarks. She was pleasant to watch. She had the address of a schoolmarm, a species apparently not extinct in Africa.

"So I gather Rev. Mathias and the others are conferring?" Mike slumped in his chair with one of his exaggerated frowns. "That should give us ample time to explore my question."

Bill laughed. "And the question is?"

"So, if I notice differences between Kenyans and us, categorical differences, am I a racist? If I am impatient, say, if our African hosts are not as efficient as they might be? By Western standards?"

"You traveled halfway around the world to join this fellowship, Mike. I think that would exonerate you of any charge of prejudice." Bill nodded toward one of their hosts. "Do you see him?"

"That's Simon," Mike said. "I'm getting the names straight. The first names."

"That's Jim Daub."

"Jim Daub?" Mike said, scowling skeptically, though he was obviously eager to be instructed. That was the name of one of their fellow session members at home.

"He's the Kenyan version. He's a windbag. An intelligent windbag, but still a windbag. I think it's a good sign that I can recognize types here. There's not just a generic Kenyan. Or is it wrong to see stereotypes? Is it all right if they're trans-racial stereotypes?"

"I wish it was that easy not to be a racist," Mike said. "The purchase of an airplane ticket. I could present my boarding pass. I'm afraid though that if you're an American you're a racist. You've been conditioned to see the world in certain terms: black vs. white. At the same time, you're taught that everyone is equal. Maybe there are a finite number of types. I'm talking about whole races. Is it possible that one race is superior to another?"

"My father has a theory," Bill said. "He concedes that there are intelligent blacks, but he has constructed an IQ graph of the two races. It looks like two parallel lines, the white line above the black line. In other words, the lowest and highest points on the black line would be lower than the corresponding points on the white line, though intermediate points would be at the same level."

Mike's frown deepened. "You have to admit that's an intelligent theory."

"That's the problem," Bill said. "It's also racist."

"So those qualities can coexist?" Mike said. "You can be an intelligent racist? Or is it that you can be intelligent even though you're mistaken about a fundamental truth? Or, in order not to be a racist, do you have to ignore certain facts?"

"People might ask all the same questions about a Christian," Bill said. They looked around the room. "Still, it would be pretty hard to argue that a race is inferior many of whose members speak three languages."

"Hey," Mike said, turning on Bill as though he had broached the subject. "You look at any human being, any color. Even though you've never seen him before, you know two things about him: God created him; Jesus died for him. Or her."

"Agreed," Bill said.

Mike relaxed. "So how come it occurs to me to compare races, which are composed of individuals? Or is that a different question?"

The knot of Kenyans at the far end of the hall loosened. One of the elders spoke to the woman who had befriended Bill. She stood at the head of the head table and waited for the room to quiet down.

"I am Zipporah Mathai," she said. "And I am saved."

* * *

"How are we this morning?" A heavy-set nurse blustered into the room. The cheerful shout must have been covered in the rehab center's staff manual.

His father had to shrug to turn his head. "Don't ask," he said.

The nurse straightened in mock surprise. "I have to ask. That's my job."

"I've been better."

"Ah. I thought you were going to say how happy you were to see us again." She pulled up a chair and sat in front of him. "I'm going to get you ready for speech therapy." She gave him a moment to absorb that thought. "How about that?"

"I can't wait," his father said.

"Good," she said. "Can you stick your tongue out for me? Not at me, now! That's it. Move it to the right. To the left. Good. Now smile for me."

"I need something to smile about."

The nurse sat up straight and made a show of looking around the room. "Your son is here to see you."

His father followed her gaze. "Try something else."

"Your father's a character, isn't he?" the nurse said. "Is that just lately?"

Bill was laughing. "No, that character is not a recent development."

* * *

At intervals that he kept pretty close track of, Bill allowed himself to look at Zipporah. She seemed to him slightly aware of being observed. As she moved from around the room, though, she looked totally absorbed in every conversation. That was partly because her eyes were slightly protuberant. In fact none of her features appealed to Bill individually. He would always have conceded that the African-American women he found attractive were what in one of their spoofs *MAD Magazine* called "TV Negroes": actors with dark skin and Caucasian features. He could not really imagine sharing her atmosphere. Kenyans did not practice the same hygiene that Americans did. Bill routinely showered twice a day at home, rinsing off in the morning and taking a longer shower after his late afternoon workout. On this trip he had cut back to a shower every other day, in between giving himself a sponge bath with a technique he had probably learned in a junior high health class. At the time the information probably seemed roughly as valuable as the difference between the governments of a municipality and a small city or the atomic weight of barium. He didn't know what it would be like to hold her or to kiss her, or if he wanted to; what her leathery-looking lips would feel like against his. What would she taste like? Did she use mouthwash, as he did after breakfast here, a bottle of Listerine in one hand and a bottle of water in the other? He had been close enough to breathe her spicy body odor. To her maybe he smelled perfumey or chemical. But every look at her gave him pleasure. It was partly that combination of briskness and alertness, her eyes full of concern when she spoke to someone. She could have been half of some of the married couples he observed who had a way of separating in groups to talk with other people yet seem conscious of each other's presence, connected somehow. Rev. Kerr and his wife were particularly good at that.

Zipporah's announcement turned out to be an update. They were trying to communicate with the vans, which had had to be rerouted, so their afternoon stops had to be reshuffled. All the elders were already back on their cell phones. Mike continued their discussion.

"Colonialism was horrible. No argument. It was unconscionable. But was it all bad? I'm talking about the effects. If Europe hadn't invaded, would Kenya have hospitals, railroads, universities? Why didn't black Africa colonize Europe? I need some answers here, William."

Bill laughed.

"And another thing, while you're thinking. Along those lines. China had printing way before Europe did. Paper. The Arabs were great sailors. Why didn't those peoples come to America and settle it? We could be speaking Arabic right now. What, were they too nice? And what were the Europeans supposed to do when they got to America? Ask the natives if the continent was taken? 'Okay. Thanks. Could you point us to Antarctica?' The Indians came from Asia themselves."

"You forgot to mention the gospel," Bill said. "Europeans brought that with them."

"And what would people say about Christians here? That they've been brainwashed, taught a couple of formulas. Could they explain what it means to be saved?"

"You don't believe that," Bill said.

Mike sat back in his chair. "No, I don't." Then he laughed. "I need a stretch." He meant it literally. At its apex, his arm outspread as though in benediction, he caught sight of Rev. Mathias. He beamed and walked over to him. Not a minute later Zipporah took his place, sitting on the edge of the chair, hands in her lap, rapt.

"William," she said. "*Kuniambia kuhusu mke na watoto wako.*"

Bill could only smile back at her.

"Tell me about your wife and children."

* * *

"Do you see what I'm saying? Bill?"

"Not yet," Bill said.

The motion on the table was to collect ties from the congregation to send over to Kenya for ushers in church to wear. The idea, as Rev. Kerr explained it, was to give elders a sense of the dignity and value of their office. What might seem trivial to us could be important to them. Bill remembered that suits were ubiquitous but that he had seen very few ties. The ministers all wore clerical collars, which you didn't often see in America anymore.

"Bill and I were talking about this before," Mike went on. "You remember, Bill."

Bill still wasn't sure what he was getting at, but he realized gradually that Mike was referring not to their discussion before the meeting convened but to one they had had in Kenya. For all the histrionics of his conversations, Mike had an uncanny ability to pick one up where it left off months before. He could listen while he hammed it up. Bill wasn't the only one at a loss. Ralph Collins, the senior member of the committee, sat across the table, eyes narrowed behind his glasses to their most oracular-looking. His face, which wore a perpetual frown, had a limited range of expressions, from alarmed to appalled, and he always seemed on the verge of a pronouncement that never came. It might just be that he couldn't hear anything. Bill could never understand why some older men with all their hair chose to buzz it into a crew cut. He had reason to be alert on this topic: he was the only committee member wearing a tie, under his cardigan sweater.

"Bill and I were talking about how superficial Kenyan Christianity could seem to the outside observer," Mike said. "Well, I was talking."

"It's only been there for a hundred years, Mike," Curt Ellis said. He was the academic on the committee, a new professor of religion at the college. "It's like the second-century church. Think of yourself as St. Paul."

Mike recoiled at the suggestion. "But the faith should be more than claiming to be saved or wearing a tie. How about some doctrine? Come on."

"The early church didn't have any theology," Curt said. "They were just following Jesus. They were scared."

"We know better," Mike said. It was everyone else's turn to recoil. As usual, it was hard to tell when Mike was just stoking a discussion. "Wouldn't this gift be hypocritical? Just when we Americans are starting to dress more casually . . . "

"Like you?" Lois Tunick interrupted. On Sundays Mike always looked as though he had stepped into the sanctuary from the pages of GQ, wearing his college tie whenever remotely appropriate.

" . . . When we are saying that God doesn't care how you dress when you worship, we're sending ties to Kenya? That's patronizing. Shouldn't we be sharing the gospel as we understand it? Send a check. I doubt they will buy ties with the money."

"We could send a check also," Lenore Towns said, supine on a nearby couch. The only African-American on the committee, she had announced that she would not be along for the mission: she was still tired from the trip over, 300 years ago. Actually she was in chemotherapy and repaired to the couch at intervals during every meeting. Many Sundays she lay down in her pew during worship.

"Stumbling blocks and stepping stones," Rev. Kerr said.

"Amen," Lenore said. They had just sung that anthem on Sunday, at her request.

"We might be mature enough in our faith"—Rev. Kerr pulled a face—"that we can be worshipful no matter how we dress. But in some places the chance to dress up might draw people to church. Where they might by chance hear the gospel."

"It still seems like hypocrisy to me," Mike said.

"Let's call it humane hypocrisy," Rev. Kerr said. "Bill and I can be guilty of it."

"Deal," Mike said.

* * *

"It had to happen someday," Bill said.

"What did?' Rev. Kerr, in the seat next to him, looked up from his book with a smile.

"For the first time in my life, my pastor is younger than me."

Rev. Kerr laughed. "Not by much."

"Are you still on the sunny side of fifty?"

"By a year."

"Then I've got five years on you," Bill said. "At least you're not young enough to be my son."

Rev. Kerr laughed again. "That would get you in the *Guinness Book of World Records*. It wouldn't get you in the Bible, though, if you're feeling old. There are fathers a lot older than you in there."

"Where are you getting your information?" Bill said. "That doesn't look like a Bible to me."

"It's not." Rev. Kerr held up *The Best American Short Stories 2010*. "Why do I do it to myself? All the anguish these characters feel. All the insights they have, and never the needful one. If they went to church once in a while instead of to cocktail parties. But I suppose if I wrote short stories all the characters would be saved at the end, and that would be predictable."

"Can't have that," Bill said.

"Actually, I think these stores are pretty predictable, too. In the last paragraph the protagonist is 'redeemed.' That means he is embittered but enlightened as he comes to his private terms with a meaningless universe made livable only by fellow-feeling among its denizens."

"Congratulations," Bill said. "You just reduced the literature of the past couple of centuries to the proverbial smoking rubble."

"That's called an 'epiphany.' But there was an Epiphany. And if they want redemption, I know a better place to look for it. But I keep reading it," Rev. Kerr sighed. "I do like good writing. And it's not that it's not true. It gives me some sermon-fodder. It's just not as true as it might be."

They sat for a minute. Rev. Kerr had turned his book open but face-down on his lap.

"I suppose I could have a pastor son," Bill said. "How old were you when you got your first job?"

"Twenty-eight," Rev. Kerr said. "I was precocious. That was maybe a little too young, even for an associate. Early thirties is probably more like the average these days."

"So if I had had a son when I was twenty-four."

"Or daughter."

"Or daughter."

"But you'd be as likely to find a pulpit starting at your age. You'd be surprised how many people take up ministry as a second career. The seminaries are full of middle-aged baby-boomers. And we need pastors. Good pastors, young or old."

It was clear to Bill that he would always feel a certain reserve when he talked to a pastor, even one younger than him. At least he called him Doug. He could never bring himself to address his former teachers by their first name no how much they insisted. Mike felt no such qualms. When they ran into their high school principal, Mike would greet him with his given name—which happened to be Homer—and a suggestive grin, presumably at the charade of formality they had pulled off for four years in the 1960s.

"So?" Rev. Kerr said.

Bill looked at him blankly, then laughed. "Me? A pastor? I don't think so. I may not have informed you of this fact, but I am a sinner."

"That didn't stop me," Rev. Kerr said. "And look at you! Going back to Africa. Anyone can go once. There are a lot of mission tourists out there. 'Vacationaries,' we call them. Are you sure you don't feel a call?"

"I'm not sure I could tell you why I'm going back."

"That sounds like a call. Answer first, read the fine print later."

"There are sins, and then there are sins," Bill said.

There was a silence, or what passed for silence in the cabin—the hiss of the engines and the artificial breeze.

"What, Bill? What's bothering you?"

"I thought Presbyterians didn't confess."

"Actually," Rev. Kerr said. "That's a bit of a misconception. We don't practice auricular confession, one-on-one, so to speak. Although they did in Geneva in the sixteenth century. Calvin and his colleagues made house calls. They assembled the members of a household and examined everyone on the state of their faith. How would you like to have me show up at your front door unannounced with the *Book of Confessions* in my hand?"

"Isn't that called surveillance?"

"We moderns would see it that way. For the Reformers, it was one of the signs of the true church, along with the sound preaching of the gospel and the right administration of the sacraments. They called it discipline."

"That's better?"

Rev. Kerr laughed. "We can't use discipline in schools anymore, let alone churches. They saw it as pastoral concern. Don't we want the gospel to apply to people's daily, domestic life? Should a Christian family go home from church after a service and be dysfunctional? If a woman comes to church every Sunday with a black eye, what do you do? Pick new hymns? Or investigate? Call it 'intervention' these days and people are okay with it. And they would say, and I kind of agree, that you shouldn't just waltz into church once a quarter and take communion. The pastors wanted to make sure everyone was prepared for the Lord's Supper, so they examined them, for the sacrament's sake as well as theirs. We've only got two sacraments left, so we've got to protect them. They didn't want the meal to be profaned, and the people didn't want to be excommunicated."

"Excommunication? I assumed we were talking about Protestants."

"We are. The Reformed Church excluded people from communion for longer or shorter periods of time, depending on the offense. True, Calvin also thought that excommunication sounded a little too Catholic, so he preferred to call it suspension or something. But it was literally excommunication; people couldn't take communion. And they were terrified at the prospect. That's how you received grace. Do you think it would bother people today if they were deprived of communion? If we just stopped having it I wonder how many people would notice. I would love it if the church had a concept of discipline. There is still a provision in *The Book of Order* for private confession. I don't know of an instance. But we practice public, generic, unison confession, every Sunday in church. In fact, this crowd looks a little like our congregation during one of my sermons. So go. Make a clean breast of it before anyone wakes up."

The cabin had gone dim, and it was dark outside as well. They had lost all sense of motion; it was easy to imagine the plane hung up in an invisible skein of time zones. Bill couldn't decide if he was tired or not. They were on the second of two consecutive eight-hour flights; he had dozed during a long layover in London. The passengers around them had fallen into every attitude of semi- or unconsciousness, some wearing a deep frown, others twisted into sleep verging on despair, head back and eyes straining shut.

"I disobeyed God's first commandment," Bill said. "The very first one: 'Be fruitful and multiply.' It's even before the Big Ten. It's like Commandment Zero. I just wasn't listening. Or I guess I didn't realize it was directed to me. I thought it was kind of generally speaking, to the planet at large. You know: 'Reproduce. Continue to exist.' Probably mostly to plants and animals. They multiply; they don't have children. I never got married; therefore, I didn't have children."

"You must have had chances," Rev. Kerr said. "Were you ever close?"

"I suppose I thought there would always be time. I should make sure the match was perfect. Meantime I would just be better and better prepared to have a family. There was no rush. To the contrary. Marriage was inevitable. It would be like the draft. Not too long after college you'd stand in line like a GI holding your arms out to get a blanket and a uniform except you'd be issued a wife, a house and kids. The challenge was not to get shoved into line before you were ready. It happened to everyone sooner or later, it would happen to me. But look how it turned out. I was the serious one in school, I was the hard worker, but all my friends got out of school all of a sudden and became citizens and heads of households overnight. One minute we were all playing pick-up basketball together and the next everyone was married but me. Look at Mike. He was a goofball in college. He's still a goofball. The world is a frat party, and everyone is a brother. And he's got three kids. Meanwhile I sowed my wild oats out of season."

"Now we're talking confessional."

"By the time I was young I was middle-aged. Now it's too late for me."

"Are you sure?" Rev. Kerr said. "Church is a great place to find a partner. I always tell that to young adults, at the risk of sounding crass. Churches are full of thoughtful, compassionate women. Those are good qualities in a wife. Do you expect to find the women of your dreams in a bar, I ask them."

"I'll tell you when it hit me," Bill said. "A few months ago I was standing in the hall outside my father's bedroom. You remember; I moved in to take care of him. We slept with our doors open in case there was some crisis during the night. I was listening to him breathe. Or, rather, I was making sure he was breathing. It seemed to me that he had developed some sort of sleep apnea; he was always spluttering and clearing his throat. That was unsettling. But it was worse when I couldn't hear him breathe at all. I realized that I should have been registering a solemn irony, remembering how I had watched over my children, and now I was watching over my father. Friends have told me how they stood by the cribs of their children, taking each breath with them, amazed that, if they stopped, their babies' breathing would continue, all by itself. I never did that."

"You were a good son to your father," Rev. Kerr said. "I'm not sure I would have wanted to be his caregiver. He was a handful on the session."

"Wouldn't it be something if all those years he wanted grandchildren?" Bill said. "How was I supposed to know? People have to tell me these things."

"Sometimes I think having children is one of those things you have to do without giving it too much thought," Rev. Kerr said. "That might sound funny coming from a father of four, let alone a pastor. Talk about pressure to have a family. Being a monk is not an option for a Presbyterian minister. But if people stopped to consider how much work children are, how much heartache they can bring, I don't know that anyone would ever get born. You may be called to be someone's second husband, some child's stepfather."

"All these calls coming in," Bill said. "My switchboard is lit up. By the time I get to the phone, though, all I hear is a dial tone. Maybe my phone is off the hook."

"Put it back on," Rev. Kerr said. "Then sit next to it. Your call may come late, like Abraham's. And stay in shape."

"Abraham's children were to be like the sand and the stars, part of the cosmos. That's a whole creation I failed to create. I would call that a major sin."

"Creation is God's job," Rev. Kerr said. "You're repenting above your pay grade now."

"I never told a child to open the car for a minute before they got in on a hot summer day, on Sunday, say, after church in the Sears parking lot. Or to leave the window open a crack before they got out. That's a little more down to earth. Or that, in a letter, after p.s. comes p.p.s., and then p.p.p.s., not p.p.s.s. I guess my wife would have told him that. My mother told me. It's the particular I think about. There are memories I don't have when I need them. How would the world have looked to my children? What memories would they have formed, where would their sacred places in the neighborhood have been, like the ones I had? All those realities that might have existed. I would have adult children by now. They could have helped with Dad. They would have. On their own. They probably would have looked like Dad. Do they? Someplace?"

"Or will they?" Rev. Kerr said.

* * *

At first, among the adjectives that Bill might have applied to Kenyan comportment, he would not have included "gracious." There was that phalanx of silent men on the sidewalk outside the airport, reaching for their bags, herding them into vans. At the group lunches, when their hosts turned to each other and broke into conversation in Kikikuyu, it was hard not to imagine that they were correcting every impression their visitors had just voiced. The Kenyans pulled out their cell phones so often they might have been calling each other with their latest observations of the Americans. Back at their houses after a day of driving around they spent most of their time on couches making conversation as best they could while the bustle of the household went on around them. One meal or another was always being prepared. When the women, who were less likely to speak English than the men, finally sat, they mostly listened in silence, as though despairing of another chore to do. It was not always easy to tell who lived in a house. The widowed mother of Rev. Mathias, his first host, shared a hut in the family compound with a woman of about her age who turned out to be her husband's and Rev. Mathias's father's other wife. They had continued to live together as sisters since his death many years before. Other women appeared from somewhere to cook the food in the back yard in pots that they rested on three stones over three sticks that they pulled in or out of the fire to regulate the heat. When at last Rev. Mathias prayed before dinner, he did it without turning down the volume of the small television on a shelf behind him that was tuned to professional wrestling in grainy black and white, broadcast seemingly not just from America but from 1960s America. They left it on during dinner. He didn't see Rev. Mathias's wife until he got up for seconds and discovered her sitting around a corner in the next room by the table holding the food. She had fixed his favorite Kenyan food, *irio*. She urged him to get more, as if he wasn't about to. He realized how at ease he felt all at once. Their hospitality, like her, had been out of his sightline.

Three days later he moved in with another minister and his wife. Their children were away at boarding school. Like Rev. Mathias, Rev. Ngigi wore his clerical collar around the house, which was full of heavy furniture in no discernible arrangement. With its cinder-block walls and concrete floor, the living room had the feel of a suburban garage back home used for storage. The walls were crammed with pictures and plaques bearing Bible verses, and pieces of fabric were draped pretty much at random over chairs and on the walls, though some of them covered doorways. Their conversation at table, just the three of them, was polite and informative. They shared the state of their respective churches. The next day was Sunday; the proprieties were to be followed during worship as well. In a tone near reprimand Rev. Ngigi remarked that he assumed Bill had brought a tie with him, which would only be fitting for someone addressing the congregation. At his full height and girth, Rev. Ngigi was an imposing man, especially in his clerical garb. He was like his own pulpit. Bill assured him he had no shortage of ties. Then, back at the house after a nine-to-five Sabbath in churches both English- and Kikikuyu-speaking, as Bill was about to depart for his next host family, Rev. Ngigi's eyes behind his small, wire-framed glasses brimmed. "My wife and I grieve that you are going," he said. "We do not want you to leave. You have blessed our house." There wasn't much question but that he meant it.

On this second trip he stayed first with the family of a high school teacher, Peter Mathai. From the moment of his arrival, Peter's two young sons flanked him, alert for a chance to carry his guitar case.

"William, is it empty?" one said. "Is there something in it?"

"I wondered when it might occur to someone to ask that," his father said. He was maybe a dozen years Bill's junior. His dress was more American than Bill's; he wore slacks, a crew-necked jersey and loafers.

"We could probably open it and find out," Bill said.

The boys' eyes widened in innocent triumph. In a minute they were trading the guitar back and forth. Bill set it across each boy's lap in turn so they could strum while he fingered chords.

"Do you need this, William?" the other boy said.

"Isaac," his father said. "Such questions."

"Not really," Bill said. "I have others at home. I thought I might find someone here who could use it."

After a moment's reflection, Isaac's brother said, "You could leave it at our house."

"Clever of you to think of that solution, Jacob," his father said.

"I'm going to play it at some churches," Bill said. "I'll leave it at one. Someone will have to play it after I'm gone."

The boys reached a consensus that one or the other of them could. Bill did not point out the make of the instrument. In that Kenyan living room the filigreed gold semicircular C. F. Martin & Co. logo that he loved to see on the headstock was mute. Est. 1833.

For the two weeks of their mission Bill visited one church project after another. His group would be ferried in by their hosts to Presbytery headquarters for prayer and tea and long discussions, then distribute themselves in groups of four or five to the matatus for a trip to a school or clinic or church under construction. The Kenyans built in stages, as they raised money. Most of the sites amounted to not much more than partially-erected walls behind the peculiar-looking scaffolding they used, gnarled branches woven together into what looked like wickerwork. There was rarely anyone working on a building; most hadn't progressed dramatically since Bill's first visit, two years before. They would all gather on the floor of a future church or hospital under the open air while parish officials pointed out where the balcony or lab would go. At every site, a committee would be waiting for them as their vans pulled in to usher them into the vestry for tea. Budgets would be reviewed, guest books signed, checks presented and pictures taken with the session or a women's guild. With their sky-blue head scarves the ladies looked like the lost order of Presbyterian nuns. There was one question Bill fielded at every stop: *Wapi Michael*? Where is Michael? They all remembered him. Mention of his name was enough to light faces up.

Bill suspected that, while their lodgings seemed rustic to them, his group stayed in the nicest homes in each parish. On the tour of his second house on the trip, Bill's new host proudly flung open a door to show him his private bathroom. It was spacious enough but contained nothing Bill would have classified as plumbing until he noticed the tank on the wall behind him. And the hole in the middle of the floor probably counted. The next house, up in the Aberdare Hills, had the feel of a cinder-block villa, ringed not with vineyards but with tea plants. The last house where he stayed was something like that, but nearer town and lower and therefore planted with coffee trees. This was one of the church's guest houses. His hosts dropped him off with a supply of bottled water and Coca Cola. His dependence on Coke was a running joke that had carried over from his first trip to this one. He had never had to worry; there was a Coke bottling plant in the city. One of the first stops on this trip was a tour for his benefit.

By comparison to the others, his last residence was palatial, a sprawling affair of two wings radiating from the living room and kitchen. Whereas at the house before he had barely had space between the bed and the wall to get into his room to sleep, here he had three bedrooms and six beds to choose from. By a fluke of scheduling, he was the only team member there. But although he was the only guest in the guest house, he was not alone. A housekeeper, a lanky young man named John, occupied the wing opposite Bill's. At, night as he closed the door between his hall and the rest of the house, he heard faint music from a radio. He had the sense that there were other gardeners and groundskeepers outside, but he never saw them. John though was ubiquitous, in and out of the house on his rounds in the kitchen and shamba. His shaved head and stern features made him look like a life-sized carving. His English was not bad, and he immediately set about ascertaining Bill's itinerary. His interest had to be mostly academic, since he would remain at the house. The simpler Bill's answers, the more sobering their effect on John. "And how will you get to the Presbytery office tomorrow, William?" he would ask.

"Rev. Mathias will pick me up a ten o'clock."

"Rev. Mathias will pick you." He pronounced it *pique*.

"Yes."

"At ten?"

"Yes."

"Oh," John said, his expression still graver as he absorbed this information. Apparently it was either more or less significant than he had originally thought. Even his mannerisms were academic; he fingered the lobe of one ear while he thought. He brightened. "Do you have children, William?"

"I do not."

"You do not have?"

"No. How about you?"

"I have three." Suddenly his response seemed grudging. He brooded over it for a moment. Or he might just have lost interest in the obvious. Conversation with him was fitful, interrupted by his duties but also by changes in topic. Bill could never be sure what John would find amusing.

"You stay here tonight, William?"

"Yes, and the next few. In fact, until I leave."

"You stay here until you leave?"

"Yes. On Sunday I'll be driven to Nairobi and fly from there."

"Yes. They will take your bags?"

"Yes. I will leave this one, and the guitar."

"You leave the guitar?"

"Yes."

"Oh," he said, as though to apologize for his surprise. "I would like to play the guitar."

"You can try it," Bill said.

"Yes," John said, though he continued just to eye the case. Then he pointed to the suitcase next to it. "What is in there, William?"

"Ties."

"Ties?" John said. This half-amused, half-mystified him.

"I'm leaving them for the elders of the church."

"Oh, William. You make me laugh."

Bill thought that it wasn't his generosity that John was struck by but his wit. In the course of their brief acquaintance John seemed to come to think of him as a kind of wag. You could never tell what that zany American would say next. Bill got to look forward to their conversations after a day of visits to churches and the rounds of formal speeches. He wasn't sure how so many adults were free of a weekday to gather for their meetings. He and John would lounge around the living room like flatmates for a half-hour or so until it was time for the news, which John liked to watch every night while he ate his dinner. Bill couldn't follow the stories, even though they were in English. Though they didn't eat together, they shared food. John would look approvingly through the bags that Bill brought back from the market and sometimes request an item for the next day. He laughed at the sight of the daily Coke bottles.

"You have brought bread, William."

"Yes."

"And bananas."

"Two kinds. My driver picked them out for me. We don't have either in America."

"Oh, William. You say such things."

Everything Bill did seemed progressively to deepen John's impression of him.

At lunch on his last full day in Kenya, the Saturday before his departure, he saw Zipporah. Or, rather, she materialized, as she had when they met two years before. He turned to his right in a crowd and found her standing next to him, her hand extended. She smiled and made a little bow. "Hujambo," she said to him brightly. "You did not e-mail me!"

"Sijambo," Bill said. "You did not e-mail me! I thought you were going to start. In fact, I think I have that in writing somewhere."

She still laughed from the waist. "All right, then. At least if you weren't e-mailing me you were studying your Kiswahili. Unaweza kusema Kiswhahili sasa. You know to say sijambo!"

"Yes, I learn one new word each trip. I will be fluent sometime in the twenty-third century. I hope I can think of something to say. I wasn't sure I would see you. We leave tomorrow."

"This is my church. We are the mother church of the parish. We knew you would be stopping here."

"What do you think of our new sanctuary?" Zipporah's pastor, Rev. Simon Gaki, was standing right next to them and had been, Bill realized, the whole time. Short and stocky, with cropped hair, he looked pugilistic in every respect except his clerical collar and his perpetual, approving grin. "When it is finished we will be able to gather the whole parish for worship. Go. Show William. Do not fear. Tutafuata. Where you lead, we will follow."

He and Zipporah stepped out of the fellowship hall into sheer sunlight. The church complex contained a number of low buildings, including some classrooms and the church office. They started out across the springy grass of the churchyard, brushing through the stench of the pit latrines as though through a cobweb on their way to the new sanctuary. Bill would have taken it for a ruin. The walls that seemed to be crumbling were actually going up. The branch-like scaffolding around them could have been an overgrowth of vines from an encroaching jungle. They entered an archway and picked their way among what looked like rubble on the ground but was the blocks that would be fitted onto the jagged walls as they rose. Bill could see that progress during his absence has been uncharacteristically dramatic. On his first trip the structure was little more than an outline, one course of stones on the ground, like the pretend houses he and his childhood friends had laid out in the woods, one log or branch high.

"Can you manage?" Bill said, touching rather than taking her by the elbow, just grazing the barky skin at the bend of her arm. She was in low heels, making her about Bill's height.

"Oh, yes," she said. "Come. I can climb stairs, too. This will be the balcony."

Weaving through the scaffolding as though it were a thicket, they started up the pebbly steps. At first they were enclosed in the grotto of the staircase, but they emerged onto an unfinished ledge, exposed to the sky. The sunlight glazed her dark skin, which up closed looked a little corky, a trace of her adolescence. Beneath them a rolling green landscape of hedges and shambas spread out beyond the compound. One of the fields was the football pitch of the school attached to the church, frayed sandy at the center.

Zipporah pointed off to the left. "Look," she said. "*Kirinyaga.*"

Against the horizon, they could see its outline, as spectral as the moon in a day sky.

"*Karibu*, Mt. Kenya," Bill said.

"Yes, welcome, Mt. Kenya," Zipporah said. "I'm sure Kirinyaga is moved by your hospitality. When the Europeans brought God, we did not need to welcome him, because he was always here. We had only one god, and we thought he lived on the mountain. Can you blame us?"

"No," Bill said.

"We were prepared to receive the gospel, because God spoke to us through our elders, who were the priests of their families. Every home was a church already. And we opened them to strangers."

"I have noticed," Bill said.

"And every meal we share is sacred. The worst thing you can do is betray someone you have eaten with. You see? We knew what communion is."

"I think I have had the same experience. Do you know that when I arrived here two years ago it was very confusing, because people kept coming up to me and saying the same thing: '*Bwana asifiwe.*' I finally asked someone what it meant."

"You say 'Praise the Lord.' Even just 'PTL,' isn't it?"

"When I was a boy in America we used to watch Tarzan movies on television," Bill said. "I wonder if you have seen any, or what you would think of them."

"Yes, we have seen."

"We used to repeat certain lines all the time. "Me Tarzan, you Jane." You could substitute another name for 'Jane.' 'Me Tarzan, you Mike.' We all wanted to be Tarzan. Or, 'Me Tarzan, you moron.' I know. We were very witty."

Zipporah smirked.

"There was another expression we used a lot. The African porters always addressed the Europeans as 'bwana.' So we used to call each other that as a joke. 'Good morning, Bwana Mike.'"

"Bwana William," Zipporah giggled.

"I didn't know it was a real word," Bill said. "I thought it was a Tarzan movie word. Then when I got to Kenya I realized that God was here waiting. I had known God's name all along."

"Yes. We say Bwana Mungu. Lord God."

"We have found you." Rev. Isaac emerged smiling from the mouth of the staircase. Bill's compatriots followed him onto the balcony and dispersed along the parapet to look out over the countryside. "Tell me, who is *mwalimu* and who is *mwanafunzi* today? Who is teaching whom?"

In a flurry of mutual deference, Bill and Zipporah got their hands all tangled up as each indicated the other.

"William is *mwalimu*," Zipporah said. "He can show his friends Kirinyaga."

"Yes, come, William." Rev. said, taking him by the hand, which he did not then subsequently release. He led him over to the other Americans, who were wearing the same expectant smiles on their faces that they had worn for the past two weeks. The smiles were a little fixed by now.

"There," Bill said, pointing with his free hand. "Mount Kenya." But by then the clouds had thickened so that only the shoulders of the mountain were visible. The arrowhead-like summit was lost in white plumes. "You'll have to take my word for it."

Back down on the ground, Zipporah led the group to the fellowship hall for lunch. Two church members flanked the door, one with the basin of water and the other with the roll of paper towels. Zipporah stepped aside for her guests and turned with a swirl of her skirt to see Bill and Rev. Isaac bringing up the rear, hand in hand.

"Bwana William," she called, with a gesture toward the ground. "Did I remember to tell you? *Ndugu ni makinya.*"

Rev. Isaac turned to Bill with a grin. "It is Kikikuyu."

"Wait a minute," Bill said. They had reached Zipporah. "That's not fair. I just learned Kiswahili."

Rev. Isaac gave Bill's hand a swing. "It means, 'Friendship is footsteps.'"

"It means you must return," Zipporah said.

* * *

Just as before, it took Bill almost the whole trip to re-regulate his bodily functions. On his first visit, in a spirit of openness, he had eaten everything offered to him. The less identifiable the foodstuff, the greater the gusto with which he consumed it. He paid for his diplomacy with a day in the middle of his stay laid up with an upset stomach. Mike, who had boasted of his cast-iron stomach, was curled up in a bed in the room next to Bill's. They passed each other on their trips to the bathroom. This time his vigilance and his ascetic diet became another running joke among his Kenyan acquaintances. They recognized just two classes of people, feasters and fasters, and disapproved visibly of the latter. Had he become a monk in the meantime? Even the short excursions he kept a wad of toilet paper in his pocket. But no matter how careful he was, he could count on a rough patch at some point during a trip to an alien climate. He just tried to minimize the damage, and he thought he had averted a crisis on this trip with a day of Coke and water. On his last night, lying in bed, he was comfortable. He was pretty sure he could time his bathroom stops through the ride to Nairobi and the two long flights to follow. On the far side lay a homeland of gleaming tile and plumbing and gushing water to every side. And on his bedside table stood a vial of the magical Cipro.

But there was the bodily function he had forgotten about in the constant motion of the past two weeks. In the dimness and quiet of his room, his groin was aglow. It had long since become difficult to tell which prompted the other: the tugging ache from his vitals or the glimpse of thigh when a skirt was adjusted. Or maybe it was the woman's smile of apology but at the same time acknowledgment that followed. In the right state of deprivation, that would be enough. The suggestion, often innocent in itself, could come from anywhere, inside or outside. His brain was a little like the fortune-telling eight ball he had as a kid: turn it over and a cryptic message bobbed up from its oily black interior. The adult version was an image of a naked girlfriend. This time though the sensation was unattached, pure longing, almost the way it was at puberty, when a new, private recreation became available to him almost on demand. It turned out all his friends had discovered it independently at about the same time. They all assumed it would be temporary, but it persisted through adolescence and even into marriage and beyond, into early middle age at least. So, his attention claimed, he lay in his bed awake a little longer, stirred to life, straining into the Kenyan night, staring into the depths for the next image. But the slide show didn't start; the screen was blank. At first he was trying not to think of Zipporah. Then he allowed himself to. To his relief, he couldn't. Her image dissolved into the darkness and left him alone, and then asleep.

* * *

On their last day in Kenya the team would all attend the same church in Nyeri and then after a meal make the three-hour trip to Jomo Kenyatta Airport. The outbound flight was always at eleven at night. By the time they reached Nairobi, the drive would feel more like an evacuation, as they inched along the choked highway when they moved at all, one of a herd of matatus full of Kenyans, assailed by young women weaving on foot through the traffic begging with babies in their arms, followed by men hawking fruit or trinkets. Bill knew from experience to keep his window rolled up.

It would be a long morning of church, first a recognizable, hour-long worship service, then a two-hour service in Kikuyu that would include everything from testimony to an auction of produce from members' shambas. The week before Bill could sense that they had reached a high moment in the service, but he didn't know the occasion until someone came forward to hand money to the usher and carry a sack of yams over to lay at Bill's feet. He also received a cabbage and an enormous melon. He waved in gratitude and later handed over the tribute to his host family. Rev. Kerr was going to speak both times, with a translator at the second service. It was as close as he would ever come to being Billy Graham, he said. Bill would play the guitar he brought at children's time and then present it to Rev. Isaac for the church. He had played at other services. The children would come forward and gather around. Their faces, smiling and wide-eyed in anticipation, would turn solemn as he began to pick "I Belong to the Band." Piedmont-style, he would explain. He was bringing their music back to them. The ranks of adults standing behind them were just as rapt. If Rev. Kerr felt like Billy Graham, he was Rev. Gary Davis for a day. After he played for the first time on that trip, a boy reached out and stroked his hand, then pulled his own back and stared at it. Bill asked Rev. Mathias if the boy wanted to steal his ability to play guitar. "No," Rev. Mathias laughed. "He wanted to see if the white came off."

At the same service he would give away the ties. He brought that suitcase into the living room of the guest house as he got ready for church.

"You leave now?" John said, drying his hands on a towel as he entered from the kitchen.

"No," Bill said. "Not until a little later. These are the ties for the church. Remember?"

"Oh," John said. "The ties."

"For the elders."

"Oh." It was hard to tell if John was clarified or further mystified. "Can I see?"

"Sure. And it wouldn't be a bad idea for me to make sure I've got the right bag." He hadn't looked inside himself since the bag was handed over to him in the slushy parking lot of his home church on the asphalt-gray January day they had left for the airport.

This thought amused John; he threw his head back and yawned a laugh. "Oh, William. How do you say such things? You make my day, you know."

Bill opened the suitcase to reveal a tangle of ties that might have knotted themselves into a net during the trip. They were all different styles, probably none terribly fashionable even when they were new. On top was some kind of envelope or maybe more like a gift bag.

"What do you have, William?"

"I'm not sure." Bill opened it. "It's a tie. I suppose that's not surprising."

It was an old-fashioned regimental stripe, but it looked bright and new. The colors were blue and orange. College colors. The tag on the reverse read, *100% Seta Milano*. There was also a note: "For your collection. The Martin of neckties. Your fellow mzee, Mike."

"John, I need my daily *neno mpya*. My new word for the day. How do you say 'tie' in Kiswahili?"

"It is *shingo*."

"*Una shingo*, John? Do you have a tie?"

"*Hapana*. I do not have."

"*Hapa*. Here." Bill handed him the tie. "You may need it. You may be an elder in the church one day."

John took the tie in both hands and held it out for inspection. "Wow," he said.

"Now," Bill said. "Do you know how to tie a tie?"

Still gazing at it, John shook his head.

"Come into the next room," Bill said.

John followed him into one of the unoccupied bedrooms. There was a mirror on the back of the door, which Bill closed behind them.

"Stand in front of me," Bill said. "Let me have the tie. Now turn around."

THE LAST MIRACLE: INCIDENT AT NAIN

"Such a shame."

The others nodded in such a way as to say they could only nod.

"A young man of such parts," Gamaliel went on. "To hear him read in the synagogue. It is to hear Gabriel speak. And when he sings . . . "

"If I had a miracle to spare," Nathaniel said.

"A miracle to spare?" Moshe said. "You have squandered how many, then? And you had so many witnesses you did not bother to summon me?"

"The age of miracles is past," Gamaliel said. "There are no Elijahs among us."

"Are you so sure?" Nathaniel said. "Or do we fail to see them? Were you watching when the sun rose today?"

"You know what I mean," Gamaliel said. "I mean the kind of miracle we read about in the scrolls, when the Lord announces his presence unmistakably."

"For what exactly are you asking?"

"How about a sea split in two? Or a sun that does not rise and proceed across the sky as we expect—yes, perhaps jadedly—but stands still?"

"The Romans will tell you of miracles in abundance," Nathaniel said.

"Which they manufacture," Moshe said. "Let those words remain in the prayer house. There are prayers to go with them."

"Nor are there Davids among us," Nathaniel said.

"Why will the Lord not demonstrate his control of the cosmos?" Gamaliel said.

"Our demeanor is so grave today," Nathaniel said. "Yet Rabbi Yonathan is smiling at us. Perhaps he has heard these questions before. Or perhaps, ancient of days, you have seen a miracle."

"A sea unseamed?"

"Or such."

"How ancient do you think I am?" Their laughter flared before he spoke again. "I have seen one only."

"On the earth or in the heavens?"

"You will be disappointed. Nothing cosmic. Only a healing."

"But that is just the sort of miracle that is called for. Tell us."

* * *

"It isn't fair."

"An only child."

"An only son."

Even if he knew their names it would be pointless to identify the speakers. If he had heard these sentiments once he had heard them a dozen times and from the moment he set foot in this nondescript village where he was stopping on his journey from Nazareth, a dusty day's walk for a scholar. It was called Nain.

"What can be more sad than for a woman to lose her son?"

"A widow. And her only son."

"How will she live?"

The grief in the town was palpable, but what he sensed when he entered the town, like a breeze on a stifling day, was the bustle. He had arrived as though on a fair day. There was an event. The townspeople had purpose. They milled around a woman and the pallet a covered body lay on.

"To the cemetery," someone said, but prematurely. His remark was politely ignored, the forgivable gaffe of an enthusiast.

As everyone looked down at the woman's pathetic burden, the rabbi looked up. It was one of those days when earth and heaven are mismatched. The gauzy blue of the sky, streaked with light clouds, seemed moist and maritime. It should have been stretched over sails and docks, not the huddled brown houses of this town.

Then one of the townspeople with lowered gaze must have noticed the hem of his garment. "A rabbi among us," he said, and the cry was taken up by others, who turned to him. "Lead us to the cemetery," they said, and, "Will you pray at the grave?"

"I know prayers for the dead," he answered.

At that the crowd stirred. It was time at last. But on the way something else incongruous occurred, something like but unlike the divergence of landscape and sky, something as subtly unseasonable. Another crowd appeared ahead of theirs, emerging over the low horizon of the rolling road as though from the other side of the earth. Or it was as if two tides were rushing at each other. This one too swirled around a central figure, but it was a man walking. He was just of average height but nonetheless striking. The rabbi suspected he was either younger or older than he looked, but he could not be sure which. At his right and left hand smiling young men skipped sideways alongside him offering up pleasantries, undiscouraged even though they met with no response from their leader, only a dreamy alertness. They could have been two unruly armies joining battle, but instead they drew up short, without mingling. Except the leader, who never broke stride. He walked between these standing waves of humanity up to the mother, past the rabbi and the vanguard of her group, as though she were the destination of his riotous expedition. "Do not cry," he commanded her, not unkindly. He reached out his hand as though to brush tears from her cheeks. But already they were dry, and her eyes bright. Instead he laid it on the bier, which brought the bristling pallbearers to a standstill.

So strange, what happened. Strangeness upon strangeness. "Youth," he said. "I am telling you to rise." Yet when the man sat up, the veil fallen from his face, he looked no younger than the other, no one he should address as "Youth." He could have been looking at himself. And straightaway he spoke, he rose speaking, with the wide-eyed indulgence of his audience of one who recounts a dream before he is fully awoken from it. So strange and yet so natural that the rabbi forgot at first to be amazed at the least credible thing of all, that one deemed dead was alive.

And did the crowd react with joy? Anything but: they were terrified. The mother, as though it was she who was revived, gasped. The man turned the son to his mother for an awkward, armless hug; the man was not yet free of his winding sheet. The crowd came to itself in its turn and began to praise God and to chant, "A great prophet has arisen among us!" They embraced their visitors, who joined in the chorus: "God has looked upon his people." They were right, whether in their jubilation they knew it or not. More than a dead man had arisen. At his appearance in a small town, two mobs had become a population.

* * *

The elders sat and gazed out the window of the prayer house. Every face wore a smile of one inflection or another—irony, wistfulness, concession. Higher in the sky now, like a full pitcher carefully lifted, the sun poured light into the courtyard. The sharp-edged shadows of the surrounding buildings retracted.

"If only he were here."

"There he is."

Nathaniel and Moshe had spoken almost simultaneously. They all watched as their visitor stepped into the incandescent courtyard, a gaggle of boys around him. They would help him bring food to the poor and the widowed; then he would help them with their lessons. His Greek was very good, his Hebrew flawless. Yet he did not teach—formally—at their school or any other, as far as they knew. He had given them to know that he would be moving on. He was not young.

"How will he ever find a wife with a withered arm?" Nathaniel said.

"A withered right arm," Moshe said.

"Anyone who can raise the dead could restore a wasted arm. If only he were here," Nathaniel said once again.

"It was a miracle you witnessed, Rabbi Yonathan," Gamaliel said. "Perhaps the last."

* * *

For a moment the commotion of the streets spilled into their house, long enough for the son, still in his winding cloth, to be set on his bed and for the mother to be led to a bench. Men carried the son on his litter as though he were the ark, fearful of the slightest stumble. Then they were alone. After a minute, decisively, the woman stood up and busied herself around the room, straightening up as though for company.

"Mother," the young man said. "Rest. I have not been away long."

"But far away."

"Yes."

"I kept your scrolls where you left them."

"I see you have. Everything is much the same."

Then they both laughed, though the mother through the tears that sprang again from her eyes. The day before yesterday he had lain on that bed, inert.

"Let me help you," she said, fumbling for the end of the winding sheet. When she pulled it free, she gasped a second time that day.

"What is it, Mother?"

"I thought he would have healed you. He touched you. Why didn't he heal you?"

"Mother, listen, please," he said, hoping to calm her. But she bolted to the door and threw it open. The street in front of their house was empty. "I can catch him," the mother said, looking in either direction. "I can find him. He can't be far." Tatters of celebration remained in the air, a shout here and there. Or by now maybe just the cry of a merchant.

"He is gone," the son said.

"Yes," she said.

He called her to him and put his one good arm around her. "Mother. How can I be raised and not be healed?"

THE DISPUTATION

Bill couldn't decide if they were caricatures or not. Irving Wachsberg was as Jewish as it was possible to be, starting with his name. You didn't call him Irv. That was made clear in various ways, partly preemptively, in that he alone among their cohort of English graduate students called Bill William. He also dressed like a professor before the fact. Even though his duties as a teaching assistant were limited to leading discussion sections of large lectures, he did it in uniform, often in vest and tie, which he kept on the rest of the day. When he wore a yarmulke it seemed to match. A sport coat was about as far toward formal wear as most of the faculty would go. Facial hair was almost *de rigeur* in the department, but Irving sported the only goatee. The overall effect was one of almost old-world distinction and refinement. That he was so obviously after the effect made it tolerable, which was not to say it was tongue-in-cheek.

Bill wasn't quite sure how they had met, let alone become friends, which he would have to say they were. They had no classes together, being in opposite camps, across the great divide of the Enlightenment from each other. About as far apart as possible, in fact. Irving was a modernist, a theorist in search of a theory, he joked. The minute he found one, he intended to read some literature so he could apply it. Bill had entered graduate school resolved to eschew all affectations and also with the foreboding that that effort would constitute an affectation in itself, which proved to be the case. In the deferred adolescence that was grad school, avoid one mannerism and you fell into another. It was a time when his peers sprouted not just beards but accents: if you spoke very softly you could sound British. Bill accepted that he looked aberrantly normal. He wore the same khaki slacks and button-down Oxford-cloth shirts that saw him through a private suburban high school and an Ivy League college and another four-year term teaching in a New England prep school as he saved money for grad school. His penchant for swimming and basketball also branded him as All-American. The odd thing was that he was a medievalist, a fluent reader of Latin, which he had been forced to learn in school and turned out to love. To look at them, you would have thought Irving spent his time with musty rabbinic tomes while Bill read Hemingway between workouts. But Bill had taken the Hamlet-like credo of one of his college professors to heart: to be a medievalist is to be a comparativist. Your learning had to be Europe-wide, which Bill took as license to study other languages as well. He just didn't look the part of a medievalist, or of a scholar, period. Law students occasionally asked him about upcoming exams. Maybe that's why he and Irving got along: they were stereotypes switched at birth.

Though he was beginning his third year, Bill hadn't figured out how friends were made in the department. People did make friends. For instance, there were the jongleurs, the jocular medievalists, as he thought of them, a group of several of his fellow students who followed each other from seminar to seminar and outside of class spent inordinate amounts of time staging brown-bag lunchtime mock conferences where they read and analyzed parodies of lays and romances they composed for their mutual amusement. Bill would be swimming at the time. As far as he could tell the protocol for conversation among graduate students was to establish that, while you found your interlocutor's subject of study profoundly interesting and self-evidently significant, you knew absolutely nothing about it and could not be expected to know anything about it, since you were in an entirely different field and with luck a different millennium. There was no chance that your work—a favorite word—could impinge on anyone else's, or vice versa. It was possible to keep up this pretense even when you were in the same seminar discussing the same book. Everyone's angle on the text at hand was utterly unique, incommunicable, though it might find its way to expression in a dissertation. No one exactly stated a view. "It strikes me that" . . . "I'm troubled by this image" . . . "I have a sense that" . . . He felt a little sorry for the professors who had to keep this quivering mass of egos in the confines of a classroom, like the molds his mother used to pour jello into. He wondered if they ever felt like therapists. But he was in no position to be satirical. Everybody there was smart; they had all been following some truth glinting from books from grade school on. No wonder they were all scared of each other.

It was Irving who spoke first. "That looks good."

They were in the room housing the photocopier teaching assistants used, just a tinge of toxicity in the air from whatever chemicals percolated in the machine. Bill wasn't sure he was being spoken to until he realized they were momentarily the only two in the room. He had seen Irving around the building but had only recently learned he was not a professor. Then he couldn't figure out what he could be referring to. Not the stack of handouts he was stapling. When he turned inquisitively, Irving smiled and nodded toward the table where Bill had set a plastic glass and a bagel. The glass contained

Coke. Bill was also pointedly not a coffee drinker and so did not carry the ubiquitous mug around with him. Irving was indicating the second course of his breakfast; Bill had already eaten an apple.

"It doesn't seem that appetizing, now that I actually take a look at it," Bill said.

"Well, when you're fasting." Irving's smile was expectant, obviously inviting questions. But then he relented. "It's Yom Kippur. I'm observing." He did a half-pirouette so Bill could see his yarmulke.

"Of course," Bill laughed, implying he wasn't sure exactly what. That for once in his life the holiday had slipped his mind? That he hadn't known it was ever actually celebrated? "Remind me which comes first, Yom Kippur or Rosh Hashanah. I know there's a week in between."

Irving brightened. "That's more than most people know. Rosh Hashanah comes first. That's our New Year. Rosh means beginning in Hebrew."

"Okay. Sure. Rosh is the first word in the Bible. Or second, in Hebrew; third in English. *Bereshit*. In the beginning."

Irving's smile broadened. Actually Bill was being modest. During breaks at college he lifeguarded at the Jewish Y where he had swum AAU in high school. He enjoyed being the butt of Gentile jokes. "Ingram? What's that short for? Ingramstein?" His teammates decided he belonged to the Chlorinated branch of Judaism. He knew all the holidays, right down to Minhat Torah, because there was no practice those days. Meanwhile life went on as usual back in his suburb, the stores open and school in session. Succoth was his favorite. He loved driving in to practice on the sunny autumn days when booths blossomed on the lawns of the houses in that part of town. It was like a late, resident alien spring at the opening of a school year that stretched ahead of him like a desert. He decided to save his Jewish lore in the event of future conversations with Irving.

"And you're a modernist, isn't that right?" Bill said.

Irving grinned. "Guilty as charged. Mr. Medievalist. When did we get so boxed in? Remember when we just liked books? So am I not allowed to read Chaucer now?"

"After sundown," Bill said.

Irving was amused by that, more amused than Bill had seen him before, though he hadn't seen him that much. It was just that he had that stately bearing, actually always incipiently amused, wearing a half-smile that might just have been suggested by the goatee. Now that he stood next to him, Bill was surprised that Irving was a little shorter than he was; the slenderness gave an impression of height. Bill wasn't sure now how much of his distinctive appearance was ethnic and how much was academic. Irving was certainly not the only Jew on campus; it seemed you could spot a yarmulke someplace almost every day. But now he saw him as downright rabbinical.

They bumped into each other regularly from that point on. Irving stopped wearing the yarmulke but maintained his three-piece look. They taught a class at the same time, so they often jostled and jockeyed with other graduate students around the Xerox machine or their mailbox outside the department office. Or they might be checking a reference in the Brooks Room, the department's library-study-lounge. It had a mustiness suspiciously akin to a dormitory's. Graduate students seemed to form a nomadic tribe, living in who knew what off-campus hovel and biking in every day with all their possessions in a backpack. You wouldn't be surprised to find an abandoned campsite behind one of the couches. In conversation Irving referred to a car and an apartment. Bill's place was fairly close to the university in a neighborhood much like the one he had grown up in, except that there he lived in the house, not the garage. He had a nice bike, though, a ten-speed. He bought it with a view to training for triathlons, in case he ever felt the need to graduate from normality to hyper-normality.

At the Xerox machine a week or two after their first conversation Bill said, "I never congratulated you."

"For what?" Irving said. "No one could ever say about me that I pass up opportunities to be congratulated."

"You survived your fast."

"You're assuming I finished it." A styrofoam cup steamed on the table beside Irving's briefcase.

"I never doubted you."

"I did. It seems to get a little harder every year."

"The not eating is not so bad. It's no water that kills you. I mean, sort of literally."

Irving's eyes widened again. "You've observed?"

"Once."

Bill told him about his year as a lifeguard at the Jewish Y. To get in the spirit, he fasted on Yom Kippur, to the delight of some of the observant staff and the amusement of others.

"I sat up in my guard's chair looking out over the pool and dying of thirst."

"Water, water, everywhere," Irving grinned. "Didn't you stick out there? Could you be any more goy? Look at you. It's October and your hair is still bleached."

"There were a fair number of Gentiles on the staff, and the custodians were mostly black, so they closed early on holidays like Christmas and

Easter. That irked the devout members. Also the devout swimmers: everyone had to work out before noon. The pool looked like a salmon falls."

Irving shook his head. "So you drank no water. I'm impressed."

"Nothing is to pass the lips, right?"

"You're a Hasid," Irving said. "Now we'll get you circumcised."

"My parents took care of that long ago."

"I drink a little water," Irving said. "Wet my whistle."

"I won't tell our rabbi."

It was true that Bill was conspicuously non-Jewish at the Y. He continued to welcome the distinction when he worked there. One of the perks of the job was that he could continue to use the facilities, in fact more of them than when he was just on the swim team, and in the steam room and locker room the older members fussed over him. "He's an honorary Jew," one of them would say. "He could never be a Jew," another answered. "Look at that face." "Put a forelock on either side. You'll see." "Blond forelocks?" "Why not?" He took to reading the stories of Isaac Bashevis Singer. Then Israel Joshua Singer. He only wished they had other brothers writing about shtetls and dybbuks. He should be so lucky. His instinct was still to ration this material, keep some in reserve for later conversations with Irving.

"Gentiles fast sometimes, don't they?" Irving said.

"Not so strictly," Bill said. "My next-door neighbor growing up was Catholic. What they meant by fasting was they ate fish for dinner on Friday night. My family always had chicken, so my friend couldn't have dinner with us Friday night. Talk about sacrifice. They were so different. How could you live like that? Now, they did some serious fasting back in the Middle Ages, when men were men."

"And monks were monks."

"That's right. All week long they ate bread and water, but on the Sabbath they had breakfast—they broke their fast—with bread and water and salt."

Suddenly Irving looked impatient. Alarmed, Bill looked at the wall clock. They still had ten minutes before class. Maybe he had finally strayed into ant-Semitism. But it wasn't impatience; it was enthusiasm.

"This is too interesting. We need to discuss this over dinner," Irving said. "I know, I see the irony, too: discussing abstinence over dinner. But we do need to sit down and talk."

And so began the disputation.

* * *

It wasn't Bill's first such experience. He could remember other relationships that carved a cleft in the rockface of his life, far above and utterly removed from his daily round. From that aerie he could almost see himself far below carrying on his normal activities. During the winter between his sophomore and junior years in high school he had somehow obligated himself to visit the house of Nick Thompson, the other bright kid in his class—to ride out to his house on his bicycle, no less, since he didn't yet have his driver's license. On sunny weekday afternoons they sat in a dim, paneled basement and listened to records that Nick found particularly meaningful, particularly Leonard Cohen. Nick would pass the album covers over to Bill so he could follow the lyrics and consult the liner notes. He welcomed the relief from the soulful eye contact that Nick maintained. He was never quite sure what was expected from him by way of reaction, if anything, since the meaning of the songs seemed self-evident to Nick. Stunned silence appeared to suffice. Nick might also pull a cubical paperback off a bookshelf (the basement was also his bedroom), something by Ayn Rand or a science fiction writer, any alternative reality to the wasteland of the school year on either side of the summer. The margins of every page were embroidered with Nick's scrawl. He should have been the one to go on to read illuminated Bibles; he wound up in law school. When they did speak, they vaulted from one theory of life to the next, as though from stone to stone across the creek in the woods behind Bill's house, which he had probably been doing at that time the year before, though it seemed a lifetime ago from these seminars. In fact, someone else's lifetime ago. Bill would start to make his apologies a half-hour or so before he managed to get back on his bike. Some days he actually had another obligation—a lawn to mow or a shift at the community pool where he lifeguarded. His mood as he left would be desolated, as he felt was expected from him, whereas Nick was always pleased with the session and expected him back the next week. He would stand at the head of his driveway and wave as Bill pulled away. For as long as they lasted the meetings seemed immemorial, with neither beginning nor end, coeval with the foundation of the universe, part of the cosmic fabric. In retrospect they were a time capsule, an embossed carbuncle in the stream of his life. And over.

Or they hadn't begun. His discussions with Irving felt a little the same. Without quite knowing how, Bill found himself committed, maybe covenanted was the word, to Wednesday evenings with a sudden friend. It wasn't so much that he lost count of the sessions; more that they seemed to begin in progress, midway through a cycle. Too, there was the fear of fraudulence, the worry that their conversation would fray and the improbability of their friendship show through at some point. The difference was that these sessions were enjoyable. They were convivial. He and Irving had plenty to talk about. Instead of two intellectual eminences speaking across the linoleum abyss of a suburban gameroom, they were boulevardiers getting together every week in a different restaurant of the many around the university, surrounded by other couples in equally earnest discussion. The conversations were parallel yet somehow performed for the general benefit. At every table an existential breakthrough seemed imminent.

"Of course you know what we have in common," Irving said as they sat down the first evening.

"Besides our marginal niche as English graduate students far down the scale of being?" Bill said. "Clinging lichen-like to the bark of one of the outermost trees in the academic rain forest?"

"That, too," Irving smiled.

Though in fact their surroundings belied that taxonomy. The inaugural disputation, though they weren't using the term yet, took place at a small Cuban restaurant on the main drag that bordered the campus. Bill had biked by it many times without imagining he would ever eat there. The people sipping coffee at the sidewalk tables in milky morning sunlight did indeed look as though they might be Cuban. Inside on that night however all the patrons seemed as gringo as they did, though actually in his vest and goatee Irving had something of the air of a grandee. It wasn't a string tie he was wearing, but it was skinny.

"To the one side, we are lackeys to professors," Bill said. "To the other, we are despised by undergraduates."

"You're saying that our enemies surround us."

"They make mouths at us."

Irving beamed. "And it's not that we're both psalmists. It's that we're both minorities." He pulled up short. "Don't you hate that expression? 'We welcome minorities.' Look at any job description. 'We particularly welcome applications from minorities.' These ads are presumably written by educated people. What, do they expect an entire race to apply? They mean 'from members of a minority.' Everyone is a minority of one."

"You're looking at job postings?" Bill said. "You must be farther along than I am. My dissertation feels like a float I got on with a volume of the *Summa Theologiae* for beach reading and then got washed out to sea. When I looked up I couldn't see the shore behind me or anything on the horizon ahead. I've got a lot of note cards. They'll make nice jetsam when I go down."

"My advisor gave me one piece of excellent advice," Irving said. "'You can't start to write too soon.' Even if you don't know what you want to say. I figure you also can't begin to look for jobs too soon. Even if there are no jobs out there on the horizon. If I may borrow your metaphor."

"We're both white," Bill said. "So are we the famous majority minority? That's what they say about California, you know. If there's not already there soon will be a majority of minorities. Still predominantly white, but whites will be outnumbered by all the minorities combined."

"That's not what I was thinking."

"Am I getting warmer?"

Irving motioned to a waiter. Bill deferred to him here; he had suggested the restaurant and seemed to know the staff.

"You're Jewish," Bill said when they had their menus. "Observant. We've established that. What am I, too average?"

"True but wrong," Irving said. "You're Christian."

"You knew I'm a medievalist. You know I'm a Christian. Am I that transparent?"

"A medievalist I might not have guessed by looking at you," Irving said. "I might have said Americanist, but that would have been too easy. Maybe eighteenth-century British. But come on. You have Christian written all over you."

Their food came. To the amusement of both Irving and the waiter, Bill finally recognized his dish as what he had ordered. Both their meals included rice and beans, but everything else was unfamiliar to him.

"So how does that constitute something we have in common?" Bill said. "Jewish and Christian. Doesn't that make us antagonists?"

"We're people of faith," Irving said. "To a Muslim we would look identical—people of the book."

"The same enough to slaughter each other."

"Voilà. Our faiths, albeit different faiths, make us both outsiders here, wouldn't you say? It's not that the university welcomes all religions, however it phrases it. It has its own official religion. And it's not knowledge, whatever their catalogues say. It's self-fulfillment. If your faith gives you a sense of identity, that's great. It doesn't matter which one it is. Naturally, the more atrophied, the more vestigial, it is, the better. You're Jewish. All right. You've been oppressed. Orthodox Jewish? Interesting. Druze? Wonderful. We can check that box. Just don't imply that your religion is true. And that's ironic, because didn't the university grow out of the monastery?"

"It did. You know something about the Middle Ages, don't you?"

"A couple of courses in college. I always thought that if I hadn't become a modernist I might have been a medievalist. I'm sure you've observed that we learned how to read poetry from the way all those monks and rabbis interpreted the Bible. We all do midrash. We're forever taking scripture—Ginsburg is holy writ for us—out of one context and putting it in another."

"Or peshat," Bill said. "That's the opposite. The Jewish version of exegesis: keep it in context, construe it in its own terms. Find out what the words meant when they were written to the people who were writing them. Explain one verse of the Bible with another, if you can. Works for poetry, too."

With one hand Irving took a fountain pen from the breast pocket of his shirt while with the other he reached inside his jacket for his wallet. "That was 'peshat?'" he said. When he couldn't find a note card to write on he pulled out a bill.

"Do you always gloss your money?" Bill said. "You didn't tell me you were a Masorete."

"That word could be worth twenty bucks in my dissertation. And you might end up in a footnote."

"I'll up the ante," Bill said. "To me all you modernists seem like kabbalists. Everything's in code. Only the illuminati can have any idea what a poem is about. Literature is a closed, arcane universe. Poems are about each other, not life."

"Touché," Irving said. "And that is the last French you get out of me tonight. You're the language person. If I haven't already, I'd like to thank you for salting my field of study and life's work as a modernist."

"Any time."

Bill liked about their agenda that it was in a field neither of them claimed expertise in. He was happy and even eager to steer the conversation away from literature in general and the middle ages in particular. He might be expected to know something on the subject. That was the thing about graduate school: everyone's dissertation topic seemed more interesting than yours. It followed that their lives were more meaningful than yours. They seemed to find your topic fascinating, too, and furthermore to know more about it than you did. They liked nothing better than to call to your attention books you were unaware of that you might find pertinent and that you suspected on the basis of the title said everything you intended to.

"It has occurred to me more than once as I sit in my carrel, or cell, in the bowels of the library under the quad, or cloisters, that we're a lot like those abbeys," Bill said. "They started so well. A few hermits in the desert (that's what "hermit" means) get an idea: Let's go somewhere and contemplate alone together. The idea was simple, to allow people to work and pray. Prayer and work, that's all life consisted of, and everybody did both. Then the fall. The original sin: specialization."

"Ouch," Irving said. "I mean, ooch. *That* will be my last French word tonight."

"Sorry," Bill said. "I didn't mean to be brandishing my fork."

"I think I see where we're going with this."

"If we realize some people are better at some things than at others, and get some peasants to do the hoeing, which they're good at and don't seem to mind doing, see, that frees up some people to do the crafts and calligraphy, and the rest of us can get down to some serious praying. Or up to something else."

"Any analogy to the modern university there?"

"Now that you suggest it, as far as I can tell our professors spend all their time at conferences or on sabbatical. Or at cocktail parties. They found peasants to till the fields of freshman composition, their 'junior colleagues.'"

"I love it when they call us that," Irving said.

"They also found their cottage industry. That's called college football. And television rights. And the tee shirts. We've got a gift shop on campus right next to the chapel. My parents get their catalogue, and I haven't even graduated yet, for Christ's sake—and in this context that's not an oath."

Irving put up his hands in mock submission. "I'm convinced already."

"Every department has its own gospel. Study literature; it will set you free. Read this novel: see how redeemed the characters are? Maybe you can be that redeemed someday. Major in sociology: you will see through the sacred canopy to the denuded reality beyond and live an illusion-free, authentic life."

"What did Chesterton say?"

"How would I know?" Bill said. "He was Catholic. So how would you know?"

"He said, 'When people stop believing in God, they don't believe in nothing. They believe in anything.'"

"Amen."

"So you're saying a Reformation is due and overdue for the university."

"Absolutely. Just don't quote me on that before I get my degree."

Irving switched the salt and pepper shakers. "Recording devices off." He had been eating during Bill's diatribe and was finishing up his dinner. "So," he said, setting down his silverware. Tonight has been an organizational meeting, shall we say? Just agenda-setting. Shall we also agree to meet for dinner on Wednesday nights to pursue matters such as how to observe one's faith in a hostile environment and whether our two disparate faiths can or should be allies in that effort or whether because of their tenets and truth claims they are irreconcilable, exploring in the process at what points they might in fact be reconcilable? To that end we will confess our faiths to each other.

"Does that call for a second?" Bill said.

"It calls for dessert," Irving said, dishes that turned out to be less identifiable still than the entrées. When the bill came, Irving put on half-moon glasses and scrutinized it. It was the most scholarly he had looked all evening. Satisfied, he pulled out a credit card.

"I'm going to get me one of them someday," Bill said.

"It help when your father's a banker," Irving said, and handed him the bill. "That's what you owe. You can just pay me."

"I hope you're not a big tipper," Bill said.

"Half a reasonable tipper," Irving smiled over his glasses.

* * *

Every other Tuesday afternoon Bill visited one of the two readers of his apparitional dissertation. Given his subject, the medieval romance, it was fitting that his thesis materialize before him, bound and sealed, as long as he talked with Frank in his office, then dissipated into the sunlight as soon as he found himself back on the quad.

"William!" Frank exclaimed when he appeared in the doorway.

Unlike Irving, Frank ordinarily called him Bill. He must just have been feeling hale that day. Bill had learned in his dealings with academics to expect long stretches of awkwardness and abstraction punctuated by bursts of comradeliness. Frank was lounging in his chair with his boots propped up on a bare, gleaming desktop. The shelves behind him held a number of massive volumes that on closer inspection proved to be bound prewar journals and dictionaries of dead languages, even an old phone book or two. Frank called the office his storefront: "I wouldn't dream of trying to do any serious work in this madhouse." Actually the building was quiet as a crypt anytime Bill got up to the second floor, which was lined with doors, all closed, their frosted windows dimmed. Each had a typed index card taped in a corner announcing office hours, indicating that the offices were occasionally occupied. Sometimes Bill saw a professor locking up. They always looked furtive, on the run. He half-expected them to throw a hand up over their eyes to avoid being photographed. In fact, their pictures were often right next to them on a poster advertising their appearance at a conference or a new book.

"Have you talked to Warren?" Frank liked to establish that first thing. Warren Hartline was his other reader.

"Day after tomorrow."

"Oh, yes. I remember. I'm Tuesday, he's Thursday. Got your swim in, I trust."

"Sure. At noon. You?"

"The lifeguards keep moving me over a lane, closer and closer to the wall. I'll be in the gutter before long. Why don't they do something about those people who keep passing me at breakneck speeds?"

Bill had seen his advisor in the pool once. In his development as a swimmer he was just on the cusp between treading water and doggy paddle, and he had not grasped the concept of circle swimming. It was just like driving, Bill had explained, down on the right and back on the right, and it worked best when everyone was going roughly the same speed. Or at least going forward, he could have added. Furthermore, the lanes were fastest in the middle of the pool and progressively slower outward toward either wall. His instruction didn't seem to be taking.

"Did they change the water recently?" Frank asked.

"I don't think they drain the pool very often, if that's what you mean. The water is always circulating."

"I think it feels all full of sweat."

"That's the chlorine, I guess." Bill meant to be reassuring, but Frank seemed disappointed. And when he mentioned his thesis Frank looked downright crestfallen. Their sessions in his office were just like his seminars, which he began by discussing any topic but the assigned one and then following any false trail available: "It's not clear what the relationship between his father and his patron *was*." He didn't seem sure why all these people had assembled around the long table when they all had such command, albeit unspoken, of the subject. After an hour or so he would offer a few observations on the author of the day, suggesting that they glance at a passage, and then end up keeping the class forty-five minutes late. Once he got going he was interesting and engaging and sometimes brilliant. Maybe he was inspired by the late afternoon fall sunlight fading into dusk and then pitch black outside the window. His specialty was penance, and he made sure his students paid it.

On this late afternoon in his office they also finally got down to business, and, typically, Frank slipped him a typewritten sheet by way of conclusion. "You might find these references helpful." It was that week's lifetime's work, a list of about thirty books and articles to read. Frank had written three of them.

"Thanks," Bill said. "Can you direct me to the nearest hermitage?"

Frank laughed. "Good one, young William."

"I only ask because I will get a similar bibliography from Warren." Which would contain a few articles by him.

"Yes, naturally," Frank said. "I think I would start with these, and my two articles in particular. Well, you won't get their full benefit unless you read my book first. It's early work, admittedly, but it will give the articles context. Please don't mistake me. Warren is immensely learned, and I have nothing but respect for his work. We owe him an enormous debt in the field. I have profited from it hugely myself. However I can't help but feel that his theories on the subject of romance are not just wrong but wrong-*headed*, if you know what I mean. The genre is ready for a different approach altogether. Are you still seeing Irving Wachsberg?"

Bill had forgotten that Frank was the master not just of the digression but of the non sequitur. "I wouldn't say that either 'still' or 'seeing' is the right word. We met for dinner last week. Were you at the restaurant?" Bill hadn't recognized anyone there that night.

"Word gets around the department. Irving is rather a presence, isn't he? As a medievalist I've had nothing at all to do with him academically. No one dresses like him. Those three-piece suits. What material are they? Gaberdine? All he's missing are the phylacteries."

"He takes his religion seriously."

"His religion or his ethnicity? It's so hard from the outside to tell the difference. I suspect from the inside, too." He shivered. "Mustn't be anti-Semitic, especially on this faculty. And I'm not." To judge from asides in the course of his seminars, it was equally important to Frank that he was raised Catholic and that he was a lapsed Catholic.

"I think in his case it's religion," Bill said.

"And I'm not criticizing," Frank said. He himself favored jeans and a leather jacket along with his boots. Bill recognized the ensemble as stylish without being sure what the style was. The look was maybe a little youthful for Frank, who was getting soft in the middle and thin on top. He could make the move to tweed at a moment's notice.

"In fact, we plan to meet regularly to discuss faith in general and each other's faith in particular."

"Just be careful."

"I don't imagine either of us will convert."

"And you might jot something down for our next meeting."

"The week after next?"

"It turns out I have a meeting that day. These committees. The university invents them all the time to prevent us from getting any work done. Let's say the week after that. Well, check with me."

* * *

They convened their second dinner in a deli. Here too Irving seemed to be in his element. He leaned back in his side of the booth and breathed deeply. "We could be in Zabar's," he said.

"Zabar's?" Bill said.

"That's a famous deli on the West Side. All kind of writers hung out there in its heyday. Jewish writers. Bellow. Mailer. Roth. You name them, they were there. Not that they were necessarily good Jews. Good writers, okay. But we've got our own cenacle going. Shall we dispute before or after our food comes?"

After, they decided, and that became protocol. Pleasantries and departmental politics first; then down to creeds and confessions. When they had arranged their plates in front of them and taken a few bites, they began to gesture rather than eat with their silverware.

"I guess we should decide whether the disputations will be binding," Bill said.

"How do you mean?" Irving said.

"In the Reformation these affairs were for real. Live ammo."

Between bites Irving's expression was dramatically quizzical.

"A town somewhere in Germany would call in a Catholic and a Protestant, they would make their theological cases, and there would be a vote. The town would adopt the winning religion."

"As its official religion? Interesting."

"As everyone's religion. It was winner take all. Naturally every citizen had to practice the same faith."

"Fascinating. Also appalling."

"It was probably an improvement over the old way, when everyone practiced the ruler's religion. There were ways for the minority to get around the ruling. You could organize an *Auslauf*. If you were a Protestant in a Catholic town, or vice versa, you could gather a bunch of your coreligionists and walk over to the next town, which very likely observed the opposite faith, and worship there."

"A Protestant parade," Irving said. "Sounds festive."

"They still have them in Ireland. Not so festive. Or you could find a hedge preacher. Follow him out of town just to the other side of the boundary and hold your service."

"So you think to have a proper disputation we need to vote after dinner?"

"I suppose so."

"I foresee a certain number of ties." Irving smiled.

"That's the first problem, though, isn't it? How do you approach interfaith dialogue? Sounds good in theory, but is it practically possible? Do you really expect to change the other person's mind? Because it's not just his mind you have to change."

"Or hers," Irving said. When that brought Bill up short, Irving winced in apology. "I'm not trying to be politically correct. Hey, it's just two guys here. I just mean there can be all kinds of dynamics in play. Sexual, social, personal. Isn't that what you're getting at?"

"Exactly. It's not as though all you're doing is asking the person to assent to an intellectual position. Jesus is divine. Bodily resurrection follows death. My religious beliefs are all tied up with the linoleum floor of my Sunday school classroom, the attendance cards in the pews, which I used to write notes on to my mother, my grandfather singing tenor. In a bow tie. God came to me in all those things. You must have equivalent memories. But they must be very different."

"Yes. You didn't mention Friday prayers chanted by my uncle. Who knew Hebrew about as well as he knew Martian. But devout? For one thing, I would say you are unusual among Christian apologists in that it would occur to you that other perspectives on the divine exist."

"Perhaps I am not called to be a Christian apologist."

"Called," Irving said. "Now you're speaking my language. Jews are called. In fact, we have all the 'c' words: call, covenant, creation. Combine them almost any way you want. Let's throw in chosen. Different sound, but we'll call it sight alliteration."

"You're the poetics guru. Or rather rabbi."

"We modernists cut some corners on occasion. And I'd better quit with the 'c' words. Or 'q.' Abraham, Moses, Gideon. All called. Not to mention the prophets. Sometimes rather dramatically. From a burning bush, no less."

"And Jesus called his disciples. But literally. In person."

"All Jews. That's what I'm not sure all Christians see. How Jewish your scriptures are. What is it with this Old Testament? What's so old about it? For Jews there is no other testament. Just the Bible. Then some commentaries in Greek."

"And as a Christian I should practice charity."

"You can start by picking up the tab."

"Not that kind of charity," Bill said, but Irving had already winced again, this time to acknowledge a bad joke. "Should I be open to every person I meet, love him in his totality, including his faith? Or hers?"

Irving raised a hand. "'Him' is good from now on. Remember, just us guys here. But you're right, if I could just pick up on one of your words. How could or should you approach religious discussion? That's something we might want to consider. Open to conversion yourself? Vulnerable, so to say?"

"Some people claim that that if you're willing to discuss religion with someone else in the first place you're already converted. That's a conversion in itself. You've opened up, turned to, oriented yourself to the other."

Irving shivered. It was Bill's turn to wince. "Other" was one of the words no graduate seminar could be conducted without the liberal use of.

"I don't know," Irving said. "I've heard theories like that. Conversion is a continuum, a process rather than event, gradual not instantaneous, a series of steps—openness, etc. All right. I still say one of those steps is a big one, across a chasm."

"I'm not saying I accept that view," Bill said. "More the opposite, in fact. I like to enter interfaith dialogue—well, 'like to'; this may be my first— admitting, announcing that I have no intention of converting."

"Wouldn't that preclude dialogue? 'Jesus is Lord.' 'No, he's not.' End of discussion."

"I knew you'd bring up Thomas More sooner or later," Bill said.

"Sooner than I thought," Irving said. "How did he get into this conversation?"

"He could turn up anywhere: he's an in-between kind of guy. A Renaissance humanist who wanted to be a monk, a Catholic on the sill of the Reformation, a lawyer who wore a hair shirt. He imagined a long religious discussion, and I mean long, called *A Dialogue Concerning Heresies*. He knew he couldn't talk to Luther, for the reason you mentioned—they disagreed on first principles. You think it's a challenge for a Jew and a Christian to talk today? From here they both look like Christians, but they each thought the other followed a false or more like alien religion. So More debated by proxy, with his son-in-law, who just had Protestant leanings. He caught him when he could still be reasoned with. But I say that's the beginning of dialogue, because I would expect and invite the other person to adopt the same stance. I would not be expecting him to convert, either. Let's just talk and see what happens. Maybe more talk. And that's good."

Irving shrugged reflectively.

"Because another thing that happens is that you learn about your own faith when you have to explain it to someone else. Your own faith is deepened."

"So, if it works the way you say, you've got two people farther apart than they were to start with. That seems like the opposite of what you intended. Maybe that's why we're not in seminary. We're studying literature. We can just express or immerse ourselves in all these points of view, then go out and teach them, without converting ourselves or anyone else. We're like evangelists who don't close the deal. I'm glad you're not hard sell. I have to say you make Christianity very appealing. I don't know how much of that is Christianity and how much is you."

"To be honest, I can see how you could convert to Christianity. Not so much how I could convert to Judaism. Is that even possible? Don't you have to be born into that faith?"

"We're Jews, not Druze," Irving said. "Of course you can convert. But that will have to wait."

"Till the general resurrection?" Bill said.

"Until after the election."

At first Bill didn't know what he meant.

"The vote," Irving said. "We still don't know who is converting."

"I forgot. The vote," Bill laughed, and then they decided they really hadn't disputed that night, they had just discussed discussion, though true enough in formal disputations all the genuine, unforced dialogue often took place during the ground rule-setting phase of the proceedings, and the ground rules set could determine the results of a colloquy before the first exchange, but none the less they would postpone the vote, and that became another running joke, the perpetually postponed vote. They had long since finished eating, and they both had meetings with their advisors the next day. Irving had a chapter to show his; Bill was just hoping to get some notes together between now and then.

* * *

His meetings with his other advisor, Warren Hartline, also took the form of dinners, which were followed by more or less withering reviews of Bill's progress on his dissertation. Convivial these evenings were not, more like entering a void out the other side of which Bill might or might not emerge intact. The challenge of these sessions was different from the one he might face with Irving. It wasn't conversion he had to resist but complete dis-solution of his ego. Warren lived in a sprawling suburban compound just within biking range of the campus, and when the weather was good Bill preferred to get himself out there, over Warren's protest at the distance. Bill would pass it off as his exercise, though he did his serious cycling during the day in full regalia with fellow triathletes. Sometimes on the way he felt he might be travelling back in time to his friend Nick Thompson's base-ment, eternally pedaling to strange symposia. When it rained, as it did on this evening, Warren came in to pick him up. They always met at his house. Bill had been in his office only once; it made Frank's look homey. "I spend as little time breathing an atmosphere of mediocrity as possible," he said on that occasion. As they drove, Bill glanced at him occasionally from the passenger's seat. It still surprised him to see a scholar of Warren's stature do anything as pedestrian as driving. As pedestrian as driving: Bill congratulated himself on coining that paradox, just for the fact that his brain hadn't seized up in the backdraft of his advisor's. Though that metaphor probably wasn't as successful. On the first such trip they had had to stop at the supermarket. It was even more of a shock to see Warren striding the aisles of the store with a shopping basket on one arm. When he stopped to take an item off a shelf and slipped on his reading glasses he could have been poring over manuscripts rather than expiration dates. For most of the drive their gazes were as parallel as the headlights, converging only in a utopian future where people understood the Middle Ages for what they were, the real Renaissance. That was the title of Warren's book in progress. Once in a while they shared a laugh, usually at the expense of other, benighted medievalists. That was the equivalent of clicking on the high beams for a glimpse onto a prospect of shopkeepers and mechanics breaking into proper middle English to quote Chaucer back and forth. "Things just haven't been right since the Great Vowel Shift," Warren liked to lament.

Somewhere on either side of sixty, Warren was a big man, even strapping, and he squeezed behind the steering wheel of his car as though into the cockpit of a biplane, glowering straight ahead into the diatribe against intellectual decline that he had prepared for the evening. Bill was glad to be to the side, out of that strafing gaze. When they reached his place they didn't get past the garage, which was also his library. The big upstairs room came complete with stacks, which held works in English; each of the freestanding bookcase was devoted to a different Romance language. There was also a reference section. His holdings in music were less organized, at least to the untrained eye: CDs lay around in stacks on every available surface. Warren picked one up and put it on. Unsurprisingly, it was a mass by William Byrd. "Listening to this is like watching a cathedral being erected in your house," he would say. He always offered Bill sherry, which he always declined in favor of a glass of water now and some wine with dinner.

Ever aware that the critique of his thesis awaited, Bill made his best effort to lounge in an easy chair across from Warren's. As always, Warren wanted to know first about his last session with Frank. "I see," he would muse. "Now, look, you're on solid ground with Frank. He can help you get a footing in the field. One thing we can confidently say about our friend Frank is that he has a firm grasp of the obvious. Vise-like, in fact. And I mean that in the best possible sense. We need people who can process and transmit information. We have our scribes. They are the ground bass of our discipline, you might say." He inclined his head for a minute to

catch a phrase of the music and smile. "That resolution. "Sacramental is
the only word for it." Then it was back to business. "From the foundation
that people like Frank provide, others can soar. The soaring is best left to
others, however, if I may be permitted a chiasmus. Mind you, I voted for
Frank for tenure. I could hardly have not: I was the chair of the committee
that brought him in. I never dreamed others would vote for him as well."
He looked over the reading list Frank had given Bill. "Let me suggest a few
adjustments." Pen poised, he seemed to have a change of heart. "Perhaps
we should just start with this one," he said, and handed Bill a fresh sheet.
"These will put the others in perspective, if indeed you ultimately need
them. We'll get to your thesis after dinner."

Bill followed him down some outside steps, across the weedy yard and
through a side door of the house, where there were some hallways to negoti-
ate, all with outcroppings of bookcases, some of them packed with old paperbacks that looked one step from compost. He knew to expect company
in the kitchen, possibly already seated, but introductions were not part of
household protocol. His first evening he and Warren had been joined at the
table by a woman Bill only gradually realized was Mrs. Hartline. The house
that seemed so deserted from the outside turned out to be swarming with
people, like one of the enchanted forests in the romances he studied. He got
used to passing people in the halls with an averted nod. They would show up
again at dinner. All table talk was conducted in asides to Warren. It counted
as a conversation in so far as one aside might allude to another. It was like a
boarding house, only less intimate. Bill assumed the other males were also
students, though he learned on one drive back that that night's unfamiliar
dinner guest was Warren's half-brother, a climatologist back from a rain forest. "The fruit of a family distressed and ultimately fragmented by divorce
and so forth," Warren said into the headlit night.

After dinner, that evening's guests dispersed again into whatever recess
or wing of the compound, while, to the strains of Gluck this time—"here's
your avant-garde, if you want one; Mozart just dotted the quarter-notes"—
Warren and he adjourned to the cavernous, dimly-lit living room. It had the
same basic décor as the library but retained a really rather pleasant smell of
wet ashes, and in fact Wesley lit a fire "to take off the chill." They sat side-by-
side on a long couch, Bill's slender sheaf in Warren's lap. Warren seemed to
like to extend an evening with these discussions, just when Bill was getting
logy. Not so torpid that his ego wasn't quivering at the prospect of criticism.
At least Warren had to be on his guard, too, since Bill had one advantage
over him that could drop him to his knees in a second: he knew Greek,
and he might have slipped a phrase or two into this instalment. Among the
books scattered around this room were all manner of Greek dictionaries,

grammars, texts with interlinear translations. "Someday," Warren was wont to say with a sweep of his arm at any nearby bookshelves, "I will set all this aside and get a real education. I will put myself on the right side, on Bernard Berenson's side. You know what he said: there are two kinds of people in the world—those who know Greek and those who don't. At the Harvard of his day, long before I got there, you started with Assyrian and worked your way on up. Learning Assyrian, he said, was as dry as chewing tree bark. Not Greek, I feel sure. It's a tough nut to crack, but the meat is sweet."

"Don't feel too bad," Bill would say. "Remember, Aquinas didn't know Greek."

"I know, I know. Neither did Augustine. Neither did Petrarch. He possessed a copy of Homer in the original. When he opened it, he wept because he couldn't read it. And look at me. I own every Greek edition of Homer there is. I should spend my days sobbing."

"You will drench your couch with your weeping."

Warren glanced at him sharply, either because he didn't recognize the allusion to the Psalms or because he did. "In the meantime, you shall be my Grosseteste."

And Bill was happy to translate words and phrases for him. For those few seconds that Warren watched Bill at work, his gaze became blissful, beatific, adoring. True, if Bill quoted from the New Testament with any trace of conviction, suspicion would flicker in the gaze.

On this night, with his shoulders hunched, his glasses low on his nose and his favored green fountain pen in his hand, Warren perused the few paragraphs Bill had managed to generate for the occasion. He could have been back in the passenger seat of Warren's car, straining his peripheral vision to catch Warren's reaction. He couldn't assume Warren was as comatose as he looked; by now he knew that his posture of profound rumination was identical to his posture of profound slumber. By contrast, not just Bill's eyes but his whole body down to the flimsiest tendon was as tense as on his first visit with the recognition that once again he had landed himself in the situation he had so often been cautioned against: he was alone with a male college professor. At night, on a couch, no less. Would his knowledge of Greek prove defense or aphrodisiac? But he gradually relaxed, too. Aside from the fact that Warren was married, albeit not very demonstrably or demonstratively, with a couple of grown children off somewhere, he suspected that for Warren these after-dinner critiques with students were not some elaborate foreplay in advance of a seduction but erotic events in themselves.

After a while Warren stirred and peered straight ahead, as though through a windshield. "Yes, quite fantastic. To see through the veil of Christianity to the foundations of a culture, which are ultimately legal, of course. Draped with covenants, swathed in liturgies and creeds, one laid over the last, which then is barely discernible. What did Mallarmé say? The sacred must be clothed in mystery? And yet, despite that, the hoi polloi—that's redundant, isn't it? As you taught me once, since hoi means 'the' in Greek? So: despite that hoi polloi believe. Because of that hoi polloi believe. And obey. Remarkable. From legal code to religion to romance. Fictions all. You may be on to something."

He slumped back into meditation. Bill didn't quite see how that rhapsody could have been inspired by anything he said in his paper, but insofar as it seemed approving he welcomed it.

Warren came to again, this time to offer Bill the highest accolade he had yet received from him. "This is reasonable," he said. "Perfectly reasonable."

* * *

"I think that Christians overemphasize faith."

For all his formal attire and stately bearing, Irving was as far from arrogant as possible, so *ipso facto* not really all that academic. He didn't have the pseudo-apologetic stammer that often went with the beard. That was one thing Bill liked about him. The veneer was high-gloss but transparent. The main thing, he would have to admit, is that against all likelihood Irving seemed to like him. Bill found it much easier to discuss matters of the mind with him than in a seminar. Maybe it was because they acknowledged they were stereotypes going in; maybe it was because Irving seemed so professorial, whereas their teachers often tried to appear as much like students as possible. Still, he couldn't imagine a more improbable pair at a restaurant table. The choice on this night was Chinese, and it was frequented by other people from the university. As they made their way to their booth they took turns waving at people one or other of them, but usually not both, knew. It had a little of the feel of a high school dance you brought an unexpected date to.

After his opening remark, Irving sat back in his seat with an expression somewhere between self-satisfaction and mischievousness.

"So *that's* the trouble with Christians," Bill said.

"Well, I didn't say 'trouble,'" Irving said, but his smile broadened.

"I know. That was a favorite expression of a pastor of mine at the church where I grew up. It was right next to a seminary."

"I'll bet that explains a lot about you."

"You could count on several theologians in the pews on any given Sunday. The sermons often nodded to them. This particular guy loved to shake them up from the pulpit. Everyone else, too. 'The trouble with Christians is' . . . Fill in the blank. 'The trouble with Christians is they want people to have sex in public.'"

"That's a topic for our next series of disputations."

"He meant that congregations want to keep a lid on sex. They want to know who's sleeping with whom. But they don't want to ask. They don't want to pry. Church discipline is a dirty word. It could be an act of love, but privacy is sacrosanct these days. So how can you know? Marry them to each other."

It occurred to Bill mid-argument that another thing unusual about their meetings was that they didn't discuss women. Two male graduate students getting together and a subtext of their conversation was not sex, its absence or imminence in their separate lives. He liked that, too.

"Interesting," Irving said. "Your pastor sounds like a provocateur."

"A prophet, I think he would have said. There's bad news, and there's good news."

"A comedian, then."

"Not really. The news comes in that order, unlike most jokes. First you have to be convicted. Scared of damnation to within an inch of your life. Conscious of your sin."

"Sin. That's another word you don't hear much anymore. Is it still legal to use? I thought it went out with 'mentally retarded.' People can't be sinful. That would be an awful thing to say about someone. Maybe 'morally challenged.'"

"I've got another word for it. But it's Greek."

"I like it better already."

"One of the words in the New Testament we translate as 'sin' is *hamartia*. It comes from a verb used in archery when you miss the target."

"Fascinating. So you might be aiming at something good."

"But fall short. It happens to be the same word in Aristotle that gets translated—not too accurately, either—as 'tragic flaw.'"

Irving raised his hands palm-upward. He looked on the point of applauding.

"So 'sin' shouldn't be so saturated with guilt," Bill said. "However, that doesn't mean that we can define sin out of existence. We still need to be saved from it, and we can't do it ourselves. What Christians worry about in Judaism is the implication that you can decide to be righteous. Just go out and follow the law. But the harder you try, the more hypocritical you get. That's a law, too."

"In California? The land of license?"

"In Romans. Paul said he found a law in his members: what he did not want to do, he did; what he did want to do, he didn't. It sounds to me like impedance."

"'Impedance,'" Irving said. "Is that Greek, too?"

"It's the one thing I remember from my college physics class. Alternating current produces its own resistance. It's proportional to voltage, if memory serves. The more juice you pump into a circuit, the harder it gets to move it through. Human effort to do good works against itself. We need to be picked up out of the whole morass. That's where faith comes in. We need to look outside ourselves."

"But maybe not that far," Irving said. "We Jews keep it simple. For us it's the three Bs. Belong, behave, believe. In that order. We put faith last, not first. Christianity is unusual among religions in that respect, you may not have noticed. I have my issues with Islam, but faith doesn't play a big role in there, either. Jews experience God in community first. We don't ask people to assent to propositions or have any kind of conversion experience, much less announce it to the world. We invite them to join. Do you know that historically one of the biggest challenges for rabbis has been to call a congregation to order so a service can begin?"

"Nothing a blast from an organ can't fix."

"What's to fix? We rejoice in being together. That's the point. There's a story about two old Jews who have attended the same synagogue for years. Let's call them Morris and Sidney. Sidney is the pious and quiet one. Morris can't stop talking. On and on, every Friday evening. Finally one time Sidney can't stand it anymore. He says, 'Morris, can't you shut up? I want to worship already.' Morris says, 'Sidney, haven't you figured it out by now? You come to the synagogue to talk to God. I come to talk to you.' So, you see? Judaism is not a religion."

"How can we be having this discussion?" Bill said.

Morris shrugged. "We seem to be."

"I thought the object was to find out which of us followed the true religion. Truer, anyway. And one of them isn't a religion. Something tells me though that you're not capitulating."

"Your intuition is correct. Maybe neither is a religion. Then we're even again."

"Well, if you're going to get Barthian on me. Many people feel that Christianity's problems started when it became a religion. Then the official religion."

"Belong," Irving said. "Belong. Then you might see how believers behave. Then you might behave as though you believed. Then, oops, you do believe."

"Fake it until you make it? That's what they say in AA. It's probably an old slogan, but I heard it for the first time just the other day."

"That's a great expression."

"I'm not saying belief is cerebral. You know you can use 'believe' in two ways. The intellectual way: you believe *that* a proposition is true. God is good. Though to my mind that statement is either false or an understatement. But you won't get much argument if you make it. Or you believe *in* someone or something. Jesus loves me. The beauty is that, when you have a hard time mustering one kind of belief, you can maybe fall back on the other."

"Believe that whatever, believe in whomever," Irving said. "I'm not saying I don't like it."

"Ready to vote?" Bill said.

Irving glanced at his watch. "The polls are closed. I've got some letters to write anyway. We'll vote next time."

"Right," Bill said.

* * *

For the duration of the disputation, Bill and Irving met only once outside the English department or a restaurant. It was one Sunday in church.

Every so often in his adult life Bill got asked if he was a Christian. The question was sometimes suspicious, but more often delivered after a pause and with a sly smile, and more as a statement, as though the too-obvious answer to a riddle. He in turn had developed a standard response: Yes, but not so as you'd notice. He felt that way about the couple of the churches he had visited around town since his matriculation into graduate school.

"What denomination is this?" Irving asked when they had found a pew.

"It's non-denominational," Bill said.

"But Christian?"

"You tell me, an hour from now."

On Sunday mornings the campus was like a drained swimming pool; the worshipers were the last puddle-remnant at the bottom of the deep end where they gathered under the colonnade to enter the church. Otherwise the vast, pebbly quad was deserted. The ushers could have been museum guards as people filed apprehensively past them through the vestibule into the cavernous sanctuary. The demography, like that of the university or a major tourist attraction, was cosmopolitan. You couldn't be sure how many of the adults were one-timers—visitors, parents, townspeople. Bill never saw any of his professors there. He was more likely to recognize someone at the church he attended occasionally just off campus. It was known as a "social justice" church. That was a new term for Bill, one that you couldn't very well object to, but he sometimes felt he had walked into a union rally. There were always petitions or sign-up sheets circulating for legislation or service days at a camp for migrant laborers. He was pretty sure his garage apartment exempted him from sheltering the Salvadoran family the pastor offered to find for any willing member. On- or off-campus the houses of worship were polite; mentions of Jesus were kept to a minimum.

The idea for the extracurricular session was Bill's. Inspiration, rather. When it came to him he would almost have called Irving, had he known his number, though that would have breached protocol. So he waited until one day before the discussion sections they led, when they both happened to be on the ground floor of the English department in the Brooks Room. As always, the air was silty with the stale odors of coffee and cigarette smoke, a subdued stench hosted by the various fabrics of rug and furniture. Even though the room was almost always empty, there was the spectral presence of generations of indigent graduate students. The couches looked slept on. The sole current occupants, Bill and Irving were looking along the shelves for the one last citation essential to their respective lesson plans. Bill wanted to share his other newly-discovered phrase, *Yom HaShoah*. Like "social justice," he had never heard it until recently and then seemed to meet it daily in some context or other. "Holiday" was probably not the right term for it. It was a commemoration of the Holocaust, and the campus church would observe it that Sunday.

Irving was receptive and even impressed. "An interfaith service."

"I guess you could say so," Bill said. "At least not exclusively Christian. Or excessively Christian. The main speaker is a rabbi."

"A worship service?"

"I suppose."

"Is the purpose to seek forgiveness?"

"Could be," Bill said. "Am I being dogmatic enough for you?"

Irving grinned.

"But, now that you bring it up," Bill said, "how exactly would that work? How could a church, or a religion, ask for forgiveness? Or be forgiven? It's an abstraction, an entity. Do I, as an individual Christian, need to ask forgiveness of you, an individual Jew? Neither of us was born at the time of the Holocaust. I'm sorry it happened. I doubt that's worth much to anyone."

"Repentance and forgiveness are in order, I would say."

"Was your family affected?"

"Rather peripherally," Irving said. "Surprisingly peripherally."

"You know, someday there will be no more survivors of the camps," Bill said. "The perpetrators will be all gone, too. No more to hunt down or root out. It sounds awful to say, but sometimes in testimonies I hear almost a nostalgia for the camps. Could good and evil ever have been more clear? In that way it seems almost an age of innocence. Can any people have been more totally wronged? Collectively or individually?"

"You've given this some thought," Irving said. "I can't say I'm surprised."

One nice thing about attending the university church was that nearly every service featured a guest speaker. It was a prestigious school; world-famous figures passed through all the time, and many got invited to preach even if it was a stretch to consider them clergy. A developing-country peace-prize winner might appear one week, an environmentalist the next. Church felt more like a lecture series. Edifying, for sure. The music was out of this world. During one stretch of Sundays, the service consisted of a Bach cantata and not much else. Then church became a recital. Undeniably uplifting, once you filtered out the guilt of not having to sit through a sermon. At the opening of every service, crimson-robed, two abreast, the choir streamed down the center aisle from the back, then split up front to process in single file up either side aisle. Their step was brisk, no-nonsense, if not a forced march, since they had to make it all the way back and up into the loft before the last verse of the opening hymn.

At the first strains that Sunday, Bill said. "This is a good one. Perfect for today. 'The God of Abram Praise.' Maybe a little lugubrious."

"You mean a little Jewish," Irving said.

"No, no. There are joyous Jewish tunes, too. And not just 'Hava Nagila.' This one has a good bass line."

Irving found the page in the hymnbook. "Ah, yes." He pointed to the top right-hand corner: *Hebrew melody.* "Good old 'Leoni.'"

Irving had a pleasant light tenor. A woman in the pew ahead of them made a quarter turn to add her soprano, so that they formed a trio. Bill wondered if the choir members could discern their voices as theirs washed over them from the aisle as they passed, section by section, higher and lower voices mingling like currents of different temperatures. With the final verse, the choir now above and behind them, the harmonization changed, and the organ's volume stepped up from triple forte to seismic. The congregation both sang the last lines and settled in their pews in unison. Their ears rang with the sudden, stony silence of the sanctuary.

The set-up was different that day. Four men about the same size and age sat in armchairs spaced evenly across the dais, two in robes and two in suits. The rabbi would be the main speaker, but instead of a sermon, or even a dialogue sermon, with one person in the pulpit and another at the lectern preaching back and forth to each other, which had been done in the past, there would be a panel discussion. The university chaplain, a silver-haired Southerner, stood. He stepped up to the lectern, gazed out over his audience, and spoke: "Two pastors, a rabbi and an urban evangelist walked into a bar. I mean, a house of worship."

Jokes in a church produce a shock wave. First the congregation has to grasp that it is allowed and even supposed to laugh. So there was a little lag before laughter rippled through the pews, front to back, to be absorbed into the walls like water into sand.

"And what happened? What's the punch line?" He spread his arms. "They talked! Surprise!" More laughter. "Yes, even on this solemn occasion. Even on this, can I say it, ambiguous occasion? Is it appropriate for a Christian church to observe Yom HaShoah? When I visited Dachau, not so very long ago, I found chapels and crosses. Do they belong there? Did I? Could you call my tour a pilgrimage? I visited Dachau on a warm spring day. It was pleasant, and I felt a sense of absolution. Should I have? In what sense and in what season can the church witness to such a tragedy? How can it worship? Should we think of the book of Job, which was all about causeless suffering? We know that Job's first response to his pain was to worship. His friends' reaction was to sit by him and observe seven days and seven nights of silence. Then there was a lot of talking. A lot of talking.

"Today we will collapse the scale of that book somewhat. As you can see, it will be a different kind of service—less music, fewer litanies. We could have worked up a liturgy. That would have been fun. Maybe too much fun. Maybe too eloquent. So this will not be our usual service of word and sacrament—that would have been a challenge to devise—but a service of words. Even on this somber occasion we gather to converse, to laugh, maybe to forgive. Or to understand forgiveness better. Rabbi?"

Across the dais, the rabbi climbed into the pulpit. "*Shema, am-haelohim, dvar-haelohim al Yeshayahu*," he began. "Hear, people of God, the word of God to Isaiah, a favorite prophet of Jesus:

> In days to come
>   the mountain of the Lord's house
> shall be established as the highest of the mountains,
>   and shall be raised above the hills;
> all the nations shall stream to it.
>   Many peoples shall come and say,
>   'Come, let us go up to the mountain of the Lord,
>   to the house of the God of Jacob;

that he may teach us his ways

and that we may walk in his paths.'

"I have words of friendship for you today," he said. "And I have hard sayings for you. The way I might for my siblings. My younger siblings." He wagged his finger; that brought laughter. "But you can cope with them. You are used to hard sayings from Jesus. I want to remind you how closely related we are." He explained that we had to speak of Christianity emerging not out of Judaism but out of Judaisms, in the plural. "Look at all your Protestant denominations today. Methodists, Baptists, Presbyterians, Episcopalians. Free Will Baptists." Now he waved his hands in confusion. That was funny, too. "Think of Second Temple Judaism in that way, too. We know better now how many sects of Judaism there were, including Jesus-followers. And I must say that even then your concern for us was touching but misguided. Today some Christians wish the state of Israel well but only in order to usher in Christ's reign. Back then, the evangelist Mark, in the 'little apocalypse' of chapter 13, has Jesus lament the destruction of the temple. But I can tell you that to Jews, who had already seen one temple destroyed, the fall of the current one would be one great catastrophe, but not the end of the world! We are survivors, then and now. We are happy to be your fellow survivors. You have suffered, too. And I hope you know you Christians are under assault from the wider culture. However, as your friends and fellow survivors, we must remind you of the undeniably anti-Semitic passages in your new testament. Or in your new covenant, as you often more correctly translate it. But it is the same covenant, friends, renewed by God for his people, if only they repent. If only they *shuv*, turn, a word heard over and over in the Hebrew Bible. Turn. Turn back."

As the rabbi sat, the associate chaplain spoke from his seat. "I have a strong feeling this is the place in our discussion for a simple-minded question." He was South African, with one of those not-quite-English accents you heard around campus. "I knew there was a reason I was invited to be on this panel."

Everyone laughed, including the rabbi, who was settling himself in his chair. "For your exquisite sense of timing?" he said.

"Exactly," the associate chaplain said, joining the laughter. "And here it is. What sense does it make for Christians to be anti-Semitic?"

"No sense," the rabbi said.

The associate pastor was already laughing and rephrasing his remark. "I mean, how is it possible? I know they can be. But logically. Jesus was a Jew. Paul was a Jew. The apostles were Jews, the lot of them. There was not a Welshman in the bunch." He said this with a look at the chaplain, whose name was Jenkins; his was Davies. The chaplain laughed along with everyone else, squirming in his chair and smirking, as though suppressing one of several possible rejoinders. "Remember that in the early days of the church not only could you be Jewish and Christian, you couldn't be Christian unless you were Jewish first. Why would Christians slander Jews?"

"To curry favor with the Romans," the rabbi said. "The Christian Jews looked to the Romans for protection from other Jews."

The urban evangelist spoke. Straight-backed and imperially calm, he looked slightly the oldest but also the fittest of the four. "I am flattered and grateful to be part of this discussion. I just happened to be passing through at the right time. I rejoice in a meeting of different faiths and denominations, but I try not to let them look too eternal to me. They are means to an end at best? Stumbling blocks at worst? I try to think in kingdom terms. Every Sunday I say, 'thy kingdom come, thy will be done, on earth as in heaven.' Am I sure I know what I'm asking for? What will the kingdom look like? Who will be there? It was so simple once. Jews and Greeks, Greeks and Jews. That covered the waterfront. Now look around at our cities, at this campus. Here are the nations. How did Hollywood put it? The empire strikes back? They were righter than they knew. The colonialists who forged paths into the undeveloped world did not stop to think that those paths would be two-way, would become freeways, bringing black and brown populations back to the home countries. You don't have to travel halfway around the world to go on mission. If you live in an urban center, just step outside your door and you will see the nations marching by on the sidewalk. As I take a step back to survey the spectrum of humanity, Jews and Gentiles seem more and more one tribe, allies, witnesses to the God of Israel. As I read the book of Romans, the Jews are in the kingdom by birthright. Jesus-followers hope to be grafted onto the stock."

"The *Shema* says that there is one God," the associate chaplain said.

"Or that God is one," the rabbi said. "Depending how you translate it."

The associate chaplain continued. "But does that mean that there is only one way of reaching the one God?"

The chaplain broke in. "I was invited to attend a conference of religious leaders once. I will always remember what one of the participants, a Native American shaman, answered when he was asked whether his religion offered the only path to God. He thought for a moment and said, 'It's the only one I know.'"

"I learned a curious fact about Mahatma Gandhi," the urban evangelist said. "He remained a Hindu all his life, but many people converted to Christianity on his example. They assumed from his ethics and his lifestyle that he was a Christian. Could it be that there is only one way to God, but there are many ways to Jesus?"

"We don't know as much about the life of Jesus as we would like," the chaplain said, "but we know one thing: he was no Christian."

"I seem to recall that you couldn't keep him out of the temple," the rabbi said.

"'I thank thee, that I am not as other men are,'" the associate chaplain said. "Lord, save us from arrogance."

"May I quote John Calvin?" The urban evangelist made a show of cringing at his own suggestion and got a laugh. "In a commentary on the Psalms he tried to assuage that very worry of believers, that their praises of God were triumphalist. It's okay to be immodest in that context, he said. You're not bragging about yourselves. You're bragging about God. That makes it a *sancta jactatio*, a holy boast."

"Okay," the chaplain said, looking around him at the panel. "So maybe we're not just a bunch of blowhards and windbags. We're holy boasters. I like that better. Just taking turns holy boasting. And shall that be the last word? In Latin, no less." He threw up a hand. "No, no. The penultimate word. I know some Latin myself. The next-to-last word. The last word will go to the rabbi. After we sing, he will offer a benediction. Let's stand for our concluding anthem. Welsh tune, Hebrew names," he said with a nod to either side. "Talk about chemistry. We can all pray, 'Guide Me, O Thou Great Jehovah.'"

After the last peal of the hymn, the rabbi pronounced the Aaronic Blessing in Hebrew. The organ burst out again in a postlude, and the congregation broke ranks and spilled out into the aisles, many ages and colors milling their way toward the back of the church.

"There are the nations," Bill said.

"Heading out the doors toward the mountain," Irving said. "Where the Torah is waiting for them."

Another thing Bill had to get used to about going to church in California was that it was also sunny after the service. In his native Northeast it was typical to enter the church under clear skies and emerge into overcast. It became kind of a joke in his home congregation. He and Irving winced in the gravelly glare of the quad.

"Now I owe you a visit to a synagogue," Bill said.

"No, we're even," Irving said. "That service ended on the right note. I'm not going to tell you what it says in your own Bible or what language they speak in Heaven. But check Acts 26.14. If I were you, I'd start practicing my conversational Hebrew."

* * *

At the end-of-term department party Bill found himself momentarily alone on a couch in the living room of the big house on campus belonging to a professor he had never met but had seen a few times around the quad. He was hard to miss, with his shock of white hair and perennial tan. He was known to be a daily tennis player. No one could remember when he had last offered a class; at the moment he was on either leave or sabbatical. Warren's current status was "on duty but not teaching." Bill wondered if he might come across him somewhere on campus in a sentry box. What the faculty was on guard against seemed to be teaching. But the fewer classes they had, the more harried they seemed. He would not see Warren at the party, or Irving, for that matter. Neither socialized. In top-to-toe corduroy that night, Frank was somewhere in the crowd.

Bill always felt pre-empted at these affairs because everyone was acting normal. Straight-faced all semester, they all of a sudden displayed personalities, like a costume party, unless the rest of the year was the costume party. The males flaunted their allegiances to sports teams: the more hapless the franchise, the better. One professor liked to wear a Cubs cap, welcoming jeers from all sides. If you chanced to mention a book to him, he would nod in exaggerated, solemn agreement with your views until the subject of baseball came up again. The women were either chic or slovenly. What disgusted Bill was that he couldn't help feel the need to grab a last-minute identity for the occasion. Usually he was the normal one, but that role was taken many times over. The party game seemed to be musical stereotypes.

For the moment he sat back and watched. From his distance the faculty looked like a grove of birch trees, all going gray at about the same time. His fellow graduate students swarmed the refreshment table as though they were blocking out for a rebound. However, basketball players didn't have the disadvantage of holding a plastic cup of white wine in one hand. There were two or three attractive female graduate students. They also had attracted a crowd, but it consisted of professors.

"In reverie? Or a mystical vision?" Vince Damico, a poet-scholar and one of Irving's advisors, sat down next to Bill in the spot that a few minutes before the eminent Victorianist, as he liked to call himself, John Schall had briefly occupied. Bill's company seemed to represent some kind of asylum from the scattered conversations in the room. Someone had put on Motown, not that anyone in that group would dance. Their milling around was already dancing compared to sitting in a library all day. "I thought you might be gazing in the direction of the radiant Regina. I might have been wrong."

"You were right."

"In your position I might be edging my way toward her."

"I am." Bill said. "Just very deliberately. I don't think she's noticed, do you?"

"Did you say deliberately or glacially?"

"It's a technique of seduction I've been working on. You might call it romantic plate tectonics."

"I see," Vince said. "No perceptible movement for a long time, then an earthquake."

"Brace yourself."

"Thoughtful of you to introduce this method in California, where we're used to them." He paused. "It's not easy being a male at a university these days, is it?"

"No, now that you mention it," Bill said. "I suppose I'm most aware that it's not easy being a graduate student, but that may have distracted me from other, more basic difficulties."

"Maybe Thomas can shed some light on the situation."

No one could remember when Tom Hart had entered the PhD program, but he was deep into a dissertation on *Beowulf* that he kept claiming to have to start over on after discovering that someone else had published his latest idea. In the meantime he had filled just about every part-time job the university offered; he could currently be found at all hours behind the circulation desk of the library. He was a deceptively tall guy and athletically gaunt, with thick, sandy hair and craggy good looks. In a cardigan and slacks instead of his blue jeans and flannel shirt he would have looked at home on the PGA tour. But his eternal thesis had given him something of an oracular air, which was enhanced by his occasional abstracted gaze into the distance. He was the Wanderer stepped out of the poem, rowing into the endless, icy fjords of Old English scholarship. Bill wondered if Tom were peering into his own future or into Bill's. For the moment he was steering an armchair over to the couch to make a group of three.

"Happy to," he said. "What situation are we talking about?"

"We were discussing the difficulty of being male at the university," Vince said. "Not all that long ago, but before your time . . . "

"There was a before my time?" Tom said. "The PhD program has a pre-history?"

Vince's laugh was surprisingly hearty. "We used to do an exercise with male graduate students when we first made an effort to rectify the gender imbalance in the department, which we should have done. You may know that there was a day when English departments were the domain of males. You may have heard such stories around campfires. One day folks noticed that most undergraduate English majors were female, but most graduate students were male, and all tenured professors were male. Even faculties grew alarmed. Something must be done. What can we do? We will do anything we need to. Anything except retire. Good God, no. Most of us are already retired anyway. Paid retirement is the best kind. But we have at least admitted as many women as men into the graduate program. We have seen to it that your generation of males will do the right thing. You gents are among the chosen few who made it in. I think a little survivor's guilt may be in order among us. Hence the exercise. Complete this sentence: to be a male at this university is to feel . . . Fill in the blank."

"Neutered," Tom said without a pause.

Heads turned at Vince's reaction, which could only be described as a guffaw of delight. "What you got, William?" he said when he had caught his breath. "Are you in? He set the ante pretty high. It used to take us an hour to get a pot that big." But he couldn't stop laughing. Bill laughed, too.

Straight-faced and sitting forward in his chair, hands on his knees, Tom said, "It looks as though my work here is done."

"No, no. Stay," Vince said, composing himself. "Elaborate. The question is just to get conversation started. Though admittedly you cut to the quick." He shook his head. His laughter was either subsiding or about to start up again.

"What I mean," Tom said, "is that at this school to ask a girl out is not just to be sexist. It's to be imperialist."

"Not to mention medievalist," Bill said.

"Who said 'girl?'" Vince said.

"Not me," Tom said.

"It was one of you. I've got it narrowed down that far. I'd write you up if I could remember who it was." Vince looked around the room. The scents of wine and cheese were in the air like a mist. He sighed. "Things are better, I guess. I don't know. I'm just glad I got my plumber's license when I did."

"I wonder how Irving would answer the question," Bill said. "Where is he tonight?"

"He's got his own schedule. And agenda. There's a guy . . . ," Vince paused. "He finishes chapters faster than I can read them. But why ask me where he is? Haven't you two been spending time together?"

Tom's gaze swung back slowly and innocently from the party and in particular from Regina, who was in the middle of another scrum of professors, toward Bill. Bill reflected that if he and Tom had been working construction instead of being immured in their separate specialties they would be buddies. As it was they had the Norman Conquest between them.

"No, no, you've got it wrong," Bill said, preparing once again to explain that he was neither spending time with nor seeing Irving. "We have a project going. You might call it an interfaith project. We get together once a week over dinner to discuss religion in general and share our own beliefs."

"And you haven't gotten to the different Sabbath traditions?" Vince said. "Excuse me. Shabbat."

"Of course," Bill said. "It's Friday night."

"Before I met Irving I wouldn't have said that there was any such thing as a Jewish evangelist," Vince said. "Of course Jews have been a presence in the academy for some time now. It's the hunkies like me that had a hard time getting in. I'm using that word generically, by the way; dago would be more accurate in my case. Maybe Jews weren't such a visible presence. Maybe they weren't really acknowledged. Ask someone the story sometime about how our former chair served bacon-wrapped shrimp for hors d'oeuvres at a department party. Now I'd say their presence is, what? Disproportionate? Would that be a fair word?"

"An evangelical Jew," Tom said. "Wouldn't that be an oxymoron? Considering that evangelical means gospel."

"Actually there's kind of a movement in that direction," Bill said. "It's a response on the part of Jews to perceived threats to their group identity— secularism, intermarriage. They have rallies. I saw a clip from one. It looks odd. A rabbi with a microphone working a crowd. It was like Billy Graham in a yarmulke."

"Those must be some dialogues you have with him," Vince said. "You two couldn't be much more different, could you? I mean, religion aside. He belongs smack dab in the middle of Manhattan somewhere. Give him a briefcase and turn him loose in the Diamond District. You're suburban to the max. What is it? Upper St. Clair? Fox Chapel?"

"The latter," Bill said.

He was pretty sure Vince knew that; he had told him before. Even though he had never had him for class, he and Vince had a certain acquaintance, having been pointed out to each other soon after his arrival as fellow native Pittsburghers and hence presumptive Pirates and Steelers fans, which they were. Vince however had grown up in a mill town, as he liked to recall. "Dormont, it was, Thomas," he said. "William here wouldn't ever have been there."

"Sure, I have," Bill said.

"Driven through it, you mean. They used to call it Doormat. The doormat to Mount Lebanon. That's where the rich kids lived. They wiped their feet on us on the way by. We were allowed to go to the same high school." Vince was working himself up into his usual gleeful paroxysm. The longer he talked the more he swallowed his *l*'s, the sure sign of a Pittsburgh accent. "Allowed" came out something like *ayyawed*, though no alphabet would be up to putting it into print. "The WASPS lived up on the hills. My father delivered their milk. In the winter we could see their houses through the trees." And that was *hawses.*

Bill was looking for another opening. He also spent a fair amount of time explaining that he didn't have a drop of Anglo-Saxon blood in his veins.

"I know what you're going to say," Vince said. "Ingram. That's better? I'll bet you're one of those god-damned rich Scotch-Irish Presbyterians." He looked up to see one of his colleagues motion him to the drinks table. He noted his own empty glass. "You'll have to excuse me, gents. We will continue this stimulating seminar at a later date. You didn't know I was a sociologist on the side, did you?"

When Vince left Tom said, "Are you going to belt him, or do you want me to do it for you?"

"What?' Bill said.

"Didn't he just insult you? Or wasn't I listening?"

Bill realized that he had been laughing. "Well, it's all true. Except the rich part. True, I went to all private schools, but on scholarship. My parents couldn't have paid for them. Actually, I felt kind of flattered. I never thought of myself as belonging to a group that could be envied. Or that I would be noticed in that way."

"Noticed enough to be negligible?"

"I guess that doesn't make much sense."

"I think he was trying to insult you. Or doing his best to turn a compliment into an insult."

"That must be what it means to be privileged," Bill said. "You welcome your stereotype. Slurs roll right off them. Have you ever been called 'Whitey?'"

"Not that I'm aware of."

"I was once. By a black guy I had kind of considered a friend. I assume it was supposed to wound me, but it didn't. I didn't even stop liking the guy. Hey, Tom, excuse me for a minute for an exercise."

They met halfway across the floor as though for an opening dance.

"You're alone," he said. "That must be a novel sensation for you. I don't mean 'novel' novel. I'm not trying to get literary with you right off the bat."

As he walked toward her it was as though she came in and out of focus. Viewed from the couch she had been stunning, trim, with straight blond hair that swung as she turned to listen to one admirer after another. Midway toward her, as he made out her features better, he wasn't sure she looked anything like he thought. Standing right in front of him she was just pretty. She had a few freckles.

"I was just wondering when we might have a class together. You didn't design your graduate studies to avoid me, did you?"

To be a male at that university was to feel that every conversation with a female was simultaneously an explication of that conversation. On further analysis, her smirk was fetching.

"You're a little on the old side to have a class with me."

"I know. I spent a few years teaching between college and graduate school. I'm thirty."

"Watch it, buster. I'm thirty."

"That's not so old."

"What I mean is, I teach here."

"You're a professor?"

"I'm a nobody."

"You attract a lot of attention for a non-entity. Including mine, you may have noticed."

"Technically, I'm an instructor," she said. "That's my title. But it means a nobody. I teach a freshman seminar. Two, in boom times. So I'm sort of a member of the department. I get invited to the parties."

"At least you can lord it over teaching assistants like me. And I thought I heard that instructors were going to be called lecturers."

She spread a hand over her chest and fluttered her eyelids. "Give me a minute."

"Since your academic rank is so clearly superior to mine, let me ask you a question that relates to a conversation I was just having. It wasn't about you. But you would be in a good position to answer this particular question. Is it difficult for a woman to be both attractive and funny?"

"Is that a rhetorical compliment?"

"I suppose it is. But I'd love an answer. I've always wondered."

"I'll have to give that some serious thought. In the meantime, were you going to offer me a ride home?"

"I was, but only after I stole a car."

"That was a rhetorical question, because I live a walk away. Would you like to walk me home?"

"Leave the party with you? I'd be a marked man. But yes."

"I'll get my jacket."

Tom was holding up his glass when Bill walked back to the couch for his coat. "What's in order? A toast? Or flames to douse? Shot down? It's only water."

"I'm going to walk her home."

"Not bad for a male. Ask me how I spent my time."

"All right."

"My advisor came by to remind me of the religious veneer over the essentially pagan core of Old English poetry, which should resonate in our increasingly disillusioned in a good sense secular society."

"Nice banter."

"Damico thought it was tough being an Italian-American male in academe." Tom surveyed the festivities. "Try being a Christian."

* * *

To their surprise, they had not yet eaten Italian. Since their inauguration, the disputations had missed only one week, over spring break, when they departed in different directions, Irving home to New York and Bill to visit a college friend in LA, a fellow triathlete. They billed it as a working out vacation. Every meeting found Irving and Bill at a different restaurant, each one more exotic than the last—Ethiopian, one night. So many cuisines were on offer in the environs of the university that Italian seemed pedestrian. But it was one of Bill's favorites. He warmed to the prospect of starch in all its forms, which he had burned off in advance with a long bike ride that day, and as he looked around at the vista of red-checked tablecloths he realized how much more comfortable he was there than he had been at the department party. It was early on a weeknight, so most of the tables were empty; the other diners were older couples rather than the college and young professional crowds at the other places. The establishment hinted at a hushed elegance, but the patrons were dressed retirement-casual. With the exception of Irving, who wore a tie.

"I suppose it's time to get serious," he said. "It's almost summer."

"It's California," Bill said. "How can you tell?" He knew though that that wasn't true; after a couple of years you learned to savor the shift from one season to the next. If nothing else, he noticed as he looked out the window to the parking lot, the glaze of late afternoon sunlight on asphalt had a different quality as spring gave way to summer. "Anyway, summer's when you relax, isn't it?"

"I mean, maybe it's time to state our faiths definitively. In light of all our conversations to date. We've done everything but, when you think about it. We've discussed the state of higher education, the distance it's traveled from its religious matrix."

"I remember that night. Cuban, wasn't it?"

"The challenge of interfaith dialogue. All form and no substance. I take your point about meta-dialogue and how deceptively substantive setting the ground rules can be. Maybe discussions of faith have to be incidental. They have to happen when you're talking about something else. But, remember, sharing is what we set out to do. And there's just the two of us. Religions, that is."

"I was beginning to wonder," Bill said. You know what they say about rabbis: where there are two rabbis, there are three opinions. That probably applies to English graduate students."

In fact in the course of the last few meetings they had granted each other the privilege of five minutes to state their faith unopposed. They never used up their time. The practice began in all earnestness but almost immediately became a benign charade, a parody of the post-work barroom confidence, each sitting back in turn as the other confessed his faith and listening with a patient smile until he stopped so he could begin. As though one of them might drop to his knees in the middle of the restaurant and convert.

"You first," Irving said.

"Wouldn't it be almost better if we stated the other person's faith?"

"I think I know how that would go. I had a teacher once who prided himself on eliciting classroom discussion, but when you made a comment he was prone to say, 'That's very interesting, but wouldn't it be more true if you said the opposite?'"

"All right. No use of that line. By now though we should have a pretty good idea of what the other person believes. Could we put ourselves in the opposite faith for a second?"

"Taste and see."

"That is probably my favorite synesthesia," Bill said. "And in the Bible, no less. I've always thought that captures the mystery of faith perfectly. The revelation is so strong it jumps the tracks of one sense and lands on another. Even though it's from the Old Testament it sounds like communion to me."

"And like a seder to me."

"A seder. Love it," Bill said. "So much about Judaism appeals to me. Like, to build a fence around the law. To have all these little laws to be vigilant not to trespass so you don't so much as graze the big ones. That's great. And it keeps you occupied. The sacred can go about its business. We disciples can't even tell how Jesus felt about the law. Did he come to enforce it or obliterate it? Or did it depend what mood you caught him in? Maybe what parable he had cued up for that day. We can let him worry about Torah. Not that we can or want to forget about it. I'm a Calvinist to the chromosome, but I quote Luther once in a while. He said that we are free from the law and free to obey the law. Now we fulfill it out of love, not fear."

"You make Torah sound like the problem," Irving said. "Torah is not an obstacle. It's a way. It's God's great gift to the Jews, who can then be God's gift to the world, drawing all the nations—all the goys, the Hebrew says—to

Zion. I'll get there someday. Everyone I've told that to must think I'm a Jonah. God called me to Jerusalem, and I went to graduate school. I will return to Israel, but only when I have something to offer, when I have established myself as a professor of literature."

"Maybe we can finally disagree about something," Bill said. "You know they say that interreligious dialogue only takes place between people who agree already."

"You said: if you're willing to talk, you're already half-converted."

"That's a different point. They mean that it's the liberals in either camp who talk to each other. Apart from their core beliefs, the fringes have more in common with each other, like education, than they do with the fundamentalists in their own denomination. We both have faith in literature. We read our respective scriptures as literature. And also as the word of God. As a pastor of mine once put it, the Bible is the word of God and sometimes the words of God."

"Not bad. You had some pastors who could turn a phrase."

"But as a Christian, on my own, I can't offer much of anything to anybody. Sometimes not even a clear statement of my own belief, which as I recall is what you requested not too long ago. I don't know that I have any confidence in the articles of faith I recite all the time. The thing about creeds is, the shorter they are, the better. Scholars think that maybe creeds arose for the sake of baptism. In Latin *credo* means 'I believe.' You're standing up to your waist in water. The priest says to you, 'Credis?' 'Do you believe?' You don't have time to say, 'Well, on balance, in light of the testimony of scripture and the Fathers . . . ' The next syllable out of your mouth will be 'glub.' You're immersed. So when he says, 'Credis?,' you say, "Credo.' 'I believe.' That's it. Spit it out."

"Interesting," Irving said. "Fascinating."

"So when we all stand to say the Apostles' Creed, I don't give it a lot of thought. Born of the Virgin Mary? If you say so. Because I'm not formulating a belief system. I'm affirming that I'm part of the body of Christ. I say what everyone else says. We're all just doing what we're told to do anyway. Called to do, we'd like to say. What we believe in is Jesus. I'm like Paul: I'm a δοῦλος ἰησοῦ χριστοῦ, a *doulos* of Jesus. That's often translated as 'servant,' but I think 'slave' is better. I'm Jesus's slave." Bill paused. "I know. I can dispute myself on that one. It's easy to say I serve an absentee master. He went off to his own banquet and left me behind to my devices. Would I obey him if he came in here right now and gave me an order? 'Drop your books. Follow me.' Would I recognize him? What would he look like?"

"You can be pretty sure he would look more like me than like you," Irving said.

"Except for one thing."

"What's that?" Irving said.

"You're too tall. According to an archeologist I read the average height of a Palestinian Jew around zero AD was five feet. Would I want to follow a five-foot-tall Jew around campus?"

"We would both tower over him," Irving smiled.

"What about you? Do you have something like that, a creed? Not all Christian churches do."

"More the opposite," Irving smiled. "We have the *Shema*. We don't say anything; we listen. Yes, though, like slaves. Our people has some experience there. 'Hear, O Israel: The LORD is our God, the LORD alone. You shall love the LORD your God with all your heart, and with all your soul, and with all your might.'"

"And every week I say the Lord's Prayer, even more regularly than the Apostles' Creed. I pray that God's kingdom come. What does that mean? Do I know what I'm asking for? What would it look like? A world where everyone acknowledges Jesus as Lord? Or a world where everyone accepts everyone else in all their particulars, including their religious belief? That's the trouble with Christians."

"They must be more trouble than I thought."

"Same pastor. He had a million of them."

"Tell him to watch out; he's poaching on rabbi territory. Every rabbi's secret wish is to be a stand-up comic."

"The trouble with Christians is that they want everything to come out right."

"I don't know that that sounds so terrible," Irving said.

"But it did come out right—on Calvary. In suffering and death and humiliation, at what looked at the time like the low point. The kingdom came. That's the punch line."

The conversation missed a beat. Something. It was a little like when an airplane drops suddenly and you can't decide whether you're out of breath or dizzy. Irving looked at him a little differently. Not exactly gently, not exactly kindly. Bill's expression may have been different, too.

"You know," Irving said, "you're not that easy to dispute with. You're not supposed to see your opponent's side of the argument. That's nice that you do. I would have to say that it is not the general perception of Christians that they can be self-critical. The trouble with Jews? I don't know that we feel it's necessary for us to point this out. Plenty of other people have shown themselves willing to do that. I would simply say that if someday Jews remember they belong to the same family and behave accordingly, if Jews should start to act like the Jews they were intended to be, that they contracted with God to be, then the world will see something. They will see a messiah. A person? Possibly. We feel you Christians were a little hasty in anointing yours. Yes, I know Jesus called himself the Son of Man. Could there be a more evocative title? Of course, he got it from Daniel. But does that name belong to an individual or to a collectivity? Israel is finally a nation. One day it will be a people. There's your kingdom. You will be invited."

There was another pause.

"People are just so different," Bill said. "Isn't that the problem? Who really knows what anyone else believes? Somebody standing right next to me in a pew saying the same thing I'm saying might mean something totally different. Somebody even in my family. That used to be a thought experiment we played at dinner when I grew up. What if you and someone else agree that the pie you're eating is good, but it tastes different to each of you? What tastes to you like apple tastes to the other person like peach. How would you know?"

"Would it matter if the result was the same? That's what it would mean. Taste and see."

"Or taste but don't see," Bill said.

It dawned on him why their expressions had changed. The sun had gotten lower, light streaming right through the window into their booth. Just then a squat, middle-aged man walking briskly by pulled up short to adjust the blinds. But it got brighter, and they both squinted as his silhouette swelled in a kind of aura.

"Scusi," he said. "I always turn that gizmo the wrong direction. There. That's better."

When it was dimmer and their eyes had adjusted, Bill saw that the man was much younger than he had first thought, though still proprietary in demeanor. His long hair was combed straight back; his wispy beard was more like a dark filigree against his olive skin. He could have been Italian; Mediterranean for sure. His vest had given the impression of girth. He was actually rather slight. Bill wondered if he could survive outside this artificial, frosted-windowed, air-conditioned enclave. He couldn't imagine him outside in shorts and a tank top in the sunlit California playland—biking, swimming, running—any more than he could Irving. Maybe in a Levantine dockside café; nowhere in between.

"Gentlemen," he said. "Have you not been waited on?"

"We didn't notice," Irving said. It occurred to Bill that this might be the first place they had eaten where Irving didn't seem to know someone on the staff. "We're having a feast of conversation."

"Yes, I see. But man does not live by words alone." He took a basket from a passing waiter and set it on their table.

"I thought that was bread that man did not live by alone," Bill said.

"That, too," the man said. He reached to another table for a small lazy susan containing some bottles and a couple of saucers. But for the short term. Menus in the meantime. And the wine list?"

"Why not?" Irving said, with a smile more at Bill than at the maitre d', which is what the man must have been. Bill looked back at him in surprise. They had been teetotaling to that point, he assumed at Irving's behest. "You can just bring us the house red."

"Very fine," the man said. "Someone will be back for your order. *I* will be back for your order. No more slip-ups."

When he left, Bill said, "All along I assumed you didn't drink. I assumed for religious reasons."

"For an occasion," Irving said.

"I meant to mention," Bill said. "I won't be able to make it next week. Due to an unforeseen circumstance. Like apocalyptic-type unforeseen."

"What could that have been?"

"It happened at the department party. I didn't see you there."

"I'm not much for parties."

"I spoke to a woman I had seen around literally since the day I arrived here without ever actually meeting. Maybe we were introduced in a group, or pointed out to each other. We sort of knew who we were. I was trying to figure out how under the circumstances to ask her out."

"There's those circumstances again," Irving said. "How did you?"

"I didn't have to. She asked me out. Well. She invited me to a dinner at the church she attends. Afterward I get to help out with a youth group she directs. Which meets on Wednesday nights. The first date should be a hot one."

"As betrayals go, that one is really rather well timed," Irving said.

"How?"

"I'll be gone, too. All week, actually. For an interview."

"That sounds like a very thorough interview."

"It's for a job I've been all but offered. It's my second interview with them. On campus. I have the job so long as I don't fall on my face and I finish my dissertation, which I can do down there. My director has signed off on it. I'll work on it over the summer, on a fellowship."

"There was one word you lost me on," Bill said. "Did you say 'job?' You got a job?"

"I did."

"Talk about a traitor. You're not supposed to do that to your fellow graduate students. You're not supposed to actually finish. Betrayal is not a strong enough word. That's heresy. Apostasy. Something."

Irving smiled. "Let's have something to eat. At long last." He handed Bill the basket of bread.

"Looks good," Bill said. "Is there butter?"

"That's what this is for." Irving poured some oil into the saucer and pushed it toward Bill. "Dip your bread in this."

The man returned with a carafe of wine.

"We'll just have tonight's dinner special," Irving said.

The man nodded approvingly. "All in due course," he said.

As dilatory as the first part of the evening was, from then on it was brisk. Their food arrived within minutes. They were hungry, and it was good. As they were finishing, Bill said, "So you're leaving for the summer? That makes this our last supper."

"Which was a seder," Irving said. "Also, ipso facto, our last disputation. Which means."

"Which means?" Bill said.

"It's time to vote."

Bill laughed. "I suppose so. You realize that, in the unlikely event of a tie, a recount will be tough to arrange."

For ballots they found a couple of paper napkins, which they would mark with either a star or a cross. Each wrote under the table and put the napkin face down between them.

"Now," Irving said. "Who will count the votes?"

"I know," Bill said. Let's ask the maitre d', owner, whatever he is."

He was a few tables away setting out silverware. Bill beckoned to him. "All in order, I trust," he said, walking over to them.

"Absolutely," Irving said. "But we were wondering if you could turn over these napkins for us."

As serene as ever, he did. Both napkins contained a cross. "Thank you," Irving said, and he returned to his chores.

Bill looked at Irving. "Whatever it was we've been doing these last weeks, I wasn't trying to convert you."

"Oh, you didn't," Irving said. "I'm the Jew I always was. And you are who you are. We can neither of us change the thing about the other we really want to. People are so different."

RAPTURE

He was almost out the door when he heard the commotion. It couldn't be anything serious, but he should probably check into it. He was also curious, and he had a little time to spare.

A minute earlier, just before noon, the Reverend Douglas Kerr had been striding down a hallway of his church toward the back door. If he left the office just a few minutes early it meant a full hour at the health club and therefore a legitimate workout. He tried to get himself in motion by 11:50. What he dreaded most was a last-minute drop-in by a parishioner, requiring him to blend small talk and counseling as his endorphins seethed under a show of pastoral patience. Some delays were his own fault, as he looked up one more reference for a sermon, tracked down a Bible verse in just the wording he wanted, leafing through one translation after another, starting with the Geneva, his favorite, the one most likely to wake his congregation up with a missing phrase, where the psalmist lived in the house of the Lord not "for ever" but "a long season." True, they had come to expect it by now. Worst was the dawning discovery that the verse he was about to quote did not exist in any translation, that he had made it up. That called for all manner of research and paraphrase that he was loath to attribute to the Holy Spirit. Next thing he knew it was ten after and hardly worth reporting to the gym. By the time he had gotten parked and dressed he was looking at a perfunctory session in the pool or weight room.

So his gait down the hall was brisk without being furtive, quick enough to get past doorways before he could be hailed. It looked like clear sailing on this day: all the lobbies and foyers he traversed were empty. He started down the few steps to the back door and the small lot where he kept his car in a reserved spot. He could see through the windows of the door that no other vehicle was blocking him in. He noted as always that the rubbery gray steps were treaded like tires. Then he heard the disturbance from below. Instead of pushing through the door, he turned the corner and descended another set of steps to the basement.

He would have loved to grow up in this church. Added onto over the years, wing on wing through the mid-century boom, the building was like a catacomb. He entered a large, low-ceilinged room of linoleum and paneling where they held church and community dinners. Through a door on one side was an equally big but unfinished room that once held a bowling alley. There was still, against all odds, a pool table inside. On the other side of the back wall a second set of steps led back up to the original structure.

The ruckus was in the kitchen, though a swinging door to his right. He entered to several turned backs. He had to join the crowd and peer over shoulders to see what was going on. Ed Murdock turned and caught his gaze with good-humored exasperation.

"It's okay, Ruth," someone was saying, over other exhortations.

Ed turned back to the woman. "It's just a precaution. It's overkill; they just want to protect themselves."

"It's safe down here, Ruth," someone else said. "It's a church, for crying out loud."

The chorus consisted of the church's two cooks and several Meals on Wheels drivers back from their morning run, some with unclaimed food, others to do chores around the kitchen or to do errands. These folks generally volunteered two or three days a week. Some women had their retired executive husbands drive them in from the suburbs; now the wives were the brisk and businesslike ones, the men sitting patiently behind the wheel while the cars were loaded for their rounds. They generally departed directly for home afterwards, while other volunteers hung around most of the day. Ruth kept the inventory. Now her coworkers formed a circle around her as she knelt on the floor in front of a large cardboard box that she might just have unearthed. Ed was making a show of his resignation. Whatever was happening, he was in no hurry to intervene. Apparently this counted as an event; events in the church were to be savored. Pearl, the heavy-set cook, was frankly amused. Like all the staff, she did not belong to the church; she was Catholic or possibly Orthodox. Between Sundays and below street level, St. Andrew's was not particularly Scotch-Irish Presbyterian. Its neighborhood, once the fashionable East End, was now inner city.

"Maybe you can talk to her, Reverend Kerr," Ed whispered. "We're at an impasse, as you can see." He managed to put quotes around "impasse."

With a quick look at his watch, Doug stepped inside the ring of spectators. "Is there a role for your pastor here, Ruth?"

Ruth looked up at him, clearly stymied, then gestured despairingly at the box. "It says right here."

"I've been telling you, they have to put that, Ruth," John Rucitello, a deacon, said. "They don't mean it. It's just paper plates."

Ruth continued to look at the box as though it were a bomb to be defused. "All I know is that it says not to use if the seal is broken. The seal is broken. Isn't it?" She pointed to a corner of the box, where indeed the tape had peeled away. "Shouldn't we do what it says? Why else would they say it?"

Ed turned to Doug in a wry but sympathetic aside. "She's got a point. You know how it is these days. You go to the store and find a jar on the shelf with a lid loose, you're supposed to evacuate the building and mobilize the National Guard."

"It is odd," Norman Flint said. He was retired also, but from the faculty at the university. He was a geologist, and Ruth's driver. "Since when did the consumer have all the responsibility for a safe product?"

"She wants to get the president of the company on the phone," John said.

"There's an 800 number here," Ruth said. Though she still looked stunned, she was taking in the conversation.

Doug knelt beside her.

"I didn't write it," Ruth said.

"Let me check," Doug said. He traced the warning with his finger, then ran his hand along the edge of the box. "I think it will be all right, Ruth. John's right: these are paper products. If it was food, we might have to worry."

"If you think so," Ruth said.

"Were you storing this? We can tape it back up."

"We're fixing some things for tomorrow," Pearl said. "We need more plates. That's our last box."

"Does one of you guys want to get this?" Doug said.

John and Ed both stepped forward to pick the box up and set it on the big metal table in the middle of the kitchen, though one of them could have handled it. Doug took Ruth's hand, and they both straightened up, and the charmed circle of workers stirred back to life.

* * *

Despite the crisis in the kitchen, Rev. Kerr got to the health club on schedule. There he was Doug. The locker room was one of the couple of places in town he did not have to be a minister. The other was the volunteer fire department, though he did not appear there daily. By now, in the few years he had resolved to get in shape, a circle of friends had formed in their bay of lockers. There was a longstanding core, to which he did not quite belong, but the configuration was slightly different from day to day, and people occasionally joined or moved away. It was always interesting to Doug to watch a new member or a guest sense the caliber of conversation in their aisle and then learn that Doug was a man of the cloth—terrycloth, that was, as he stood in the hooded bathrobe he favored; and then a familiar sequence of jokes ensued. Baptisms would be performed in the whirlpool, confessions in the sauna (never mind that he was Protestant). Doug took them in good humor and shrugged off the frequent apologies for a cuss word or an innuendo. A locker room has its liturgy, too, he might have said.

None of his gym friends belonged to his congregation; in fact, he rarely ran into them outside the health club. He had the sense that some of them attended a church. What struck him here as elsewhere in the world was the implied piety, the tacit acknowledgement of God's existence, but only tacit, as if God would be belittled by a mention outside church. It amounted to a consensus if not a creed. Yet except for Doug this was the place they attended religiously—and of course only he was paid to be in church every day. Nonetheless he embraced this chlorinated cloister, this monastery from which women and work were banished. They could talk like high school teammates again, as though lives of possibility lay ahead of them and they weren't going right back to their offices and their families after they worked out. Here allegiances were easily claimed and automatically respected. After they dressed, they went off to different sports as though to different branches of the service, some to play racquet ball or basketball, others to lift weights, and they regrouped in an hour to share their veterans' exploits.

Apparently they had acquired a new member that very day. Doug arrived to find the lockers swarming like a metal hive, combination locks snapping open and doors clanging shut as his friends changed into their workout clothes, and, like the still center of a storm, a rotund man sitting in shorts on the bench in the middle. Smiling beatifically at no one in particular, as though balancing his nearly spherical belly on his lap in a spiritual exercise, he was Buddha-like. His face was so full that you couldn't be sure if his eyes were open or shut. At the same time, there was something mischievous or apologetic in his smile, as though his appearance was belated and he should have been there long since, or perhaps had been, unnoticed in his serenity.

"New man in the squad," Rick Campbell said. In a church he would have been on the fellowship committee; he saw to it that the patrons of the locker room were introduced to each other. He was a swimmer by health club denomination. Doug had him pegged as an Episcopalian.

"Buck." The man raised his hand at the elbow as though calling his own name on a roll. Doug shook it, whether he was meant to or not. It was well padded, more like a paw.

"New man in the squad," Jim Veltri said. "Sounds like an episode of *Combat*. Anybody here besides me remember that show? Every week there were a couple of replacements. They were there for one reason, and one reason only, whether they knew it or not. Their life expectancy was not good."

"I might not last a week," Buck said. He was the kind of joke-teller who gathers himself before a laugh after a punch line, his own audience. Then he did close his eyes; he couldn't have seen or heard if anyone was laughing along. It was a nice, hearty laugh, though, making it hard not to laugh along. Your laugh became kind of presumptive. "I'm so god-damned out of shape."

"Don't worry," Sid Gillispie said. "This will be a good place to go. Doug can give you last rites. He's a minister."

"Did I mention I was so gosh-darned out of shape?" Buck withdrew into that booming laugh again. It might have been a form of meditation.

"It's all right," Doug said. "I'm as off-duty as I get here."

"Doug's no stickler," Jim said. "He might let's just say mutter emphatically once in a while on the basketball court when the shots aren't dropping. What were those words you were saying the other day? Father, son and holy ghost?"

In truth, cussing didn't much bother him; he could appreciate its creativity in the heat of sports. Or in the workplace: on his summer jobs in college he knew construction workers whose command of profanity was Homeric. He did have a problem with casual blasphemy, which they were currently skirting. "It's one thing to countenance someone else's swearing, another to do it myself. I try to refrain."

"Slippery slope," Jim said.

"Stumbling block. That's the theological term," Doug said. "St. Paul is very sensitive to it. I might be strong enough in the spirit to swear and not do myself any damage, but for someone else it might constitute a sin, or encourage related ones. Like drinking. I like a glass of wine at dinner. Call me anything you want, but don't call me a Baptist. But I remember a wedding I conducted once. I was standing at the bar at the reception about to order a glass of cabernet when one of my parishioners, your stereotypical elderly female saint, approached me and complimented me on the fine example I set at an affair so prone to licentiousness. I called the bartender back. 'Make that a ginger ale.' Baptists are all right, by the way."

Buck proved more judicious in laughing at other people's jokes. He registered Doug's anecdote with a squint, or a slightly deepened squint, since his face was so full as to have a permanent squint. "That's called hypocrisy," he said. Then he laughed. Once activated, his laugh had the one volume and duration.

"Granted," Doug said. "But benign hypocrisy. It would be as though I went into a weight room, did some curls with real heavy dumbbells and then left them lying around where other guys . . . "

"With less massive biceps," Jim said.

"Exactly . . .would be tempted to lift them and injured themselves."

"In the law that's known as attractive nuisance," Phil Kyle said as he opened his locker. He had just arrived, as though to offer that comment.

"Or, look, there might be an alcoholic at the reception," Rick said, taking Doug's part. You could count on an advocate in the group whatever your position. "You might be able to loosen up and have a drink for the occasion, but this guy doesn't need a test. AA has a neat way of putting it: fake it till you make it. There might be someone there faking it. You're doing sort of the opposite, Doug. You don't have their problem, but you pretend you do."

"Right" Doug said. "For their sake. We need to bear each other's weaknesses. I've got my share." He stopped and looked around. "This was all on the record, wasn't it? I'm quoting you all in Sunday's sermon."

Buck had already lapsed back into apparent rumination on the subject.

"Who's going to bear my weakness?" Hank Fister said, walking in on them already dressed in his training gear. A retiree as long as anyone could remember, he lived close enough to the club to bike in. He just kept some equipment in his locker, like the gloves he was putting on. He kept to some inscrutable schedule, though he often stretched a workout over an entire day, sometimes making two trips in. He clenched and unclenched his outstretched, gloved hands. "I'm lifting today, as you can see. Who's joining me?"

"I am," Jim said.

"A natural-born spotter," Hank said. "Follow me. What about you, Tony? You're dressed for the occasion. It's bench press day."

"Legs today," Tony Caro said, frowning and shaking his head almost before Hank proffered his invitation, clearly in the throes of some private imperative sure to be respected in that company. "I've got to do legs."

"I'm headed for the pool," Jim said. He had looped his goggles over his wrist. They clicked like castanets. Others declared for the indoor track.

"What's your line of exercise, Buck?" Rick said, still the host.

Then they realized that he was still in his shorts and in fact was finished with, not starting his workout. He pointed to his left. "If I shower long enough my body thinks it must have exercised."

They dispersed to the echo of his laughter off the lockers.

* * *

The church was still quieter when Doug returned from his workout. This was his favorite part of the day. He went downstairs and retrieved a yogurt or a sandwich that he had tucked on a shelf beside the bulk foods in one of the massive, humming refrigerators in the kitchen, which would be deserted by

then. In the next room over there was a Coke machine of a couple of generations earlier, probably the same vintage as the pool table; he could still get a
twelve-ounce can for a quarter. Then he would repair not to the church office
but to his study, an obscure room along a hallway over the chapel where he
read scripture and worked on his sermons.

After the flurry of the morning, when he looked after the business
of the church and made most of his hospital calls, and before the tedium
of evening committee meetings, he could nurse his late lunch with a book
propped open on his desk. Since he worked on Sunday, the aftermath of
which always extended into Monday, his nominal day off, these early afternoons were as close to a Sabbath as he got. In fact at the moment he was not
reading the Bible but a life of John Donne, which he was anxious to get back
to. The church was just a block away from the seminary, so his congregation
was a funny mix of academics, young professionals and street people. He
could afford and was indeed obliged to be a little literary in his preaching.
The biography was full of good stories he could use in his sermons, and it
quoted Donne's own sermons at length. He had read a few in their entirety
in the stacks of the seminary library. Even he could not imagine sitting
through one. He envied the old timers, who had an hour to work with—for
the sermon, not the service. Donne might begin, "In our hour today . . . ";
Calvin turned an hour glass over when he started preaching and when the
sand ran out might stop in mid-thought. He would take up where he left off
tomorrow. Doug's listeners got antsy as he approached twenty minutes and
annoyed when he went past. He like to think that he and the Dean of St.
Paul's were kindred spirits, though he could not claim to have been as amo-
rous in youth as Donne or as contemplative a clergyman. He did not keep his
coffin in the study to take naps in so as to be ever mindful of his end. Soon
enough after he sat down to read he would feel his afternoon energy dip
come on. A fit pastor will be an energetic pastor, ran one of his rationales for
his midday trips to the health club. An athletic siesta he called them, though
the siesta was literal. He was useless in the middle of the afternoon; then he
got a second wind and closed the church down around six. His reputation as
the Protestant Work Ethic personified would not have held up to investigation. About two-thirty he would clear his desktop and lie down on his back.
That was asceticism enough. Twenty minutes usually did it, which he had
a hard time extrapolating into eternity, because he always came to revived
and ready for the world as it was. He would stand up and stretch, then walk
over to the window of his study, which looked out onto a side street where
deliveries were made, shoppers returned from stores to squeeze into their
cars with their packages, police cars parked only to move on—routines that
from his steeple-like vantage point seemed an inner city Sabbath. If only he

could instill in his congregation that sense of God's abiding presence on a Sunday. Now that he thought about it, maybe Sunday wasn't just his work day. He often wondered what kind of day of rest it was for whatever group was hosting fellowship hour downstairs, the service piped in over speakers setting up coffee and pastries, which got more and more ornate; for the fussy choir and especially the middle-aged bachelor tenor he could picture finishing every anthem breathless and wide-eyed, all but shuddering in relief at musical disaster averted once again. Even the peace-passing in the middle of the service could seem strenuous.

On this day, though, he heard a rustling as he turned into Calvin Chapel and made for the back stairs up to his study, where he was less likely to be intercepted and drawn into small talk with a parishioner, his Coke inexorably returning to room temperature in his coat pocket. The sound came from the other side of the hallway, what they called the Knox Room. They had the Reformers pretty well accounted for in the church's floor plan. He found a scene reminiscent of the morning. Ruth sat at a table, absolutely immobile, a closed book in front of her. At her right hand was a stack of five or six more.

"Hi, Ruth," he said softly, so as not to startle her.

"Oh, Reverend Kerr. You gave me a turn." She did seem startled, though brightly and pleasantly so. And she might after all have counted on the pastor to appear in the church. But whatever mood he had found her in seem dispelled. There was no consensus on his name among members. Some called him Pastor Doug, the more jaunty, Mr. K. Some Dr. K., though he didn't hold a doctorate of any kind. Ruth remained formal, despite his repeated invitations to call him just Doug if she wanted to.

"Is everything all right?"

"Oh, yes," she said, coming to herself with a chuckle, suddenly aware that her presence in a big, dim room in an empty church might call for an explanation.

"Do you have enough light?"

The halo cast by the floor lamp created a midday chiaroscuro. Her corner of the room was all gleam of woodwork and maroon of rug. It would have taken a Caravaggio to depict the scene; too bad it wasn't a Catholic church.

"I didn't want to turn on the overheads and light up the whole room. That would be a waste of electricity. I just need this little space. I was doing some work on the collection."

"As befits the church librarian. Who is the Meals on Wheels coordinator, and head of a prayer chain. Just think how you've been sustaining the church today alone: feeding bodies in the kitchen, minds in the library.

What else is there? I'm not sure the church could stand without you. If any one of those people I mentioned is a pillar of the church, what are you? At least an aisle."

By the time he had finished his compliment-cum-litany, Ruth was rocking in her chair with silent laughter. "I guess I'm a one-woman colonnade," she said. "But I'm not holding up much weight today."

"How do you mean?"

"She sighed. "For one, I'm stumped with the first book. What should I do?" She held the book up for Doug; its title was *Religion and Literature*.

"Let me guess. A donation from Jim Burgess."

"Oh, yes. And these others."

Jim was one of the seminary professors. He often gave new books sent to him for examination on to the church library, so that the shelves that ringed that end of the room held a combination of cutting-edge Biblical scholarship and Edwardian-era devotional literature and mission journals, all equally untouched. The books that moved, according to Ruth, were the contemporary Christian fiction. A bunch of paperbacks were set up on display on a separate table. To judge by the covers, there was an unusual and Doug wasn't entirely sure healthy interest in the Amish.

"It looks interesting," Doug said. "I may be the first to check it out."

Ruth threw her hands up weakly. "But first I have to catalogue it. Where do I put it? With the literature or the theology? It falls right between. I've been debating since lunch. The table of contents isn't much help, or the introduction. I've practically read the book by now."

Doug dragged one of the heavy armchairs across the deep rug and sat down at the table. He pulled the book to him. The effect he intended was of holding her hand. She sat with both hers in her lap.

"Ruth, I am about to offer an observation that is the fruit of my many years of pastoral training and experience. I'll have to get a little theological and use some technical language. Are you prepared for that?"

Ruth bowed her head, half chastened, half amused. His counseling sessions with women often had an edge of flirtation.

"On the basis of our association over the past few years, I have concluded that you are a worrier."

She was laughing her silent laugh again. "So I've been told. And not just by pastors."

"Let me tell you a story on Betty. Just between us."

"Betty our secretary?"

"Have you gotten to know her?"

"Especially since I started with Meals on Wheels. She's great. I never see her in church on Sunday."

"She belongs to Grace Methodist. It's our policy for staff members to be Christian but not members of our church."

"Why not?" Ruth sat up, then relaxed. "The story."

"She's a dear woman, and very protective of me. She would hate to see me in an awkward situation. So. One Sunday I got up in the pulpit prepared to deliver a sermon that I had entitled 'Worry Is a Sin.'"

"That's harsh." Ruth feigned affront.

"Betty thought so, too. When I looked in the bulletin I discovered that she had taken it upon herself to revise the title to 'Excessive Worry Is a Sin.'"

"Oh, that's great." Ruth laughed and was as quickly serious again. "But did you mean it? Your original title was rhetorical, wasn't it?"

"I did mean it, and the title was not rhetorical. Provocative, sure. But that's what the Bible says."

"You mean like the lilies of the fields? That's such a beautiful image." Ruth and her cohort in Sunday school weren't like the women of the church of his childhood who knew their Bible chapter and verse. When they cited scripture in his class they were almost apologetic, as though they were resorting to cliché or even cheating, like looking up the answers to problems in the back of your math book. Many of them were college-educated and professional. The problem now was to get them to take anything the Bible said literally. "But how can worry be a sin? If you're worried, doesn't that mean you care? You want things to come out right."

"Is there any possibility things won't come out right? The problem is that when you worry you imply that God is not in control. Remember the rest of that passage. You can't add a minute to your life by worrying. Did Jesus worry?"

"Well." Ruth frowned in thought. Her face might have been pretty if it were more often in repose. But she was usually either laughing broadly or thinking intently, so that you didn't get a good idea what she looked like. Doug suspected she didn't give much thought to her appearance. Surely her hairstyle could be more flattering. She wore bangs that she might have trimmed herself and that made her seem more plain than she was. There was still some blonde in her hair; Doug couldn't figure out if it was not dyed or intentionally obviously dyed. Her dresses were probably more shapeless than she was. She seemed generally unconscious of herself, not just of her looks. Some of his colleagues would have advised against meeting a female member of the church of any age alone anywhere other than in the office, with the door ajar so that the secretaries or anyone else could observe an interview. In their church it was not confession, after all. That was Billy Graham's practice into his eighties. Generally Doug followed it. Ruth however was about the least seductive woman he could imagine. She was without guile. "To be fair, what did Jesus have to worry about? He didn't have a job."

"He had a task. But that's a fair point; I've wondered about it. His ministry wasn't a paying gig, and he had to eat. Did he have rich backers? Or did his family and his disciples provide for him?"

"Don't worry. Let other people worry."

"Pastors used to have wives."

Ruth looked at him sharply. "Meg will be interested to learn that fact."

"No, you're right. I'm one of the lucky ones. Meg always saw being a pastor's helpmate as her calling in life. We knew we would be a team since we were in college. She's responsible for most of what goes right in the church, and I get the credit. And she doesn't mind. These days a pastor's wife often has her own career, inside or outside the church, for better or worse. And a pastor's husband. Talk about a rare bird."

"But on the other hand, there's a source of potential stress out of the way. If Jesus wasn't married."

"If."

"Oh, right. Jesus was married. I guess I never got to the fifth gospel." Ruth laughed her broadest laugh, the one meant to show she was in on a joke. Predictably, her expression then went blank. "You're not serious."

"I wouldn't make the claim. But scholars have. Let me show you." Doug got up and beckoned Ruth toward the shelves along the far wall. "While we're at it, let's file this book in the literature section. I'm going to go ahead and turn on the overhead lights."

"Okay," Ruth said, suddenly purposeful. "Let me get my pad so I can record where we put it."

"Roughly," Doug smiled. "I don't think we're going to the Library of Congress system anytime soon."

"I suppose not," Ruth laughed. "I'm still learning ours. I just started, and I don't get to spend much time up here. We do have a literature section."

Every so often shelves were marked with handwritten labels under aged, speckled scotch tape. They must have been the work of a seminarian in years gone by, or more likely of his wife. Patristics. Homiletics. Doug led her to a range in a corner of the room. They had to close a half-door to the hallway to get at it.

"Someday I'm going to look these words up," Ruth said. "'Soteriology.' What in the world?"

"It's from the Greek word for 'savior.'" Doug said. "That's the branch of theology that investigates how people are saved, what it means to be saved."

Ruth scanned the spines of the books in front of them. "That's where Jesus comes in."

"There for sure." He stopped and peered and slid out a slender volume. "This is a book that made quite a splash when it came out thirty-odd years ago. Forty. Every decade or so a theological issue makes headlines. Do you remember the "Is God Dead" issue of *Time*?"

"Oh, sure. The black cover? I was in, what, my first year of college?"

"This controversy was almost as big. I forget now if it came before or after. This congregation followed it closely, because the author attended. He couldn't belong, not because he was a professor at the seminary but because he was ordained."

"A minister can't belong to a church?"

"No."

" I never knew that." She sagged at the revelation. She obviously loved to be corrected. Her jaw dropped when he handed her the book. It was entitled, "Was Jesus Married?" "That might cause a stir," she laughed.

"Especially when the answer is yes."

Now Ruth both went limp and dropped her jaw, leaning with one hand on the nearest table. "I'd better sit down," she laughed again.

"Let's," Doug said.

"Can they prove that?"

"The author makes what you call an argument from silence. It runs like this. It was customary for a rabbi to be married in New Testament times. Jesus was a rabbi."

"Therefore Jesus was married."

"Or put it this way. If Jesus had not been married, the gospel writers would have touted his bachelorhood as one more of his distinctive attributes, along with the miracles and healings and riddles."

"Jesus told riddles, too?"

"Well, parables. It's the same word in Hebrew. And since the gospels don't mention that he was not married, we should assume he was."

"I had no idea."

It was Doug's turn to laugh. "It's just a theory. But it's a good book, with all kinds of information about Jewish practices at the time Jesus lived. As a Jew, Jesus would have followed most of them, though, again, we hear about the ones he broke."

"Oh." Ruth shook her head. "I knew he was Jewish."

"Many Christians don't, or they don't stop to think about it. We don't know a lot about Jesus that we would like to, but we know one thing: he was no Christian."

"No," Ruth said. "I guess he couldn't have been. He was too early."

"Or married, I don't think, and I don't think the author really thought so. It was just a pretext to delve into Jewish lore. An attention-getter. And it worked, for a while." Doug slid the book back into its slot on the shelf. "And it ended up on Tombstone Row in the library of St. Andrew's Presbyterian Church. Jesus isn't married anymore. Now he has to be gay. He was human—fully divine, fully human, as we believe—and therefore he had a sexuality. But maybe he just didn't have a very strong one. Some people aren't very highly sexed, even today. They're not as obsessed with the subject as the society they live in. There's a group with some explaining to do. Maybe Jesus had some self-discipline or, God forbid, modesty. But, sure, marriage would have complicated his life. He might have worried."

"No," Ruth said. "His wife would have worried."

* * *

Buck was almost always already there when Doug arrived in the locker room and almost always in the same Buddha pose, seated naked and bemused on the bench with a towel draped over his lap while others milled around him, clanging locker doors open and shut. Doug couldn't resist checking every time to see if his legs were tucked up under the towel in the lotus position. But his columnar calves were always visible, feet planted firmly on the tile floor. His routine must have long pre-dated his arrival among them. They soon realized that he took a shower before as well as after his swim. It was true that a pre-swim shower was stipulated by a notice on the door to the pool, but that injunction was honored more in the breach than the observance by the regulars. Most people dashed though the gauntlet of showers, catching a little spray, maybe. Buck soaped up with his shower mitts and dried off before he put on his suit, a heavy garment of some canvas-like material with all manner of pockets and zippers, more appropriate for the beach than for the pool. After he swam, he pulled a cardboard box off the shelf of his locker that was full of toiletry items, from toothbrush to nail clippers, various talcs and ointments. He ran through the towels stacked around the room like Kleenex. At least one of their group was ritually pure. He was ready for the inner temple.

Doug became fascinated with Buck's hygiene, which actually left very little time for a workout. Perhaps it constituted a workout. He was only apparently abstracted while he performed it; he held up his end of the locker room seminar throughout. One day Rick set down his recent absence—all absences were noted—to jury duty, opening a fresh topic for discussion. Everyone had an experience or a near miss to relate, and Buck took his turn. "The first time I was called, the defendant was black. The judge said, 'Do any of you feel you could not return a fair verdict due to prejudice?'" Buck snapped to seated attention and raised his hand. "'I'm a racist,' I said." He laughed gleefully. "That got me off. I was ready to say I belonged to the KKK. The next trial I got called in on, surprise, the defendant was black again. It didn't work this time. Same judge. He said, 'You're no more prejudiced than I am.' Well, I tried." He bellowed and returned to his grooming.

Doug swam only a couple days a week; on the advice of his buddies he was trying to add it to his regimen for the sake of flexibility. "Cross-training" was the mantra-of-the-month at the health club. When he was showered and dressed in his suit, Buck would shamble along the deck past the baby pool to one of the main pool's end lanes, designated for slower swimmers. Doug, a novice but reasonably fit, was usually the next lane over. His goal remained to swim steadily for twenty minutes. If he could ever master the flip turn he would consider moving even one more lane over toward the masters, but he had been counseled that you had to be going a certain speed before that technique was advantageous. It was true that on his few previous attempts to flip his turn he sank before he made a full revolution. After observing his form from the deck, his swimming friends had diagnosed his stroke as "slow."

Even so, he was quicker than Buck. Buck's routine was to lean with his back against the end wall after each length, meditative again, until he gathered himself and pushed off for another. He lumbered when he swam also. His head out of the water at all times and thrashing from side to side, he clawed his way to the other end as though through quicksand. "Don't struggle," you felt like calling out to him. His baggy suit didn't help; his feet all but dragged on the bottom of the pool. The effect was of hydroplaning in slow motion. On a given day he might complete a half dozen lengths, each an exercise in survival. Another thing that was different about swimming since Doug's childhood, besides sharing lanes and even swimming in circles if there were more than two of you, was goggles. Doug had played as a kid with diving masks, but now everyone had goggles to keep water out of their eyes. Even Buck, though his were superfluous, since he rarely put his face in the water. So were the nose plugs he wore; you rarely saw them anymore. But the goggles only made him look more visionary when he paused between laps. With his own goggles, Doug could see when Buck was resting at the wall and turn and keep going to avoid the risk that Buck would greet him with a pleasantry. Mid-swim conversations were hard to break off; your partner was prone to make a comment just as you pushed off, the last few syllables submerged. How and when to respond politely was a problem.

Buck always seemed satisfied with his workout when the squad reconvened in the locker room from their various stations in the health club with stories of their exploits.

"You filled it up today, Mike," one of the basketball players said to his teammate. They were the sweatiest as a group and maybe as a result a tad self-righteous.

"Well, once in a while I can turn back the clock," Mike the former college player replied.

"Oh, yeah," Buck said from his seat on the bench. "And you pay for it the next day."

Doug couldn't help but cherish the club's unspoken myth of the Golden Age, the presumption, never challenged, that to a man they could look back to past sports prowess, as though there was any comparison between the athletic abilities of Buck and Mike, who was lithe into middle age. But Buck's real service to the group was to uphold another locker room tradition: he could give any discussion a sexual slant. He was never obscene but could recognize the latently raunchy in any subject, the way they raised filed-off serial numbers from murder weapons in TV crime dramas. He gave hints of his earlier amours, like the story he told about taking a date to a restaurant only to be waited on by another girlfriend. "Awkward!" he exclaimed, leaning back to laugh. From some of the details—it might have been a prom night—Doug gathered that this incident dated to his high school days, which was fair enough, since the group dipped at random for anecdotes into its vague collective history. Other episodes were harder to situate. He was the first to gloss someone else's story about a friend of his spotted with another woman by a coworker who happened to be vacationing at the same Caribbean resort.

"Bad move," Buck said. "If you're cheating on your wife, go to the motel down the block. Less explaining to do in the long run. If you meet your girlfriend in Timbuktu you'll run into your next-door neighbor."

You couldn't tell if he was speaking from experience or from common manly lore. As Buck laughed, Doug noticed that the tip of his tongue was just visible between his teeth, so that it seemed pink and seemed beaded at the end, like a parrot's. He resisted picturing it seeking a partner's tongue in a kiss, though it must have, if his allusions were authentic. Luckily to date in Doug's church, as opposed to his denomination, the issue of gay marriage had not arisen. He was less troubled by it theologically than in the flesh. He was okay as long as he just theorized about it. All through his life in the church, the cohabitation of male or female members was common, like Esther and Audrey in his present congregation, whose fling every year was to travel to Florida to see the Pirates in spring training. Who knew what their living arrangements were in the big old two-story brick house they shared, and who cared? If they were married, you would know. That's what he meant when he said, to shake his parishioners up—in a class rather than from the pulpit—that the church liked people to have sex in public. Esther and Audrey were the salt of the church; their identically short and white hair brought home to Doug Jesus's metaphor, which he had never quite understood in its gospel context. The particular generation of vipers (that metaphor he got) that he squirmed along with in discomfort at the prospect of homosexual union might have to pass before the question could be resolved.

But he had to admit to himself that he couldn't much more easily contemplate coupling between certain men and women. Occasionally when an unattractive pair sat with him in his study for pre-marital counseling he wondered how they would bring themselves to make love. It was no part of his job to prepare them for that shock. Often it was clear from their demeanor that they had consummated their relationship long since. It might emerge that they were living together; sometimes they weren't even apologetic about it. One might joke about the other's snoring. Not that he routinely imagined friends in the act, but the idea of Buck aroused was if not repugnant then ludicrous. He had children, but they heard less about them than about his old girlfriends, embalmed though they might be in a high school yearbook. To his credit, he didn't gloat. To the contrary, he managed to convey his recognition that continuing female demands on their attention was a problem they had in common. In a couple of cases he might have been correct. But in his?

* * *

"But if Jesus was married?"

You could count on Ruth's comments to cause an uproar around the table, God love her. It struck Doug again how regularly this harmless woman was the eye of a maelstrom, collecting people anxious to direct her, correct her, remind her of the obvious, in a funnel cloud of witnesses.

"Jesus was not married," Dot Moore said.

"Remember, that was just an idea someone floated," Doug said. "That writer wanted us to see Jesus as a Jew."

Dot simply straightened in her seat at that. She was one of a dozen-odd women who met in the Calvin Room on Wednesday mornings to read and discuss the scripture he would preach on the following Sunday. The class included a solitary man, Ben Jacobson, a bachelor of late middle age, a former engineer and a genuine student of the Bible who had taken up on his own a study of Greek and Hebrew. He rode an old three-speed bicycle all over town and even into the hilly countryside, presumably for exercise, though he was always in street clothes. He was an anomaly in the congregation, but he never missed a service or event. That in itself was somewhat anomalous. His ancestry had a Jewish strain. And there was an irony in the fact that he was surrounded by females in the class, because he obviously followed a policy of avoiding even casual physical contact with the opposite sex. During the passing of the peace on Sundays he would shake the hands of the men and bow to the women. He could probably have produced scriptural warrant for this practice.

"Our passage today gets us thinking about the family in general," Doug said.

"Who picks these passages anyway?" Imojean Jones said, setting off another gale of laughter.

"Not me," Doug said. "Blame the lectionary."

"I would, if I knew who that was," Imojean said. She pronounced the first syllable of her name to rhyme with "eye."

"It's a schedule of readings many different churches follow, an attempt to cover the whole Bible in a certain period of time. It's basically a Catholic practice. Calvin the Reformer preferred to work his way straight through the Bible, starting with Genesis and going straight through to Revelation. Then you start over again."

"We should probably do that," Ruth said. "We are in his room."

"I'm not sure anyone would prefer that particularly," Doug said.

"First we're Jewish, then we're Catholic," Dot said. "I didn't know we were either."

"The gospel passage for this week is sad," Judy Griffin said.

"Would you read it to us, please, Judy?" Doug said.

"I'll cry," Judy said. But she laughed along with everyone else at the idea. "This is Mark chapter three, verses thirty-one through thirty-five: 'Then his mother and his brothers came; and standing outside, they sent to him and called him. 32A crowd was sitting around him; and they said to him, "Your mother and your brothers and sisters are outside, asking for you." 33And he replied, "Who are my mother and my brothers?" 34And looking at those who sat around him, he said, "Here are my mother and my brothers! 35Whoever does the will of God is my brother and sister and mother."' It's sad to think that Jesus had no use for his family. I mean his biological family. His mother must have been hurt terribly."

"He was a problem child," Imojean said, sitting bolt upright with her insight.

"His family worried about him," Doug said. "They worried that he was possessed. What would they say today? He was 'acting out?'"

"What happened to the Holy Family?" Dot said. "All those Christmas cards."

"Yet all through the Bible God worked through the family," Doug said. "Abraham and Isaac, fathers and sons. How can we explain Jesus's attitude?"

"He was following the Old Testament," Ben said. "God was willing to jeopardize the family. He told Abraham to sacrifice Isaac, his one chance for descendants. What if Abraham had not listened to the angel and actually killed his son. Could God have found some other way to work?"

"Or will the family look completely different to everyone someday?" Doug said. Remember what else Jesus said: in heaven, no one will be married."

"First everyone is married, including Jesus," Ruth said. Now no one is married. I'm confused." But of course she loved to be confused, because then she could be instructed. And people loved to instruct her. She gathered instructors like chicks to her breast.

"Look around you," Doug said. "Look around the sanctuary next Sunday. Are you seeing your family? Does it look like a family? What's missing?" His students looked at him expectantly, ready to laugh. He sometimes felt the class was like children's time for adults, comic relief in church. Adults say the darnedest things. "Where are the spouses?"

That hushed the group. It was hard to imagine another gust of hilarity kicking up amidst those chastened faces. If he ever wanted to get his congregation's attention of a Sunday morning all he had to do was preach on the physical loneliness of widows or remind his listeners that the Reformers held that meeting sexual needs was a mutual duty of spouses. Widowhood could be pre-mortem. Afterward, during fellowship, he would be asked laughingly whether future sermons should have a rating. "Might have to give that one an R, Pastor Doug." With one or two exceptions, these women attended church alone. A couple were widows, a couple of their husbands attended another church, but the others simply did not exist as far as the church was concerned. The men couldn't plead work; most would be retired. It worked the other way around, too: some husbands came alone. Bill Miller was his stalwart on Sundays, arriving sometimes before he did to get the bulletins and offering plates in place for the ushers. He might not light the altar candles, but he would make sure that they were lit. Doug had lost count of the duties Bill performed around the church during the week. Although he was a retired banker, Doug was just as likely to pass him in a hallway swinging his tool box as to find him in the office checking the books. He was an elder by title, but he remained a deacon in spirit even though the church had eliminated that office. From the pulpit on Sundays Doug could observe the rest of the ushers seated in the back pews, like a Sanhedrin. They were all business: getting a head count, going over to hold the door for latecomers or check the sound system, then taking up the offering. And they didn't hear a word he said. They were all spouseless as well, at least for that hour.

"It's hard, isn't it?" Doug said. "Mary knew. Where was her spouse?"

"Who was her spouse?" Ruth said, and shrugged.

"Well put," Doug said. "It must have been confusing for her. And what happened to Joseph? He just disappears from the gospel accounts. We never learn about him after Jesus's childhood. Mary was to all intents and purposes a single mother." Every teacher needed a Ruth in his class. She didn't say anything but collapsed in her seat at the force of the revelation. "It's hard to be a single wife on Sunday. It's hard when husbands and wives don't share their faith."

"I've stopped trying to get Arden to come to church," Ruth said. "Even for a picnic or a play. He went to church with me once, he'll say. When we got married. He doesn't seem to mind that I go. I think he thinks of it as an activity, like bridge club. Then every Sunday when I get home he'll say, 'Did you get me off the hook?'"

"My husband says he takes the Bible literally," Dot said. "The Sabbath is a day of rest. So he sleeps in."

"My husband says that's his only time to himself," Imojean said. At around fifty she was the youngest of the group. She was married to a teacher. "He listens to NPR all morning. Since they talk about serious things, I think that's a little like church for him."

More husband stories followed. After a few, his students were shrieking with laughter again. They couldn't volunteer their stories fast enough, usually dissolving in laughter themselves before they could get their punch line out. Doug suspected that the class cherished a self-image of zanies, women of a certain age who had realized that the Bible could be fun. Who would have thunk it? They seemed for this session to have absorbed about the most painful passages he could have produced.

"I have a question," Kay Baker said, then cringed. "It's related, I think." She always raised her hand, though not above shoulder level, to be recognized. "Someone told me that in the Bible it says that if a wife is saved, her husband will be, too. Do you know where that is?"

"Really?" Dot said. "What about children?"

"And pets?" Imojean said, to laughter. "I'm sorry. As long as we're asking."

"Do you mean to tell me that as a group you want everyone to be saved?" Doug said. "That's all right. God does, too, apparently. Paul says all creation will be redeemed. And I have heard that said, too, about spouses—not just husbands—Kay, but I'm honestly not sure if you can find it in scripture. I'll have to look. And on animals, Imojean."

"Could you check on husbands first?" Ruth said.

* * *

"Look. You can only lower interest rates so low and for so long."

Wheeling on him, jabbing a finger for emphasis, Ed Olson admonished Doug on the subject of fiscal policy. Not Doug's, necessarily. It was fairly clear that Doug was not the object of his caveat. Neither was under the impression that the other had a seat on the Federal Reserve Board. Rather, Ed was being rhetorical and assumed that Doug like any right-minded person would agree with him. The locker room was full of them; it was a forum for words to the wise, though you could never be sure what the day's topic would be.

It was equally a place for daily breakthroughs. Notwithstanding that its main source of humor was the patent disparity between the members' current shape and their physical prime (purely presumptive in some cases), there was the unspoken assumption that that prime could be recovered if the proper regimen were instituted.

"I know what I have to do," Sid announced. "Cut the carbs. Back in my triathlon days I bought heavily in to carbo-loading. Trouble is, I stopped training, but I didn't stop loading."

"We can't burn them off like we used to, face it," Rick said. "The trick is not to let your core muscles go. Running's not enough by itself."

"I know my downfall," Joe Biola said. "Two words. Ice cream."

Once you had castigated yourself for your physical decline, a little indulgence was in order.

"It's when you eat it," Sid said. "Don't eat anything after six o'clock. Problem solved."

"And lots of water," Sam said.

"It's the same amount of calories." Jeff White, silent until now, appealed to Doug with a smile and a shrug. "Why does it matter when you consume them?"

"Late-night desserts get me, too," Mike said. "You say there's cheesecake in the refrigerator? Two pieces. Right here."

"Who are you kidding, Mike?" Sid said. "You couldn't get out of shape if you tried. Why don't you age a little? Gain some weight. Lose some hair. Something."

"You mean some more hair," Mike said, though he was youthful there as overall. The myth also worked the other way around: some guys complained they were in worse shape than they were.

It was a house of vanity, for sure. At the end of every range of lockers hung a full-length mirror, consulted by some with scrutiny that looked like suspicion and passed by by others with averted gaze. Some mounted and some skirted the scales at the door to the shower room. And why might that Palace of Pride be frequented by a pastor? Though he had never been heavy, Doug wasn't athletic, either. Meg was the jock in college. The last pastors' retreat he had attended included a physical exam and a fitness workshop, where he was advised to pay a little attention to his blood pressure and his cholesterol. Meg seconded their prescription of regular exercise, noting that improved muscle tone would be an added benefit. He did feel better when he worked out, and he liked the way it broke his day. So within a year he went from doing no exercise beyond yard work, which since they lived in a manse maintained by the church he had to manufacture, to his religious attendance of the health club at noon. Plus these days a pastor had to project the same youthful vigor as a politician. When he was a kid, the more cadaverous the preacher, the more convincing. If you wanted a good-sized church now it helped to look like a professional golfer.

Given that there were fifteen regulars in their bay of the locker room give or take and on and off, all of the same age cohort, though at forty-eight Doug was maybe a hair on the sunny side of the mean, he found himself alone with Buck more often than was statistically likely. But then Doug had discerned his pastor's call, or curse, early in life. People liked to confide in him; anyone with a story to tell could pick him out of a stadium crowd as a sympathetic listener.

"It takes me a little while," Buck was saying. "I'm even slow getting dressed, I'm so fat."

It was the first time Doug had heard him acknowledge that he was more than allowably out of shape, beyond the group standard exemption. Doug was dressed, the others having left virtually at once in a glissando of clanging locker doors, but it seemed unmannerly to leave Buck alone. He had his pants on, at least, and was pausing between socks.

"Do you want to use my hairdryer?" Doug offered.

"What's the use?" Buck said. "I think I'm just going to get a buzz cut next time."

Now that he looked, Doug saw that Buck had lost hair from the inside out, so to speak—from the crown down. He still had a perimeter of a hairline. When it was combed back you didn't realize it was hollow. Fresh out of the shower and lying flat, it looked like a tonsure.

"I'll get a move on here and walk out with you," Buck said. "Or do you have to get back to work? Oh, I forgot. You're a preacher. You only work on Sunday."

That made him laugh.

* * *

She swung into the hall from the direction of the office, heading straight toward him. When she saw him, she glanced to one side. With her bouncing stride, it looked like a fake or a cut, but it was just her sign of recognition.

"Hi," he said.

"Hi to you."

They met by one of the archways to the Calvin Room and its congregation of mid-afternoon shadows. He loved her air of breathless preoccupation—the less urgent the situation, the more breathless. He leaned forward and kissed her.

"Why did you do that now?"

"Is this a bad time?"

"My lips were all scrunched up."

"I thought they were puckered."

"There's a difference."

"So am I in trouble? I mean, I can see I'm in trouble. What I'm really asking is, will there be consequences?"

"Later, yes."

"In a house full of children?"

"A house full of drugged children."

"I set one out that says 'Number Nine' on it. Don't give them that."

She put her hands on his chest where she could grab him by the lapels if he were wearing a jacket. "Were you under the impression that chlorine is an aphrodisiac?"

"That's what they told me at the club. It's in their literature."

"Maybe suggesting you start exercising again wasn't such a good idea."

"You're scrunching up your lips again."

She tapped him twice on the sternum. "Why don't you just go about your business, and I'll go about mine? I have a women's circle to run."

From the far end of the hallway, as she turned to go upstairs, she waved without looking back.

* * *

This time when Doug walked in on her Ruth did not seem surprised. To the contrary, she seemed to be expecting him, her expression contrite. She was at the same table in the Calvin Room, which was still set up from a talk on Sunday with rows of folding chairs. The table where she sat held several stacks of books and an open laptop computer, as though she were a teacher at her desk waiting for her class to arrive.

"Another donation," Doug said.

"Oh, no." Ruth shuddered in denial. And, Doug thought, a little relief. It was something else. "I'm reclassifying the books we already have. Did you know that the Library of Congress has a web site? You can find the call number for any book. Except . . . " She paused and looked around at the book-lined walls.

"I did not know that," Doug said, finding a seat, her early, eager student. These were nice for folding chairs, with velvety seats. They were stamped underneath with the name of a funeral home long defunct itself. "But I thought we were kidding about reorganizing the library."

"But then I got to thinking about it. Why not? It can be done. Except there are more of them than I thought."

"Some of these books are pretty old, Ruth. Pre-Library of Congress? Pre-Dewey Decimal?" Doug reached for one with a grainy maroon binding and pages that looked powdery along the edges. He hesitated to open it for fear it would disintegrate. "I doubt they all have dates."

Ruth perked up. "There's a way to handle that. There's another site that explains how to document books. This is all coming back to me from college. If there is no date, you put 'n. d.'"

"Hey, I could have thought of that," Doug said.

"My big problem is that after I got started I saw that the call number can be different for different editions of the same book. Some of these are second editions. So I had to start over. I put the call number in pencil inside the book cover so I don't mark the books up. Then I enter it in the computer. We'll be able to find any book we have."

Doug raised his hand. Ruth looked at him quizzically, then got the joke. "Yes, young man?"

"It's a lot of work for one person. Maybe we need a committee. We have one for everything else. Or maybe we could make do with our own system after all. I'm not sure you could scrape these labels off the selves."

"Maybe," Ruth said.

"Here you are, you two bookworms. I should have known where to find you." It was Meg, on her afternoon rounds. "You look like you found some light reading, Ruth. Headed to the beach?"

"Really," Ruth smirked. "Rev. Kerr is probably here to do some homework I gave him."

"Mine first," Meg said.

Doug looked as baffled as he could.

"We have a situation in the office."

"He was going to find out for me if it says somewhere in the Bible that if a wife is saved her husband is, too."

"I see why that would be a priority for him," Meg said. "He's got a lot at stake."

Ruth looked blankly at them both, then rocked with laughter. "I didn't mean you two. It's my Arden I'm thinking about."

Her laugh was not the most attractive thing about Ruth. It had a suggestion of collapse, a surrender of all self-awareness, as though she were somehow the butt of whatever joke had just been told. It was too innocent. It was one way she and Meg differed. They were both cute; Meg was also pretty. She was probably ten years younger than Ruth and more fit. Even after bearing three children she retained a college girl's energy. Her figure had subsided a little, but she was still trim and seemed even at rest to be bouncing lightly on the balls of her feet as though still at the net waiting to volley. Of course, he loved one of them.

"It's only about money," Meg said.

It had to do with the way she set her mouth and shifted her weight slightly, signaling that in the direction from which she had just come things were completely out of control and that her response was to strike out into fresh chaos. It was a good quality in a mother, too. Along the way the needful things got done.

She plopped down beside Doug. "Let's see what our pastor has to say." She twisted the chair around to face him so that now he was the teacher, and she and Ruth were the class.

"But if it's important," Ruth said. "I can work on these books."

"The office can wait," Meg said. She put her chin in her hand and gazed at Doug attentively, adoringly. Now Doug was laughing.

"Or I can go down to the kitchen for a while. I still have Meals on Wheels things to do."

Scanning Doug's face, Meg said, "I think what Rev. Kerr wants to convey is that perhaps Arden is due for a pastoral call."

Calling on parishioners was admittedly not Doug's long suit. In his experience, it was more a chore for them than for him. He was more comfortable on hospital visits, where it was not clear who was receiving whom.

"Did Arden grow up in a church?" Meg said.

"He was raised Catholic. He went to parochial school and has the scarred knuckles to prove it. He knows the length, width and diameter of all his fingers because the nuns applied their rulers to them so often. Every day was Sunday, so he had his life quota of church in by the time he graduated from eighth grade." Ruth paused for effect and breath. "He's got a million of them."

"I can hear him now," Meg said. "But I can't picture him. Usually we see the spouses once in a while. Christmas Eve, say."

"Not Arden. Every so often he'll have to drop me off at church, but he won't come in."

"Well, I'm going to drop in on day care," Meg said. "Things are really no more in an uproar than they ordinarily are." She reached over and laid a hand on Doug's knee. "Do I have to tell you you needn't rush? I didn't think so."

After Meg left, Doug said, "Let's just leave these for now." He picked up another book. It seemed fresh but not new. It was probably about his age. "*Desert Streams: Devotions for Housewives*," he read. "I doubt anyone is looking for this one."

Ruth laughed. "Probably not."

"At least it can wait till tomorrow to be filed. They may still be working on a call number for it."

As they walked together down the hall, Ruth said, "I feel I should be doing things. Sometimes when I'm driving to church on Sundays I see people working at a recycling center or tending a garden in a traffic circle, and I think, they're doing more good than I am sitting in a church. They're doing something."

Doug stopped in mid-stride and grimaced, mock-pleading. "Ruth. What a thing to say to your pastor."

"I'm sorry," she said. "But I wonder. When we're just standing up and sitting down, reciting and listening."

"You're describing our liturgy," Doug said. "You know, in Greek that word means 'work of the people.' It may look to God as though we're busy."

"I don't know."

"I agree that it's a mystery. We Reformed types put all our trust in faith, so to speak, and none in works. Yet it's clear in the Bible that works are important. Jesus says that your smallest act of kindness, like giving someone a drink of water—shelving a book?—gets you into the kingdom of heaven. But he adds that it must be done in his name."

"How does that make the deed any different or better?" Ruth said. "The effect is the same. It's still kind. And how do you do something in someone's name anyway?"

"Ruth," Doug said, inviting her to resume their walk. "I haven't completed my first assignment yet."

* * *

"I'm going to make a wager with you this morning. Have I got your attention? Because you know that, unlike some among us, I am not a betting man. I know that some of us do not share my qualms about this pastime and in fact occasionally play the Pennsylvania State Lottery."

A voice came faintly from the back. "Benefits senior citizens." It was George Siple, on cue. There was laughter. That was good.

"I'm not going to bet that you don't know the story of Mary and Martha. We all know it, right?"

"All right, Pastor Doug. We all think we know it." He could count on Pearl Filbert, too. "Is that what you're waiting to hear?"

"Thank you, Pearl. You obviously know how I operate by now. I'm not sure I'd want to bet against you."

More laughter. But not too much, also good. He would need it later.

"You're right, though. I'm betting there's something you never noticed about the story. It's not very long. That surprises me every time I read it. Five verses in the middle of Luke's gospel. Listen:

> Now as they went on their way, he entered a certain village, where a woman named Martha welcomed him into her home. [39]She had a sister named Mary, who sat at the Lord's feet and listened to what he was saying. [40]But Martha was distracted by her many tasks; so she came to him and asked, 'Lord, do you not care that my sister has left me to do all the work by myself? Tell her then to help me.' [41]But the Lord answered her, 'Martha, Martha, you are worried and distracted by many things; [42]there is need of only one thing. Mary has chosen the better part, which will not be taken away from her.'

It would be too easy to guess whose side you're on."

"Martha's," a couple of voices said.

"Me, too. It's her house. She's doing the work. Meanwhile her sister is languishing at the feet of their guest. She's like the guy you work with at the plant, or the cashier in the next aisle who always has to go check on something important in the office, ask the boss for some clarification, something you wouldn't think to consider, more important than the job you're supposed to be doing. She's lollygagging, our grandparents would have said. We'd say she's loafing. But you've been around Jesus long enough to know we're being set up, right along with Martha. It's not as though Jesus hasn't wrong-footed you before. You're the older brother, aren't you? You're steaming at the end of that story, when your younger brother gets the homecoming party. I know you. You're the one with the buried talent, the one griping because you only got paid as much as the guy who showed up an hour before the shift ended. Where's your union rep, for crying out loud? I know you're there because I'm standing right next to you, clutching my pound in my napkin, grousing because I didn't get time-and-a-half. And maybe you have noticed how Luke fits the story into his gospel. Look with me at Luke 10."

He would resort to calisthenics rather than laughter at this point to wake them up. With an inaudible grunt people sat up and reached a Bible from their rack. Half of them or so.

"The story of Mary and Martha comes right between two of the most famous passages in the New Testament. We don't always think about the context of Jesus's stories. Our lectionary clips them out of the Bible and sticks them up on the refrigerator for us. We read them as more self-contained than they are. Right beforehand, Jesus tells the parable of the Good Samaritan. Like the Martha and Mary story, it appears only in Luke's gospel. It answers the lawyer's question, who is my neighbor? Ask Jesus a question, you get a story. And all you wanted was a straight answer. The answer is not so obvious: it's not the person who lives next door. So who is my sibling? The one I should be helping in the kitchen? Or the one who enthralls me with his words? The one who shows up with all the good stories?"

He must have been getting through; Ruth had stopped taking notes.

"Jesus is nobody's brother in that house, is he? But when Jesus has come and gone you're not sure of much of anything. Everything gets shaken up. It's a chaotic day in the neighborhood. And what comes after the story of Mary and Martha? Well, probably not in real life. There's not much of a segue. One minute Jesus is in a house; the next he's in 'a certain place.' It's in a new chapter, but remember that chapter and verse numbers came along long after the Bible was written. We don't know what happened in between; Luke has just put them back-to-back. So immediately, as far as we know, after Jesus has commended Mary for listening, he teaches his disciples how to speak—to pray the Lord's Prayer. Take them together, and we're conversing with God."

He had Meg's attention as always, her loving smile of incipient disapproval. Her eye was on the sparrow of his sermon, which she would not let fall.

"But there's more. Let's say you noticed all that. There's one thing I will bet my last denarius you don't know, because no one knows it but me. Last night as I was reading today's scripture I had an insight into this text that no theologian in the history of theology has ever had, and I will conclude by sharing my revelation with you."

That was not gospel truth. He had a little more to say. But he had learned from hearing someone else that it helped to give some hope that the end was near. And he needed their attention for this one.

"I alone of all the readers of the Bible who have ever lived have recognized this fact: Martha was a Presbyterian."

It worked. He waited for the laughter to subside.

"Yes, we're in the wrong. Jesus nailed us again. We're in a committee meeting, we're preparing the refreshments for fellowship hour, we're stuffing envelopes when we should be listening to him. And I think that somewhere a couple of millennia ago there was a Presbyterian scribe somewhere who thought maybe Jesus had gone a little too far, overstated his case, and decided that what he really meant to say to Martha was that 'few things are needful, or only one.' You'll see that you have that listed as a variant at the bottom of the page. Thanks for the thought, but let's leave it the way we have it. There is one thing needful, and let's remember that in Hebrew, the language Jesus would have been speaking or thinking in, the same word can mean 'thing' and 'word.' There is one needful word, and it is capitalized. You have God's word for it.

"So we've heard the story of Mary and Martha. Let's finish it the way Luke does, with needful words. Let's pray."

* * *

It looked again that Tuesday as though Doug and Buck would be the last to leave the locker room. Buck was ahead of his usual schedule. His ablutions concluded, he sat fully dressed on the middle bench, pleasantly withdrawn from the conversation around him.

When he wasn't talking or guffawing, he was entranced, though still vaguely indulgent of the ambient cacophony. It was possible he was waiting for Doug.

Doug enjoyed the daily coda of their workout, the flurry of farewells punctuated by lockers slammed shut, the assurances they would all see each other tomorrow, as if there were any chance they would not. They often departed in random pairs, grimly companionable as they set out for the implicitly shared problems they faced at work or at home. As he watched them disperse Doug noted that he had missed one more chance to throw a "Jesus saves" into the repartee. He wondered how that thought might be absorbed by the group, whether they needed it. The life of the locker room was abundant in its way; its congregants were in better shape in every way and every day. Maybe the context would present itself next time.

Buck stirred when Doug closed his locker. "Where are you parked, Rev?" he said.

"I'm on foot, unless someone called in a miracle for me. My car died. Very peacefully, right in the parking lot out front. Faithful to the end. I coasted into my parking space."

"Let's take a look," Buck said, and a couple of minutes later Buck was holding the outside door for Doug and saying, "Which is your vehicle?"

Doug pointed.

"Go ahead and pop the hood."

That much Doug could do.

"You say it just stopped?"

"That's right."

"Try the lights," Buck said, suddenly very clinical. "Alternator. Where's your garage?"

"Just a few blocks from here. Pugh Exxon."

"That's about the most expensive place around. But close—that's good. I'll jump you, and we can make it that far."

"That's nice of you, Buck, but you don't have to do that. I was going to walk back to the church and call the garage from there." He wondered if Buck caught the note of concession in "was going to." He suspected Buck's favors were not easy to turn down.

"No, no. You've already got one workout in today," Buck said, jovial again. "I'm retired. I've got nothing but time. Time and more time. I'll swing my car around. I've got cables. See, the battery's good; you've got a few more years on it. But it's not being recharged as you drive. When we get you started, I'll follow you to the gas station. If you don't make it, I'll jump you again. It will save you a tow. He slammed the lid closed. It usually took Doug two tries. "You say it stopped right here? You used up your miracle for the day."

They made it to the garage in one go, and Doug was content to sit in what passed for a waiting room, a couple of metal-tubing chairs with cracked leather seats and a coffee table covered with auto parts catalogues, while Buck negotiated the repairs. "Tomorrow afternoon late," he said as he beckoned Doug to the door. "Best they can do. They can get a rebuilt alternator for you."

The interior of Buck's car was not what Doug would have predicted. A box of Kleenex in a metal holder was attached to the dashboard; a cross on a beaded necklace hung from the rearview mirror. "I never asked what you retired from, Buck," he said.

"Engineer."

That term had always seemed a catch-all to Doug. "Not a car mechanic?"

"No, you pick that up. You buy enough junky cars as a kid," he laughed.

"This is a nice car."

"That would be one word for it. It's my wife's. Mine is in the shop, too. Looks like we've got a plague going; maybe you should look into that. I'm going to pick her up at her church, and she'll take me to get it. Which is your church again? There's one on every block in this part of town. Sometimes two."

"It's just two lights down on the left. It's good of you to do this."

"You told me that already. The question is will you remember it on Sunday. Maybe it will get me off the hook for a week anyway."

By the time they pulled into the church lot Doug wasn't surprised to see Ruth waiting for them by the back door or to see her mouth surprise as he emerged from the car. Buck stayed in the driver's seat. Surprise was not in his repertoire of emotions.

"Talk about awkward," Doug said. "You realize, Ruth, that as a man of the cloth I am obliged to tell Buck about your other husband, Arden."

Ruth laughed at that. "If anyone calls on the phone and asks for Arden I'm supposed to tell them he's not at home. I'm the only one allowed to call him that. And his mother."

"So, your labors are done for the day?" Doug said.

"No." Ruth indicated the bags on the steps behind her. "My driver couldn't make it. Judy dropped me off earlier. Now I've got my car but no one to deliver. I'm way late already."

"I can do it," Doug said. "My afternoon is pretty free. Let me just explain to Betty where I'll be."

"I'll get the bags loaded." She leaned into the car. "I feel sure Arden will help."

"At times like this I go by Buck," he said. Then, "All right."

With Ruth at the wheel, Buck in the passenger seat and Doug in the back, they set out on their rounds. Buck made the two deliveries on the way to his garage. When he got back into the car after the second, he said, "They don't seem to complain about the food when I deliver."

"I wonder why?" Ruth said.

They laughed together, each at their own joke. The conversation along the way was steady but did not stray into theology any more than it did at the health club.

The garage was one of those franchises, a wing of a big mall store. They threaded their way through solid ranks of parked cars.

"You can just drop me off," Buck said. "They told me it would be ready right about now."

"We can wait to be sure," Doug said. "We wouldn't want you to be stranded."

"It will be okay," Buck said. "They know me. That means they know I don't like to wait around."

He heaved himself out of the car with a parting laugh. Doug took his place. Just in case, in a remote fringe of the lot, right before the exit, Ruth and he parked.

"As long as we're stopped, let's change places," Ruth said. "The clients will be expecting me."

Rearranged, they watched from their distance through the big front window of the store—the wall was all window—as Buck approached the counter and pantomimed with the clerk. He appeared to pay. Then he walked back outside and stood with some other shoppers on the sidewalk that ran the length of the building. It could have been a train platform; a steady stream of shoppers entered and exited the double door to Buck's left. The effect was enhanced when Doug eased them into gear, as though the building was pulling out of its berth rather than them.

"Maybe we should pick him up," Ruth said. "At least drive by to check."

"I think he's all right," Doug said. "It looks like maybe he does have a wait, but he doesn't look upset."

"You can tell?"

Buck looked around him, alert but complacent. After a minute his face settled back into a squint, as though signaling his assumption that he was no longer in anyone's view, or no longer needed to be, and he turned to join the flow of shoppers into the store, and they lost him.

THE RECOMMENDATION

To his chagrin, as he stood in the office of the philosophy department, Jim couldn't tell which of the two reactions to the news of that June morning was the more ignoble, his teachers' or his. Chagrin itself was hardly the appropriate feeling for the time or place.

At this point in his college career he was used to finding himself on the high road, his professors far below him, mired in pet theories and worldly concerns. By the end of his junior year he was long past disillusionment. When he arrived, one summer removed from his senior year at a high school two counties away, he was relieved to find that conversation was not conducted at an unbroken academic intensity in every corner of the campus. He had assumed that his every pleasantry would have to be original and insightful. Eventually he found that it was up to him to ratchet discussions with his teachers up intellectually; they seemed content to talk about sports. He could remember walking behind one of the faculty superstars, a professor of Italian, and a younger man, probably a graduate student. Aimless that day as he often was, Jim trailed them across the quad for the gleanings of their conversation. The professor was recapping a police show he had seen on television the night before. When his presumed student compared a plot point to a scene in Dante, the professor's smile crumpled as he conceded the point. "I suppose so," he sighed. You could tell that *The Divine Comedy* was the last thing he wanted to talk about. Once, in an unbelievable windfall, Jim was sitting with a philosophy professor at a table in the cafeteria when two other professors joined them. It was almost a bad philosophers' joke: I went to lunch and a symposium broke out. He did witness a dialectical display of sorts: in the space of three sentences they moved from Hume to the prospects for a local chapter of a teachers' union.

Professor O'Rourke was not like that. But then he had never seen Professor O'Rourke talk with either professor or student outside the classroom.

So in retrospect he was more surprised at his own response than at Professor Weiss's when he walked into the department office in East Main that day. School was out; grades were in. Jim's were good. Summer had arrived punctually; maybe a bell had gone off overnight. Finals week had been fittingly grey and drizzly. Now suddenly the sunshine outside was incandescent. If there were any doubts about the season, they were dispelled by Professor Weiss's attire: Bermuda shorts, sandals and mid-calf black dress socks. Jim stood beside him at the counter, inside the glass door. The room was institutional in décor and atmosphere; he and the professors could have been lining up to renew their driver's licenses. The two desks on the other side of the counter were occupied by women who looked like schoolteachers of an earlier era. Usually one or the other would stand up and approach you, ready to produce any form for any occasion. On this day they sat stock-still and half-smiling. Professor Weiss stood next to a colleague Jim didn't know.

"Pills?" the other man said.

"No," Professor Weiss said. "He was old school."

And, when Jim found out, he thought, Well, I guess I'll have to ask someone else for a letter.

* * *

When Jim explained to the room at large that he was looking for Professor O'Rourke, it galvanized the nearer of the two secretaries. She sat straight up and gestured as though semaphoring, one hand beckoning Jim and the other pointing toward Professor Milnes's inner office. He was the chair of the department. As Jim swung the counter gate open and walked through it, Professor Weiss observed him with a blank expression tinged with suspicion, as though he were watching a chair moving of its own volition. It did not follow either from his stupefaction or from the fact that he had not had Jim in class that he did not know who Jim was.

Although he had had Professor Milnes only in a huge lecture class, he was greeted familiarly when he entered his office. It was probably his job to know all the philosophy majors and even the minors, like Jim. The professors were comically overt in their efforts to recruit majors, whom they joked (the students assumed) they outnumbered. Jim had been on the periphery of several conversations including Professor Milnes that actually had some substance. He at least made him feel involved, creating the illusion with a look or a nod that Jim had a comment on his lips. He almost convinced Jim that he did.

Jim classified Professor Milnes as a normal professor. That was good and bad. He may not have been any younger than Professor O'Rourke, but he was blond and trim; his two children sometimes played in his office while he worked. He was almost always there. A nine-to-five philosopher, he said freely and ruefully. He said something in that vein to Jim that day. "The department of philosophy. You would think that you've come to the right place. We should be philosophical. You have inferred what happened?" He smiled at Jim and as suddenly set his chin on his hand and gazed out the window, like someone nodding off, except into consciousness. He looked back. "You would not have deduced it. Bart could be a difficult man. Not communicative. But tenacious. Not one to let matters rest."

Jim suspected it grated on Professor O'Rourke when his colleagues called him Bart. He didn't look like the kind of person who would go by a nickname. Barton wasn't his first name anyway. Thomas Barton O'Rourke. T. Barton O'Rourke. He probably went by Barton to avoid a nickname, as though a middle name would be immune to abbreviation. Bart was maybe marginally less prosaic than Tom. He remarked once when they were covering existentialism in class that Camus said that people had only one decision to make: whether or not to commit suicide. All subsequent decisions depended on that one. Existence before essence. He must have considered his name one of those choices.

"What bothers me," Jim said, "is that I came in just to see if Professor O'Rourke had written the letter of recommendation I asked for. That suddenly seems kind of trivial. Who cares?"

"You asked Bart for a letter?"

"Just for a summer job. I'd be a teacher and counselor at a school I used to go to. He was maybe an odd choice. I had just the one class from him."

"We can put something together for you as a department. We can look at your grades, maybe some of your work. Bart mentioned you. The class was Philosophy of Religion, I believe? A paper on Augustine, I think it was, you wrote for him? I remember you from the lecture course, though I didn't do any of the grading. You were on our radar. We're always trolling for majors." He came down heavy on the "trolling," an academic's way of both telegraphing and apologizing for a witticism. Even normal professors did it. "And mixing our metaphors." He lapsed again into seriousness. "You're worried about a letter. As well you might be. It's your future, at least one step. I'm thinking how glad I am this happened after the school year. It can be a nightmare to decipher someone else's grade book. Give me Linear A."

Normality did not always translate well to the classroom, Jim had found. True, this was not Professor Milnes's only office. The steel shelving here held more binders than books; his green metallic desk could have belonged to an accountant. He had another office upstairs. His cave, he called it when he lectured on Plato's *Republic*; he wanted to run back into it when he saw the cruel light of the classroom. It was one of those teachers' jokes Jim got a couple of years later. Jim had glimpsed the piles of books inside, the couch and the floor lamp. In class he was surprisingly formal and dry. You could tell he was trying to connect with the students, but he had a way of seeming to be on the brink of a breakthrough or a confidence without ever quite producing it. If he broke a sentence off short and started a new one with, "Look," you could expect to be more rather than less confused afterward. Whereas you never knew where Professor O'Rourke was going next, if anywhere.

* * *

Jim recalled the first day of their class. At some point in the course of his college education he had heard that you remembered in black or white. Or maybe it was dreamed. Or both. He could not recall if one of his professors or another student had told him this. He wouldn't have known enough to dispute either. Whatever its source or validity, that theory would be moot in the case of that colorless January day. The branches of the leafless trees on their Appalachian campus gleamed like coal against a sodden gray sky. It was a Tuesday-Thursday class and therefore scheduled for an hour and fifteen minutes. The first day of a course was always an exercise in apology. The lesson plan was to scrutinize a syllabus into pointlessness. The organization was so obvious and the goals were so modest that there was hardly a point in meeting again. That analysis took fifteen minutes. So you would walk out of the lecture hall into a meaningless void with an hour to kill before your next class.

Not in Professor O'Rourke's class. If there was a syllabus, they never heard about it. He sat at his desk with a smile of anticipation as students wandered in, as though he had some gossip to share. When he looked at the clock behind him, it was a couple minutes past the hour. The class was hushed. Latecomers sidled along the walls looking for a seat. He stood up and began to pace. "I have never for the life of me figured out the appeal of Dwight Moody." He recalled for us an event he had read about as a child. A revival attended by thousands. "Dwight Moody must have had something to say they were awfully anxious to hear." Every time he pronounced the name it was with the same conspiratorial irony, as though appealing to the class for help. "What was it about Dwight Moody?" Not that he stopped talking, wide-eyed with delight at the conundrum, long enough for anyone to opine. Jim had heard the name, he wasn't sure where. He was pretty sure that even so he was better informed than his classmates. The room was packed. Rather than desks it contained benches, which felt on this day like bleachers. After fifteen minutes or so students began to exchange glances. They were neutral at first. Jim had long since lost the thread of the lecture.

A few minutes later a student raised his hand and said, "Could you remind us who Dwight Moody was?"

The question seemed only to heighten Professor O'Rourke's delight. His jaw dropped. It was possible the student was joking. He would play along. "He was an evangelist, of course." He continued. The more restless the class became, the more rapt he seemed. "And all on account of Dwight Moody."

A couple of girls in the first row on the other side of the room, who had been taking notes from the start, laid their pencils down. They still sat forward in their seats, but their smiles of attention seemed enameled on their faces. Professor O'Rourke had not consulted the wall clock since he began lecturing. With about fifteen minutes to go in the class, the students became transfixed by it. The problem was that it had one of those jerky minute hands, so you couldn't be sure when it jumped past the three that it wouldn't jump back again. Finally there could be no doubt that the last quarter hour had passed; the minute hand had broken clear into the next quadrant of the clock's face, as all the students had registered.

Sometime before that Jim had become aware of a counterpart two rows back on the other side of the classroom, a guy about his size, comparably semiformally dressed. Their eyes met every so often. Jim got the feeling that he had singled him out, too, as perhaps the one other right-minded individual in the class. After a while Jim felt he could read into his expressions a sequence of emotions—exasperation, amusement, resignation, outrage— each shading into the next. With nothing better to do than be flattered, Jim was doing his best to acknowledge and reflect these expressions as he also tried to pay attention to Professor O'Rourke. When class should have been over for ten minutes, the guy began to twitch in his seat. His last look toward Jim seemed to be one of betrayal as Jim sat still. But Jim was right up front, and this was his last class of the day.

Finally the other guy grabbed his books and bolted. He might have uttered a soft groan, more defeated than defiant. That started the exodus. In twos and threes, then whole rows at a time, students peeled off like fighter jets from a formation. Professor O'Rourke was sitting at his desk by this time, smiling paternally at the departing students as at wayward youth. He had more to say about Dwight Moody. Jim realized he had not consulted a note throughout. In fact, he didn't have any books with him. Eventually Jim and he were alone in the room. Professor O'Rourke turned and looked at the wall clock. "Do you think that worked?" he said.

* * *

Ironically, even though he was the first to leave the room, Jim's alter ego was sitting on the bus back to the main campus that Jim caught. The shuttles ran less frequently after the rush when classes let out. They had all missed that wave; Jim saw several other classmates scattered around the bus. As soon as he boarded, it lurched into gear and set off. He swayed his way down the aisle and sat next to the guy, who was gazing abstractedly out the window. He seemed to know it was Jim without looking at him. He shook his head. "The two most interesting topics in the world, philosophy and religion. How could you kill them both in one class period? Is that what you thought Philosophy of Religion would be when you signed up for it?"

"I wasn't sure. I probably assumed they were sort of the same thing. Philosophy of Religion sounded almost redundant."

"I mean, you want to like the guy."

That was true, too. Professor O'Rourke was big and rumpled-looking, with a spring-like forelock of curly hair that dangled almost to his glasses. But not quite, so that didn't explain his occasional squint. You couldn't be sure if he had a gut or not, because he was sway-backed when he walked, and one tail of his shirt was habitually out under his sport coat. You knew the sorts of thing about him you knew about professors. He had written a book. He was divorced. He had a degree from either Oxford or Cambridge. He stayed in town during the week but lived on a farm a county over where he had grown up. As he lectured, he was clearly amused at much of what he said and seemed eager to share that amusement. Or maybe the joke was too obvious, or maybe it was on him. That seemed to amuse him, too.

* * *

Something occurred to Professor Milnes. "So, school is out, but you're still here. Will you stick around this summer? Or are you local?"

"I'll be here for a couple of weeks. I won't know exactly where I'm going until I hear about the job."

"Of course," Professor Milnes shook his head. "The recommendation."

"I think it's perfunctory. I'm pretty sure I'll get the job. They know me. They just need all the forms. In other words, I don't think it has to be a glowing recommendation. I could ask someone else."

"We can take care of it. Where can we get hold of you? On second thought, could you stop back here in a couple of days?"

"Yes. I'm pretty free."

"By then things should have settled down. It wasn't as messy as it might have been. I'm sorry. Not a happy choice of words."

* * *

At the second meeting of Philosophy of Religion the classroom was full but not bursting. No one had to lean against a window sill or sit on the floor. Jim's acquaintance sat in his same seat, looking no more comfortable than he had on the bus. When Professor O'Rourke began, "I think one proposition we can safely make is that we have exhausted the subject of Dwight Moody," there was laughter, about half relieved and half nervous. The latter reaction proved the more justified. The subject of the lecture that followed was if anything less identifiable than that of his earlier one. Initially it seemed to be pedagogy. "What is my role as a teacher?" he asked. The class sat back collectively at what seemed a confidence. Pencils were laid down. Jim had a pretty good sense of these things, and he judged from this preamble that nothing note-taking-worthy would come up for a good five minutes. While earnest, however, Professor O'Rourke was not especially lucid. Only an occasional phrase stood out, not always in English. "*Weltanschauung* . . . upwardly mobile . . . *ennui* . . . a simulacrum of philosophy, hedonism in effect . . . I ask myself if it is my calling in life to provide an intellectual *frisson* for students on their way to a seat on the Stock Exchange."

It was right about then. Something like a pulse. A wave. That was all that occurred to Jim at the time. He wasn't sure what it was, but he was sure that everyone in the room felt it. It must have been with Professor O'Rourke's next sentence that for a second every peripheral vision in the room merged into one concerted gaze.

"There are suspiciously many of you."

One minute the class was lulled into the anticipation of another obscure reflection; the next it was tensed with the current of collective recognition that they were listening not to a confession but to bitter invective of which they were the object.

"For students to throng to hear about the philosophy of religion is a sign that many of them are profoundly confused about the nature of the event, which is not a happening but a course. So I supposed you will be requiring these."

He picked up a stack of papers from his desk and began passing them out. Students took them from him numbly. It was the syllabus. As he paged through it in a monotone, the sensation ebbed. By the time he was through, the students had regained some composure. A few clipped the syllabus into a notebook. Then, with forty minutes left in the class period, he exited the room. No one moved.

"He's not coming back," someone finally said.

"Did that just happen?" someone else said.

As before, people left in twos and threes. Once again, his buddy was out the door first. Jim had to jog to catch up with him as he strode purposefully for the bus stop, where they found several shuttles idling. This time they were too early for the rush. The class spread out among the vehicles to sit and wait. Jim followed his friend to the bus at the head of the line.

"He's a jagoff," he said, again before he turned to look at Jim.

"A what?"

"That's a Pittsburgh variation of a standard term of abuse. It refers to someone who habitually and fruitlessly engages in a solitary activity that should involve some other human. I came all the way down here to college to get jerked around."

"I just wanted to compare notes with you."

"Notes, right. What's there to take notes on? I still don't know who Dwight Moody was. Except now I don't want to know. I'm dropping. If this bus ever starts I should have time to get to the registrar's office before my next class. You coming?"

"That was my first instinct. I was insulted, like everyone else. I wanted to walk out then. Like everyone else. Then I got mad. If that was a trick to get me out of the class, I'm not going to fall for it. I want to know something about the subject."

"Good luck. He'll make you work to get anything he knows out of him. I know that kind of teacher."

"Give me one more class."

"Give *you* one more class?

"Come on. There's another week until drop-add is over."

He didn't tell him his theory about what happened back in the classroom. He had just formed it and would have to sleep on it. He suspected you would have to call what they had just been through a religious experience. Maybe it was in the course description.

* * *

Jim became something of a fixture in the office of the philosophy department over the next couple of weeks, all but a staff member. The secretaries routinely nodded him into Professor Milnes's office, where he took a seat until Professor Milnes hung up the phone or straightened up whatever documents he was working on and set them aside. Then he would sit still. Jim could have been counseling him. It seemed to help him to have the letter of recommendation as the office's most pressing item of business. One day as he was thinking he pushed an envelope around the top of his desk with the eraser end of a pencil. A smiled played around his mouth, but the kind Jim had observed on people when they suggested an idea undeniably to someone else's advantage but even more to theirs. "Do you expect to be around for another week?" he said.

"Oh, sure."

"It's just that we are in the process of putting together a memorial service. We thought it best not to wait until next academic year. It would be nice to have student involvement. Do you think you could participate? Be an usher? Maybe offer a reading? Good. Keep stopping back, if you would. This is a good time."

* * *

Timing seemed to be an issue for Professor O'Rourke. On the third day of class Jim was among the first few students to arrive. The classroom door was closed, but from the hallway they could see through the door's window that he was sitting at the desk. When they finally opened the door and entered, they seemed to be joining a lecture in progress. "If that was all I had to worry about," he was saying. "If that were the greatest of my worries." He welcomed them, wide-eyed as always, as he would have latecomers; he might have been addressing the empty classroom for some time. He seemed eager to share if not reveal his thoughts. He would at all costs avoid stating the obvious. "A dramatic exit I can cope with, even appreciate." Some days you waited for his classes to end; other days you waited for them to begin. This was one of the latter. They could afford to wait; nobody much was there. Eventually Professor O'Rourke descended to detail. "Just last period I went a few minutes beyond class time, which I admittedly am wont to do. A young man got up before I had quite perorated and when he left slammed the door behind him. I believe I was to interpret that as a sign of annoyance. If only that were the greatest of my trials."

Meanwhile, they were ten minutes into the present class period. Only the first couple of benches on the far side of the class contained students. They looked around at each other with the intimacy of survivors. The atmosphere was ark-like, as though Professor O'Rourke had preserved two of every kind of student, like the two studious girls who still sat opposite Jim. He counted a couple of preppies, a couple of hippies. The effect was heightened by the icy rain falling outside. If nothing else, these random students shared their uncertainty about the subject matter of the class. Then Jim's counterpart walked in. His pair was complete.

Professor O'Rourke eyed Jim's friend as he found his seat. He probably thought he was late. And that's when the class became interesting. Mesmerizing. Call it their second religious experience. "I could see from Mr. Mentzer's expression the other day that he was a skeptic," Professor O'Rourke said. Jim now knew him as Mike; he was surprised that Professor O'Rourke knew his name. "Perhaps he remains agnostic."

"Deeply," Mike said. "Watch." He shrugged. A couple of students laughed.

"You didn't believe me when I told you that God exists by definition, did you? And it takes only a good-sized paragraph or two to prove it. The class can hardly complain about the length of your reading assignment for today." He drew himself up in his chair and looked around. "What was that? Someone made a comment. I believe that is what is referred to as 'classroom participation.' That is a desideratum in higher education these days. I will report it to the dean and get it on my record. Who said it?"

To Jim's surprise, it was Jim. "Still, it was long," he said. "For a definition, at any rate."

"'Still,'" Professor O'Rourke said. "'At any rate.' Can we be any more academic today? Can we hedge any more? What are you saying?"

"That when you look in a dictionary for the meaning of a word you don't expect to find even a paragraph. You expect a sentence. Not even a sentence, a fragment. God—a being who controls the universe. Just a word, if there's a synonym."

"How about a picture?" Mike said. "It's always seemed to me that dictionaries tend to wordiness."

"By definition?" Professor O'Rourke said, to more laughter, and a groan or two. "But I think Mr. Fuller is longing to say more. What is the logical destination of this juggernaut of analysis?"

"Maybe the longer a definition is, the weaker," Jim said. "Maybe even no synonym would be best. Then a word would have to mean itself. It would really be true by definition. It would be its own definition."

"I would say then it would be self-evident. And therefore meaningless?" Professor O'Rourke said. "But if a definition is called for, a single word would be best?"

"Yes."

"Provided we knew what that word meant?"

"Yes."

"What might such a word be in such a case as this?"

Jim looked out the windows at the dripping, bare black branches they framed. "How about 'nature?'"

"Nature!" Professor O'Rourke said. "A second Spinoza! I did hear you say *Deus sive Natura?*"

"That's what I heard," Mike said, and there was more laughter.

"Not five minutes ago, though, didn't you say that God controls the universe, which I take to be equivalent to nature, and now God *is* the universe?"

"Didn't hear that," someone else said. Jim didn't realize there were a couple of people behind him. The laughter was spreading.

"I sensed as soon as Mr. Fuller began speaking that we were dealing with one of the great minds of the seventeenth century," Professor O'Rourke said. "Sir, you have anticipated Baruch Spinoza—a few hundred years after the fact, it is true. You were early late. Spinoza let slip the phrase, *Deus sive Natura.* That is Latin for 'God or nature.' God *or* nature. He seemed to equate them. Take your pick. And would you like to dismantle Anselm's argument any further? You seem to have scant respect for this particular saint. Are you content to have reduced his reasoning to rubble, or would you prefer it granulated and commingled with the dust? Just to remind ourselves, I believe the definition with which we are concerned, as we have it from St. Anselm, represents God as that entity than which no greater can be conceived."

"I'm also not sure what it adds to the definition to say that something already good is even better when it exists. Wouldn't you assume that? If anything is true by definition, I would think it is existence."

"Congratulations, Mr. Fuller. You are making century-long strides. You have just vaulted into the Enlightenment. That is the approach of one Immanuel Kant, who can be said to have refuted Anselm. It took seven hundred years, so you're not far behind in the scheme of things. He indeed asked how the attribute of existence altered a concept. Anything else, Mr. Fuller?"

"One thing. Just because you proved God existed, would everyone necessarily believe in him?"

Professor O'Rourke peered at him, then at the clock. There were ten minutes of class left. "I would love to take this matter up with you, but I see our time is up. Or very nearly. I think that today, in contradistinction to you, I will be late a little early."

Jim had to catch up to Mike again on the way to the bus. It was harder because he dodged the puddles that Mike charged though in his boots. Jim just had loafers on. He had to get in front of him to get his attention. "What do you think?"

Mike shook his head, not so much disagreeing with anything as preoccupied.

"Better, wasn't it?"

"I still don't trust him. I haven't heard anything about a paper or exam. I just have a feeling the hammer is going to drop."

"You chimed in today."

"Tell me one thing," Mike said. "I'm asking myself, why now? Is there some reason the first class couldn't have been like this?"

* * *

Jim began to organize his days around his standing appointment in the philosophy department. It was the closest thing he had to an obligation for those couple of weeks between the end of term and any prospect of employment. After a late breakfast he spent time in the library, sometimes wandering in the stacks—but safely now. The books were defused; he could pick them up without having to write a paper about them. The pleasant weather outside seemed to have penetrated the building; the air conditioning was balmy with the scent of old book bindings. In the main rooms he browsed among the journals on display, discovering in the process several subjects he hadn't known existed. With students no longer milling around, the librarians noticed and occasionally smiled at him. In the afternoons he went across campus to the athletic complex and lifted weights or played pick-up basketball. Most of the players now were locals, and he passed for one.

On one of his trips to the office he walked into a scene. The secretaries expected him by now, but on this day one of them shrugged and the other winced as he let himself through the counter gate and headed to Professor Milnes's office. Seated in the chair Jim usually occupied was another professor visibly younger than Professor Milnes, whom Jim had thought of as the minimum age for a professor. He realized he and this professor had passed each other in the halls during the school year, acknowledging without ever quite greeting one another.

When they were all three together he was surprised there were so many years between him and Professor Milnes for this guy to fit into with so much room on either side.

"No one told me that," the young professor was expostulating, his expression suspended between outrage and amusement. "No one explained that to me." As soon as he saw Jim hovering in the doorway he included him in his appeal.

"We need to consider the audience," Professor Milnes said. He was looking down at a sheet of paper.

"The term is 'congregation,'" the other professor said. His name was Watkins. "It's church. This will be a church service, and the mourners will be its congregation. *Ad hoc*, it is true, but still a congregation. What did you expect?"

"A eulogy," Professor Milnes said. "This is to all intents and purposes a sermon."

"It's the university church. I attend it. We preach the resurrection. Are we supposed to espouse beliefs except when we really need them?"

"There is a committee," Professor Milnes said.

"That's reassuring. There must be Presbyterians in charge."

"We want to be sensitive to all perspectives. We felt . . . If you could say the same thing without being so . . . particularist."

Professor Watkins sat back in his chair, eyebrows raised.

"Certainly there are values here we can all endorse. This was to go in the program, after all. If we could manage not to be Christocentric. With a little tailoring to the occasion it could be a departmental statement."

"So if I edit Jesus out it would be all right? Then it would be spiritual but not religious. It would be philosophical."

"Yes," Professor Milnes said after a pause, then laughed, half reluctantly and half in relief, as though Professor Watkins had articulated what they had both been agreeing on all along.

"Right," Professor Watkins said, reaching for the paper. "No editing. Someone else can write it." And he left.

Professor Milnes paused again, then motioned Jim to the vacated chair. "That was not the demeanor of a man who is unmindful that he was just recently not denied tenure," he said. "Not to be too apophatic. I supposed we'll need to get used to it. People do acquire principles along with tenure. We're better off without an altar call, though I suppose it stopped short of that. We have a few reminiscences. Still, it leaves us with a void. You said you could offer a reading? An appropriate reading? And a memory or two?"

* * *

Jim had no shortage of material. Philosophy of Religion was easily his favorite class that semester. After its truly bizarre start it just got more and more interesting. It raised every question about religion that bothered Jim and some he had never thought to ask. Furthermore, Professor O'Rourke proved capable of histrionics over and above his baseline eccentricity. One day he came into class straining under a load of books. As often, Miss Satterwhite, one of the class scribes, was taking notes before class even began. When she looked up and saw Professor O'Rourke she groaned, either in sympathy with his effort or in dread of a weighty lecture. That gave him his opening. He tottered over in front of her.

"Help me, Miss Satterwhite," he said. "You seem to be feeling the burden of this dilemma as much as I am. Is something carried because it is a carried thing, or is it a carried thing because it is carried?"

In answer, Miss Satterwhite groaned again. Everyone laughed. By now they all knew each other by last name at least; the students who had stayed in the class after Professor O'Rourke's withering first lectures never missed. They laughed at Miss Satterwhite's reaction and also at the discovery that she had a sense of humor.

"Nicely negotiated," Professor O'Rourke said. "You have avoided falling into error. You share the practice of the skeptic who would not risk making a statement, which might be false, and so in response to any question would only point." He set the books down on his desk with a thud. "Now, all together. Is a thing carried because it is a carried thing, or is it a carried thing because it is carried?"

Maestro-like, he waved his arms until everyone caught on. One after another, the students looked alert and sat up. Then, on cue and in unison, they pointed at the books.

"Splendid," he said. "And we all know where we're going from here, because we all did our reading, yes? These books don't look so carried now, do they? They were only carried things so long as someone, in this case yours truly, carried them. There is nothing intrinsically carried about them. They might be carried; they might not. But, you demur, and I tend to agree, who really cares about a pile of books? What, though, if we changed the verb? What if we said 'love?' Are things loved because (and only so long as) they are loved, or are they loved because they are loved things?"

A guy behind Jim offered his first remark of the semester. "Hank Williams would say, the former."

"Another great philosopher," Professor O'Rourke said. "And contemporary. I somehow omitted him from the syllabus. What did Mr. Williams have to say on the subject?"

The guy answered in a sing-song. "'My hair's still curly; my eyes are still blue. Why don't you love me like you used to do?'"

"And you would interpret those lines how?"

"You're only a loved thing as long as someone loves you. My argument would be largely empirical. That is to say, I speak from experience."

"I might quibble with you," Professor O'Rourke said. "By Mr. Williams's own account, is there not something inherently lovable in the subject that someone responded to? The quality inhered in the subject before he knew the other party, and it persisted after they broke up."

"That reasoning didn't work on the other party," the student responded, to laughter.

"And what if we changed the object? Let's make it the gods. Are the gods loved—worshiped, if you prefer—because they are worshiped things, or are they worshiped things because (and only so long as) they are worshiped? There is perhaps more at stake here?"

"The gods should be lovable by definition, shouldn't they?" Miss Satterwhite said. "They couldn't depend on anyone for anything."

"The Greeks used our word 'therapy' where we might use 'worship,'" Professor O'Rourke said. "Humans give the gods therapy—service, we could also translate."

"It wouldn't make any sense to say that God is lovable," someone else said. "As though that is one attribute of God, separate from everything else. Love must pervade God."

"It must?" Professor O'Rourke staggered back a couple of steps.

"God is love," someone said. "It says that somewhere."

"Where?" Professor O'Rourke said, looking around.

"In the Bible somewhere," someone said.

"1 John," someone else said.

"So God does not receive love at all, but gives it, even to himself? God is not a loved thing at all but a loving thing?" By this time Professor O'Rourke had collapsed in his chair as though cowering under an onslaught of insights. The fact that they were mostly his made it funnier.

Their assignment was a dialogue by Plato called the *Euthyphro*. That was a character's name, but it was still called "the" *Euthyphro*, like the *Phaedo* or the *Gorgias*, which they also read parts of. Professor O'Rourke said it was common in Greek to use the definite article with a proper name. Jim liked the idea. He and his buddy took to greeting each other that way when they ran into each other on campus. "How are you, the Mike?" "Not bad. Thanks for asking, the Jim."

"So the *Euthyphro* is one of the early dialogues of Plato we like to call aporetic," Professor O'Rourke was saying. "Why do we like to call them aporetic? Because that is the Greek word for 'dead end.' Where are we at the conclusion of the conversation? Your impression is correct: right back where we started. We still don't know what holiness is. Was it a waste of an hour and fifteen minutes? I knew someone would ask that question, if only me. Did we learn anything along the way? Do we know what holiness is not?"

* * *

"Good," Professor Milnes said, despite the episode with Professor Watkins musing with a smile over the draft of the service in front of him. Some of his professors seemed unaware or unconcerned how long it took them to think in the presence of their students; Jim suspected Professor Milnes didn't mind others' watching his mind at work. "And, let's face it, you owe him a tribute."

"What do you mean?" Jim said.

"The investigation at the farm is over, if that's what it was. Inquest? Bart didn't leave a note. But we did find this on his desk."

He handed Jim an unaddressed envelope. It was official university stationery. On the bottom left-hand corner it read, Re James Fuller. On the other side a signature was scrawled across the seal.

* * *

Not that every meeting of Philosophy of Religion was an hour and a quarter of sustained cerebral bliss. One day Professor O'Rourke lectured for the entire time on a philosopher named Plotinus. This figure, they learned, had set out to harmonize Plato and Aristotle and ended up producing his own, original philosophy. It was the first they had heard of him and the last. There was no context for the lecture they could discern; it had no connection to the class on either side of it. As Professor O'Rourke expatiated, Jim could not have been the only one wondering whether they might be witnessing the second coming of Dwight Moody. The students were not so much attentive as vigilant. Because there was the palpable worry that the class would snap back to its original awkwardness, like a spring you have almost hooked into place before it slips from your grasp. They were all straining together in silence as the clock twitched.

Two days later, the next time they convened, it was as though that lecture had never occurred and Plotinus was a phantom. "I'm going to tell you a story," Professor O'Rourke began. "I had it from a philosopher named John Wisdom. Poor fellow never had a chance: with a name like that you have no choice but to be a philosopher. So. Two imperial British explorers find themselves in an impenetrable jungle, when they break through the bush into a clearing and see in front of them a beautiful, formal garden. Row after row of multicolored flowers. They pull up short, looking at one another in amazement. When they climb a nearby knoll and can look down on the garden, they see that the flowers are arranged in such a way as to produce the Union Jack. Their amazement increases.

"'We are not alone,' one explorer says, elated. 'A Briton lives in the vicinity.'

"'We are not alone,' the other says, despondent. 'That means someone has preceded us. Remember, we are explorers. Our job is to discover things. We are supposed to get places first.'"

"I know," one of Jim's classmates said. "Plotinus got there first."

"Plotinus was not British," Professor O'Rourke said with an upraised finger, less amused than the rest of them. "The first explorer said, 'Well, obviously there is a gardener hereabouts. Flowers don't spontaneously grow in the patterns of national flags.'

"'Why not?' said the second. 'Given enough time and space, the odds are that every possible pattern will be produced somewhere or other in the jungles of the world. Most of them will not be observed. There is no gardener.'

"'You don't *want* there to be a gardener,' the first explorer said. 'You are ambitious.'

"'You do,' the second said. 'You are lonely. But there is none.'

"'Let's wait and see,' the first explorer said. 'We will pitch camp here for the night. The flowers will need to be watered. We'll take turns watching for the gardener.'

"'Fair enough,' the second agreed.

"They waited, but no gardener appeared, and the flowers seemed just as fresh the next day.

"'You see,' the second explorer says. 'No gardener. The flowers grow at random and on their own.'

"'There must be a gardener,' the first explorer insists. 'But he must be invisible.'

"'All right, then,' says the second. 'We'll build a fence around the garden.'

"And they do. Still the flowers thrive. The second explorer feels vindicated anew.

"But the first says, 'There is a gardener, but he is invisible and he can fly.'"

"Something doesn't add up," Jim said. "I'm not sure they're disagreeing."

And at that moment, for that moment, they were all back in the ecstasy of awareness of the second session, but this time Jim thought of the analogy that had escaped him then. It was not to a garden but to a touring bus. It was as though the students were the passengers, cruising along, forgetting they were in motion and that there was a driver up front at the wheel, when all at once they realized eerily as one that the wheels were not in contact with the road and they were not driving but skidding.

Not that Professor O'Rourke snapped, any more than he did the other time. He turned slowly to look at Jim and said, "And I'm not sure why you would make that comment at this point in the story."

Then it was over. The tires grabbed the road again. Someone behind Jim said, "Put a roof over the garden."

"Capital idea," Professor O'Rourke said.

Then, as he liked to do, he waved his arms like a conductor, and the class said in unison, "But . . . "

In unison except for Jim. He listened along with the class as Professor O'Rourke reviewed and reflected on the story. It was a good exercise, Jim could see, a variation of the argument from design: surely a cosmos that functioned as well as theirs had a maker. Professor O'Rourke was building to his climax. "It *turns out that* the two explorers were coming to opposite conclusions based on the *same evidence*. Were there other forces than logic at work? Prejudice? Patriotism? Self-interest? Something you'd call faith, though it might take the form of doubt? One wonders if one could even say they were disagreeing."

It was one of those rare classes that ended just about on time— in this case with a minute and only a minute to spare. A couple of students stayed behind to press Professor O'Rourke on his last point, which sounded to Jim like Jim' last point. One did wonder if they were disagreeing; Jim was the one. He did not linger, though he had planned to. He had planned to ask Professor O'Rourke for a letter of recommendation. The deadline though wasn't for a month. He had time.

* * *

"It looks ready to go out in the post," Professor Milnes said. "All it needs is a recipient."

"I was going to bring him the address," Jim said. "That's what I was coming for that first day, after school let out."

"We can send it for you. But I'm just wondering. It might be a good idea for us to vet it for you."

"Vet?" Jim said. "I'm not sure what that means."

"We can read the letter to make sure it will further your candidacy. We do it routinely for our graduate students when they apply for jobs."

"The seal would have to be broken."

"I think we can explain that under the circumstances. Bart was eccentric at the best of times, and, hard as it might be for you students to believe, he was on his best behavior in the classroom. With his colleagues he veered from the eccentric to the erratic, especially toward the end. There were scenes. He accused the secretaries of things. Our selfless secretaries. They keep the department sane and afloat. Who knows but that he didn't turn on you in the letter?"

"I think I'd rather just send it as is," Jim said. "I'm funny about recommendations. I feel unworthy to ask for one, can't imagine how a teacher could vouch for me, then I worry that it will be too good."

Professor Milnes barked a laugh. "Your grades suggest you'd make a good academic, but if you join our ranks you'll have to acquire a skill you seem to lack: self-promotion. But as you wish. You say you think you probably have the job? You're a known quantity at the school?"

"Yes, though that would make a bad recommendation worse in a way. I care what they think about me. And I thought I might use it later, for other jobs or for grad school."

"On the other hand, you have the academic's gift of seeing an issue from two sides, both bad. If you get us the address, we'll send it along for you and with luck send you along to your next port of call. You have another year with us, however?"

"I'll be back in the fall."

"Good. I'll be offering a course in phenomenology next term, if that subject holds any interest for you. You'd be welcome. And of course we may have a new faculty member when you get back, if we can mount a search in time. You know you're just a few credits shy of a philosophy major?" Jim saw that the document on Professor Milnes's desk beside the draft of the service was his transcript. Professor Milnes tapped it. "It's been good to have you with us the past couple of weeks. Around the office. That was fortuitous. You can leave the information about your reading with Mrs. Blount. She's the secretary nearest us. The service is all set except for that. That's the finishing touch."

Mrs. Blount sat straight-backed in her chair, unsurprised at Jim's approach. When he reached her desk she swiveled and smiled brightly at him. Her hair was a swirl of gray and blonde. Sherbet-colored, maybe, Jim thought. He realized that he thought she was pretty. Trim—he had heard middle-aged women with a figure called that. He handed her a sheet of paper. "This is my contribution to the service. It's not terribly original. Maybe someone is doing it already."

"No," she said, looking it over and smiling again. "And someone should."

* * *

Jim had little experience with funerals, still less with suicides. But he felt reasonably sure he would never attend a stranger memorial service than this one.

The university church seemed especially cavernous when the crowd was small. On Sundays it was quite full, not only the pews but the aisles, when the choir processed before a service all around the sanctuary and back to the loft at the rear of the church. This was a Friday afternoon during summer break. Clumps of people were scattered around, barely within hailing distance of each other. He took a bulletin from one of the two young men at the door, no doubt graduate students, even shadowier presences than professors during the year. He hadn't been told to sit anywhere in particular, so he walked halfway down the center aisle and took his usual seat on the right. The two departmental secretaries sat side-by-side farther down on the other side. They might have been in prayer. But then they seemed at prayer even at their desks. The front row on his side must have been designated for family members. The result was that they seemed marooned, with a gulf between them and the pulpit on one side and another between them and the nearest other attendees, several pews behind them. The man standing up could only have been Professor O'Rourke's brother. The resemblance was almost comical, down to his half-bewildered, half-belligerent expression as he peered into the sanctuary. He was a little taller and leaner than Professor O'Rourke, but he had the same forelock and heavy black glasses. A woman and three children sat alongside him.

Jim looked to the right and saw Professor Milnes sidling the length of the long pew toward him. He sat down breathlessly. He was fidgety. "You're here. Good. More than I can say for some of my colleagues. You would think organizing a memorial service would be straightforward," he said, continuing to look around. "It's about as easy as mounting a production of *Aida* in Nigeria. With a native cast." He paused long enough to grin at his joke. Jim would have said that *Aida* was an opera. "No one on the faculty had any idea what it should look like, least of all me. The chaplain was good," he nodded. "He offered his help but was not overbearing. This is an impressive space. I wonder if it has plumbing."

"There's a men's room downstairs through the door to right of the pulpit," Jim said. "There's a bathroom upstairs by the choir loft, but it's unisex."

Professor Milnes looked at him quizzically. Then he glanced at his watch. "We have a little time. I'll just be on the safe side."

A few more people came in during Professor Milnes's absence, but not many. Jim recognized a few professors among them. When Professor Milnes sat back down beside him with another glance at his watch, he said, "I was thinking. Tell me. Your reading is not"—he searched for a word—"inordinately religious? I suppose I could look. I haven't had a chance."

"It's from the Old Testament."

"That's safer, I suppose. Bart wasn't Jewish, was he? What am I thinking? O'Rourke?" He opened his bulletin. "Oh, yes, I see it. Psalm 23. We've printed the whole thing. Well, that's almost proverbial, isn't it? 'The Lord is my shepherd . . . He restores my soul . . . ' Still, if it's a question of the soul, there are some sublime passages in Plotinus."

Thanks to the honoree, Jim knew who Plotinus was. He made a show of rummaging in the pew rack in front of them. "There don't seem to be any copies of the *Enneads*."

Professor Milnes sat back with a smile. "Point taken."

After a last pause he sat forward again and glanced around, then squeezed past Jim into the aisle. By the time he reached the lectern that had been set up at floor level in front of the steps up to the altar he was perfectly calm and composed. He was good. "I welcome you all here today in my capacity as chairman of the philosophy department. More than that: I welcome you into the philosophy department. Today we are all philosophers. Those who, as Socrates said, may logically not fear death. Philosophers are those who know only one thing: that they know nothing. If they fear death, they disqualify themselves as philosophers, because they are acting as though they know something they do not know. They are assuming that death is a bad thing. They are not in a position to assume that death is a bad thing, never having experienced it. Socrates loved to reduce the complicated, harrowing situations life confronts us with to simple choices. Death is either nothing or something. If it is nothing, if we never wake up, it can be neither good nor bad. If it is nonexistence, it will have no attributes at all. If it is a translation to another place, that place will be good or bad. For all we know, it is devoutly to be wished. Socrates thought so. He imagined an endless dialogue. What could be better than to explore our ideas with new friends, arriving all the time, forever? We may someday join Bart in discussion, and, if it is a much better place, we may even follow his reasoning."

It wasn't just that there was no music that made the service seem strange, and no clergy; the pulpit was empty throughout, the Bible resting on it inert. All the faculty who followed Professor Milnes were good; they all had a distinct point to make. None was what you would call mournful. Professor Weiss, whose job it was to talk about Professor O'Rourke as a colleague, looked on the point of exasperation as he shook his head and said, "I won't pretend Bart was easy to work with. But we can understand his behavior better now than we could then." This was the only allusion to reports that Professor O'Rourke had been suffering from a brain tumor.

Jim wasn't sure from whom he heard them; as of the past few days they were suddenly public knowledge. Another professor discussed Professor O'Rourke's "work," always a mysterious word to Jim when applied to his teachers, since it seemed to refer to everything they did except teach, which is all he saw them do. "We all owe a debt of gratitude to Bart for the work he did on the topic of other minds. The question fascinated him. How can we know what other people are thinking? How do we know that the meaning we attribute to their words is the meaning they attach to them? Isn't what troubles us today the thought that we could neither sense nor share the pain that he must have been feeling?"

What was strange was how obvious it was throughout that they were holding a service in a church in honor of someone no one particularly liked conducted by people none of whom believed in God. At some point during one of the speeches there was a single sob from somewhere behind Jim. Probably behind; there was an echo in the sanctuary.

* * *

"Now that you have completed the course," Professor O'Rourke began, "it is comforting for me as your teacher to know that you are absolutely convinced of at least two truths."

It was, indeed, the last session of Philosophy of Religion. Though that was not likely one of the truths he was referring to, it was inarguable. They would meet again for the final exam in a week's time. It had gotten to seem that the course would go on forever in its cycle of tedium and fascination, terror and exhilaration endlessly alternating. Spring had set in. Outside classes occasionally met in circles on the grass of the quad, while, ten feet away, stray students sunbathed with their books.

"You may still be wrestling with some minor questions of theology and philosophy, but you know with perfect certainty that these two propositions are true. First, God exists. Second, God does not exist."

* * *

Standing at the lectern, surveying the sanctuary from the front, Jim discovered that he was not nervous. It helped that he seemed to be facing a number of separate, isolated audiences rather than one large one. The scattered faces turned to him, even those of the professors he was used to being lectured by, were more pleading than demanding.

"I am the student, if that's not obvious" he began. "Professor Milnes asked me to offer a reading and a remark. I chose the twenty-third psalm. That choice involved a twofold risk. First, although we mentioned the Bible a lot in Professor O'Rourke's class, we didn't read it, so it's not really appropriate in that way. Though we are in a church. More misleading, it is so familiar that it might seem a cliché, and Professor O'Rourke was never a cliché. I suppose the eccentric professor is a stereotype, but he was an original stereotype. I think he would like that oxymoron; he had a taste for paradox that he often indulged with his students.

"He could probably have found one in this psalm:

> The Lord is my shepherd; I shall not want.
>
> ²He maketh me to lie down in green pastures: he leadeth me beside the still waters.
>
> ³He restoreth my soul: he leadeth me in the paths of righteousness for his name's sake.
>
> ⁴Yea, though I walk through the valley of the shadow of death, I will fear no evil: for thou art with me; thy rod and thy staff they comfort me.
>
> ⁵Thou preparest a table before me in the presence of mine enemies: thou anointest my head with oil; my cup runneth over.
>
> ⁶Surely goodness and mercy shall follow me all the days of my life: and I will dwell in the house of the Lord for ever.

"Like many people here, I would guess, I know those lines pretty well by heart. If it ever occurred to me as I was growing up to ask if I understood them, I would have worried that analyzing them like a poem would mean the Bible was a fiction, just one more storybook. I should just recite verses, not try to explain them. What college has shown me, and Professor O'Rourke in particular, is that it's all right to ask question about your beliefs. Faith can absorb questions. Doubt is a foreign matter, but it can strengthen faith, like rebar in concrete.

"I came to see that the Bible invites questions. In my Old Testament class, Professor Jenks defied us to explain what the first verse of Psalm 69 means: "the waters come up to my soul." Obviously the speaker is in a dire predicament, but it's not as figurative as it sounds in English. It's not even that spiritual. The Hebrew word for "soul" is *nephesh*. It's very physiological: it means your nostrils and your mouth, that part of your face—your breathing apparatus. The speaker is up to his chin in water; he's worried about his next breath. That's the same word in the third verse of Psalm

23: he restores my *nephesh*. He lets me catch my breath. The portrait of the believer in the Bible is not always very flattering. It is hard to picture Professor O'Rourke as a sheep, one of the flock, waiting for commands from his shepherd. But that's what the psalm says; the Hebrew word for 'lie down' is used especially for animals. But then all of a sudden at the end the sheep are in a house sitting at a table.

"So I have more questions, and I have questions today. Why was Professor O'Rourke part of my life, and why did we lose him? Wherever Professor O'Rourke is now, I hope he is breathing easy. In the meantime, I can do the believing for him. Because I'm guessing that he and I arrived at different answers to the same questions and even on the same evidence. My faith is only stronger because he was my Socrates, checking at every turn to see if I really meant what I was saying, or more usually thinking to myself. I hope I'm not a disappointment to him, I doubt I am. I'll still have to trust to my faith. Trust to my faith: Professor O'Rourke was less fond of tautologies than he was of paradoxes. I hope he'll excuse that one. He may be in a place where reason can rest by still waters and believing is as automatic as breathing."

When Jim returned to his seat, Professor Milnes said, "Well, okay."

* * *

The class responded with mingled laughter and good-natured mutters.

"But which is truer?" one of Jim's classmates said.

"Is one proposition really, really true?' someone else said.

"Did someone hear a bell?"

"This is college, Professor O'Rourke. No bells."

"Oh," Professor O'Rourke said. "Well, according to the clock, time is up. Or very nearly up. Fifteen minutes is not much in the scale of eternity. I guess you'll have to choose on your own. After hours, so to speak."

This provoked a cascade of comments.

"But can you tell us which way you might be said to tend to incline, Professor O'Rourke?"

"If you were a betting man."

"The least you could do in decency is point."

Professor O'Rourke threw up his hands. "I can offer this. Follow me to the window. Observe the clouds."

The late spring sky was a bottomless blue. Not a grain or crystal of a cloud.

"No clouds," Professor O'Rourke said. "Where are they when you need them? The winter was quite overcast, as I recall. But this is better for our purposes. Look closely. What if, literally out of the blue, clouds appeared, swirled into shape and spelled, 'I EXIST?' Then would everyone believe in God? Or would they resort to meteorology? And if there were no meteorological explanation, then would they believe in God? Not necessarily. Just because you proved God's existence doesn't mean you would believe in God. As someone here once remarked, I think." He turned to look at Jim.

"All these reasons," one of the girls said. "I already thought God existed, but I kept finding better reasons to believe. So I was wrong in the first place?"

"But if all the reasons are true," Jim said, "wouldn't that mean that no one of them is true? Then have you really proved anything?"

Professor O'Rourke looked out the window. "You all are dismissed until the final exam. I'll stay here and watch."

Jim had the feeling that as Professor O'Rourke was gathering up his books from the desk, his back turned and looking hunched under his tweed jacket, he sensed that Jim had stayed behind. "Can I ask you something, Professor O'Rourke?" he said.

Then his back hunched.

"Would you be willing to write me a letter of recommendation?"

Professor O'Rourke relaxed and turned around. "Better than recommend you do something. Are we talking about graduate school? In philosophy?"

"No. I have a year left."

"Because I'm not sure I would wish that on anyone. In today's academic climate. Not that you couldn't do it."

"It's for teaching in a summer program. These would be junior and some senior high school students. Helping teaching, really."

"Certainly I will write you a letter, once grades are in, if that's soon enough."

"Sure. I'll get you the address."

"I was worried that you would ask me which of the two true propositions I would be inclined to believe. Off the record, of course."

"I'm sure everyone wonders."

"Let them. If you don't reveal my choice, I won't reveal yours. Promise."

Jim wasn't sure but that that should be the other way around. But he wouldn't pursue it. He would settle for the letter.

* * *

After about ten minutes Jim could be reasonably sure nothing he was saying was getting through. The three girls on the couch were still leaning forward, bright-eyed. With a little mental effort he could project them into the place of the girls in Professor O'Rourke's class. Except that he realized they were alert not because they were interested but because they were encouraging him. Every couple of minutes though one of them would think of something important and whisper it to her neighbor, who would nod. That was serious. One of the few boys had commandeered the only easy chair in the room. He operated it like a crane, pulling on a lever and twisting a knob until he was pretty much supine, his limbs lolling off the edges of the chair. But he lolled respectfully, twitching in response to some of Jim's points.

Jim had wondered how he would act once he got in front of a group of students, if he would emulate Professor O'Rourke or go out of his way to be different.

He was not in a college classroom, however. He was in the educational wing of the church he grew up in. For six weeks in the summer it hosted a series of camps for kids in the area that included a couple of sessions of Bible study every day. Teaching the classes was one of Jim's duties; he also led a few of the activities. Right after this session on Hosea—Prophets and Peer Groups was the theme that week—they would all pile in the church van and head to the community swimming pool. So the kids could afford to be indulgent. He was a college kid. Let him talk. The church's full-time youth director, apparently with nothing better to do, was sitting in. He would take over after the class. He was if anything less engaged than the students, though equally pleasant, but he perked up when Jim wrote a few Hebrew words on the blackboard.

"Those are letters?" one of the kids said.

"That's not all," Jim said. "Watch what I learned to do in college."

"Congratulations," someone said. "You can write backwards. And, don't tell us: you're really left-handed."

"These two letters—you're right, they are letters—are the Hebrew word for 'not'—*lo*. It rhymes with 'no,' which it also means."

"Hey, that's an easy language."

"Not all Hebrew words rhyme with their synonyms in English, unfortunately. If you go into a synagogue, you will see this word written on the wall, over and over again." Jim copied the word on the board in a column. "*Lo. Lo. Lo.* Not quite ten times, but almost. Why?"

"Thou shalt not. The Ten Commandments," one of the girls said.

"Exactly," Jim said.

The girl snapped back in her seat in delight.

"I knew that," the reclining boy said. "But I shalt not look smarter than the girls in the class."

Jim did neither. He neither mimicked nor avoided Professor O'Rourke's mannerisms. He felt as comfortable as he had at the lectern at the memorial service. He could see that he would do these students only so much good, probably none of it through what he taught them about the Bible. In a few years some of them would be in college, on the brink of mysteries. He could only mouth them from his side of the chasm between them.

"*Lo* was the first name of Hosea's children, too. That's what God told him to call them. Not Pitied. Not My People." When he explained that God instructed Hosea to marry a prostitute to symbolize Israel's unfaithfulness, concern replaced indulgence in the expressions on the faces of his audience, including the youth director's.

As the class left the room, one of the boys turned to another and said, "After you, Not My Hero." He waited until he was sure Jim would hear him. Jim laughed. In half an hour the students would all be thrashing in the water like salmon.

* * *

"How is the exegesis going?" Rev. Corbin said. Jim had reported to his office for his weekly debriefing. "I understand you have our campers reading the Old Testament in the original. We didn't even charge them for that."

"I thought they would enjoy seeing what Hebrew looks like," Jim said. "That's what hooked me on learning. Glimpses I got from different teachers of subjects way over my head at the time. I'll try not to conduct college-level classes. It's hard to gear down, though. At school I'm always worried I'm not being profound. Now that I'm teaching I get the feeling my professors are sitting out there in the seats."

"I'm just kidding," Rev. Corbin said. "Our camps should be seminaries. I'm perfectly serious. If we remember that 'seminary' means a place where seeds are germinated." Rev. Corbin liked to clarify when he was joking and when not. He waved his hand at the floor-to-ceiling bookcases that lined the walls. "If you do wind up pastoring a church you won't have much need for these. I'll adapt my favorite line from *The Grapes of Wrath*. Nice Biblical title; it's up there somewhere on one of those shelves. One of the migrant workers says that if he was rich he would stack pork chops up around him like firewood and eat his way out. I've already stacked the books around me. When I retire I'm going to sit here and read my way out. I don't mean to discourage you. Seek your students' level, and you'll do good. Or your congregation's. Instruct, exhort, do what you can. I try to work a little Barth into my sermons, try to let the folks know there is such a thing as liberation theology. But it seems to me that for most of my parishioners the sermon is a kind of penance they pay. Sitting through one is good for the soul. Really I think my job is to remind them that God loves them. Not much more than that. I do my best to." He straightened in his chair, as though getting down to business. "The kids like you."

"I'm glad."

"I knew they would. You come highly recommended, you know. Or maybe you wouldn't. The letters are all confidential."

"I think I'd be embarrassed to know what the letters said. I always check the 'confidential' box."

"Yes. The confidential letters are best. It's counterintuitive, I suppose. But if the writers know the candidates will never see what they wrote I think it allows them to be more natural, unguarded. Not just that they won't have to answer for it. And if you're careful and make a candidate sound flawless, he won't be very believable. One of your letters is particularly good. I don't mean good in the sense of complimentary. All letters of recommendation are good in that sense, and that makes them all sound the same. I mean good in the sense of memorable. If a letter stands out, the candidate does, too." Rev. Corbin was obviously holding the letter in front of him, scanning it with a smile. "So I can't read it to you," he said, though Jim could tell he wanted to. "You beat Spinoza and Kant to the point, sort of. Those are names I haven't heard for about a hundred years. Since I was in college, in fact. Very good. See, it's very specific. So you finished some of his thoughts for him? All right. Just the last sentence. He foresees for you a brilliant career and a good life. Nicely turned. They're not always the same thing, are they? I'm sure you'll be able to guess who wrote it. You should be sure to thank him."

"I have more than that to thank him for," Jim said. "He convinced me that God exists."

That caught Rev. Corbin between breaths. "Yes, that's something," he managed to get out. You couldn't be sure if he was having trouble starting or stopping laughing.

"I suppose what I mean is that I wasn't sure I knew God existed until I had his class. Then I realized I had known all along."

Now Rev. Corbin was mostly nodding. When he composed himself, he said, "Too bad you can't pay him back in kind. A recommendation is a funny sort of favor, isn't it? I mean, it presupposes the superiority of one party; it concedes it. There could hardly be a mutual recommendation, could there? If that makes sense."

"It does," Jim said. "But I did have a chance to recommend him once. I did what I could."

THE PASSENGER

WHO ELSE WAS IN the car? It would help to know that. But even so he should be able to make some sense of the situation.

It wasn't as though he was entirely sure of the identity of the others, but he was sure he knew them.

Before, he was talking to a friend on the phone. He was having trouble making the point he had called to make, and then he was talking to his friend's wife. If his friend hadn't understood, he wasn't sure how he could explain himself to her, though the point was simple. She not only did not understand; she was becoming offended. She may already have hung up. It was so frustrating, because he could hear his friend talking in the background. He was there.

And he was at fault. Another group of friends was arriving at his house, so his attention was divided. His friend's wife may have sensed this. He had to yell in delight and surprise when he saw his friend, though the surprise was feigned, since he saw him coming. He had to. The yell may be why his friend's wife was (understandably) offended.

He was pretty sure his friend was married, though he wasn't sure it was to this woman.

His other friend's profile edged into the doorway at the bottom of the stairs at the top of which he was using the telephone. He didn't remember his friend's profile being so distinct, almost chiseled into a smile of self-satisfaction at imminent surprise. Though he hadn't seen him in a while either. Not Easter-Island-statue distinct, but approaching it. His friend didn't know he had seen him already.

Himself would be the obvious answer to who the unidentified person in the car was. In the corner on the passenger side of the back seat, which was full if not over-full. Himself was often the answer in cases like this one.

They were to meet at the car dealership to exchange the cat. They must have piled in the car and driven to the spot. It was not a long drive, but they arrived in an utterly different landscape, of tiny manicured lawns outside cubical buildings. It was a bright beautiful day. The dealership occupied the ground floor of one of the quite substantial buildings, maybe a bank from the second floor up. Yes, a bank. The name of the brand of car being dealt, in huge colored letters on the side of the building, was not quite legible. He was out of the car, holding the squirming cat. There had been talk of putting the cat in a plastic bag. All but a consensus, really. But he worried, in fact he could see, that the bag had been dented but not perforated, so there were no air holes for the cat, which may already have been in the plastic bag. They were very late. His friend must have promised, very generously, to be waiting for them. And he may have been; there were cars around. He couldn't be sure he would recognize him. He hadn't seen him for a while, either. The other people in the car with him were very supportive. They were family or friends, with the possible exception of the blank face in the back seat. He was pretty sure he saw the proceedings from behind that face, which however was not his.

He wasn't sure how he felt when he woke up.

"Good or bad? Let's start there."

"Not bad," Mark said.

"Now we're getting somewhere. You felt good."

"Not good. Better than that."

"Ecstatic, then. Euphoric."

"Sorry, I didn't mean better," Mark said. "Different. I felt different afterward. The feeling still comes over me, sort of in waves, but a little weaker and at longer intervals."

"Aftershocks."

"Yes," Mark said. "That's a good analogy."

It was funny how they had fallen into this skit, client and analyst, Mark struggling for words, Luke looking sage and patient. Mark was impressed. Luke and he were better friends than he thought. Even funnier, the act helped. He really wasn't sure how he felt.

"I'm actually not that much of a dreamer," Mark said. "Sometimes it worries me. People tell me these very elaborate dreams they had the night before, and I don't have any."

"That you remember," Luke said.

"What's the point if you don't remember them? Did you ever really have them, then?"

"Maybe your brain has a mind of its own," Luke said. "It's got to keep itself entertained somehow."

"Or, if I do remember, it will be in the middle of the day, when I'm walking down the street. Something will pop into my mind, and at first I'll think I'm recalling an event. But in fact it's a dream, or a fragment of one, like debris floating on the top of my brain. I reach for it; for a second I see the whole thing below the surface. Then it's gone."

"Interesting," Luke said and, still in character, stroked his chin.

"But not this one. This one is different. I remembered it from the minute I woke up in the morning."

"There's something you're not telling me," Luke said.

"No, I think I got every detail."

"Not about the dream."

It was Wednesday, which meant they were in the basement of the Presbyterian church on Main Street. Fellowship Hall, Mark thought they called it, though a) the church seemed to be full of rooms people referred to by name, and he couldn't keep them straight, especially since this was the only one he had been in, and b) there was nothing particularly warm or religious-seeming about this room, with its linoleum floor and folding tables and chairs. It had the slightly acrid odor, some combination of mothballs and cleaner, that told him he was in a church—almost antiseptic, one step short of a hospital. He rather liked it. His office, two blocks away, smelled more like a motel, with the massive furniture and perpetual air-conditioning to match.

For the past couple of years he had come here for the weekly soup-and-sandwich lunch, billed as something like "Bread and Broth." He always saw some old acquaintances and made some new ones, often people like Luke he had seen around but never met. He hadn't known the person who invited him all that well, a neighbor and member of the church who since had moved away. He once in a while made a business contact, which didn't hurt. There was a service in a chapel (or chapels, he gathered) upstairs at noon, which Luke attended. It was all surprisingly casual, which was what Mark liked about it. You could put money, if you remembered to bring any, in a can on your table to pay for lunch. That had a name, too, with "cents" in it—a "centsible meal," maybe. There was no pressure to go upstairs. They could even joke about how he came only for the gourmet cooking. When he arrived early (though never early enough for the service; he would not want to interrupt it by coming in while it was in progress), he helped set pots and plates on the serving table. He overheard people talking about the service as they came downstairs to join the latecomers. Mark wasn't the only one who arrived just at lunchtime. Apparently there weren't proper sermons at the service but rather "reflections." Judging by the conversation, they were often interesting.

"The people in the dream," Luke said. "They're real?"

"Oh, yes," Mark said. "I should have said that, if I didn't. They're my two best friends. Although actually I might not have known that at first."

"You just said your friends and your other friend."

"Like I just have two," Mark laughed. "I don't know when I realized that's who they were. Maybe just now. By 'best' friends I mean childhood friends."

"Sure," Luke said. "They're the best. Did they know each other?"

"Oh, yeah. We were a pack."

Luke seemed to reflect. "There's still something you're holding back. Or maybe you're saying it but I'm not hearing it. However," he said, thrusting his index finger professorially in the air, "that will have to wait for our next session."

The women of the church, the group he was told organized the meal, were circulating with their dollies to pick up dishes. Gray-haired and sweat-shirted, they were of that indeterminate time of life on the outskirts of old age. Their jeans were tight across the hips, loose at the calves.

"Same time next week?" Luke said.

"Count on it," Mark said.

It was fifty-fifty that he and Luke would see each other on the sidewalks of town and exchange pleasantries between now and then. Luke was a fairly visible citizen. He and another set of friends jogged every afternoon. When they passed under his office window, Mark knew it was about 3:15. They were like a locker room on wheels, in a portable atmosphere of banter. They ran the same route every day, setting out from the YMCA, of which Luke was the director. It was probably expected of him, as of gym teachers and coaches, to stay in a modicum of shape. Even if he had been a runner, Mark could not have joined them. His was a classic nine-to-five job. He sometimes wondered how many of them were left. Everyone he knew seemed to have more leisure than he did. They worked "on flex time" or "from home." The runners included a couple of teachers at the local college and a couple of early retirees. There must have been a thirty-year age difference across the group, but they had found a shambling pace that seemed to suit them all. They started out ostentatiously slowly, as though collectively amused at their distance from their physical prime. Mark had seen the leaders finish an hour later in a sprint, though, Luke among them. They staggered loose-jointed around the Y's parking lot or bent over with their hands on their thighs. For those few moments they were dead serious, like witnesses of a revelation.

Mark couldn't help but marvel at the way, with very little effort on his part, his life had filled up. At work the orders just kept coming in. Complications kept arising, almost identical but not quite. About once a year he was sent off to a conference to master another revolutionary software program or marketing technique. Family took the rest of his time. He and his wife had settled in this town because she had many relatives thereabouts;

his family was small and far-flung. His father lived in a nursing home far from his birthplace near his only sibling, a sister, who was a nurse herself. He felt that his life was missing something and, at the same time, that there wasn't room for anything else.

He had come to look forward to the Wednesday lunches and even just the walk down there along what he thought of as Church Row. On that same block of Main Street three churches adjoined each other, Methodist, Baptist, and Presbyterian. Someday he would like to find out what the difference was. Members of all the churches came to the Presbyterian church for the lunch. He had the impression that they all shared other activities as well. The Baptists had a big affair at Christmas. The preachers took turns delivering the reflections upstairs.

He couldn't justify a whole hour away from work, but he always ate lunch, even if he didn't leave the office. He now resented it if a meeting or appointment kept him from the church meal. And in fact the very next Wednesday his boss called a lunch meeting; he announced it as though it were a treat. Mark seethed throughout, rehearsing the dream to himself. Atypically, he had had a couple in the meantime, but they hadn't effaced this one, and he made no effort to remember them.

On his return to the church the next week, though, roughly the same group of men was discussing another reflection. "Do you still remember your dream?" Luke asked as he straddled his folding chair while setting his soup gingerly on the table. The bowl was both hot and full. There was potato salad today. Often the women threw in an extra dish.

"I do," Mark said. "Except . . . "

"Except?" Luke said.

"Except at this point I don't know if I'm remembering my dream or my memory of the dream. You know, the way I told it to you. My account of the dream."

"Did you write it down?"

"I thought about that. But then I thought that might kill it. Even more than telling it."

"Did you tell anyone else?"

"No. My wife's not in it. There are really three kinds of people in it. Me and my friends. The other people in the car. They're all individuals I know from somewhere, but they're interchangeable. They even switch places in the car. I'm never sure who's where. Then there's the guy in the back seat. The blank."

"You're sure it's a man?" Luke said. There was no role-playing this time, Mark realized. Luke sounded interested, or concerned.

"Yes, I can tell that much. He's always in his spot."

"What are we talking about here? Dreams?" Al set his plates beside Luke and across from Mark. A half-generation older than them, he, like Luke, attended the services. He wasn't one of the runners, but he could have been, tall and trim, with shoulders that were sheet-metal sharp under his short-sleeved shirt. His gray hair was the same color as the frame of his glasses. He had some sort of part-time or volunteer job in town. "You set any store by them?" he asked Mark. With his imperious stare, Al seemed to see it as his calling in life to bring even the most casual conversation to a crisis. By now Mark had concluded that was just his natural expression. "What does the Bible say? Are there dreams in the Bible?" At that his eyes widened, as though he was brought up short by his own insight. "I don't know. I'm just asking."

"Are we maybe looking for a scriptural basis for dreams here?" Luke was smiling; he had just preempted Al's favorite phrase.

"Wherever possible," Al shrugged. "We ought to look there first, maybe? Sometimes that's the last place we look."

"There's not an answer in there for everything, is there?" They had been joined by Holt, whom Mark also saw whenever he represented his business at the Rotary luncheon. They were on Mondays. He hadn't noticed Holt sit down next to him. "If my DVD player is broken, I'm not going to look in the Bible for how to fix it."

"But maybe for what you should be watching on it," Al said.

"I hope they're not going to make a movie of First Chronicles anytime soon," Holt said. "I've been following one of those read-the-Bible-in-a-year programs. You know the ones. I'm into the histories now. You want to talk about gore."

"I hope they do make it," Luke said. "I've got the sequel."

"Second Chronicles?" Al said.

"And I thought I was the first to think of that," Luke said, grinning at Mark.

Mark liked it that they didn't take everything seriously here. Even Al broke down in laughter at some point. Also jokes didn't actually have to be funny to be good. Now that a crowd was forming, Mark hoped the conversation did not get back around to his dream.

"Here's someone who can tell us," Luke said as Curt approached.

"About DVD players?" Curt said. "You've got the wrong guy or I've got the wrong table. I can plug one in for you." But he sat down.

"About dreams in the Bible," Luke said. "If any."

Curt was about as much below the average age at the table as Al was above it. He was a new professor of religion at the college. He was also both a runner and a member of the church. To Mark that combination was a little unsettling; it seemed one association too many.

"There are dreams in the Bible." Al had a way of making questions sound like statements, and vice versa.

"Of course," Curt said. "Some famous ones. Just think about Joseph. The thing is . . . "

The thing was, with Curt it was as though you pushed a button and a lecture played. He knew his stuff, though.

He adjusted each of his plates but didn't eat. "First off, it's not always easy to tell the difference between a dream and a vision in the Bible. And in the Bible God speaks directly through dreams. The dream might be symbolic, but it's also transparent. It doesn't demand interpretation. That's true in the ancient world generally, what we call the Greater Mediterranean. Do you remember your Homer?" He finally took a bite, though he had gotten no response. "In the *Iliad* people appear in dreams in disguise, but the dreamer sees right through it. Nobody's fooled. Agamemnon knows that Nestor is really Zeus. It makes you wonder why they bother. Same in the Bible. The message is clear. God just uses the dream as his medium. We moderns do the opposite: we focus on the details. Everything has to mean something; we like dreams to be cryptic. I think they're more like parables. The meaning isn't in the details; it's holistic. Dreams have morals. No matter how bizarre a dream is, don't you always really know what it means?" He was looking at Mark when he finished.

Neither he nor anyone else could answer this appeal, because the pastor of the church reached their table on his patrol of the luncheon. "And to what might this group be up?" he said.

"We were analyzing Mark's dream," Luke said, as Holt and Curt mugged their surprise.

The pastor picked up the offering can and shook it. "We don't charge enough for that," he said. Rev. Cobb was what Mark would call recently youthful. His thick hair was now probably more gray than sandy. He wasn't heavy, but he looked as though he had once been lean.

"We got off task," Luke said, then smirked. "That's not like this group. Next week we'll get to the bottom of it. Right, Mark? Can you keep the dream fresh for one more week?"

"If I can stay awake that long," Mark said. The laugh that followed was satisfyingly final. Rev. Cobb walked off, and a couple of people pushed their chairs back to get up. Holt and Curt could get down to eating.

Mark had friends. He came away from the lunches elated, and when he returned to work he was surrounded by people he felt comfortable with, especially afterward. In fact he had a sense of homecoming. Back to the actual world. The conversation was nothing like as stimulating, but they shared all the same stresses in unspoken sympathy. He and his wife, who administered a county health program, spent most of their time together scheduling their children's activities. They both brought work home. With all these demands, lovemaking became first hypothetical and then mythical. Sex belonged to a golden age populated by a different race in which younger versions of their selves numbered.

What he lacked was buddies. All his best friends were the ones he made in school. Grade school, junior high at the latest. He often found himself laughing at thoughts they were the only possible audience for. He repeated stories to himself as if to them. Those relationships had been covered over by the lava of his adult life; they were preserved like fossils. You couldn't cultivate that sort of friendship. It was a given. It moved in next door. Most of the guys at the church had known each other for years. They seemed to share a life outside the lunches. When he arrived in town he was already married. He couldn't just start running. He couldn't initiate a formative stage of his life. He couldn't turn at will into someone else. Except that he was turning into someone else—his father. Unless all the mirrors he caught glimpses of himself in as he went about his daily rounds in town had been left behind by a traveling circus, his outline was changing. He was appreciably rounder, thicker—stooped? Something. A little less hair, a little larger waist. It wasn't any one thing.

He had friends. But not like his wife had friends. She must have spent two hours a day on the telephone. He didn't think he was exaggerating. When she got a call, she lit up like the cell phone. Her demeanor became animated; she paced all over the house as she talked. He became a piece of furniture to be negotiated. Family members seemed to check in with her daily. He called his father once a week and had to work to prolong the call for ten minutes. Sometimes his sister was there visiting. He preferred to e-mail her.

The following Wednesday as he went about his chores in Fellowship Hall he was surprised by a male voice emerging from the kitchen. "I was wondering whom we had to thank for those impeccable place settings."

It was Rev. Cobb. Mark laughed and said, "Shouldn't you be upstairs?" It was barely 12:15; he had arrived earlier than he realized that day.

"Bill Calhoun is preaching today. We're doing a series, and we get the day off when it's the other guy's turn. We know each other's theology pretty well by now. Once a month all us pastors get together for lunch. You think these affairs are wild."

"I can only imagine," Mark said.

"Besides, I like to help in the kitchen once in a while. I hope there's still a little of the deacon in me." He was wheeling plates and bowls in on a dolly.

"I'll get to a service one day," Mark said.

"We're glad you join us for lunch," Rev. Cobb said. "It's all bread. A sermon is like a meal. You don't remember the menu of every lunch you ever had, not even the good ones. I couldn't tell you myself what I preached two weeks ago. Meals and sermons. Their job is to tide you over to the next one. So have you made any progress on your dream analysis?"

"Did Luke tell you about it?"

"Oh, a little. No seal of the confessional here."

"It wasn't exactly a confession."

"Of course it wasn't. Although isn't that what dreams are? In a way? Confessions to ourselves? I would say that confession is a basic human need. We Protestants think that we did away with all that in church, but we didn't. It's true that we don't practice auricular confession, private sessions with a priest. We confess in public and in unison. Though the second kind of negates the first, since we're one body."

"Collective bargaining?"

Rev. Cobb laughed. "Too late for that. The deal's already done. I have to remind my people: we're not forgiven because we confess; we confess because we're forgiven. Without God's grace we could never bring ourselves to acknowledge how far we fall short. We confess out of gratitude. Do you know Dietrich Bonhoeffer?"

Mark had heard the name.

"You'd like him. He made one of the stranger claims for the church I've ever heard. He said the church permits people to be sinners. I would have thought the purpose of the church was to prevent people from being sinners. What he meant was that among other believers no one has to pretend that they are righteous. You are seeking God's grace as one sinner among many. Confession is a sign of the true church. In fact, he called the true church the confessing church."

"Funny basis for friendship."

"I think I would say fellowship rather than friendship," Rev. Cobb said. "I don't know that I necessarily like everyone who comes to church here. What did I hear someone say once? As a club, the church is unique: the only requirement is a professed unworthiness to belong." He reflected. "Maybe I do remember last week's sermon."

Just then they heard the drumming of feet on the stairs down from the chapel. A few men were also coming in the door from the street.

"I'd better get these tables ready," Mark said.

"Right," Rev. Cobb said. "Enough theology for the time being."

Mark still hadn't told his wife about the dream, but he routinely re-counted each Wednesday lunchtime discussion at dinner, sometimes over several evenings, as points came back to him. He shared Rev. Cobb's characterizations of the church. They sounded revolutionary to him, though apparently he got them all from other people. One night she said, "Do you want to go sometime?"

At first the question confused him: he hadn't missed a Wednesday for a while.

"To church. On Sunday," she said, amused at his reaction. "I used to go at home, as a child and on up into high school. It was one of those things like eating the same cereal for breakfast or practicing piano. For a long time you do it every day, then you miss once and you never do it again. My parents put up surprisingly little resistance when I went agnostic on them. They just went off to church and left me in bed."

"I never knew you played piano," Mark said.

That particular conversation took place on a Sunday evening. A quiet Sunday evening: their children were gone for a two-week summer camp sponsored jointly by the churches in town. They had been the past two years and seemed to enjoy it. The following Wednesday was different, too. He got a call from a client right after noon, just when he usually left the office, "for church," as his coworkers kidded him. He quick-stepped along the sidewalk under a bright blue sky. It would get hot again, but this day was cool, almost autumnal, after a sweltering week. Lunch had already started by the time he arrived. The places were all set. The room was less full than ordinarily, since some people were away on vacation. Mark wondered if he had always unconsciously assumed that churches closed for the summer, like school. His circle was intact, though, as if awaiting him as he sat down, and a conversation was under way. Curt had the floor; the others leaned in to listen as they ate, except for Al, who leaned back in his chair wearing his usual dramatically thoughtful expression, as though recoiling from Curt's line of reasoning.

"The prodigal Mark," Luke said. "We figured you ran off to squander your father's estate."

"He must have taken care of that himself," Mark said.

Luke had spoken aside, but now Curt turned to him. "We're still on the forgiveness series. The title of the reflection was 'Conditional Forgiveness.'"

"Who gave it?" Mark said.

"Reverend Cobb" was the unison response. Some of his friends nodded at the obviousness of the answer, some at the reasonableness of the question, or some combination. Luke took up the synopsis. "The way he reads scripture, you need to ask for forgiveness. The onus is not on the injured party. That would only compound the injury."

"Or blessing," Curt said.

"That's what the Bible says," Al came in. "The evidence is there. What do we pray every Sunday: 'forgive us our sins, as we forgive those who sin against us.' That says to me we have to forgive if we want to be forgiven. If that's God's policy, shouldn't it be our policy, too? The person who injures you has to ask to be forgiven. He has to at least repent. At least apologize. Come on."

"He said it could be read that way," Curt said. "But I just don't think that's the spirit of what Jesus said. I mean, it's obviously overstatement. Forgive a member of your congregation seventy times seven times? If you saw him once a week, on Sunday, that would go on for nine and a half years."

"My Bible says seventy-seven," Luke said.

"That's a textual question," Curt said. "You can look at other passages. You'll always find some multiple of seven. It has to do with Jubilee. So the number is symbolic, too. In Luke it's seven times a day. The Gospel of the Nazaraeans, for what it's worth, combines them: you're supposed to forgive an offender seventy times seven a day. Assuming you're expected to be forgiving just during the waking hours, that's thirty times an hour."

"Don't forget, if they ask," Al said.

"All right," Curt said. "So they're asking you every two minutes. That could get annoying. Then you'd have to forgive them for that."

"Hey, I thought you were a religion teacher," Luke said. He looked around for an audience for his witticism. A few people from a depopulated table had joined them. Al continued to frown, but not in disapproval. Mark had come to the conclusion that his dogmatism was all show: the more inconclusive a conversation, the better he liked it.

"I have my students do the math in class. Any way you work it out, it's a lot of forgiving."

"Maybe forgiving isn't an act but an attitude," one of the newcomers said. "You're prepared to forgive."

"Disposed to forgive," Luke said, returning to the discussion. "Always forgiving? That makes 490 an understatement, not an overstatement."

"People are pre-forgiven?" Al said, adjusting his frown upward.

"So many questions," Curt said. "Can you forgive a collectivity, like a government? A disease? A natural disaster? You lose a loved one to a flood. A race? Do people need to repent for what their ancestors did? One thing forgiving is not is forgetting."

"Which brings us to Mark's dream," Luke said.

"It does?" Mark said.

"Nice segue, Luke," someone said. Rev. Cobb was passing by. "We would like to lay the dream to rest, though, Mark. So to speak. Do you remember it?"

"I do," Luke said. "Let me see if I can get the gist of it."

"It's the detail that's important," Al said.

"Yes and no," Curt said.

"Well, it's what's interesting."

"Let me try," Luke said.

When he had finished his rehearsal, to Mark's satisfaction, one of the new members of the group said, "That's what we've been praying about, isn't it?" Mark had never seen him outside the church, and only recently there.

"You've prayed about me?" Mark said.

"The conversation doesn't have to end here," Rev. Cobb said. "We can always include God. Or maybe that's vice versa."

"What would you pray for? We don't even know what the dream means. Obviously." At first Mark didn't know how to feel. Words beginning with *b* shouldered their way into his mind: breathtaking, betrayal, badgered. They all contained an *r* also. It seemed that everyone in the room was surrounding him. As he looked around he saw that that was not exactly the case. Some members of the reduced crowd had left. As the other tables emptied, more stranded diners gravitated to theirs. And a couple of people had arrived even later than him.

"I imagine we must have prayed to the general effect that the issues the dream represented or raised for you be resolved," Rev. Cobb said. "Something like that. Here or at home. We keep a pretty good-sized prayer list going."

"You got the details, Luke," Curt said. "The events, if that's the right term."

"The plot," Rev. Cobb said.

"All right. But you left out the feeling. What was bothering you when you woke up, Mark. First thing. Something was."

"I want to know about the friends," Luke said. "That's what sticks out to me."

"Here you go," Al said. "How did you feel about the friends? Friendly?"

"The opposite," Mark said. "I don't mean unfriendly."

"That is the opposite of friendly," Al said.

There was a clearing in Mark's memory. The images were orderly, like the plazas around the cubical office buildings in his dream. He could walk through and around them. They were orderly but inert. He was glad he had left them.

"It was how they felt," he said. "The feelings were going in that direction. They were friendly to me. Why? Was it because they didn't see each other? Neither knew the other was in the dream."

"What does that have to do with anything?" Al said.

"Did either of them actually see me?" Mark was on the edge of his seat. It was as though the dream had opened and popped up in front of him, like one of those elaborate birthday cards. Or the dream flanked him, like a diptych in a church. He was back inside it, but from the outside. "See, you wouldn't know this. I said they were my best friends. But that didn't make them best friends with each other. I was the one that held us together. It was important to me to have them both there." Others might have been about to speak, but the dream kept reassembling itself for him, images composing themselves as though on an altarpiece. "And then they weren't both my best friend. That's impossible. That was a lie. My lie, all for me. I liked one less well. He was less best, and I think he knew it."

"The one you delivered the cat to," Curt said.

"Yes."

"He took it," Luke said.

"I suppose," Mark said.

At that juncture Al produced one of his explosive insights. "All this time I thought we were talking about dreams. We were talking about forgiveness!"

"But who is forgiving and who is forgiven?" Mark said. "My friends had done nothing to be forgiven for. I didn't ask to be forgiven."

"Have you spoken to them since?" Rev. Cobb said. "Since the dream?"

"No."

"Call them," Luke said.

"What would I say? I haven't spoken to them since our last high school reunion, let alone the dream. That was, when, three summers ago? And I call them my best friends. How could I let that happen?"

"Call them," Rev. Cobb said. "Tell them the dream. Maybe they can figure it out. Even if they don't have a dozen psychologists on retainer, like you do. And, Curt, you have homework, too, pal: Hebrews 8.12."

He had just enough time to call one of his friends on Sunday morning. It was another bright day, but palpably closer to the end of summer. Cool sunlight washed through the room's windows from the side yard, like waves. It was the kind of day on which you left the beach, home to the dregs of vacation. Even in early middle age Mark felt the chill of school in his bones, as though the lingering effects of a childhood fever. His wife was still getting ready; briskness radiated from that end of the house in the form of closing drawers, a whiff of perfume. He wasn't clear of his confusion, he knew. He would call his less best friend first; he couldn't bring himself to say second-best. It would be easier that way. It was the prospect of emotion of any kind as well as the obligatory catching-up—reports on parents, siblings, children—that made the call seem a chore. He could only talk for so long. They had to get to church. He could always call back. He had resolved not to mention the dream, this time.

For all his trepidation, he was almost laughing as he dialed Bill's number. Now that he was down, the memories piled on. Bill's wife answered the phone. When Mark identified himself, there was a pause. Then she said brightly, "Mark from the reunion!" It was like a clap of the hands. He couldn't quite picture her, either. He just remembered she wasn't quite the match he expected for Bill. They had been married abroad, though she was American. He had received an announcement with a note from Bill. The few times he had seen Bill since, he had been alone. And at the reunion she had assumed the reticent observer status of the classmate's spouse. He could sense her smile, though. "I had never seen him laugh so hard," she said. "Or in that way. Especially you three. Who else was at the table?"

"Marty, his name was."

"Yes, of course. Bill talked about him, too."

She was kind when he asked to speak to Bill. "Oh, Mark," she said. "It's been a year already. Almost to the day. We weren't completely unprepared. His father died of the same thing, at almost the same age."

So he had, during their senior year of college. Mark had learned only later, too late to offer sympathy.

After they hung up, with promises to stay in touch, Mark sat and waited. He would call Marty in the afternoon. Now he had a reason: he would have news for Marty, as Bill's wife had had for him. But there was no rush. The news was not new.

His wife called from the front door. "There you are," she said. "I thought you might be in the car."

This was the perfect day to go to church. The children from the camp, theirs included, were to arrive midway through the service and participate somehow. Then they were to go home with their parents, or friends' parents.

He and his wife didn't talk in the car, but it was as though they shared an alertness. Mark was reflecting that now the mystery of the dream was solved. The blank-featured passenger in the car had to be Bill. He was there and not there, as in a sense he had been all along, blessing him in his absence. The fact that he also appeared as himself in the dream posed no problem to that interpretation. In dreams people often showed up as both themselves and/or someone else.

They arrived a few minutes early, but the service seemed already to be under way. One person was replacing another at a lectern. Apparently they were making announcements. There was scattered laughter from the pews. As they found a place halfway down on the left, they passed some of his lunchmates in the midst of their families. Mark registered Luke's grin,

Al's mock surprise. Nicest of all was the lack of any reaction from others. For all they knew he belonged. There was some standing up and sitting down, some singing, before Rev. Cobb took the pulpit. He looked toward Mark. "As pastor," he began, "I try to avoid unseemly theological disputes with my parishioners. One of us might turn out to be a heretic—or both. But one of your fellow congregants made a statement the other day that brought me up short. I hesitate to identify him." Mark hadn't seen Curt two pews ahead of them. He cringed comically against his wife and raised his hand. She laughed. "Yes, it was our friend Curt who said that, though we might not know what forgiveness is, we know what it is not: it is not forgetting. And I thought to myself, 'That's right.' I also thought to myself, 'He's a professor of religion; I'm not.' And then I said to myself, 'That's wrong.' Those are my two usual positions on any difficult scriptural question. I think what Curt meant is that forgiveness is not a reaction but an action. It has stages—acknowledgement, acceptance, repentance. It is mutual; it invites the offender to participate. It is creative; it continues or revises a story. The original act has a new context, a new frame. It is not the same event. Is that what Curt meant, Aline?"

Curt's wife nodded emphatically, to laughter. Mark and his wife laughed.

"That's not even the sermon yet," Rev. Cobb said. "That's a little bonus sermon. You can kick in a little extra at the offering. In fact, this is a series of sermons; we have been exploring the topic at our Wednesday sessions. How can it be both true and not true that forgiveness is not forgetting? Is it a partial forgetting? Or could it be in this way: there are two perspectives. We humans need to be mindful of our failings. We can hardly not be. They are our nature. As Paul tells us, reminds us, we humans operate according to our own law. Faced with a choice, we say, 'I should not do this. I think I'll do it. I'll do this. I shouldn't.' To forget our own sins would be to forget who we are. By the same token, if we deny the sins of others, we would think that we alone are sinners. In either case we will be isolated, from ourselves, from our fellow humans. We must forgive so that there is forgiveness. We will need it. But God has no sin of God's own to remember. How does God regard this thing that is utterly foreign to God? What does the Bible tell us? As I read scripture, God seems a little embarrassed by sin. God covers it. Another time in the Bible God is like a parent playing with a child: God puts sin behind God's back. 'Oops! Where did it go? It's gone!' Not that God is always so kindly. The image of God the judge is everywhere in scripture. He can be scary, arbitrary. But it gets worse. You remember that Job has his defense together; he can't wait to lay it out. But the judge doesn't show up. There's no one on the bench. That's Kafka before Kafka. But why isn't he there? We may have to wait one more testament to find out. A new testament. Now, I gave Curt some homework for today, but I've picked on him enough. Why don't I ask a visitor? Mark, I should have told you that when you come to this church you get put to work. Could you read Hebrews 8.12 for us?"

Mark blanked. Hebrews. Wouldn't that be the whole Bible? Or half of it? Rev. Cobb said New Testament. That meant toward the back. Except he was looking in the hymnbook. Someone nudged him. His wife was holding a Bible out for him, open to the page, pointing to the verse. Mark stood and read: "For I will be merciful towards their iniquities, and I will remember their sins no more."

"Thank you, Mark. You just read one of my favorite verses. What kind of judge is that? A forgetful one. He forgets to show up in court. He forgets the evidence. Some people say he doesn't forget, he chooses not to remember. Same difference, as far as I'm concerned. So, what, the case is thrown out because of a technicality! Or God forgives us out of the goodness of God's heart? In all our worry we forgot to look to our right." Rev. Cobb did a double-take. "We had a good defense attorney all along. Jesus calls himself our advocate. But he's more. He turned himself in and paid the price for us. We were guilty as sin, but God forgot. Jesus put in a good word for us. That, God remembers. Amen."

Rev. Cobb spread his arms. "Friends. You've probably noticed that we're doing things a little differently today." Mark and his wife exchanged glances. Different from what? "I hope you'll forgive me. If you forget, that's okay, too. I have delayed the passing of the peace, which we ordinarily have after the prayer of confession, which is a good place for it. But today we have reflected at length on our need for forgiveness. You entered the church today as families and friends. You may not have seen one another since last Sunday, much less wronged one another. But I invite you now to stand and greet your neighbor as a brand new creation, whom you are seeing for the first time, a brother or sister in Christ. Introduce yourselves with a sign of peace and forgiveness."

As Mark stood he thought he might be light-headed and need to sit back down. But it was not that. Rather, he felt, as much as saw, a clarification. He knew that the passenger in the car was not Bill. Everything in the dream was reversed, like a picture developing. What was dark became light. The back seat was the front seat. The empty face became full; it was fullness itself, fullness and frontness. The dream flared into fullness. And then it was gone.

Mark turned and shook hands with his wife.